THE
UNDERSIDE
OF
STONES

George Szanto

THE
UNDERSIDE
OF
STONES

A STORY CYCLE

A Cornelia & Michael Bessie Book

Harper and Row, Publishers, New York
GRAND RAPIDS, PHILADELPHIA, ST. LOUIS, SAN FRANCISCO
LONDON, SINGAPORE, SYDNEY, TOKYO, TORONTO

The author wishes to thank the Canada Council for an Arts Award, 1987–89, which gave him the time to complete this book.

Several segments of *The Underside of Stones* first appeared in magazines in slightly different form: "The Grace" in *Descant*, Summer 1986 (reprinted in *Iron*, Winter 1988); "Sálome" in *Canadian Fiction Magazine*, Summer 1988 (reprinted in *Telling Differences*, 1989); "How Ali Cran Got His Name" in *This Magazine*, 1987.

"The Sweeper" was presented to Geoffrey Andrew on the occasion of his 80th birthday.

"The Grace" was written for André Claude.

FIRST EDITION

Designer: Nancy Eato

Library of Congress Cataloging-in-Publication Data

Szanto, George, 1940–
   The underside of stones: a story cycle / George Szanto.
      p. cm.
   "A Cornelia & Michael Bessie book."
   ISBN 0-06-039108-1
   I. Title.
PS3569.Z3U5   1990
813'.54—dc20   89-45723

90 91 92 93 94   MV/RRD   10 9 8 7 6 5 4 3 2 1

For Eugene and Jo,
for grace and for wisdom

Contents

Arrival

MICHOÁCUARO, THE EVENING of September 18, 1985. I unloaded the car, drank a cold beer, another, fell asleep early.

Woke before the sun. Washed, boiled water for coffee—

The world shook. Walls swayed, graceful, mysterious. For more than three minutes.

I ran to the rooftop patio. People, on the street, in the plaza. On the cathedral dome the clock said 7:19.

It has remained 7:19 all year.

ONE

The Sweeper

🦂 DEAD. I KNEW he was dead, I'd helped put him in the ground. An honor for any gringo, my neighbor Pepe who runs the Telecable told me. Except I hadn't understood the dead man's son Tomás nearly well enough to grasp the nature of this honor. Tomás was the eldest. "My father willed it."

You don't argue with the eldest son of a dead man, not after less than three months in a town and your sweeper dies and the responsible son says you are a pallbearer, his father willed it. Despite too much recent contact with death, you go.

The culture about me is so foreign I could be in Kabul or Papua. I'm trying to write a novel. But the dead man, my sweeper, often interrupts. "You would like a story? I have a few little stories, let me tell you a story or two." This he'd said while he was alive. After he was dead he told me, There are hundreds of stories going on under your nose (under your eggs, he said; that took me a few seconds to figure out). Tiny stories and volcano-size stories, he said. You gringos are blind.

He's much ruder dead than alive.

When I'd learned to argue with him dead I said I thought most people were blind. After a while he conceded yes, I was right, partly; except I from my culture was blind in a worse way.

He does have a lot of stories. Anecdotes, anyway; rambles. Mostly I only have to listen. A few he's dragged me into the middle of. Like this one, about the statue. He wouldn't leave me alone about it: That's a man inside there.

Come on, it's a statue. Look, I said, its feet are poured cement, reinforced, it's only steel bars that're inside there, all the way up to its outstretched hand. Look.

He laughed. All you gringos believe that. Why are you only a stupid gringo, you, a writer, a professor of criminología?

3

I am, as charged, a criminologist; I have a split teaching position, Boston and Montreal. I'm here for a year in Michoácuaro in the Sierra Madre Occidentale mountains of Michoacán, to withdraw. Michoácuaro is a hillside town of thirty thousand where the streets were paved just three years ago for the first time in its four-century history, where burros mingle with muffler-free trucks, where pigs are allowed by ordinance to meander through town only on the end of a piece of clothesline held by kids not less than eight years old. Far from office meetings, from my telephone answering service. From hospitals. Not far at all from television, but at least that I can keep out of the house. Time to escape from a life of slow death. Time to write a novel.

What kind of novel?

I tried to explain. It would be about victims. And why certain people become one kind of victim, and others become different kinds of victims. That was my specialty in criminology, I told him. Not guns or police. Victims.

People don't *become* victims, he said. So there can be no reasons.

Of course there can. I began listing a few reasons—

Slowly he shook his head, and again. Those aren't reasons. Some people *are* victims. Those are excuses.

I got more technical. Talked about different theories of victimization—

I don't understand. Why do you want to write about victims anyway? Write a story about me.

I said maybe I would, one day. When I'd finished my novel about people becoming victims.

It'll be a lie.

Like this he insinuated his way into my life from the start.

Then there was his death. Monday he was there, Tuesday he wasn't. I was informed. I made the proper noises, the brief visit to the family and so on. Then came the invitation to the funeral. Command performance it felt like, with my specific participation. Dealing with death—

I asked advice from the jefe de policía, Rubén Reyes Ponce; I was renting one of his houses. Having already accepted, of course. There'd been no room to refuse the son's polite restrained insistence during the ten minutes of his visit. The advice I got was, "Wear a dark suit. Give the family five thousand pesos for refrescos. Maybe you

4

can use what you see." Cynical smile, broken bits of laughter. Michoácuarans have an off-center sense of humor.

I helped carry the coffin. Gilt grey, worth—not worth, actually, just costing—more than I might pay him in a year, even two, of sweeping. They opened the coffin. I touched his cheek like a hundred fifty others. Some kissed it. I wasn't up to that myself. It was a tough face, lined, a worker's face. Thin nose and lips, eyes closed now but in life dark brown, thin grey hair brushed flat and trimmed since his death, the lobe of his right ear cut off—a barroom fight when he'd worked the docks in Veracruz. He wore a light-green formal shirt. The rest of the body, rigid, stiff, was covered. They closed the coffin, we carried it to the hill and halfway up. The old man weighed mightily. As did the gilt box his family had gone into debt for.

"Death? Death?" He'd spat it at me once, a late afternoon as I was trying to get to the beer depósito quickly, back in time for sunset and a drink with friends down from Colorado for a few days. "Death belongs to the dead."

My problem was I'd tried to dismiss him in my dreadful Spanish by saying—wrong idiom—I was dying of thirst.

"Death, we felt it around us all the time when I was a stevedore. On the docks death was easy. Everyone died, sooner or later. They didn't know what dying was so they gave themselves up and they died. They lost. You cannot die of thirst. You can die of letting thirst take you over. If you refuse to lose to death you can't die."

I'm pretty sure that's what he said. More or less. My comprehension was still pretty bad and I was only three-quarters listening because my friends from Colorado were dying of thirst even if I wasn't allowed the privilege. They hadn't been due till the next day so there was no beer in the house. Now I didn't want their even metaphoric death-from-thirst on my hands. "Amigo, amigo, you will live forever, but I have to go buy beer. Walk with me." With him this was the only way of not standing around all afternoon, me listening and barely understanding.

His (alive) stories go on; not just the ones he told me, also some I've gotten in exchange from other people since his death.

I found out he was still around through the sweeping. Sweeping was the link between death and life.

I think he saw me, three minutes after I got to Michoácuaro, as a great possibility. For him I represented money; however slight my means this unpaid year, they were far greater than his own. Also perhaps there'd be advantages, later, for his sons.

The day after the earthquake he'd helped me move in. Unrequested. He appeared at the gate and started lending a hand. He participated in placing the couch; he knew I'd like it better away from the window, more looking out, more down here so the TV (I didn't have one? "Get a set, Jorge, help you learn Spanish") could sit with its back to the light, good for the eyes, help me see what's going on in the world.

My Spanish then, less than seventy-two hours after crossing out of Texas, was so awful, gestures and miming television-watching were the best I could deal with. I guess I didn't understand ninety percent of his actual words.

He suggested the movers, the other movers, the ones I'd actually hired, might like a beer. He knew where to get cold Superior. He gestured for me to come along. He stopped off at his son's place—Tomás, the eldest of eleven—to pick up half a dozen empties so I wouldn't have to pay the depósito. "Entiende depósito, Jorge?" I understood; he'd saved me twenty pesos times six.

We got back with the bottles. The movers had my stuff in, they drank the cold beer gratefully, unquestioningly. I had done what was right for a gringo to do—or for any person, I realized, after my sense of being a total outsider began to diminish. I paid the movers and tipped them a thousand pesos (road-back-money, English for a single word in Mexican Spanish); I'd been advised it was the appropriate amount.

He hung around. Suggestions for plants, ideas about where to place the lounging chairs in the courtyard for maximum sun—"Your face is pale, Jorge, you do not look well"—or maximum shade. He refused to leave. Finally I realized what had to be done—after three days in Mexico some sense of how to proceed does set in, especially once polite norteamericano patterns have failed so dreadfully. For Moisés de Jesús (I'd learned his name only after he'd repeated it four times; Moisés de Jesús Gutierrez Humberto), for him a gratuity was appropriate. I brought out my wallet. Mute, I handed him a thousand pesos. Folded in discrete quarters. He took it. I said, "Muchas gracias."

Well, he was either insulted (friendship is not to be paid for, and never never in this manner) or deeply appreciative and thankful (a thousand pesos could buy his family twenty kilos of tortillas). My negligible Spanish left me with nothing to say. His immediate emotion took him, too, momentarily out of the conversation.

But he pulled himself together and stepped close. Suddenly his face was six inches from mine. With a curious twist of his head he was looking directly into my right eye, and then as with a shrug his hands were holding my upper arms, squeezing gently. "We are amigos, are we not?"

His lunch had included raw onions. I grinned. Feebly, I suspect. "Yes. I think so."

His two eyes never left my right one. "It was me who swept your sidewalk for the week before you arrived. It was me who organized your house so it is right for you. I will keep your sidewalk clean for you forever. I will help you in many ways while you are on my street. I am your amigo. Does one pay an amigo a thousand pesos?"

This came through not in a single exchange but from a series of stumblings. On both our parts. "I—I don't know." I was feeling, curiously, afraid.

His grip tightened. "A thousand pesos. It is not much money."

That I understood. And with instant relief. I realized I'd been terrified we were about to be locked into some kind of blood brotherhood forever. But a larger tip I could handle. "Amigo, I am new in Mexico. I do not know the customs of your country. What is good money for your work?"

There was no change in his expression. I'd expected a gentle smile—yes, he had finally got through to the ignorant gringo—or an embarrassed glance at the world beyond my ear. He never took his eyes off mine. Then my arms were free as his hands rose to my head. He pressed, lightly, index, middle and ring fingers of each hand to my temples. "Between you and me, Jorge, there is good friendship. I do not know the answer to your question. Only the gods know. The gods will bring you their answer." He closed his eyes and remained motionless.

The gods didn't bring me a damn thing. Except a couple of moments to reflect on how easy life suddenly was: just give him another thousand.

Which I started to do. I reached for my wallet. My right shoulder ached mightily, I'd gone that stiff.

The difficulty with the great solution was this: after all my other tipping I had only a five-thousand-peso note left. But anything to be rid of him. "I hope this is good." His open eyes blinked several times.

Yes, his gods-of-wallet-fortuna were watching over him and he knew it. "If the gods say this, then it is good." No gracias now, no bowing or scraping. That would be inappropriate among equals. He stood back proud. "Hasta la vista, Don Jorge." He left. It seemed I had bought myself a title.

A title, and his recognition that I was his great good luck, his patsy.

During the next weeks he thought of a dozen services he could perform for me, from providing a tour of the countryside to doing my shopping. All of course with the appropriate compensation; the gods would no doubt inform me of the amount. I wanted only a bit of peace to write my book, so after a couple of weeks of saying no to everything else I acceded to the sweeping: all the sidewalk, and halfway across the road, by eight every morning, according to the town ordinance. He would charge me four thousand pesos a month.

I had asked advice from the jefe. Yes it is an ordinance. His price? Steep.

"Okay, you're hired. A thousand pesos a month."

"Oh no, three."

"The gods have told me: fifteen hundred."

"Surely they must have said two thousand."

"Perhaps. Two thousand."

"Don Jorge, as you know, I have been sweeping your sidewalk since you arrived—"

"But I did not ask you to—"

"Your sidewalk is clean every morning at eight, you will pay me now a thousand pesos for two weeks."

The battle was between resilient pride and beating an old man out of three dollars. If I were going to be in Michoácuaro for more than ten months—five years, say, or a lifetime—I would have refused and fought. I gave him a thousand pesos.

We had put him in the ground with all his medals. He'd been dead for eight days, buried for five. I asked, "Why didn't you keep them, a memory of your father?"

Tomás shook his head. "It was his will to be buried with them on his chest."

I concurred as to how you can't argue with a man's wishes once he's dead.

The medals were for pistol competition. Tomás told me that three years in a row, when his father was twenty-six, twenty-seven, twenty-eight, he'd been Michoacán Champion both for Air Pistol and Conventional Pistol and the middle year also for the Rapid-fire Pistol. Each year he had been in the running for Mexico's national team, but never had made it. Later, as a stevedore, he'd won half a dozen more ribbons and four little cups for his pistol expertise. All these trophies were buried with him.

It had been my habit since arriving in Michoácuaro to jog around the plaza ten to fifteen times every morning before the town began to stir—that is, at the least hint of light, enough so I didn't trip myself up—and I would see, three or four times a week before he died, Moisés de Jesús sweeping away or washing down the dust. We'd chat briefly and I'd head in to take a shower. For the last week naturally I hadn't seen my sweeper, but the sidewalk was continuously clean. Probably one of the sons, I figured. An early morning, a Friday, I'd been up at four to make some notes and wasn't able to sleep after so I headed down to the plaza for my run.

A mistake. In front of the dark tostada stands my foot squished into the middle of a dropped soggy item, forgotten five or six hours ago, now found by me. My foot shot sideways and I landed flat-handed and hip down. I swore, picked myself up, checked the damage—mostly a skinned palm, a hip that'd complain for a couple of days and an agony in the right shoulder from jerking my arm trying for impossible balance. The shoulder wanted streams of hot water and I wanted to forget being sensibly healthy. I walked slowly up the hill to the house. And there he was.

In the barest pre-light I assumed it was the son. I began, "Buenos días, o buenos noches—" when he turned, and it was old M. de J. himself.

Buenos días, Don Jorge. I am glad to see you. You owe me two thousand pesos. For the month.

Naturally I assumed I was dreaming. Which would've been fine because then I'd have been dreaming the pain in my shoulder too. I tried the usual check-out-if-you-are-asleep devices, speaking aloud: What're you doing here? and thrashing my arms, which hurt, and the cliché of pinching. But I was wide awake.

9

And he answered my question: Sweeping. You can see that. He spoke clearly, normally.

Look, this may sound foolish, but—well, aren't you dead?

You buried me. I was pleased you did. Tomás told me he did not think you would. He was wrong. As usual.

I suppose among my reactions there might have been fear. But no, none. I remember telling myself, you're talking to a ghost—ghosts being one of our normalizing categories for irrational phenomena. I touched him. No ectoplasm. Solid, like in life. I wondered if he'd fade with the coming light. The sky was barely dark gray.

I could make no intelligent sense of this. The worst, somehow (thinking back now, to have reached for instant better/worse gradations seems weird, but I suppose so does the rest of this on those scales of reason), was I'd always thought, according to our Judeo-Christian folklore, death was a release. Moisés de Jesús was dead. Yet he was getting up at this ungodly hour to sweep my sidewalk for two thousand pesos a month. I asked him if he minded.

No. If you are dead you don't sleep. So you don't have to get up.

In a perverse way that was a relief. Had he been around, well, ever since he died?

I can't remember much before yesterday. But since then, yes.

Always here? In town? I meant, I supposed, had he been to what gets called heaven or hell.

Of course I've been around here. I am from Michoácuaro, where else should I go?

Do you talk to many people? Like this?

I told you before I died. He looked angry now. Most people are blind. They are also deaf. They cannot hear me so I cannot talk to them. They are blind, so they do not know I am here.

Everybody?

Not everybody. Obviously not you, Don Jorge. Two or three others. Two friends, the ones that listened. Before. Also a woman. Sometimes she sees me, mostly not. Not my wife. I did not expect you would be able to.

I wasn't sure I wanted to be the exception. I wasn't sure I wanted that kind of honor. I was feeling the offer of blood brotherhood again and I didn't understand its implications. Or maybe it had already gone beyond the offer stage.

We continued to talk, the longest conversation of our acquaintance. The day got lighter. He didn't disappear. A couple of cars drove by, one backfiring like a burst of gunfire, neither paying any attention. I wondered what would happen if people walked past. The miracle, looking back, was more my ability to understand his Spanish and to make myself understood than the fact that this conversation was taking place at all. Did that mean it's easier to understand the dead than the living? Because they focus more? And what kind of metaphor was I letting myself in for here?

I don't remember how we stopped talking. Nothing like, Will I see you again? or, Have a good day, in any of their Spanish forms. Just the vaguest memory of opening the door and passing through the courtyard to turn on the water heater for the shower. No sense, either, of the fifteen minutes or so it takes for the water to get hot. The first clear subsequent image was me in the shower and the relief of a hot water spray massage on my shoulder.

We kept on meeting. There was usually no one else around. When I tried to get him to explain why he preferred seclusion he avoided the question. I suspect he was a bit afraid of being seen, and heard. It'd maybe disprove his absolute theories about people being blind and deaf. I asked him once, If gringos are so damn ignorant in the senses, how come I'm one of the few select? and if he wanted complete freedom for wandering around in the open, why didn't he go to the U.S. or Canada?

All he said was, Too cold.

Too cold for a dead man?

He looked at me as if I were stupid.

Often he appears, just like that, in my courtyard, the door locked, for a chat. Several times we've run into each other, if that's the right phrase, at the market. Shopping?

We all have to eat.

If it were only his one-liners I think I'd find him tiresome, whatever his state of existence. But, as I said, he has stories. I've spent months being his audience.

I wanted to know about being dead. Alaine, my wife of nineteen years, had spent the last four of them dying—being kept alive, dying with infinite slowness. Only a few weeks after the funeral I had left her there, up north, to come here. I had thought she was gone from me. Now— I pulled my courage together: Could you get any sense of her, being dead too?

11

Don't use me, Don Jorge.

Look, I'm sorry—

I can't see or hear other dead people. Anyway, not now. And if I could why should I tell you? If I wanted to be with dead people I wouldn't bother with you. Don't use me for a connection. You want to talk to me, go ahead.

Alaine's death, supposedly permanent. Then for a moment, the tiny hope. Now suddenly, a curious sorrow; new, yet less pain—

He was insistent too about the statue. I made him meet me there one morning while I was jogging so we could take a good look before people came into the square. It is a statue of Abelardo Carosuelto Núñez, an obscure lieutenant who served with Benito Juarez in the 1860's and later became part of his government. After Juarez's death Abelardo returned to Michoácuaro, his birthplace, married the heiress to a huge sugar cane plantation and died wealthy. To his honor, his unearned wealth one presumes, the statue is dedicated. It stands on a pedestal nearly two meters high. Lieutenant Abelardo is dressed in full uniform, his long coat coming down to his knees, Hessian boots rising to the hem of the coat. He is hatless, has flowing hair, a graceful mustache and a goatee. His left arm hangs at his side. His right is outstretched, rising above shoulder level. In this hand he holds a pistol. I am told it's an old Colt .45 but given my specialization I know even less about antique firearms than of contemporary ones. The pistol points across the breadth of the plaza. There, in the early morning moonlight, it glowed slightly.

Look, I said. Solid. Here. Feel it. I jumped up on the base of the pedestal. Touch the boots.

Boots are hard. Touch the coat.

I pulled myself up to the top of the pedestal. The statue is probably half again as tall as me. I held it around the waist. Solid poured cement, I said. It felt warm, as if it had soaked up the day's hot sun and was releasing it slowly. A kind of capacitor.

Maybe it feels solid to you. I know it is a man.

Amigo—

You can see me. Others cannot. Yet you refuse to believe it when I say that is a man.

Follow a path like this, you go crazy. In fact, some days I wasn't sure I wasn't there already. Talking with dead men is usually understood as some kind of aberrance of mind. When it isn't a religious act, anyway. None of which kept me from asking, Can you talk to him?

No.

Then how do you know?

I can see him.

Can he see you?

How should I know? Just because he's in a statue doesn't mean he isn't blind. Or deaf, for that matter.

Stone deaf! I laughed.

Moisés de Jesús didn't find that a bit funny. Alive he hadn't had much of a sense of humor either.

We weren't getting anywhere. I quickly found myself jogging again.

In early January a man was found dead on the plaza with a bullet in his skull. No one knew who did it. Someone claimed to have heard a shot, about three in the morning. But the sound could just as easily have been a car backfiring. Moisés de Jesús told me the statue shot the man.

Why?

Target practice.

Come on.

Sure. You get rusty, standing on that pedestal all day, not being allowed to move. Besides, they were both drunk.

A statue? Drunk? I laughed again, more uncomfortably.

Again irritation from him. You haven't learned anything at all, Don Jorge. Someday soon you won't be able to see me anymore.

And I knew I'd be sorry. It was becoming a strange kind of privilege. I've tried to explain to myself, dozens of times, how it could happen that I, a rational norteamericano, could have these conversations with Moisés de Jesús after he died. But there's no clarification that makes sense in our terms. When we talked it was as friends rather than acquaintances. Yet I would hardly have called Moisés de Jesús a friend, we'd barely known each other; still, now we talked And it was with the openness of friendship, I mean; letting nothing stay hidden; nothing conscious, anyway. I mentioned Alaine now and then, when I couldn't stop myself. He wouldn't follow in this direction. Still, he'd got me over one hurdle: I was after all talking to him.

They'd found out in town that I am a criminologist. I'd given two talks, one to the Michoácuaro Lions Club and one to the Law Enforcement Association—I think that's the right term—of Michoacán; both with simultaneous translation, though by then I was getting so I understood some of the less complicated questions. My neighbor Pepe asked me if I would talk on television about the murder—the local news, put on by Telecable Michoácuaro.

I didn't much want to. You look like a fool when you can't really speak the language, and television exaggerates that. But Rubén, who as jefe of police had been very helpful in getting my tourist card renewed (knew a man who knew the man who with just a few thousand pesos—), Rubén urged me to; he hadn't found the killer and I sensed he was losing face. He didn't say so of course but he was asking me, a gringo, if I wouldn't mind mentioning something like how baffling this case was, and probably even with the most sophisticated methods of criminology it'd be very hard to find the killer, and so on. I agreed to the interview.

The case had become deeply disturbing to some of the citizens. It was all very well for campesinos to kill each other out in the cane bush, or for a couple of drunks to go at each other with knives or machetes in one of the cantinas. Somebody gets killed that way on an average of once a month. But when people start shooting each other in the town plaza? Across from the kids' library, and the cathedral half a block away? What was happening in town?

No one had been able to learn anything about the dead man either. The postmortem showed he'd been drunk when killed, as expected. Shot by a bullet from a nineteenth-century Colt .45.

Moisés de Jesús laughed darkly when I told him this. And did he become a victim?

What do you mean?

It doesn't matter. On the television, how will you explain it?

How did you hear?

Word gets around.

Among your dead friends?

What will you say?

I suddenly wanted out of the conversation. The truth.

How a statue shot him and made him a victim? Ha!

Go away, amigo.

In there, it is a man!

Should I say that?

14

Of course.

Who is he?

Moisés de Jesús suddenly looked grim, very uncomfortable, and stayed silent.

Well? You can't expect me to say there's a man in there unless you tell me who he is. That would be stupid.

It has been—different people.

I laughed. What people?

He glowered. Dead people.

Oh. Great. Dead people living inside a statue. Terrific.

Dead like me.

Look. First of all, there's nobody inside that statue. Secondly, if there were and it made any difference, they'd have to be alive for me to worry about it. Dead men in statues don't concern me, okay? If somebody in there were alive, well, we'd try to get them out, I said. I couldn't believe I was prattling this nonsense. It starts when you talk to dead people, I suppose. We'd pull the statue down, we'd shatter it so nobody, dead or alive, would— Which was when it hit me. You! You're afraid of being in there yourself!

Now he wouldn't meet my eye at all. He folded his arms and looked skyward.

Don't worry, amigo, because there's no one, *no one,* inside that statue. And you never will be.

When it is dark, come. I will show you. Suddenly he wasn't around.

It was all becoming, improbably, a story I might want to write one day. And who was the victim? I thought, Okay. I really will go down to the plaza, look at it again, fix it in my mind.

I got there about eleven. The tostada and carne asada stands were closing up. People loitered in the lit center of the plaza around the fountain. There was no one by the statue.

Moisés de Jesús stepped out from behind it. I didn't think you would come. He was almost angry. Look. Look at it. Do you see the light from the inside? There he is.

I looked. True, the statue was caught in a curious light, especially at the folds of its coat. But that came from the moonlight. I said so.

Touch it. Climb up and feel it.

Look, I did that last time.

Do you want to remain stupid all your life?

It was as if his words scraped, I don't know why, a raw nerve. I sacrificed my dignity and climbed up. I touched Abelardo on the hips. He was indeed warm, certainly warmer than last time. But it was also six or seven hours earlier and the statue still retained a lot of the day's heat. I climbed down and explained that to M. de J.

You are lost, he said. And walked away.

I worked out what I would tell the interviewers. First I'd outline my procedure, then explain how usually some knowledge of the victim leads to an understanding of the purpose of the crime, which could result in finding the perpetrator. In this case, with nothing known of the victim, the police having done all they could in trying to identify— And so on.

About two in the morning on the day of the interview, I was awakened by, I figured, a truck backfiring. I guessed what M. de J. would say and couldn't get back to sleep. All the night-thoughts roared through my head: Alaine before the cancer struck, before the chemotherapy, before her hair— And the novel that was proceeding so slowly, and the interview itself, and Moisés de Jesús in his coffin. I got up, made myself a flour tortilla with melted cheese, wondered if my typewriter would wake anybody up at nearly 3:00 A.M. and heard the backfire again. Or—the statue shooting at someone else? I tried to read. No concentration. Maybe a little tequila? No, I wanted to be clear-headed for the damn interview. So I did the only thing a fool would do, I got dressed and walked—slowly, it was a cloudy night, dark—down to the plaza to check out the statue. Which wasn't there.

That's not exactly correct. The pedestal was there. On it, a kind of shape like Abelardo, except it was a glowing outline of the statue. I don't want to exaggerate this, it was hardly a fireball; much more a brighter version of what I had seen a few nights before. Except I couldn't explain it away by talking about reflected moonlight because the moon was behind thick clouds. I reached up. I was unable to stop myself, I put my hand into the glow. A sharp clip of fear hit me between the shoulder blades, passed through my gut and fled down my legs—fear of being burned, or just plain afraid, I don't know. I had the unexplainable sense of passing my hand through flesh that wasn't there— Then out the other side; and nothing.

No burn, no explanation. I dropped to the ground. What to do? Wait? I sat, focused on the glow. It changed very little. Or maybe not at all. I waited possibly half an hour. Then something, somebody, human in shape, wearing the same kind of glow, appeared at the far end of the plaza. He approached, fifty feet, thirty, twenty. He looked respectable enough in clothing, slacks, a shirt. Except for the glow it could have been any Michoácuaran. Except also, I noticed then, he carried a pistol. I couldn't swear it was a nineteenth-century Colt .45 but it looked a lot like the thing the statue always held. I couldn't help myself. I stepped out of the shadow. He saw me. And pointed the pistol.

Panic. I turned and ran. I heard a shot, no car backfire this time, but didn't feel anything. Except, now, pure fear. I kept running, reached the first cover, the tostada stands, dived around the nearest and bashed my head on a kind of sticking out counter. I remember thinking, if all I get is a bang on the skull I'll be lucky. I stared out at the pedestal. Carefully. There was the statue, standing on top, dull now in the dark light, pointing its pistol out across the plaza. Unless it shifted its traditional pose I was out of the line of fire.

I stayed beyond it, kept to the shadows for three blocks and got home. How to understand, by what process, the last hour? I half expected Moisés de Jesús there, grinning gleefully, bantering, See? See?

Then I was stuck: Forget all this for the interview and retain my credibility? Or tell Michoácuaro they had a ghost of a sniper in their statue?

Only one possibility, really. After explaining everything that was appropriate from my professional perspective, and it being line-for-line translated, I would tell the reporters and the TV audience, wryly, another explanation was also possible: The dead man had been shot by a statue.

In the studio everyone laughed. A little nervously, yes, but they must have needed to fill in more airtime because they followed my, so to speak, line of reasoning.

"Why would the statue do that?"

So I went on about the man in the statue. That since it had been put there, there were always men in the statue.

"Who kill?"

"Only sometimes. When they are seen."

"Why are they there in the first place?"

"I don't know."

"You've seen this man?"

"Well, I happened to be out on the plaza at three in the morning, and—" We went on for another ten minutes, me recounting the night's events in bravura style. The two reporters were delighted; usually their interviews proved a lot more, well, usual. I told them I'd had fun too, thank you.

The producer, Pepe, drew me aside. He wasn't sure my tactic had been wise, a long time since anybody took the ghost-of-Abelardo stories seriously, Michoácuaro was still in many ways fighting its way out of the Middle Ages, now my joke would revive all that superstition, and so on. But it was done. So he thanked me too.

I was fascinated. An ancient story. And old guess-who was waiting for me in the courtyard: I had almost lost hope, Don Jorge. But he said it with a grin and a shrug. There was something curious, different, about him. I realized what only after he'd left. The right earlobe, it was all there.

My friend the jefe laughed and slapped me on the back and told me I was terrific, best joke he'd heard in a long time. He thanked me too for the good word about the difficulties of the investigation. I couldn't help thinking I heard a nervous edge to the laughter.

People stopped me on the street for probably three weeks after. It was as if they knew me, I was a friend, talkable to. Two groups of people: I had a fantastic sense of humor, a humor fit for a Michoácuaran, how could a gringo have such a fine sense of humor? That was the larger group. The others would shake my hand and nod wisely, pull me aside and tell me I was a brave man, not often did one hear the truth on television, it was good to speak the truth even on television. These were mostly older people. I would thank them in return for their kindness, the appreciation. Terrific, that. I'd never been so popular before.

I still jog in the mornings. But only after first light. Moisés de Jesús comes by from time to time, and I meet him in accidental places. The sidewalk is always swept. With the inflation here he demanded, last week, three thousand a month. I've agreed to twenty-five hundred.

18

How Ali Cran Got His Name

THE CURANDERA SAYS if I am stung by a scorpion, kill him and cut in half his corpse, then with a mixture of lime juice and garlic stick down the head part on the wound and this will save my life. In fact in twenty minutes I will be cured. Maybe half an hour.

I can imagine my doctor back home, Bob Carson who's done a bit of alternative medicine, going so far as to concede something like antivenin might really be present in the head. Or that maybe there is real curative power in the garlic-lime glue. But I also know how talk of magic potions and country cures leaves him uncomfortable and in about three minutes he'd make it clear that really the whole business was absurd: If you're ever stung, even just a nip, instantly, *instantly,* get yourself to a real doctor. Don't muck around.

Myself, I think the cure comes from revenge: one bite, one dead scorpion. But having so far avoided being stung I have no personal experience. Therefore I listen to all advice. So when the time comes—

Listening to tall tales is how I began to hear the stories of Alejandro Cruz Ocampo, known here as Ali Cran or Alicito by those who claim to be his friends. More people than I'd have thought possible say they're close to him. Before anybody put scorpions and Alejandro Cruz together for me and I learned how he got his name, I'd heard half a dozen mentions, bits of stories—because Ali Cran is a kind of reference point for the citizens of Michoácuaro. His name began to reach me from the edges of gossip or from recited memories.

For example, when María-Cecilia at the beer depósito became pregnant, the story was mainly how Cecilia's mother would at last get a new baby in the house, the mother having been barren since Cecilia's sister Guadalupina, ten months younger than Cecilia herself, was born. Cecilia wouldn't say who the father was, so people blamed Ali Cran and, to my fascination, that seemed appropriate. Similarly, when years back Sebastiano broke his leg and couldn't get his avocados picked and couldn't afford to hire, he woke one morning out of a sad pulque dream and found the trees bare and all the fruit piled below. He was so happy he got drunk again and the next day he found the avocados boxed also. The town agreed: Ali Cran. Or when Nisi Calderón's ancient truck was forced off the road into a ditch by a jeep, the old man, with a smashed arm and broken ankle, tried to get the police to find who had careened the jeep against him. The jefe de policía explained to Nisi the jeep was stolen. But Nisi said people had seen Ali Cran admiring it earlier in the evening. What proof was that, the jefe asked; and anyway there'd be no finding him—if it was him, well, madrecita! by now he'd be deep into tierra caliente, the hot country to the south and west of us. Ali Cran seemed to be the source of both blessings and disasters.

It was Rubén Reyes Ponce who told me about Alejandro Cruz as a boy. We were sitting in the courtyard, Rubén and I, sharing the last quarter of a bottle of good dark tequila, Commemorativo. I had learned the hard way to keep my tequila bottles no more than a third full because whatever was in them when Rubén came by had to be finished before he left.

And no less than about twenty percent full: Late one morning, thinking I'd be really smart—I was at a piece of the novel that felt like it was moving well—I brought out a bottle with only a couple of sips left in it. Rubén made that gesture, thumb and index finger two centimeters apart held toward me, hand jagging back and forth half a dozen times, which means un poquito, just a tiny bit. Specifically, here, of time, just a few seconds . . . He turned and went. This is the gesture which has impressed on me completely that in the state of Michoacán the time-space continuum is a living and breathing reality. Rubén was back in five minutes with a full litre. But of the cheap clear stuff, the kind that's aged to its particular local perfection maybe five seconds before it's bottled. Naturally we had to finish what was in front of us.

That was the first time he told me about Ali Cran. The story, paid for with the drinking plus a full aftermath in the head and stomach and joints, cost me a day and a half's worth of writing hours.

It seems Rubén and Alejandro had been at the same school, Alejandro twelve, Rubén ten. Alejandro was a skinny kid, good at math but barely literate, lousy at soccer, always wearing clothes at least four of his older brothers had worked their way through at the elbows and knees. That wasn't particularly abnormal—most boys wore whatever their mothers could find for them, and few were exceptional in their schoolwork. Most prided themselves at being good at sports, though. What distinguished Alejandro was his interest in details, in colors, textures, plants and especially insects: ants, grasshoppers, wasps, even cockroaches—the three-inchers that come out in April and May, Rubén said; details, and a tendency to daydream. His reveries would be either active or passive. That is, he might be sitting at his desk in school or on the steps of the arcade of the plaza or by the fountain in the middle of it, and for fifteen minutes, half an hour even, he'd be connected only to his thoughts. Anybody looking at him would know his mind was in its own world. Where, nobody could guess; just, away. In class his teachers didn't bother him at these moments—at least one of the kids was keeping quiet. Who cared what was going on upstairs.

He would daydream actively, also. ("Daydream" here is Rubén's word. I'd call it concentration.) For example, there was the time Rubén saw Alejandro sitting on the crumbled curb in front of his house, watching the ground. And what was happening now? A centipede or a scorpion, dying slowly? No, a regiment of ants dragging a dead wasp to their nest. The wasp would have outweighed the fifteen or so ants maybe ten to one; undaunted, the soldiers pushed and pulled, making slow headway. Rubén had watched Alejandro with nearly as much fascination as Alejandro had ants. With less patience, though; breaking into Alejandro's world was necessary. So Rubén came up behind Alejandro and with a blade of grass pretended some bug was tickling the back of his friend's neck. No response. Rubén found a small pebble and dropped it down the back of Alejandro's shirt. Nothing. Finally he pulled open his fly and peed in the dust, spattering mud directly beside Alejandro, splashing the procession. The ants struggled on. Alejandro's concentration remained intact. Except, when the peeing stopped, Alejandro without shifting his eyes from the ants said, "Go away." Rubén left in frustration, Alejandro's eyes followed the ants. Rubén wondered what would have happened if he'd peed on the wasp itself. Now he is much happier he didn't.

For his daydreaming and for his absent-mindedness a lot of the kids gave Alejandro Cruz a hard time. Once he came to school wearing a shirt that had belonged to his sister Camilla. Before Camilla it had been his brother Arturo's. That made no difference. Camilla's friend Silvia remembered the shirt because Camilla had once unbuttoned it to show Silvia how her breasts were starting to grow from out of nowhere and now Silvia told everybody Alejandro was wearing a girl's shirt and there were probably breast marks on the inside. So, Rubén said, because the fool kid had that morning put on a one-time girl's shirt, probably while thinking about bees or silverfish, they all called him Alejandra for days.

The best joke was to snap Alejandro out of his reveries, bang, like that. He'd be shocked back to the daily world as if he'd fallen off a cliff and down into icy water. He wouldn't have any idea where he was, everybody laughing ready to burst because they'd been holding their giggles in till he plunged back to their world. This happened so often Alejandro learned to hide most of what he was feeling, he'd wait with faked calm till his burning red cheeks and neck went away and the pouring sweat started to clam into his shirt-back and he'd figured out how to hold in the tears this time. He didn't run away anymore; though he still wanted to, as far as possible. Not home. Into tomorrow, if he only knew how.

One January around nine in the evening the full moon was high and its reflection off the still water in the big fountain down at the plaza was of a silver purer than any from the mines of Taxco or Guanajuato. Now and again a slight breeze would press down the top of the water as if enraptured with the moon. Alejandro knelt on the rim of the fountain and watched enchanted as the silver formed and melted, patterned and resmoothed. What was in his mind, Rubén said, was impossible to know. It mattered not at all who else, at Alejandro's side or over across the fountain's pool, might be glancing at the glimmering water; Alejandro and the moon were unquestionably separate from everyone else.

The culprit this time was a mean little kid, Nabór, a cousin of Alejandro's. Nabór remains to this day unequivocally nasty and, though in his late thirties, still a repulsive kid, Rubén tells me. It being a few nights after Christmas, Nabór had firecrackers. Not his; those had blasted the early mornings three days running. Forty-five minutes before the churches sent off their own into the heavens to wake the population for 4:00 A.M. mass, Nabór's explosions had driven two of Michoácuaro's earliest risers, the Vargas Martinez sisters, pious ladies who liked having time to wash before early mass, to complain to the Bishop about the sleep-shattering blasts. No, Nabór had stolen these firecrackers, little ones, from his younger brother Angel; Angel was the hoarder. Is even today, according to Rubén.

So, firecrackers in hand, Nabór, true to form, found his moment: the spellbound Alejandro, the silent evening, the argentine water. Coming up directly behind Alejandro, Nabór dropped a small jacaranda twig, a test-twig, between Alejandro's motionless shoulder blades. No reaction: moon and Alejandro in mutual admiration. Nabór took a match, lit the fuse and let it sputter. As the burn reached the first two crackers—one of those cheap strings of ten, five pairs of two—Nabór dropped it on Alejandro's back and leapt away. The first pair exploded nearly simultaneously. Alejandro remained kneeling. Suspended. Nabór stared, amazed, even an explosion hadn't— Then, with nearly the slowness of leaf growing, Alejandro curved lightly forward. His face was halfway to the water as the second pair exploded, his forehead and hair touched the water with the third, and there was time for two more to go off before Alejandro's skinny body submerged head to knees in the fountain pool. The final crackers fizzled to wet silence.

Nabór laughed and laughed. Two other boys ran to pull Alejandro out. By this time the sopping kid was standing in the pool, dripping silvery water. The story was the buzz of the school for a week, really hilarious.

I broke in at the end of that tangent. "But what about Alejandro's name, Rubén."

Sure, that was the best part of Ali Cran's early life, Rubén was just getting to that, the next piece of the story. We'd been drinking for two hours. Rubén took a bite on his lime, dunked a finger in his tequila, stuck the finger in the salt, sucked off the finger, drank down the glass. I poured him another, wondering how much of all this I'd remember in the morning. He toasted the young Alejandro and we sipped.

All the kids and the teachers at the school were off to Cerro Madre, a good-size hill a few kilometers from Michoácuaro, for the annual picnic. It was early May, summer vacation around the corner, the rains would be here before long, the sun shining defiantly through the smoky haze of nearby burning cane fields. Everyone was feeling rambunctious. The teachers kept them in check.

Alejandro too was in a great mood. An uncle who'd gone north, his favorite uncle, Pedro, his mother's brother who mailed home a hundred dollars a month—which was her only income, though Alejandro didn't know this at the time—Tío Pedro had sent Alejandro a New York Yankees baseball cap. The Yankees were Pedro's team—Pedro worked, illegally like so many from Mexico, in New Jersey as a painter's assistant. The Yankees were doing fantastic that year and Pedro wanted to send his favorite nephew an early happy birthday present. Alejandro's birthday was in November but by then the season would already be over and the Yankees probably world champions, so Pedro's early gift meant Alejandro could start cheering for the Yankees right away.

Well Alejandro was even worse at baseball than at soccer. When he had to play in school they always stuck him in right field, deep right if there were too many on each team and they could double-platoon the position. But he loved the cap. These days you can buy Mexican-made American baseball caps and tee shirts or whatever you want here. This cap, though, this was the real thing. It made Alejandro feel as if he belonged, not simply to the daily activities of his street or his school or Michoácuaro, but to a bigger world, one that really mattered. So on this day when he wanted to pretend he was as okay and as happy as all the others, planning their special games and secret walks and hunts, he wore his Yankees cap. He knew it was a good choice as soon as he got on the bus and started to get compliments—from some of the boys, even from a couple of the girls. He let two of them try it on, those who'd sometimes been nice to him, who'd talked about themselves to him, helped him with his verbs. The bus wound out of town, across the narrow valley the stream flowed through, and up Cerro Madre. The top was level, another volcanic cone, this one filled in over millions of years to leave a flat surface. Clumps of pine trees created special sitting places. A tiny spring burbled out of the ground there, the water not clean enough for drinking but great to stick your hot feet in. It flowed into the stream below.

The happiness was catching. Boys teased girls as they usually do at eleven, twelve, thirteen, feeling juices they don't know the meaning of but have to do something with. Girls giggled together about

24

boys, knowing a bit more but for all that not having much more control over their feelings, let alone knowing how to deal with them. No one was unkind to Alejandro. He felt pretty good, though the initial enthusiasm with his cap had worn off. There were tortillas and gordos and enchiladas and soft drinks. Rubén and Arturo caught a scorpion and a centipede and put them in a glass bottle and tightened the top, and after watching them fight ran with the bugs after two girls they liked, to frighten them. Despite the haze the sun got hot. Everything slowed down. Kids sat in little groups and gossiped: boys and boys, girls and girls, two small groups of boys and girls. And the teachers were at last off by themselves.

Nabór was bored. He tried to convince Silvia it'd be great fun to steal Alejandro's Yankees cap. Silvia didn't know what was so much fun about that. Nabór said it'd give them something to do. Silvia said it was too hot. Nabór said they wouldn't have to run very hard, Alejandro probably wouldn't even notice, he'd be watching some birds in a tree or some clouds or something. Silvia finally agreed. So they snuck up behind Alejandro, he was just on the outside of one group of boys, right at the edge of the shade. Nabór came up quietly from behind, grabbed the cap and stepped back, raising it high to show Silvia. Suddenly Alejandro was on his feet. "You—give—me—that—cap!"

"Come get it! Run and get it!" Nabór held it out, Alejandro lunged, Nabór pulled to the side, Alejandro's thrust missed, Nabór ran. As he passed Silvia he grabbed her hand with his free one and together, laughing so hard they nearly fell over themselves, they ran down into the valley where there were more trees to hide behind.

Alejandro waited while the blood drained from his face and the sweat soaked into his shirt. He clamped his fury inside. Only the cap was important. All else would come later. He stared downhill, saw no one. He willed himself: Find the cap.

He searched for more than half an hour. Finally he found them. They were behind some bushes beside the stream. He heard them before he saw them. They were groping at each other and panting. The cap was on the ground. He tried to be silent but they saw him before he reached it. They pulled apart. Nabór grabbed the cap and held it out: "You want it? Swim for it!" and threw it into the stream. Alejandro watched. It floated. Slowly water soaked in. Soon it would sink. He ran into the water, shoes, pants, everything. It was still ahead of him, caught in the current, turning slowly—then it disappeared. He got back on the bank, ran downstream of where it should be, splashed back in, through the water, fished about, saw something white—and found it! Caught along a submerged branch. The white was the cloth. But it was in bad shape. The cloth would dry but no way would it ever be really white again. The cardboard in the visor was sodden, probably ruined. He stared at it, his only real friend, squeezed it to his chest— Slowly he walked out of the water. He sat by a tree, dripping water. He held his cap to his face and cried into it. He leaned against the tree and lost himself, first to anguish and despair, soon to all the psychic exhaustion of his brief lifetime, at last to sleep.

Which was the way Nabór and Silvia found him. They hadn't bothered chasing him, they'd returned to their exploration of each other's bodies. Then the drives and urges had reached a very strange state, the feeling was familiar yet unknown, then suddenly it was gone. They were uncomfortable with each other. Neither understood, neither admitted ignorance. Neither wanted to go back up the hill to the others. They found some blackberries and ate them. They poked gingerly at two scorpions hiding in the cool crack of a rock. They threw stones at a family of finches.

Then they saw Alejandro. The baseball cap lying by his side gave Nabór the idea. Alejandro was, this time, deeply asleep. Nabór stole the cap a second time. He returned to the rock where they'd seen the scorpions. One was gone. Silvia banged the rock on the opposite side. The remaining scorpion, disturbed from its warm afternoon peace, panicked and rushed the other way, into the Yankees cap. It was a big fellow, over two inches long from the tip of its claws down to the dark brown stinger. Nabór held the edges of the folded cap firm. They ran back to Alejandro, hoping he was still asleep. He was. Quietly again Nabór crawled up to Alejandro and placed the cap on his chest, opened it, crawled back to Silvia. They watched, breathless.

The scorpion, probably stunned, slowly meandered out of the hat. Scorpions like to choose their own dampness and this one was no exception. It seemed to look about proudly, as if thinking, Who could have dared do that to me? Perhaps at this moment it realized it was on something breathing. Certainly at this moment Rubén, under orders from the school principal to look for the three missing students, came up behind Silvia and Nabór. They knew he was

26

there, he started to speak. Nabór tapped his fingers to his lips, "Sshhh!" and Silvia giggled silently. They pointed.

Rubén saw.

Alejandro was awake. His eyes were wide open. So was his mouth. He was trying to stare down to the bottom of his chin. There was a scorpion sitting there, tail wound tight over its head. Slowly it crawled, one tiny tickling leg, then another, another, up Alejandro's chin. It stopped for a moment, as if considering the possibilities of the face; where next to test this immediate landscape? It started the journey again. Its pincers reached Alejandro's lower lip. Nothing moved. Only Alejandro's eyeballs.

Rubén panicked. We must do something! Silvia and Nabór were choking back uncontrollable giggles, wiping away tears to see better. Rubén could do nothing. Alejandro! Only Alejandro could save himself. How? Instantly. But Rubén knew as well: if Alejandro moved to swat the thing the tail would lash out and the stinger would stab through the skin and into the flesh of the chin before the hand moved three inches. Frozen, Rubén watched.

Alejandro was stiller than time. Only the scorpion moved. Slow, like sweat. Inexorably forward. Its front part stood in fine brown contrast on the lower lip. Still it moved forward. The head and claws were hovering now above Alejandro's tongue—

Instantly it happened. Quicker than any eye. Only the result told. Alejandro's teeth snapped shut and bit the scorpion in two. The tail, arrested before its adrenaline could signal a strike, fell down the side of Alejandro's chin to the ground.

Rubén remembers he peed his pants.

Nabór and Silvia were so shocked they couldn't move. They lay there, their mouths open, as if waiting for scorpions of their own.

Alejandro got up slowly. He walked toward the three. With his soaking wet shoes he kicked Nabór in the head and then in the side and, when he rolled over, in the shin. Silvia was getting to her feet, she was off balance, Alejandro grabbed her by the wrist, bit her forearm, broke the skin, dragged her to the stream, threw her in.

Rubén, shaking, embarrassed, walked slowly to the tree to pick up Alejandro's cap. The tail of the scorpion lay on the ground, less than an inch long. Alejandro came over. Rubén handed him the cap. "What did you do with the head?"

"I swallowed it."

That story went around the school and stayed there. Even after Alejandro Cruz Ocampo graduated two years later it remained, handed down, as permanent as the passing generations. After the picnic on Cerro Madre they didn't call him Ali Cruz anymore, he had become Ali Cran. Alacrán is the Mexican word for scorpion.

THREE

Eliseo

🐾 WITH A VERY few exceptions I've not felt afraid in Michoácuaro—
in fact anywhere in Mexico. I can live with ants, roaches, scorpions,
and they let me be. I cope with the obligatory drinking and the
drawn-out stories. And at this point I have my rudimentary Spanish
under some control, though it keeps me from saying two-thirds of
what I'd like to share and from understanding half of what I want
to hear—the subtleties, the innuendoes and quadruple meanings
everyone explodes into laughter over, the histories of cures and
battles and debts and love affairs. I can grasp some parts of these
but never down to ground level, let alone at their roots.

But I don't know what to do with uncertainty. Am I in the wrong
line? Will there still be a hotel room available when I arrive after
dark? What is this new pain in my back or shoulder? Why is old
Nisi Calderón across the street watching my front door, then me,
whenever I come out, what is he trying to see? More worrisome,
what is he seeing?

I have always found some kind of hotel. The pain will eventually
go away. I know Nisi Calderón is there because he has nothing else
to do, he drives his wife crazy, he has long shouting arguments
with himself and he takes all five sides. His wife won't have him in
the house.

Which doesn't explain why he's always watching my door.
Knowing part of the reason for something doesn't change the chills
I get the next time it happens, or the next and the next.

One Monday morning they were pulling apart the street in front
of my house: an ancient pneumatic drill, half a dozen men supporting themselves on picks and shovels, an ancient ghetto blaster
with its volume turned to Kill. I ambled easily, a kind of self protection, across to Nisi. He told me his nephew's brother-in-law said
the job would take till tomorrow.

"To the end of the week, then." I shook my head.

He said, "Who knows?"—quién sabe, that strange phrase used in Mexico to send all possibilities back into mystery.

Depressed and irritated I marched back to my gate and slammed it behind me. Nisi's eyes had followed every step.

I sat at my desk. Writing fiction under the best of circumstances was proving difficult—my memory of people at home, their victimization, very hard to get on paper. Now, outside, staccato pounding fought cacophony. My story muse was untold miles away.

An hour or so later, my jefe friend Rubén came by. The son of a campesino, Rubén is in his middle or late thirties, his lank hair shines blue-black, he's broad in the shoulder, is working on a paunch, the pistol sits on his hip even when we're talking and drinking, and he's given to pointed-toe western boots. He intrigues me but I never feel completely at ease when he's around. I appreciate him for a number of reasons, not the least being he speaks slowly and clearly to me, as to a child.

We had ten minutes of polite chat, at least a third of it drowned out by mariachis overwhelming the drill. He came to his offer: "Jorge, you must go for a few days to my little house up on the hill. It will be quiet."

"That's very kind, Rubén, but I couldn't—"

"But certainly. My little house is your little house. Especially if I am not there and my wife is not there."

We laughed, his guffaws far more eloquent than mine. I find myself, most often, discomfited by the pervasive machismo here, its constant stress on challenge, on a comparison of strengths. Even more complex is my sense of disquiet at Rubén's kindness, his generosity; I don't know how I can repay it. I started an excuse, true enough but it served my real purpose, about my car not working, a piston shot, waiting for the part from Mexico City— I was drowned out by guitars electrified to the heavens.

"It is always true, Jorge, that you will not drink with me properly, each time you stop many hours before dawn. Why? Because you must write, it is so important to you. Do you want me to think you can write with this impossible noise on your street?"

I'd been to Rubén's "little house," his casita, twice, first when he drove me out to show it off, then for a fiesta one moonlit night with a band from Veracruz, a nonelectric Caribbean beat. The place could perhaps be called little if one considered only the rooms hab-

30

itable now, four, with high ceilings. At least nine others, large, their plastered adobe walls crumbing, angled out and across, six of them producing a fine courtyard, at its center the ruins of a fountain once tiled in red and yellow. Before the Revolution this had been the hacienda of a wealthy sugar cane family. One night they were dragged screaming from their beds, the old man found guilty by a revolutionary tribunal and shot beside the fountain, the mother and daughters tied together and shipped in a hay cart to Mexico City, propertyless but unraped. With land reform the acreage was divided into small plots. The household quarters and the fields had served as squatting grounds for sixty-five years. The adobe outbuildings had long since collapsed. Rubén, his police privileges helping him uncover who hadn't, over the decades, paid taxes on which land, bought from Michoácuaro, for uncollected debts figured in preinflated pesos, the ruined building and twenty-two acres. He was restoring the place, a room at a time. His great triumph, six months ago, had been to "organize" electricity in. He'd elaborated on that a couple of weeks before: "It is good, sometimes, to have light during the night. But the darkness is much better."

Moments like this were my cue, I'd learned—a reason he enjoyed talking with me. I was both willing audience and semicritical respondent. "Better?"

"There is evil in the light. More than in the dark. I can observe this, every day, in my work. In the light people see what they are doing."

Rubén Reyes Ponce, the philosopher-cop. I remarked, appropriately, "Then why did you bring electricity to your casita?"

He waved me off, the father—grandfather—to the small boy. "Evil in the light is worse. In light people defeat their humanity with rational thinking. In the nighttime they defeat it with the less fearful passions."

We would go on like that for a good while.

Now Rubén organized my return to work. A long pneumatic blast convinced me repaying could be secondary, I'd find a way to, sooner or later. When he offered a car to drive me up, there was no refusing. "I have plenty of food in the kitchen, Jorge, take what you need, I was there yesterday, we left everything, Bárbara and I." I should be ready at three in the afternoon.

The incessant radio and erratic drilling pummeled me in the head until two, when the crew broke for lunch. The silence was unspeakable pleasure. Sufficient to make me wonder if I couldn't actually stand five hours per day of this noise, I would find some other work or go for exploratory walks during the morning, I'd been planning to for a while. Did I really want to be in the casita for several days, far from town, no car, alone? But I couldn't find a polite way to say no.

I would think rationally. Three or four days of truly uninterrupted peace. The pleasure of sitting, totally alone, reveling in the moving pictures of the imagination. Michoácuaro had given me a lot of this already. But I was eager for a greater dose. An equation formed in my mind: Rubén's casita is to Michoácuaro as Michoácuaro is to my daily life in Boston and Montreal. Terrific.

Rubén came by around three-thirty. He pointed to my large bag. "You are taking very much with you."

"Notes. And my typewriter."

"And what do you carry in your head?"

I suddenly didn't feel up to any of Rubén's theories. "Just the imagination."

"Very heavy baggage, Jorge." But he backed off, handing me the key. "Everything is arranged. Pedro is not there on Mondays. You will be completely alone."

"Good. I'm looking forward to this." I offered a beer, he accepted, we drank and talked. We'd finished two by the time the pick-up arrived. The driver was one of three middle-aged young men who hang around Rubén's office, wash the two ancient police cars and the old truck, run errands of undying importance and call themselves, with no legitimacy apparent to me or others in town, deputy. I've never been comfortable around any of them—high school dropout types who hadn't bothered growing up would be my norteamericano category. Walk along any dirt road, meet a donkey carrying a mountain-stained campesino with a frown mustache to do Zapata proud, all it takes is a single buenos días to turn the mean grizzled face into a lantern of smiles and a wave that says, I know you are a foreigner in my land, how can I help you? But passing the police station I rarely evoke more than a grudging nod from one of the deputies; as if, should they receive my greeting, the veneer of their superiority might somehow implode.

The driver's name was Eliseo. I thanked Rubén again, again he told me it was nothing, truly nothing at all. Eliseo gunned the accelerator the moment my door was closed, throwing me backward on the seat. He grinned, but not in my direction. No doubt he had to be back in town as quickly as possible for an extremely important job for Rubén. I wondered if I should have offered him a beer as well.

We bounced hard on the truck's squashed shock absorbers. The disks in my spine were cushioning the vertebrae poorly. I needed distraction and reached for some easy conversation: "That drilling on the road makes a lot of noise."

He didn't answer immediately, as if he hadn't heard me or couldn't understand my Spanish. It might have been a minute before he said, "The road needs the work."

I nodded. Tried again. "What are they doing?" Silence. "With the road?"

Again the silence. I felt a little bit of the creepiness I mentioned before, suddenly finding myself in another uncertain situation. Was he ignoring me? Were the questions so difficult he needed time to figure out what to say? Or was he silent because giving answers to a gringo wasn't worth the trouble. I spoke again. "Is it for water pipes?"

Now he shrugged his shoulders.

I waited six-eight-ten seconds.

He said, "Quién sabe."

I sat back and looked out the window. Rubén's casita sat at the edge of the tierra caliente, now light green with young cane. The road stopped half a dozen miles after the turnoff to his place. Beyond lay warrens of donkey trails, millions of acres worth, motorized vehicles and the law unknown. We'd have a trip of about thirty-five minutes, at the far end three miles of well-rutted road impassible in the rainy season without four-wheel drive and even then you'd need to winch a couple of times along the way.

It was dry now and the dust on the oiled road leading out of town flew in swirls behind the truck. I've often wondered why Michoácuaro was built here, sliding down this hillside, when there is so little water. Perhaps the natural world of its sixteenth-century forbears was wetter, there were more springs then. Or more people now.

Eliseo swung around two oxen hauling a plow and the truck lunged ahead. I tried to think through a tricky part in the chapter I'd be working on out there. I must have succeeded in immersing myself in it: suddenly he was watching me and the road with equal curiosity. I realized he'd asked a question—possibly twice, some echo at the back of my head insisted. So: I'd just treated him to a version of his stance toward me. Embarrassing. "I'm sorry, what—?"

"What do you write, señor?"

"Oh— At home, articles. Here, a novel—"

"They must make you very rich."

"Oh no." I smiled, too broadly. "It is not an easy way to earn a living." I don't like chat moving in this direction.

He nodded. "There are not many good ways to make a living these days." He shook his head. "It is difficult."

A sympathetic response, enough to take advantage of. "And you. Is it a good job, working for Rubén?"

He shrugged. "For el jefe? The work, yes, it's good to work every day. It is not much money, not for a family."

Did he mean himself? I'd never thought of any of Rubén's helpers as domestic types. "You have a wife? Kids?"

"Two little ones." He nodded. "And a baby. Four years I am married to the mother of my children." He turned the grin on me then. It wasn't friendly, more—I'm not certain—self-satisfied; perhaps, thinking of his wife's receptive form, lascivious. Or maybe I was overreacting. "And my father-in-law, he lives in my house too. He has a pension. It is very little."

A man of family, responsibility, a place in the community. Had I misjudged completely his—

"This is not a good time in Mexico, señor. Not a time for us to live in dignity."

A subtle phrase, that, for Eliseo. Or a cliché he'd picked up somewhere. "It must be very difficult. But I do understand what you are telling me."

"It is different. To have a few dollars is different than to have a few pesos."

I conceded the point. Denial could lead to dangerous ground. "Have you worked for el jefe a long time?"

"Yes." He let the short Sí lie between us. Nowhere for the conversation to go. His silence brought back my discomfort.

Half a dozen miles down the road we reached the turnoff. Already the land was richer and wetter. This is the other side of the hill range, about a thousand feet lower than in town. And much greener: over a hundred springs rise here, water burbling out of the ground, it seems, behind every other boulder and out of the closest notch. Where it catches, ponds form, sometimes ice-cold when they are deep, sometimes so swampy cattle will wade in, become trapped in the mud, stumble, break their legs trying to escape, and drown. A complex of irrigation systems, some predating the Spanish conquest, controls the flow during the dry season, as now. The springs feed the valley below.

Eliseo gave gullies and potholes the largest part of his concentration. At many points the road was no wider than the truck, at others we had just enough width to maneuver around ruts and age-old washouts. Luck or some form of natural organization had somehow guaranteed the ongoing possibility of passage—traversable stretches where the road narrowed, obstacles appearing when maneuvering room, discerned with great difficulty, was also provided. I felt each thump along my back and in my shoulders.

Fifteen minutes of low-gear roaring and bouncing brought us to the gates. I got out, swung them open, and Eliseo drove in to the external court.

The hacienda must have been elegant once, lush gardens spreading before a fine old mansion. In the front it had risen to two stories, ruins of a curving balcony still visible. What had been least altered was the magnificent view: over a hundred miles of hills southwest to the coastal sierras.

I took in the view with proper appreciation. Landscape can be shared by strangers and antagonists, no quarter given or taken.

Eliseo turned off the engine, stayed in the truck, stared into the distance.

I pulled my bag down and smiled up. He took no notice. I followed his gaze. I had to say something, some few words, make amiable sounds. The mountains, sideswept by the sun, gleamed ore-filled in the low angles of light. Closer, the bright green of the young cane swayed gently in a late-afternoon breeze. "It is very beautiful, this county of yours."

He nodded then, as if to himself. As if I had discovered him basking in some unmanly pleasure. "Very peaceful," he said. And a few seconds after, "Very tranquil."

I suddenly had yet another image of my implacable driver, Eliseo the deputy: like too many of us trying to function in worlds of stress and little respect, he was thankful for a few moments of silence before the last of his duties, however trivial in my eyes, called him back. And afterwards he'd go home to a wife who threw his pride in his face, who couldn't control her children; perhaps she cuckolded him. And a father-in-law who had perhaps rejected his daughter's marriage, and now— I nodded my agreement. "Yes, very peaceful." And stared out into an unspecific beyond, letting the echo of my words die away.

Again the silence.

I was here to work. I added, briskly, "Muchas gracias."

"Por nada."

Not so much as a glance, let alone a grin. I felt a taunt in those two words and was once again uncomfortable with him. But at least I had arrived.

I figured I'd work in the kitchen and headed that way. I set my bag down, unlocked the door, realized the engine hadn't been turned back on, glanced around and waved. I did appreciate his concern, waiting to see whether I'd get in okay. Through the open truck window I saw him raise a hand, the slightest acknowledgment of my presence.

I called, "Hasta luego," and went inside. It's a pleasant kitchen, large, a chopping block/worktable in the middle, designed to accommodate, without them bumping elbows, a cook, her assistant and a serving maid. For total comfort, along one side a couch. For when the cook's assistant fainted? A place for me if my back got bad to lie down without leaving the room. All was polished clean. On the counter by the sink a few scout ants searched in vain for a crumb or two. On a shelf below the little window three large black fellows were carrying off a fly that must have died of starvation.

I organized myself at the central table—notes, paper, machine. I found a high flat stool, excellent surface for dictionary and thesaurus. I sat, surrounded by the returned pleasure of silence. All concentration could at last return to the chapter. Over the next few seconds the pieces of my body and reborn imagination settled comfortably into place—

Which was when the two bottles of beer, my hospitality to Rubén, made their reappearance—a sharp insistence low in the gut. I headed for the bathroom, accessible directly from the kitchen as well as from outside, and already felt partly relieved recalling the gringo sanitation features. I peed, marveling again that here in the hills there could be a Universal Standard flush toilet, a hot water shower, elegant blond clay floor tiles— At the corner of my eye a strange spot, glossy black, a couple of feet across which—

36

Which moved.

I screamed a tiny "Eeep!" and sprayed the floor.

Movement; shimmering.

Sweat came, cold wet points.

Moving like fur in the wind.

I stopped short, shivered— I took a step back.

Ants. A thousand. Maybe two, how do you measure a mass in motion? Step back, get away—

But my fascination inched me toward the spot. Till I could hover nearly above it. Two-thirds of the mass was immobile. The rest, bodies clambering over bodies in silence, prickled with work. A trail about eight ants wide stretched from the spot to the courtyard door, exiting beneath it. More than half were leaving, the others coming in. Their target was a sodden layer of purple glop. Closer examination—not too close—showed me the end of a Popsicle stick.

I laughed aloud. I could nearly reconstruct yesterday evening: Rubén and his wife Bárbara ready to go, the maid Concepción has everything cleaned, Lazarito the three-year-old or maybe little Mercedes who always looks too perfect has stolen the Popsicle from the freezer, hidden here to finish it, is called to come instantly, in panic of being caught sets it down very carefully and runs to their jeep. During the night or this morning along came nature's scout patrols, a veritable cleanup unit.

Their job was three-quarters done. On one side of the spot the tile was stained a patternless maze—traces of grape sugar-water, all color licked away.

I've had enough experience with ants to know not to interfere. These fellows wouldn't bother me anymore, from now on I'd use the great outdoors.

But they had made me thirsty. I'd get a beer, mull my chapter, drink, write, go to bed. In the morning the bathroom would be clean, the team's task completed. I wondered if refined sugar was as bad for ants as for little Mexican kids.

The fridge stood next to the window. I started to open it, glanced out. The truck was still there.

Strange, that. Easily ten minutes since we'd said goodbye. Maybe the truck wouldn't start. I stood at the edge of the window and watched.

Eliseo still sat behind the wheel. He seemed to be leaning back, feet possibly on the dashboard, his sombrero pulled low on his forehead. His glance, as much as I could tell, still sought out the greying mountains. I thought I could detect the truck radio, guitars strumming and a bit of a beat. What was he doing, lazing the late afternoon away? All those responsibilities in Rubén's office, why wasn't he rushing back to be important? I recalled his shrewish wife and riotous children, the financial worries— I would get him a beer, he'd drink it quickly, be newly relaxed, then he'd leave.

I brought out a Dos Equis, wonderfully cold, yellow and sparkling; an advertisement of a beer, an advertisement to take him elsewhere, to a place of beer-drinking fun. None for me, I could wait, I didn't want to get into a booze session.

He looked at me, moving only his eyes under the low brim of his sombrero, a strange stare, seemingly resentful, yet displaying no understanding of what either he or I was doing there. He got out of the truck, took the beer, raised it to his mouth, stopped for a moment to remember politeness: "Salud." Then he drank. Only a small sip. As if he were doing me a favor.

I was pretty sure I could establish some new ground rules: I'd hang around, we'd talk, he'd finish the beer and leave. No doubt his difficulties were many. I said if he wanted to talk I would be happy to listen even though, I insisted, I didn't understand many Mexican customs and my Spanish was not very good. He looked at me so strangely, I couldn't tell what he was feeling—did he think I was prying or was he amazed at my generosity? Overall I think he was pleased, though I don't imagine he understood or would have cared much for the norteamericano notion of psychology.

We hemmed and hawed as I probed more about the difficulties of the economy and how this affected his life. Nowhere to go, no other jobs were possible, he said. He leaned against the truck and sipped his beer. Very slowly. And might he one day do Rubén's job? Rubén had nowhere to go either, Eliseo and Rubén were the same age, Rubén would die when Eliseo died. He seemed to enjoy talking about himself, was speaking quickly now. What would he like to do, if he could change his work? Own a small restaurant, have a place his friends could come, argue with him, everyone would drink together. His speed of speech increased, I was only grasping small parts of what he said. But, he explained, no restaurant, no good in life would come, not without some money, some real money, not what Rubén paid him. No, not Rubén, I tried to explain, but Michoácuaro, Michoácuaro employed him. But he would have none of this, there were those in the world who always had the same great luck—he waved his hand toward the hacienda—and those who would never succeed, would always work for others. He sipped beer. The bottle was barely a third empty.

I shifted my strategy. I explained about my work, I had written nothing all day, I had my quota, if I did not get to work now I would be up all night, already my back was beginning to ache—another excuse, but true. He nodded, impressed by my resolve if the weariness on his face wasn't faked.

A small unease had settled on my shoulders. He fell silent but didn't go anywhere. Failed tactics. Admire me though he might, he wasn't budging. I said I hoped he wasn't uncomfortable in the truck. He again mentioned the view, the peace. I gave up. I wished him a good evening and started to move away. Sideways. Because I would have to turn my back on him to get to the kitchen. A curiously difficult decision, this tiny one: walk away backwards and act like a fool, or stroll off normally and leave myself in his power. Power? I asked myself; and: What's there to be afraid of? I forced myself to smile, to wave lightly and, with the flash of mind it takes to dive into cold water, to turn. I knew his eyes drilled into my back. A normal pace felt like dreamwalking through nearby marshlands in leaden waders. I dare not fall down, I dare not fall— The doorhandle, eons away, finally reached my fingers. I twisted, pushed, walked in. He was still staring. I needed to return the evening to casual, one last friendly wave. I couldn't. I shut the door, locked it. There. Nothing to be afraid of.

My back ached, merciless. I blamed it alone for all that nonsense. I had to lie down, there was nothing else. I blessed Rubén and his cook for their couch. My heart pounded so loud I was afraid I'd not hear Eliseo start the truck and drive away. After some minutes the beat slowed, softened. Not a single mechanical sound. My ears worked so hard they silenced the other organs. Far away, as if in a better world, a dog barked. A confused rooster crowed. I could hear water murmuring and for a moment was convinced it had started raining, which would explain why I hadn't heard the truck start. But the season was wrong, the burbling came from a spring and the damn pickup still sat in the entry yard.

The whole situation was ridiculous. I blamed my greed. For silence and peace beyond Michoácuaro. I hadn't understood the bounds, I was being punished like some new convert to a powerful

39

drug who's experienced remarkable highs and now wants more, still more. And gets it. I was in. No way out. What the hell was he doing there? Guarding the only escape—

So easy to imagine reasons for fear.

I have a small cottage in northern New Hampshire. Before Alaine became sick I used it for working and mulling, to be alone. After, when she needed constant care, I ran away there for short periods, to avoid the responsibilities. No phone, either. A little more than a year ago I went out there to write a report, promising to return to town in three days. All was magnificent September foliage. The third day and my work had gone well the whole morning. So much so I said to myself, to hell with getting back as promised, let Alaine worry about me for once. Another day and I'd have the whole project done. I was on a roll so fully—I recall thinking somehow I must've sold the devil a piece of my soul, it couldn't be this good naturally. The whole project was completed by six. I could still have headed back then but a storm was coming on, the sky across the lake had already darkened beyond normal twilight and anyway, I told myself, I needed a reward.

A Mozart sonata on the tape deck, a bottle of Lafitte-Rothschild '77 saved for an important occasion; what friend could be more special than my finished work. The wine went magnificently with steak and sweet potato. A terrific day, and evening. I felt wonderful, high on the whole world. Then came the first ping. On the roof. As if someone were throwing small stones. I waited. Another ping. Same place. Very strange. The light was on, seeing out wasn't possible. A third ping, a kind of double one. The curtains on the large window overlooking the lake were drawn wide open. I hunched down to cross the living room, feeling simultaneously foolish and careful. Two more pings, this time on the window. Who was throwing things at my cottage! I reached the light-switch and turned it off. But I could see nothing more in the outside darkness. Another ping. Ridiculous. I grabbed the flashlight from the shelf by the entry. I'd sweep the whole area. In one movement I opened the door, flicked on the power and stepped outside. In the next instant lightning lit the whole world brighter than noon. I was sure I saw a dash, a leap, some shape I couldn't describe spring into the trees at the edge of my land. As instantaneously it was again dark except for the beam of my feeble lamp. I leapt back inside, slammed the door, found the single malt and drank two large swallows from the bottle. An amazing electrical charge? No more pings. Someone who meant harm? Clumsy squirrels dropping nuts meant for winter storage?

When I got home Alaine wasn't there. A note: they'd had to take her to intensive care. She came back five days later. Even less well.

Now I lay down. No roosters. No dogs. Silence. The stream gurgled on. No truck engine turned over. This time I knew someone was out there. I closed my eyes. I would try the self-hypnosis I use occasionally for my back.

It didn't work, I couldn't concentrate. I lay still, keeping thought at bay as much as possible. The stream gurgled and sloshed—

I must have slept. My eyes opened to complete darkness. I had only one thought. Carefully I got up, walked to the edge of the window, looked out. It took a while to focus, there was no moon. Then I saw movement. The glint of a match. He was lighting a cigarette. The lower half of the window framed his profile. I pulled back.

I admitted it openly now, I was dangling at the spooked end of very uncomfortable. This time, all too likely, with reason. Either the deputy policeman had truly serious domestic problems and didn't want to go home—too late for his jefe's work—or he was planning something downright evil.

I forced myself to think clearly. He had been there for over an hour. It was dark out. If he was intending me harm would he already have acted? Or— Possibly he had reason to wait. For? Help. From? An associate. A partner. No, Eliseo would give orders. Or take orders. From? His boss. The jefe! Come on, not— Rubén had loaned me his little house, he'd organized— No. He had not set me up. I refused to believe it. For what, anyway? Harm me? Kidnap me? Hold me for ransom? For the millions my novel might one day bring? Ridiculous. But who else knew I was here? But Rubén might have told anyone. But why? I knew he wasn't a particularly honest man, at least not according to our back-home standards. Still—

Stop.

I couldn't remember if the backache had gone away while I slept but it was certainly there now. My heartbeat hacked into my spine between the shoulder blades, sending nasty curls of pain down my right arm to the wrist. I lay on the couch. Unchanged darkness. It was a time for strained notions. If I could see my forearm, what color would it be? If daylight suddenly shone its friendly warmth

41

through the window, would the world be a great place? And if I knew what was going on would I really feel better? Rubén could maneuver through tax records but how had he managed to tap into my nervous system?

Sooner or later I'd have to make a move. In the darkness, in the silence, my bladder had refilled. The bathroom, the ants, without turning on the light? Or—outside?

What could he take from me? Not Alaine, too late for that, I was alone. My reputation and good name? Only by forcing me into acts immensely unnatural and then not without tortures I couldn't get close to thinking about. Dying before finishing everything I wanted to do? I'd been around before on that one and concluded that, whenever the last moment comes, either there's nothing so important, or there'll always be more to get done.

So? Nothing to fear.

Suddenly, out there, voices. Quiet, speaking quickly. They would act now. It was almost a relief.

Should I wait here, silent, passive? Or fight back. With what? I stood up then. To get the knives I'd have to force a pathway through my memories of the kitchen. I moved slowly, hands reaching into the air, fingers groping, searching for landmarks. My shin hit something soft which I knew couldn't be grabbing my leg, but it felt malicious, I jumped back, then reached my foot forward again. The stool.

Outside, the voices. Louder. Closer?

The side of the table. My hand found a chair, I worked my way around, over to the counter, somewhere was the sink, then I'd need the drawers—

A single voice, directly behind the door. Didn't sound like Eliseo. Not loud. Just, there.

And if I found a knife? Which I had no experience with. Against two men? One supposedly trained in restraining drunks and more dangerous types, in small-arms combat, in who know what else—

Someone turned the door handle.

Such wisdom to have locked—

A push on the door. Nothing. Another turn and push. The lock wouldn't be easy to open. I was safe for a while. They couldn't—

The outside door to the bathroom! That pile of ants was no blockade. I groped my way along the counter.

A whisper, further away. Then silence.

42

I reached the opening, pulled the door closed. I felt for a latch, a key. Nothing, nothing at all. And it hinged away from the kitchen so even a blockade was impossible. But the door from the bathroom to the outside, was it locked? Stupid, I should have tried. Likely it was. Would Rubén leave a door unlocked?

Were they regrouping? I was certain they'd try the bathroom. It made all the sense in the world. And if it was open—

For some minutes, no movement. I worked my way back to the couch, sat, tried to think. Maybe they wouldn't come through the bathroom, maybe they didn't know there was another way in, maybe they were watching only the kitchen door— Watching. If I couldn't see them, how could they see me? Instantly the darkness was a newfound ally. I could get out through the bathroom, work my way in absolute silence along the hacienda wall, over to the edge of the garden, down to the fence; a large circle to the gate which I didn't think Eliseo had closed. It felt simple enough. A long walk to the highway but the dirt road was an easy pathway. Unless I had to get off the road, then I'd end up in the marshes, sink into the mud— No. It wouldn't happen like that. I could stay on the road with no difficulty, what was three kilometers, get to the end and hitch a ride to town.

I smiled, reminded myself to step carefully, thought about peeing as I passed through the bathroom, decided it'd be my reward when I was clear of the gates. The hardest obstacle would be the ants. I shook my head, building a reserve of courage. Ants? No problem.

The bathroom entryway swung open, silent. My hand slid along the wall, found the corner, followed the surface, located the door. The handle. I turned, pushed. Locked. I felt for a bolt, a turnscrew. Found a keyhole. Keyless. Maybe hanging on the door frame—

I could feel the sweat break out. I groped. A spiderweb. I hoped its owner was far way. My sides, my right leg especially, low down, itched from panic. Where could the key— Without thinking I scratched my prickly calf. Then it wasn't fear, it was ants. Two, three, five— Stop! In the split second between realizing and knowing they were climbing up my leg I forced myself into a superficial calm. Slow. Easy. They were only ants. I rolled up my pant leg, pinched them off. I scratched. A problem solved. But the next one—

I was locked in. Simply that. Shouldn't I just stay as I was? What choice? I scratched my leg, my thigh. In my pocket, the kitchen key— I worked my way back to the bathroom door, key at the ready. The lock turned! With very little noise. A tumbler clicked. I twisted the handle, pulled lightly. The door moved. I opened it an inch, two. Outside, darkness. The only sound the stream's burbling, louder here.

Okay. A moment to think. I could feel another ant, maybe two, on my ankle. I bent down to brush it away. A new sound, mechanical. I held still. An engine! Had they started the truck, were they driving off? I opened the door a touch wider. No. Headlights. Bouncing, down on the road. Someone else. To rescue me? If not—

If I ran now I'd be seen, certainly.

The headlights bobbed and turned and missed the bathroom door by a dozen feet. I shoved the door shut, hard, too loud, but the sound was drowned out by the roar of the engine. I worked my way back, easier since the headlights were now trained directly at the kitchen window. The engine roar suddenly cut away. The lights stayed on. A car door slammed. Shouts in fast Michoacán-accented Spanish. Answering shouts. I couldn't understand a word. Should I open the door, step outside— I wanted to look out the window. The light shone in so sharply I'd see nothing. Then silence. Then a shout: "Jorge! Are you in there?"

Rubén. I was okay. Or—

I edged to the window, peeked around the side. Rubén stood between the headlights and the door. Two others behind him, one on either side. Rubén took a step toward me. A silhouette against two high-beams. In his hand the pistol.

"Jorge!"

How was I supposed to answer? You'll never take me alive! What is the meaning of this outrage?!

"Jorge!"

I couldn't say a word.

He was at the door. The key scraped in the lock. The door opened and he stood outlined in yellow light. He flicked the switch. I honestly didn't know—

"Are you all right?" He stepped in.

"Uh—sure."

"He is so stupid, Eliseo. When he did not return, his wife was certain he had an accident, she knows how he drives. He did not listen to me." He put his pistol in the holster. "He thought he was to bring you back this evening. When you were finished. He is very stupid. He could not imagine you here alone all night."

I heard the truck engine start. "I tried to explain—"

"Yes yes, he told me. He thought you were exaggerating. It is his way."

The truck was driving toward the gate. Very slowly.

"He saw my bag. And I told him I'd be working all night." I was winding down enough to feel indignant.

"Yes, and when he could not see any light he was certain you had lied."

"I was sleeping."

Rubén nodded a half a dozen times as if he were duly tired of the whole mess. A campesino, dirty straw hat, unshaven face, bare feet in huaraches, appeared at the door: the second man. Rubén introduced me to Pedro, who looks after the hacienda. Pedro would get me everything I needed during the next few days. "If you still wish to stay."

"Of course. Yes. Unless the street repairs are finished."

Rubén grinned. "They have brought in a second pneumatic drill."

"Then it'll be done in half the time?"

"I think they will work only a quarter as fast." He went to the refrigerator. "Would you like a Dos Equis?"

We sat silently and drank.

FOUR

Nagual

🐾 DOES ALI CRAN have a tail? Did he once?

For some here such questions take on a kind of transcendent meaning: if there is a tail, we can believe in his power; if not . . .

One evening I asked Pepe, "If it matters so much, why doesn't someone just ask him?"

Normally he takes my shows of gringo ignorance in stride. To my question about Ali Cran's tail he pressed his eyes closed, shook his head and turned to leave.

I made light. "No, come on. What?"

"Jorge—" He paused. Then he sat and sighed deeply. "Jorge, even in your country, would you speak so to another man?"

"Look, I was just curious about—"

He was waving his hand from side to side, the gesture that brooked no argument. "Amigo. To ask this of Alicito, it would be like for a woman to say to you, 'Jorge, pull down your pants, I want to see do you have a machine.' "

I grinned; then forced a laugh to cover my lack of rejoinder. "Would you like a beer?"

He shrugged. "If you are having one."

Nodding, I went to the kitchen. I felt uncontrollably foreign.

That evening made it only ten weeks since my arrival. Tending plants and flowers in my courtyard had reduced both the stress and the sorrow I'd brought with me. And I'd fallen in love with the town and surroundings—flowering trees everywhere, the gentle pace, the kindness of the people. Over the weeks I'd learned some of their histories—a satisfying diversion since the novel remained slow in coming. Ali Cran stood out increasingly as the most fabled of Michoácurans. And the most mysterious. Rumors abound, stories have melded together. He fomented Michoácuaro's most famous feud. For breakfast, mixed into his beans, he eats scorpions fried in lard.

46

He can make himself invisible at night and in bright daylight. His children people the countryside. He knows many worlds because roosters and burros speak with him daily. He takes counsel with certain mango trees. Furthermore he has a multipurpose tail.

No one seems to know, conclusively, if such a feature really exists—though, living here, I'm far more ready to accept a wide range of realities. The stories, old reports and new sightings, have come, since soon after my arrival, from every direction. But Pepe was right: I could not, and least for factuality's sake, see anyone ask Ali Cran outright, Hombre, do you have a tail?

Some people concede there is a tail. In fact, several tails, all removable, each with a specialized use. A sharp spiny one for revenge, a broad fleshy one for comfort when he rides his horse, a soft furry one for his amorous adventures. A tiny one to set in place when he needs to look normal, as here in town. Because everyone agrees, when in Michoácuaro or the times he has been spotted in Morelia or the time Nisi Calderón caught him at six in the morning paddling about the pond of sacred water at the Shrine of María de León at Aguafría wearing only his undershorts or the many times he's been seen swimming in the volcanic lagoon, no tail was noticeable. When he strolls about the plaza or shops in the market, he usually wears a shirt with three open buttons exposing his not unusually hairy chest, his jacket hangs to the sides of his hips and his jeans aren't particularly loose. No attempt, in effect, either to conceal or raise the issue of a tail.

Yet such questions persist. Constanza who arrives at eight four times a week to clean swears she has seen him at fiestas in tierra caliente. "He sat on his horse, Apostata." She spoke of this memory with respect. "He looked so high in the saddle I could think only of the animal I have seen in the movie when the man with the blue eyes is riding such an animal, the man wears a cloth wrapped many times around his head, he rides on the animal's high bump."

Not trusting my Spanish I checked the dictionary. "Un camello?"

Constanza thought that was it. Anyway Ali Cran sat up high and she knew Apostata didn't have a bump on his back. Twice she saw this with her own eyes, Alicito riding much higher than normal.

About two months after I'd arrived I overheard a doomed flirtation at the beer depósito, the outlet where I get my Negra Modelo. I suspect it was allowed to continue in my presence because I was already well known in town—best known probably—for dreadful

Spanish. Still, though my speaking ability remained poor, I'd begun to understand increasingly well. Here is what went on:

María-Cecilia, a buxom young woman whose hair always shines with a thick black light, runs the depósito. She has a child, a handsome boy of four, Aurelio. She was never married and lives with her mother and two younger sisters. Though the Church frowns on children born beyond sacramental legitimacy, in Michoácuaro many people accept daily needs, bodily desires and their consequences, as normal. Ali Cran is rumored to be Aurelio's father. Apparently Cecilia has never admitted to this. Nor has she denied it. I'd been told she could go into a kind of light reverie, broken by wordless happy giggles, should anyone allude to Aurelio's parentage. Now, in the doorway of the depósito, she was being teased by a slender young man with a catching grin. I'd not seen him before. She called him Carlos. They sat on the stoop, the beer refrigerator behind them, watching Aurelio pull a tiny car on a string down the sidewalk.

Carlos asked her why she wouldn't go with him to the dance.

She said maybe someone else had invited her.

He said who was it, he'd have to fight to take her.

To me she said, slowly, "A dozen Negras, señor?"

"I'll need two dozen this time, please." I never know if I should call her señora or señorita.

She started to stand up. I told her I could get them. She left me to it. I began to load my basket.

"Are you going with—" Carlos mentioned three names I didn't know.

"No."

"Then it must be Ali Cran."

She said nothing.

I turned. Here was one of the loveliest smiles I'd ever seen. Her black eyes, looking at no one near, drew me in. Her face glowed as with a soft fire from the tip of her nose to the lobes of her ears. In that instant I felt I'd seen into the heart of Michoácuaro. She must have sensed me staring because suddenly she glanced in my direction. So, foolishly, I grinned at her.

Instantly the glow heated to a flaming blush. She looked out along the sidewalk, stood up, called with great gentleness, "Aurelio, too far. Come back."

Carlos said, "With Ali Cran I cannot compete." And in some

despair he added, I'm sure I understood it, "Even if I bring you rose petals to lie on, what could be so soft as the fur on Ali Cran's tail when it is wrapped—"

She disappeared from my view, running after Aurelio. Carlos jumped up and followed. I waited with my bottles, cash ready. She returned, her squawking son in hand. I paid, she thanked me, I left. I have assumed Carlos did not take Cecilia to the dance.

Of another group of stories, that Ali Cran's tail has to be cut regularly or at least trimmed, only the locale, the rim of the volcano, is agreed on. In what was millennia ago the cone, there is a lagoon about half a kilometer wide and so deep oceanographers from the National University in Mexico City have not been able to sound its bottom, their diving instruments too weak to withstand the surge of unusual currents down below. Deaf Gertrudis who presides over the flower stall at the market swears she has seen a monster with many heads and countless arms rise from the water. Pepe, who swims in the lagoon, says he's been warned by many, starting long ago with his mother, that the water can turn into a whirlpool. He isn't prepared to discount either the whirlpool or the monster, arguing that much of Mexico's geological foundation is unstable, as the September earthquake demonstrated again; and since underground connections between the lagoon and the sea might exist, and given certain conditions deep beneath the surface, a vortex certainly could be created. "Like in your bathtub, Jorge. When you pull the plug. Except here maybe water comes in as well. And the hole closes up again."

"And the monster?"

"It is very deep down there, no?" He paused, then spoke with great placidity: "Can we believe all life-forms have already been discovered?"

I couldn't tell if he was putting me on.

At any rate, the volcano was the site of the supposed operation on Alicito's tail. In most of the stories someone else does the job for Ali Cran; in some he cuts it alone. Two partners are mentioned most often. The first is Serafina, a young woman who, years ago, came to town for several days. About her there are further rumors too. The other, one of Ali Cran's compadres, Migro Cardo, is a large, slow man whose appearance, Moisés de Jesús's son Tomás says, can be deeply deceiving. Ali Cran is supposed to have had a brief but passionate affair with this Serafina. Some say she returns twice a year for the trimming, during Holy Week and on the Day of the Dead. There are more supporters for Migro Cardo, however; they argue that Serafina disappeared long ago and no one has ever claimed to see her by the volcano's rim, not even Nisi Calderón who keeps his eye on everybody's business and, old as he is, six years ago sat out on the rim each night of Holy Week. Nothing happened. So, maintain the Migro Cardo backers, the Serafina stories are at best secondhand and more usually third or fourth.

I have tried in vain to find anyone who has ever seen Migro Cardo snipping away, so I'd guess the story retains its believers because Migro lives right in town and can be found at his combined garage and metalwork shop, building strange machines. Whenever asked, mostly by the little kids who hang around, whether he cuts tails, he smiles as if hiding a hoard of private knowledge, laughs lightly through closed lips and returns to his work. So Tomás tells me.

I've met Migro Cardo several times, first when he and I were two of the eight who carried the casket of Moisés de Jesús. Then the time he invented a motor-run spit for me, an amazing device using a series of belts and gears, including a bicycle wheel, to slow the motor's turning ratio. It stands at the end of my courtyard. I use it for roasting chickens over a wood fire. Much easier than turning it by hand, as I've told Constanza; who disapproves. Most people say of Migro he's crazy, a dabbler, if he spent more time repairing cars and less on his inventions he might even get rich because he's a first-rate mechanic. About our only topic of conversation, when we meet in the market or on the plaza, is our friend the late Moisés de Jesús.

Depending on the storyteller, the tool used for the actual tail-trim can be any blade, from a field machete to a silver knife. Those who favor Migro Cardo argue for a pair of snippers with handles a meter long and a blade of just fifteen centimeters, a powerful unit which Migro put together, he claims, for cutting metal cord; ask him for four meters of cable and he'll bring the clippers out. Even those who've examined the tool carefully won't swear they've not seen traces of blood. Yet the blade, this group will explain, is always with Migro Cardo when he meets Ali Cran at the rim of the volcano. Some insist Migro became Ali Cran's compadre precisely to perform this act.

For days afterwards, supposedly, the water remains tempestuous even if there isn't any wind. Pepe, who claims he's not at all superstitious, refuses to swim there at such times.

There's another kind of story, all its versions by and large similar. Rubén says some in Michoácuaro take this lack of variance as blatant proof of Truth. The gist is this: Ali Cran's renown as a lover of women is immense—the reputation is well founded—and of course the tail hangs not over his rump but in front. That this version is, in my terms, far more naturalistic has never been cited in the attempt to legitimize it as the real story. Ali Cran's exploits are described with mirth or envy, with delight or anger, or with praise. Depending on the relation of the teller to the woman involved.

One sweaty Sunday late afternoon Rubén and I were sitting in my courtyard, both of us bent to dwelling on tragedy. He spoke about Marta, his beautiful first wife, and showed me her photograph, a woman in maybe her late twenties, long hair, instant lively eyes. The only real passion in his life, ever. One morning she kissed him goodbye when he left for work; early in the evening a neighbor rushed to his office, Come quickly, Marta is very sick. He carried her unconscious to Michoácuaro's small hospital. In an hour she was dead, her spleen had burst. He did remarry but could never truly love again. For myself, I couldn't bear to speak about Alaine so I told him about a girl, Becky, whom I'd met when I was nineteen. We knew we'd love each other forever, she went away for three months to her father in California, when she came back she was engaged to a carpenter from Santa Monica. I cursed them both and wished her dead. Five weeks later a truck smeared her VW and she was.

It had been that sort of talk all afternoon. We'd done some drinking and words were coming out slurred and I was forgetting Rubén's stories of only an hour before. But our exchange had brought with it the pleasure of sharing old sadnesses, and new roots of affection were being planted.

I found the courage then and told him of meeting Alaine, loving her and marrying her, waiting to have children, then not being able, and how one of the many examinations found the tumor, early enough we'd thought—

Rubén cut me off, insisted we stop talking about sorrow.

I knew he was right. Still—

He said I should immediately find another bottle of mezcal and he would grant me the privilege of hearing some of Michoácuaro's deepest secrets. As jefe de policía he knew them all. Yes, a fine escape. I couldn't get closer to the town's pulse than Rubén. But I had no more mezcal.

"Is this a problem? Surely you can mix us some of your famous martinis."

"Great idea." I spoke the words but already my head wasn't so certain. I forced my brain to work as hard as its sodden state allowed. "One of the stories about Ali Cran's tail, I've heard people chuckle over it, little references, Ali Cran and the pure-blooded Indian woman."

Rubén's eyebrows rose very high, he suddenly grinned with a kind of crinkly delight, then his chest shook with slow, thick laughter. "You like dirty stories, Jorge? This is a nice dirty story. It will make your white gringo cheeks a nice shining red."

"None of your fabrications, Rubén. Just tell me the truth." A mezcal challenge.

Rubén's grin was suddenly gone. "You make the best martinis in Michoácuaro, Jorge. That is your responsibility now. Mix. I will use your elegant toilet."

So I brewed up a large icy pitcherful of martinis and returned. He too was back, grinning broadly. I ceremoniously presented the glasses, poured, sat.

He leaned forward and sipped. Sat back, sighed his compliments: "Wonderful." Grinned, mostly to himself, as if previewing the story behind his eyes. "My friend Alicito is a strange man, Jorge. You have heard much of him."

It wasn't exactly a question, yet Rubén's pause called for a response. I nodded, waited.

Rubén sat back, stared at a space above my head and years away, and began. After a few moments I realized the slur in his speech was gone, replaced by immense clarity, great empathy. I've seen this before, here in Michoácuaro—in Pepe, in Moisés de Jesús. Something strange happens to a man when he tells a good story about a friend, he fills with deep pleasure, a shimmer of respect—

"Before he was twenty Ali Cran had already gained much fame as a lover. A dangerous thing in these mountains, Jorge. As you know, our women belong to their man—to their husband, to their father, or if he is dead or has gone away to the eldest brother until he can find her a husband. Alicito in his adventures always chooses with care, especially from the ones who come to him, which is most of them. His women are those who want revenge on their men. Or widows, of course. And women with husbands everyone knows are at the cantina drinking or have a woman in town. Ali Cran also has a taste for women who think they are somehow modern. Or women whose husbands do not rise hard, or with husbands that beat them—and Alicito is a gentle lover, it is said. Or a woman who has seen the father beat the mother every day so never wished to marry but did want to have children. Have I forgotten any? Probably. But you see, there are many women for Ali Cran." Rubén sipped and nodded, in agreement with himself.

As I waited for him to continue I realized my head, like Rubén's voice, had cleared.

"This you should also know. Until 1974 Michoácuaro was the last town on the road, the trucks could go no further. Santa María de León and Ojo de Agua were villages, places to walk to or ride to on a burro for a pilgrimage. Michoácuaro was not yet the metropolis it is now."

The towns he mentioned are eleven miles to the southwest and sixteen to the southeast respectively. There the roads still do stop. Beyond lies only more tierra caliente, down to the next range of the Sierra Madre, then a hundred fifty more kilometers of mountains and plains and hills falling away to the final range before the sea. The whole area is riddled by donkey paths connecting tiny villages and even half a dozen towns, some centers of close to five thousand people. Still today all outside goods are brought in by burro caravans.

Rubén went on: "A man did not have to travel far to lose himself. At the places where trails cross they will tell you a hechicera lives only three villages away, and you will find no one who has not heard a nagual story from someone whose brother or grandmother has actually seen the nagual with their own eyes. You understand hechicera, Jorge? A bad witch. A nagual is a half-man, half-beast."

I nodded.

"So you will understand, these adventures of Ali Cran with the señoras and the señoritas, they were perhaps dangerous. But not so very dangerous, because until the time of this story which happens when Ali Cran is about twenty-two these ladies would be in a conspiracy—you understand conspiracy?—a conspiracy with Ali Cran.

53

There was a reason, a large reason, I will come to it." Rubén sipped again. "Ali Cran was still very skinny, the hair was soft on his chin and around his eggs. His eyes were deep in his head. He always looked shy or nervous. But never afraid, you understand. Already he had known many more women than he remembered. He was a great expert, what he could tell is undreamed of by the normal man. The only experience he had not had, he had never been with a woman of pure blood, una india."

I sipped my martini, waiting.

Rubén bent toward me and his words were quieter. "Before I tell you about him, there are three pieces of information on Ali Cran's life you should know. First, he came late to his puberty. Till seventeen no hair at all grew on his body except on the top of his head. In the beginning his father, Don Martín Cruz, wondered if the boy's stones had come down yet from inside. The father examined Alicito with the boy's compadre Migro Cardo. Finally they could not say for sure. Yes the pouch was there, but. . . . They took Alicito to the hospital in Morelia. Two doctors looked at him very carefully. The organ, the doctors agreed, though assuredly small, was perfect. Of course the whole examination, you understand, was so embarrassing to Ali Cran he spoke of it to me, his best friend at this time, not until months later. I myself never forgave Don Martín. Even then—I am two years older than Alicito, you understand—I believe I understood the problem." He sighed.

I was impressed by Rubén's ability to organize his information. Especially in an oral account.

"You see, Ali Cran in those days was still very interested in insects, in looking closely. Once when I was with him we watched a squadron of ants locate an immense dead butterfly and carry it to the nest and try to pull it in by a hole that was too small. Finally, together they tore off the wings and dragged the body underground. He said many times how he wished he could crawl into the ground with the ants. He taught me to look at these things."

The inclination to keep sipping my drink was strong. Desire to remember details overcame any thirst.

"I feared for Ali Cran; that Don Martín, not a wise person, you understand, would think his son was not man enough. I thought I could help. I tried to discover from Alicito if he had ever been with one of the girls from school or at his rancho, any of them. I had not talked of such things before, not with him. With other friends, of course. But with Alicito— He said no. It was a simple statement of fact." Rubén leaned back, paused.

If he was expecting me to act surprised I disappointed him.

"I said to Alicito, would he like to do this, to put his thing into a woman. He told me he had thought about it, that maybe it would even be exciting. Still, he said, the world was filled with so many amazing details he did not think he needed to discover the inside of a woman. One day perhaps, not now. But from the way he spoke, so much unusual control, I was thinking, He is embarrassed, perhaps frightened, maybe he does not know this but he is. So I talked more, how it felt and so on. Then he told me he was having dreams he did not understand, dreams about himself with women. Many women. I took that last part as a clear sign and consulted with my cousin Rafael Mirate. Rafael was older and very macho in such things and at the same time he wrote poems and songs. Very sad, very beautiful songs. At his funeral four years ago we sang only his songs. Rafael had once explained to me how he understood everything about women, so I assumed he was the right person now. Rafael took his responsibility seriously and brought Ali Cran together"— Rubén chortled at his little joke—"with an excellent señora from the Hotel Domicilio. She was no longer thirty and they called her La Bondadosa."

Rubén's earlier wistfulness threatened a return.

"We had all heard of La Bondadosa, some of us had known her. This is the kind of woman whose many years of expertise make her very wise. As an initiator, I mean. Generous. La Bondadosa was in this way soft and strong, she would bring a young man to his satisfaction, sometimes hers, and all the time he would think he alone was responsible. She was also successful in raising life where it had not been for a long time or the man feared there would never be. Every town has such a woman. Or needs one."

I wanted to ask what happened to her but figured the question could wait.

"Ali Cran and Rafael became very close. In some ways Rafael took my place as Alicito's best friend. This was a sad change for me. What I know of the rest of the story of Alicito and his india is what Rafael told me."

And a moment later I began to feel the narrative slipping away, as behind veils. I wanted to ask why Rubén used the term india, which I'd been taught was deprecatory. I caught myself, however, and stayed silent.

Rafael had confided in Rubén: There was little doubt that the hair everywhere on Ali Cran's body had started to grow and the part of him that was most a man had begun to increase.

Rubén drained his martini, refilled the glass, leaned forward again. "And increase, Jorge. The experience with La Bondadosa awakened a great appetite in Ali Cran."

Rafael said Ali Cran's discoveries were wide and deep. He became afflicted with a great hunger, and his tail kept growing. Rubén leaned back, his head shaking as if he still couldn't believe it. "Don Martín and Migro Cardo had noticed. They took him again to the doctors. Four times in the next three years. The tests proved only what Ali Cran could see by looking."

I folded my arms and sat back.

"Now is the important part, Jorge. Alicito had never slept with a woman of pure Indian blood. This was not because he had avoided such women. There are not many such women, you understand, Jorge? not many of us who are not a bit mestizo—you understand mestizo? the Spanish blood mixed in, maybe even a little gringo. Why would such a woman come to him? And he did not go in search. He went only where he was invited, where he was wanted. The women came to him, those who needed him, because they knew his reputation. A very respectable señora—her husband works for the federal surveyors so he spends much time away from Michoácuaro—in those days she explained Ali Cran to me this way, that he shares what he has. I will not bore you, Jorge, with the accounts from many women who have spoken to me of Ali Cran. In my professional capacity."

I noted a sad hint of a smile of Rubén's face.

"From these women he received many offers of marriage. But to each Ali Cran said no. There were so many, how could he limit himself to one. And how about love? This love, whatever it was, it had never made its appearance in his years of growing. Pleasure and friendship, but no more."

Ali Cran told Rafael he doubted he would ever find love. He wondered sadly if, at the age of twenty-two, he would recognize it.

Rafael apparently advised him: You are young, hombre, you have much time. Why do you wish to spoil a good life?

Ali Cran spoke instead of growing old, of sharing more of himself than his tail. A woman to love, to love him in return for more than this burden of a machine. Perhaps children as well. Because this was truly strange: For all the seed Alicito had sown, not one child was produced. Much plowing, no crops.

Rafael asked, You have tried each sort of woman?

Young, large, old, every shade.

It was then Rafael wondered, had he been with a pure woman, one who was truly india.

Ali Cran shrugged. Why should this make a difference?

You would learn from a woman who is perfect in one way.

Perhaps. But how could he, who never went in search, ever find one of these? And why would she want him?

Rafael said only, Wait. He disappeared into the tierra caliente.

In three days he was back. At his side stood a young woman, her skin a burnished brown, he called her Serafina. She was slim-boned, her breasts were small, her legs slender. In her eyes lay centers so black they were invisible. He stared through open space onto a spirit a thousand years old, never even in his dreams had he looked into a place like this. Yet as his own eyes explored that space be knew he remembered it. Instantly here was his only passion. And the start of his pain.

Serafina's mother and then the nuns had raised her as a proper young woman, untouched by the daily world. But to Rafael it was clear she was virginal only in the flesh; behind the eyes raged a great torrent, an old fever.

Ali Cran was nervous, Rafael said. Also he said Serafina's breathing trembled, as with tears. She wore a simple skirt, dark blue, over her bare legs. And a blouse with ruffles at the wrists and at the collar and along the front; two buttons were open, Rafael remembered, and a tiny silver cross lay flat on the dark skin where her bosom—

Rubén stopped, reached for the jug. It was nearly empty. "Jorge, I believe we need another drink."

"I'll mix up some more." I pulled myself to my feet. A profound depression seeped through me.

I withdrew to the kitchen. Waited. For what? I opened the re-frigerator, reached for the ice . . . And stopped. I breathed hard. My shirt was stuck to me with sweat, my heart pounded blood and gin and mezcal through bone and muscle. Because the evening is so hot, I said nearly aloud. And knew I was lying. I stopped, took a moment. Clearly I had stepped into far more than an evening of comradely drinking. What, then? Some kind of participation, of private entrance to Michoácuaro?

I poured the gin, the vermouth; I mixed, hurrying now. To return—

In the courtyard Rubén was finishing my martini. "An excellent idea, to make more. You see?" He held out the glass and I filled it. "I was saying—?"

"Telling me of Serafina."

His sigh was thick, the nod of his head slow. "I never met her, you understand, but Rafael remembered and described each detail. I learned a little from him. A genius, while I—"

"Come on, you're a first-rate storyteller." On with Serafina. While clarity lasted.

They made love that first night, Ali Cran and Serafina, and many times the next few days. When Rubén described the congress he used phrases quite foreign to the way he usually spoke—direct from Rafael, he said. For example, in his love for Serafina, Alicito had found the place where "sight begins"; in their passion Serafina and Ali Cran had "spiraled eternally downward"; and Ali Cran had now experienced "ancient love." There was more; I cannot, sadly, bring the language back.

When I tried, in the days that followed, to get Rubén to repeat parts of the story, he got angry I'd asked about such a thing, then claimed none of it was true, finally denied having said anything in the first place.

But it's impossible to forget. Serafina and Ali Cran: the need of the one for the other proved immense. And here came a curious detail. After their first union as they slept for many hours, Ali Cran dreamed of himself as his father's father's father. In Serafina's dream she walked away from her mother's garden and down a road.

Over the days they were together a strange thing occurred. After each lovemaking session the famous tail would shrink, a bit at a time, till finally it was no more than a man's normal presence. Ali Cran never expressed relief, or regret. But Rubén would not admit telling me about this either.

One morning when Ali Cran awoke she was gone. He never went to look for her.

When Rafael heard a piece of news about her, that she was here or there, he would say to Ali Cran, Should we go to find her? Always the answer was, No.

Rubén poured more martini down his throat. His speech had become scratchy. He told me Ali Cran gained some weight then, started to fill out in the chest, and his beard grew thicker.

"And Serafina?" I remember how dry my own voice had gone.

There were accounts of her also. Difficult to take seriously, Rubén noted. She may or may not have had a child from Ali Cran. From time to time she would leave this child with the nuns and wander about tierra caliente. Some say she entered a convent, some say she became a whore. But, Rubén emphasized, these are foolish stories, fantasies— One day the child, Rubén heard, ran away from the nuns, disappeared. Still now, supposedly, Serafina wanders about in the Sierra Madre. She searches for the child and on the way she takes young men who have never—vehemently Rubén claimed Rafael had said it best—young men who have never believed their great-grandfathers too were once young men.

I smiled then.

But, Rubén insisted, it is only people like Nisi Calderón who tell these stories. Campesino stories. There is no truth to them, I had to understand this.

Again my head nodded.

Then he spoke carefully. Offhand, yet polite. "Jorge. You have no more mezcal."

I shook my head. "Sorry."

He nodded, as with great understanding. "Yes, it is late. Tomorrow I must work." He drew himself up. With only slight unsteadiness.

"Can I walk you to your home, hombre?" I could stand but wasn't in terrific shape.

He smiled, a touch crookedly. "I think I will not go home, Jorge. I think I will see if there is a bottle of mezcal at the Hotel Domicilio."

Watching him weave down the street I doubted he would find the Hotel entryway. But I wondered if, this evening, he spent a few minutes with Serafina, maybe even with Marta, while I sat in the courtyard, alone, silent, listening . . .

FIVE

The Grace

🐝 MARK REMEMBERED THE drive, the whole trip, so clearly—described it so well—even now I can see them in his Caribe, winding down the hills out of Morelia and on to Mexico City. Dolly would be delighted, driving being one of her favorite activities. Because then she was inconspicuous; mostly. Otherwise people stared. She was six feet tall. With Mark who was six-four the height didn't matter and she could wear heels three and a half inches high. Then she seemed feather-light and willowy, took his arm and felt his love. She must have wondered for that moment how the previous life could ever have been.

I'd met her four times. She was quintessentially Mexican. But a woman, six feet? Easy enough to see her feeling self-conscious. Walking alone in, say, the marketplace, no attention went to stands of fruit, shirts, canned goods. Everyone stared. Her height? Certainly a part of it. But when she walked with her escort, her man, in her shoes she nearly his height, they were giants. It was wonderful at those moments: the immense and frightening had become grand, proud, contained a new (always new; always . . .) majesty. One could say this.

No, not one—she. She could, and did. More than say—cry, aloud, in her courtyard, with pleasure and love. A liberation from twenty-five years of this immense visibility her body imposed.

(If she'd thought the sense of it through—as Loris had, often enough—would she have concluded that she and her body were the same thing? Because often she *felt* otherwise.)

Through the Morelia hills, constant curving, a slow descent, Loris slept. Dolly would take Mark's hand, gently. Both had big hands. Her touch was the gentlest Mark had known.

She'd told me on my last visit, with Mark she felt human. It was as basic as that. Even more: she felt heady, to be actually seen with him, two towering—some said epic—creatures in a marketplace, or a restaurant, patio, café. And funny too, when the colannades curved so they'd both have to bend over, nearly crouch. Still, who wants to act like a goddess? All she ever asked was to be human. A woman like any other.

Somewhere, hidden, sometimes recallable, she felt this couldn't ever be. Not so long as Loris was around. Loris knew this too. Loris was closer to her than a twin, such terrible closeness. Even closer than Mark. At the same time, far more distant.

Encased by the little car they spoke of the sweet dry exhalation of the pine forests; of the majestic old mansion turned hotel where they'd spend the night; of the Museum of Anthropology where Mark had never been. She was frankly afraid of the place, it made her dream her history, but she insisted on taking him there. They spoke in Spanish. Dolly didn't know English but since they'd been sharing a bed (seven months; a large bed) Mark's Spanish, three years' worth at Boston University during his basketball days, had improved, he liked to say, with giant steps.

"Watch out!"

Coming toward them, thirty feet in front, closer, then by tree trunks with a head at each end, a grotesque huge wooden creature snaking down the curves on eight-inch wheels: a cart, propelled by the decline like a soapbox racer of bygone times. The logs were far longer than their cart, and the two boys, one up front, one on the back, what would they be steering with? And their dragging feet for brakes.

Mark's foot hit his own brake pedal, his hands swung the wheel. The Caribe swerved round the clumsy cart and laughing kids. Did the laughs say, We do this all the time?

Mark's adrenaline drained away. God!

Then Dolly was asleep, Loris awake. Mark glanced over, smiled. "Did you see that?"

"When you pulled around?"

"They're crazy."

"It has to be done."

"Doesn't make it less crazy."

"Any other way would cost too much."

"But risking your life?"

"We all do."

"Who?"

61

"Oh . . . us. Driving along these roads."

"We're careful."

"So are the boys."

"Didn't look it."

"Wonder how we look to them."

"You look great."

She put her arm around his far shoulder, grinned. "That was corny enough even for Dolly." And her head on his near shoulder, Mark recalled.

They drove into Mexico City late in the afternoon. He had the sudden sense the city would bring them great changes. This pleased, even excited him. Still, at the back of his mind, a hint of fear glimmered. Which—he might have admitted had someone else been around, me possibly, to help make the connection—was part of what excited him.

They carried their bags into the hotel. People stared. More or less as usual. Their height? Or just Dolores (her real name)? Mark honestly couldn't be sure.

Yes: how Mark came to be with this strange woman Dolores, how they came to be lovers. It was, finally, much the usual process . . . But, looking at them together in the beginning, I was hard-pressed to admit normalcy here. My fault, culturally, coming from the north? Of course, you would say immediately. But after some thought— I'd known Mark off and on for six years, Dolores only these last months. Since my arrival here our paths have crossed more often.

One of the advantages of narrative, I've now discovered, is its selectivity: I send pictures to your mind with words, letting you imagine even more than I tell you. But I can also choose—I hide pieces of information. And, excuse me, this is what I've been doing, thereby creating an absence of a sort in the story so far. Because if I had described the situation of Mark and Dolores more fully, more honestly, I would have taken attention away from the immense attraction, the love, that held them together.

Have I explained enough so she seems normal, female, human? There was more. You see, she had two heads. I don't mean this metaphorically. Empirically, two heads. Two necks—one, two—growing from the shoulders. Each topped by a head, each face smooth light brown skin. Two sets of brown eyes, doe-like in Dolly and penetrating in Loris. The hair on each head was deep brown with

62

a surface of polished maroon when sunlight struck it. Dolly was given to dangling large decorations from her earlobes, Loris was more comfortable unencumbered.

"Two different people?"

"Course not. Different moods, sure, often enough. But aren't all our friends, our lovers, like that?"

"How do you deal with it?"

"I love her, you see."

I should have asked more. But it's hard to ask even a good friend about the woman he lives with and says he loves, "Why do you?" or, "Do you know where this is taking you?" Because you care for Mark. For Dolores too. Normally Mark appreciated my probing. This seemed the wrong time.

When Dolly was awake, Loris slept. Always. And the other way around. One active, the other not there. "Not there" is a better term than "asleep." Because Dolly and Loris did sleep also. Her body and the one head or the other would awaken in the morning, refreshed, wonderfully clear-minded, alive to all the nuances, kissing Mark with a sweetness of passion, pride, relief. Then the other—let's say Dolly—was simply not there. Though her head was, in that way.

On the surface Dolores, now that Mark lived with her, remained unperturbed: her body was formed like this, nothing more. But below the surface lay striations of fear: put there, as if centuries ago . . .

The presence of the other head isn't easy to describe. If you think of it as deflated— But not like a balloon. Rather, very much present; just not participant. Like someone in a many person conversation whom you ignore. Not because the person is unworthy. But because that person, though physically with you, is herself right then in another reality. More a meandering of mind. More like a mind that has wandered elsewhere, arrived at that other place, is happy there, yet the body still stands around in your conversation.

In fact Mark wished she, whichever she, too could be there; yearned for it, for all kinds of projected reasons. Think of it, he said to me several times: in bed or at breakfast, or just casually with you, Dolly and Loris both there, both of them!

She refused, always: "I have to choose, Mark." But Mark said it could be otherwise. He talked to her, insistent, intelligent, insightful. And, after, to her partner, her rival, her opposite, her twin, her other self. One at a time.

Their hotel room was large. It looked out on the central courtyard—palm trees, green bushes with red flowers, yellow flowers, lilies in pots on ledges. They had a small porch. Birds chirped, swooped. The bed was huge, the sheets soft. Mark and Dolly made love: the usual, and always brand-new. You are wonderful, she would tell him. He always heard it differently because she was always referring to a different moment, touch, bit of exchange of breath or mind.

At dinner, a lovely quiet evening, it was Loris. When Mark chose the red snapper she spoke wittily of, "according to Chac the water god and forebear of us all," the six ways of making Huichinango Veracruzano, the ultimate in fish cuisine.

He enjoyed her wit. But when she finished her discourse he asked, "What d'you mean, Chac our forebear?"

"Something like great-great-great-grandfather."

"*Your* relative?"

She ignored that. "Chac is powerful and graceful and vengeful, demanding—"

"Some kind of allegory?"

"Much more."

"What?"

"He's there!"

"At least say, was there."

She caught herself. Shuddered, blanched; whispered, "Exists."

"Come on."

Mark had told her he wasn't much interested in archeology, old vases, old gods; old pyramids were impressive but once you've seen one— Anyway, every year he was getting more afraid of heights and precipices. So tomorrow's visit to the Museum was decidedly for Dolores.

At night Mark fell asleep with Dolly. In the morning he and Loris made love. I wanted, perhaps perversely, to know: was there a difference in their lovemaking? I asked; once only, after much tequila. Mark said, "When you screw with your sweetheart on Tuesday, isn't it different than when you did it on Saturday?" I shouldn't have expected anything else. But I felt uncomfortable when he talked like that about her.

Have I made Mark sound contented? He wasn't. He had not come to Mexico by chance. From the beginning it was a search. "For my health." A statement of fact.

64

"You're ill?"

"Not specifically."

"Metaphorically?"

"Stop thinking like a writer."

"Sorry." I waited.

He sipped his beer. "The shoulders, mainly."

"Yeah?"

"Calcium deposits."

"Arthritis?"

"Nothing in the bones. In the muscles. Layers of calcium striated along the fibers."

"The result being—?"

"Hell of a time using my shoulders."

"You done anything about it?"

The usual, he explained. Cortisone killed the pain for a while but broke down muscle tissue in the process. And acupuncture and physiotherapy and shiatsu and acupressure and hypnosis and massage hadn't worked.

"So?" This was Dolly coming in.

"A warm climate."

"Simple as that?"

"Simple as that."

"You think it's a straight line, my love? From here to death?"

"What d'you mean?"

Mark was good at thinking in straight lines, his success was based on this ability. And he'd chosen a straight line, as well, away from that success, so-called. Because the line—as he'd abstracted it for, first, Loris—also led away from his sanity. He couldn't function anymore as a "brilliant young architect." He grew less and less young every day. Brilliance was a sham glow he could exude without a trace of inner flame—he was clever at faking, long practice. Others called it brilliance but what did they know. And architecture? A way to earn a living but best if done without pretense.

She smiled. "Think other ways."

He put his arms around her, kissed her mouth. "And just what are those?"

"Just like that." She kissed him back.

"Tell me."

"My death will be different."

"Are you being dismal?"

65

"Happy." She grinned, a flirting tease.

"How?"

"Mine will come from nowhere."

"Death always comes from somewhere."

"All right. From hatred. From love and total pleasure. Or from instant horror."

"A strong brew."

"Death is."

They joked in that way about death. At least Dolly and Loris did. Mark said to me once, Mexicans are much easier with death. And about Loris he said: She has no fear of the future, only of what's been. He asked this of her once: "You're afraid of the past, aren't you?"

She said, too lightly, "Me? 'Course not."

He let it drop.

But it stung her, she told me. Yet why should it? She lived only for now. In the present. Fearing the past was fearing ghosts. None of which kept her from excusing herself, to go out into the sunlight: make the shuddering stop! Did her twin ever shiver like this? If Mark should see them side by side—

I set Mark the obvious question: How did Dolores come to have two heads? First, he said, he'd asked her mother, a short, broad woman always in black. He lived in an apartment in their old hacienda. He had rented it soon after arriving in Morelia. An accident, finding the place; these things usually are, a set of coincidences. Inevitably he met Dolores, there in the hacienda's lovely courtyard. She had rarely gone outside its walls, and almost not at all by day. But she liked the sun.

The mother had said. "You must ask Dolores. It would not be right for me to talk to you of this."

"Not right?"

"They would not wish it."

By "they" the old woman meant the two heads, Mark had first thought. Later he came to interpret (not really understand, no) "they" as the ancestors: images, some three millennia old, all like her in that one way, the women of Dolores's strange genetic line. A throwback?

Loris had admitted, twice, she was terrified of them. Dolly was enthralled, she would not admit to fear, thinking they'd been like her.

Why two heads, and how? Mark had asked them both. The answers were of five sorts.

Dolly had said: I was born this way.

Loris had said: I was born with one head, then a second started. At first nothing but a pimple on the neck, a mole, slowly growing, with precise features.

Which head first?

I don't know.

Loris had said: I was born with one head. Years later it began to split. It took two months. It was like cell mitosis, or the healing of a wound, or a moth's metamorphosis. Not painful to experience; but for her mother, for her doctor, painful to watch.

Dolly had said: I don't know. I always had one head, then woke one morning and two were there.

Loris had said: I don't have two heads. People who look see only one head, like on everybody else. Only you see two heads.

But people do stare.

They would at any woman six feet tall. And in her spike-heeled shoes, which Mark wanted her to wear, as tall as him. In Mexico, this made them giants.

When was one head there and the other away?

This did not work by clock time. Impossible to say, for example, one was a morning head, the other an afternoon head, one a head for the sun, the other for artificial light; one a winter head, the other a spring or summer head. There, or away: these came about arbitrarily. Arbitrary anyway to Mark's attempts to figure it out.

Despite all this he came to feel, beyond comprehension, as if a system were here; but unlocatable. By him anyway. A logic, a meaning as to which head withdrew, which was with him. The cycles of the moon, its waning, waxing? Nothing explained one's absences, one's presence. Shifts projected by his moods, his shoulders, his pleasures? No. For example, he would come home in the later afternoon, aglow from a good day of walking, reading, consulting—

As he had a few months ago, he told me:

A plate of slices of the ripest papaya, with sweet yellow lime. A glass of Victoria beer right from the freezer—put in half an hour ago, she knew how cold he liked it; removed instants before, she'd felt him approaching. Her kiss the sweetest undulation on his mouth. The love that followed was the love that had preceded, Dolly's desire for him as he'd never felt needed before, not a demand at all but a gift that said, Here, I can do this for you, and this; more than this when I learn more. I need nothing more than to give, nothing except the future. He took; and gave; and she would say no one had, ever before, given her such love, not really. Because she was, yes, a freak; how could you love a monster? and yet he did. She said the two heads only doubled the love it was possible to feel, and to give.

A day later, again late afternoon:

Same glow. Same consulting job and well done too. Now a week to spend reading, maybe at last their trip to Mexico City. The papaya as ripe as yesterday, the beer as cold, the evening as lovely and quiet, and Loris's kiss as sweet; and longer. It proved to be one of the moments when he wanted, desperately, to ask, Why Loris, not Dolly? But wouldn't that seem a complaint? Unhappiness with Loris, now, here? He didn't dare take the chance. If only it were both . . . Anyway, a week together.

"A week!" Delight. "What'll we do?"

"Let's not plan."

"But we might waste it."

"Not if we're together."

"You can be so romantic, my darling."

With Loris he was usually careful not to be. Easy enough, he wasn't very romantic. "Sometimes."

"Oh yes. Quite often."

"Does it upset you?"

"Of course not."

"I don't want to upset you." He had heard something else; not the full opposite of the insistence but strange pieces of it.

It might have been that she knew where she had to take Mark; and was terrified.

But they were calling to her . . .

No! She would not herself plan this.

But, they had called, there is so much more than this little bit of good . . . bring him . . .

No!

Yes.

She fought a smile to her face. "What'll we do all week?"

They did decide on Mexico City. And some of what they planned did happen, some with Loris, some with Dolly. And the one unpredictable event.

As clearly as I can understand, Loris and Dolly each refused to talk about the other. It would have been unfair: the other wasn't there, really, to cope with insinuations, to accept compliments, to ponder hypotheses or explanations, to answer charges. I am also Loris, Dolly had said. And Loris: Dolly is also me.

Mark lived on relatively little, at least in comparison with his previous life in Boston. He consulted on a regular irregular basis with a large architecture firm in Guadalajara that had close relations to the place he'd been with in Boston. Eight to ten days per month, and he could live well, if simply, in Morelia. It was, he told me, one way of having a life beyond only the work.

Years back he'd played basketball at Boston University, been drafted by the Lakers. Said, finally, no, he preferred to study architecture. He could always be an architect, he couldn't play basketball forever. Architecture would last a lifetime.

This was both a lie and miscalculation. Already at twenty-two he had felt his knees rusty in the bounce. New rust, yes; but there already. If it hadn't started, maybe he'd have turned pro. Maybe playing would have ground the rust away. Or maybe just ground away at the cartilage. He had no glorious parallel life, he'd said, no simultaneous but alternative life, watching as his clone took the other choice, so no way of knowing. First the knees. Then the shoulders. What next? Later he wondered, was he alone to blame for living that single life.

And the miscalculation. Architecture proved less than the eternal passion. At thirty-five he was, precisely, burned out; well-known and respectable and well-to-do. A lot of the money from this went for alimony to Doris—and wasn't this name, given his new love, an irony—and to the support of little Markie. They had left him, because he had left them for fourteen-hour days at the prestigious office. A usual enough story; not the present one.

He went on as usual, for weeks. One day I'd said—we'd run into each other on Commonwealth Avenue—something simple like, What the hell's the matter with you? That was the moment our friendship was sealed. He'd seen me as having wisdom and insight, just for asking that question at that time.

Dolly, Loris had listened. He told it all so clearly. He knew, simply knew, how to regain control of his life. She loved this in him.

Hence a leave of absence. Hence a flight to Mexico. It could have been Greece Morocco Hawaii Rio, any straight-line flight including the North Pole if it'd been warm enough for long walks, his single enduring commitment then: at first for simple reasons of health, his father obliterated by a heart attack at fifty-nine; and then for pleasure, looking closely at fences, bushes, flower beds: real things one after the other, one at a time. A shift from commuter trains and eighty-four hour Boston weeks. Grotesque, he came to call the shape of his previous life. In those days the grotesque, embodied, had for Mark no right to participate in human activity.

In the morning it was breakfast at the hotel's rooftop restaurant with Loris, the drive to the Museum of Anthropology with Loris, entering with her. Somewhere between giving up the tickets—of course people stared, here as in the restaurant—and gazing up as the magnificent fountain in the immense courtyard softened and cooled the mighty stone column supporting its own protective shield, somewhere in that space Loris grew away, Dolly emerged. With her Mark went into the pre-Classical room and she led him directly to the center case, designated Middle Period Ceramics.

Did she that day take her companion fear and simply hide it deep down? It was, as the room surrounded them, nowhere to be felt. Instead, an excitement, an expectance. Which may have been, for Dolly, another face of the fear.

There in the case, to the right side surrounded by half a dozen larger and more imaginatively executed figures, six inches high, clay breasts smoothly prominent, naval at dead center: a woman with two heads. Dolly stared at her, Mark stared, their concentration so complete they could never know, were they too objects of fascination?

Both heads stood erect. Both pairs of eyes—slit wedges in the terra cotta, eyeballs deeper circular holes—stared out. Both mouths smiled lightly. Marks' hand, Loris's hand, touched; their fingers held each other's. The figurine gazed at them both, one head for one, the other for the other.

Loris said finally, "They make a good couple."

"Incredible." Slowly Mark turned to her. He whispered: "Dolly. Loris. Together."

"No—!"

"You have to."

"Why?!"

He knew then. "I want you. All the grace. The glory."

70

She squeezed his hand white. This is what they, the old ones, wanted too. But differently— But: was it different?

They left. Nothing else to do. Dolly sat silent all the way, not the breath of a word. She went up to the room, she'd leave the door unlocked. She had to lie down. Mark parked the car.

In the corridor he reached for the handle. Stopped himself. Inside, voices. The wrong room? Correct number— He turned the handle, walked in. Dolly and Loris faced each other. Phrases came from one mouth, from the other. The left hand touched Dolly's cheek, the right stroked Loris's hair. How—?

"Dolly? Loris?"

Both heads faced him.

"Are you okay?"

Both heads smiled. Loris said, "Wonderful." Dolly said, "At last." They lay their cheeks against each other. "My sister," said Dolly. Loris said, "My other self."

"What happened?"

"We're finding out." (Dolly)

"What?"

"A lot." (Loris)

"We need—" (Dolly)

"—to be alone." (Loris)

"I'll—I'll be back. Soon."

"We know." They spoke simultaneously. The one scowled, the other giggled.

Mark made a conscious decision: back to the Museum. Did he know? (I have felt since, surely he should have . . .) But everything was new.

He spent half an hour in front of the case. He had a catalogue now. The catalogue referred to the two-headed figure as a grotesque. This offended him. Viciously. Mark, who had lived with, loved, Dolores for seven months, was now faced with objectivity, so-called: all sensory interference between himself and the woman with two heads eliminated. Dolores a grotesque?

What is "grotesque"? Does grotesque mean a negative thing, something dangerous? Where? In Mexico? When? Staring at the terra-cotta, Mark had in his own terms discovered this: no, there is no place in the world for an idea like "grotesque."

That was what I learned from Mark.

How could there be? What would it be?

A thalidomide child? Loved by its parents? For the years of its life? Or many children, birth defects by the thousands? What, curse the victim of radiation for his stumps, for her humps, for their added features? Many do. Some never could, they would instead love the imperfection for its uniqueness. As we all love our beloved, really. For his, for her uniqueness; isn't it? And at moments, the other side of love: hate, that too, for such immense difference.

(Once I saw, on the beach, Playa Azul in Michoacán, an embrace that weighed six hundred pounds (an estimate, standing in the surf), his weight easily three fifty, her delicate-by-comparison form squeezed in his arms; a kiss so fleshy, afterwards two grins so tender it could bring tears to your eyes; I came close.)

Quadraplegics are fallen in love with, lepers are in these and even earlier times embraced, and logicians dine with mystics. Mark falls in love with Dolores. Dolores has two heads. Mark falls in love with very much more.

He suddenly had to be with her. Run! But his hips had caulked his muscles with layers of ancient clay. It took years to get out of the Museum, centuries to the parking lot. He roared the Caribe through the choked-up streets, left the car at the curb, thought his legs into the lobby, pulled himself up the stairs, pushed the door open.

She lay on the bed. On the pillow, both heads. Asleep? They faced each other. Their eyes were open, staring. Their lips, Mark told me, explained it. The mouth of the first pressed fast to the mouth of the other, as if the heads were trying to become one. By swallowing each other: the hands pushing the heads into one another through the mouth. Was their love so great—sisters, complements—there was no need for breath? Their mouths, finally, had to be pried apart.

Mark telegrammed me in Michoácuaro. The funeral was in two days.

I dreamed, that first night, Mark had asked me to see her just before their wedding. I came to her mother's place; the final glance. She had one head. Had the other been removed by the priest? No scar. Had they merged? Which head, Dolly, Loris, was still there? *Mark couldn't tell.* How was it possible, if he loved her?

I went to the ceremony. I couldn't keep my eyes off her. Mark seemed afraid to look.

SIX

Sálome

  AMONG THE VICTIMS I've known of perhaps the most complex has been Sálome Rivera the moneylender. I needed to learn more than necessary about the woman before writing down her story. Some put her death in the hands of Ali Cran. Such people would kill him painfully if the occasion arose. They say his tail is like a curved knife, it slashes and poisons.

About fifty when she died five years ago, Sálome had greying black hair which she would streak strawberry blonde, and chocolate skin. Pepe swore she put so much red on her mouth she must've gone through a stick a week. And those layers of face-grease and powder, seven-eight-nine veils' worth easily, he said laughing. Her pants, usually white or black, fit tight enough to get her juices flowing just by walking. And men's juices too. Above she'd wear a low-cut camisole or half-open blouse. Her shoes had heels so high and tiny-tipped it was a miracle she didn't catch their spikes in the cracks of Michoácuaro's mostly unpaved streets. No doubt she'd have fallen a hundred times, Pepe added, if she wasn't on some man's arm. And she usually was.

Rubén Reyes Ponce tells me that as sexily as she presented herself, the señora's greatest allure was her wealth. She had arrived in Michoácuaro many years earlier. No one can say where she came from exactly, or why. Some insist Umberto Ponce Alvaréz imported her. Rubén denies his great-uncle had anything to do with it, but concedes the old man did visit her regularly. A number of men seem to have been crazy about her, from Nisi Calderón of whom it's said he has second sight, to sullen Arsenio who runs the Larga Distancia. Some claim Sálome arrived with a stake of a few thousand pesos, some that her fortune began with gifts from Umberto and from Isidoro Lopez, otherwise known for his double devotion, to the Aguafría shrine and to his stomach. Most everyone agrees that from the start people in need of quick cash would go, usually with discretion, to the small side room of her elegant colonial home. There, recording every detail in a ledger covered in cowhide and embossed with gilt swirls, she would make loans at interest ranging from a hundred percent a year up to twenty percent a month.

"She was a pain in the eggs, Jorge," Rubén explained. "Legally everything was always correct—those stupid campesinos, hacendados too, signed her contracts. But there is no doubt she cheated them. All entirely legal." He grimaced, as if he'd now have to solve the Sálome problem over again. "At the same time she was, in her way, I would say a romantic." He went on at impressive length about how she believed, every time a man courted her, he loved her only for her physical charms, her intelligence, her—as Sálome apparently put it—delightful personality. Seven houses in Michoácuaro, one in Uruapan, three haciendas in tierra caliente, cane fields totaling seventy-two hectares either bought legally or signed over to her a little here, a little there, when a loan couldn't be repaid, the vast sums, as rumor had it, in her bank account: these, while she was being courted, would disappear from her mind.

In Michoácuaro she married three times. The first husband, Alfonso Vargas Valenzuela, was a small landowner whose previous passions had been raising and matching fighting cocks and arm wrestling with pigstickers. The second, Luis Parada, had been in town less than a year when he fell under Sálome's sway. After the marriage she investigated his history and learned he was a one-time mendicant friar from the state of Veracruz who had fled charges of accidental homicide, his fellow celibate dying of razor wounds allegedly inflicted on him, as he on Parada, in their arcane love-play. The third, Sergio Chavez García, one day bought four hundred grams of arsenic from Constanza's daughter Elena, who works at the Farmacía. "To kill the bats in the señora's rafters," Sergio told Elena. Elena mentioned this to her mother, who passed it on to her friend Teresa who cooks and keeps house for Umberto Ponce. Old Ponce was ninety at least but, said Constanza grinning, Sálome remained his friend. And he told her of the arsenic. Sálome went white under a smear of rouge, sucked her breath in sharply and whispered, "There are no bats in my house."

The bishop annulled the marriage for "nonconsummation," as he had the others before it. The ex-husbands left Michoácuaro, though not without swearing some dreadful form of vengeance. After each annulment, Rubén explained with a twitch of a smile, a new stained-glass window appeared in the cathedral, the gift of an anonymous donor.

A few weeks before her fifty-first birthday Sálome met Sebastiano Hernandez, Basta as he was known, a chubby, friendly man one year less than half her age. She was the first woman who had ever captivated him, possibly because till then he'd been protected by his father Enrique's wealth—coffee, pigs, mangoes, avocadoes, cane— or because shyness had limited Basta's sexual activities to irregular escapades with the ministering ladies of the Hotel Domicilio; he went sometimes when mezcal sharpened his desire and loosened his pants. Now he found himself in love. With Sálome. For herself alone. "Do you know?" he confided to those who asked. "She wants me to give her a son."

Ali Cran was a close friend of Basta's. Something had to be done about this Sálome.

At the time of Basta's infatuation Enrique lay ill, some said dying. His wife, twenty-five years earlier, had produced the one heir. (Serious doubt, of course, exists as to Sebastiano's biological father.) Only hours after Basta came into the world fat and screaming, his mother died, an internal hemorrhage. Given Michoácuaro's sense of humor, Sebastiano's nickname followed—basta meaning "enough."

Sebastiano grew up sheltered and pampered by Enrique and a string of housemaids. When he was fourteen one of these women introduced him personally to the private language of chickens and burros, and adults. Enrique, learning of the initiation, employed no further housemaids, saying the boy was old enough to do without.

Ali Cran, I am told by Moisés de Jesús, had worked for Enrique several times during the avocado and the coffee harvests. Basta, younger than Ali Cran by about ten years, came to look on him as a kind of wise brother, counting on Alicito's advice in both important and minor matters. Along the way Ali Cran himself must have decided Sebastiano badly needed some guidance. One night, talking and smoking out by the lower rim of the dead volcano, Basta had pulled his courage together and asked Ali Cran if they could be compadres—if they could, through a set of sacred promises, become as close as blood. Pepe says Alicito felt deeply moved: many people draw back from the notorious Ali Cran, but here someone was trusting him in the most essential manner. So Ali Cran agreed, much impressed by Basta's self-confidence, even bravery. Usually the compadre relation is arranged by a third party, a father or uncle; Basta, making the move himself, had broken tradition. They gave each other secret gifts, affirming their special friendship.

When Sálome, as Ali Cran saw it, pounced on Basta, here lay great danger. Sálome had been long and well hated by many in Michoácuaro. She had ruined over a dozen families with her usurious loans, had destroyed nearly as many marriages with her packaged body and, claimed the meaner tongues, was spreading several diseases. For Ali Cran the worst, Pepe told me, were the bankruptcies. Two of his cousins had been ruined by this woman, they had lost their lands to her, and the sister-in-law of another cousin had lost her betrothed. A casual theft, of momentary interest to Sálome; but it destroyed the coming marriage. And now Enrique's lands would become hers when he died if Sálome had Sebastiano's child. She was fifty, but still— Ali Cran spoke harsh words to Basta. Angry words.

In Michoácuaro, Pepe says, grinning, you hear much.

Ali Cran took Basta back to the volcano rim. "You must forget about her."

"But she's wonderful, she understands me, she's all of life!"

"Did you wait till now to discover sex, Basta?"

"She's the only person I live for."

"Thank you." Ali Cran's irony sliced nerve.

"Compadre, no, not you, I mean *woman*—"

"Her parts that give you pleasure will destroy you, compadre." Basta shivered. "How?"

Ali Cran folded his arms and stared at Basta.

"When?" Only twelve hours earlier—

"Slowly."

Basta's terror fought with the intensity of his memories—never, not even with the Domicilio ladies, had he experienced such absolution, such victory. From his fingertips to his balls.

"Why would she do such a thing?"

"She cannot help herself," said Ali Cran.

Despite his dreams, Basta knew he had to listen to Alicito. Alicito was a true compadre, who else could he turn to in his agonies about Sálome, her passion, her gentle— A word to anyone else, instantly the whole town would see him naked, terrified. He'd be even less a man than if Sálome did what Ali Cran spoke of.

76

Then Sálome disappeared. Where, no one can tell me. Or wants to.

Basta, torn between relief and despair, outwardly showed himself devastated.

His father told him to stop whining, he was well rid of the woman.

Ali Cran gave no sympathy. "She wasn't for you."

Rubén, as jefe de policía, investigated the disappearance. "As thoroughly as possible." The complete professional, he nodded with great solemnity as he spoke; but added, shrugging, "I cannot say I wept at her absence."

Early one morning two old ladies, the Vargas Martinez sisters, present still at every predawn mass, found Sálome Rivera on the steps of the Santa Rosarita Church. The younger sister fainted, the other ran for Padre Alfredo. Sálome had been stabbed several times with a curious curving slash. When the body was removed, two scorpions scurried from beneath her. The autopsy revealed arsenic in Sálome's stomach, but in the end she'd bled to death.

Rubén Reyes Ponce couldn't find the murderer. No one spoke of this in terms of negligence except Umberto Ponce to his great-nephew, but Umberto was too old to make a case. Isidoro Lopez never publicly mentioned the death, a blessing for which his wife a year to the date gave thanks in the form of a pilgrimage to the María de León shrine. A small fire broke out mysteriously in Sálome Rivera's grand parlor, destroying her records. There being no heirs to claim Sálome's wealth, the Municipal Council voted to cancel all known debts and to distribute her lands among as many of their former owners as could be traced. A few of these came forward. Rubén had the task of finding the rest. He located only one. The unclaimed properties reverted to the town and the Council gave Rubén Reyes Ponce a commendation for his balanced efforts.

"Sálome's death," I said to Rubén. "What caused the wounds?"

Rubén shrugged.

Respect for Ali Cran, together with fear of him, increased visibly. And, Pepe told me, rumors of a curved sharp-edged tail attained great credence.

But Sálome's story is more complex, at least in the minds of several who shared with me their gossip and insight. One, María-Silvia Carranza, known as Silvia Loca, visits me occasionally; less often

77

now than when I first arrived. The other, Arsenio de las Casas, together with his wife Elena, provides me a link to the outside world.

With no phone at home one heads down to Arsenio's dingy dry goods store on the plaza, and if there's a line available from here to Morelia, and if the operator in Morelia can get through to the international operator in Toluca, and if the internacionalista figures out what to do with the norteamericano number, then for a few moments one is hauled into a world of science and supermarkets that makes Michoácuaro seem arcane, an illusion. That is, if Arsenio's hand doesn't slip and pull loose the cord he's plugged into a switchboard surely stolen from the set of a thirties Bogart movie shot in the Sierras, or if Arsenio's five- or two-year-old doesn't knock the cord loose as she climbs over the shelving, I mean if the line is free, which is rare since the switchbox is the link to all the telephones in town and funnels in every call from Guadalajara or Bakersfield, California.

At the center of all this sits Arsenio, ancient earphones clamped to his skull, purportedly waiting for the Morelia operator to answer, in reality switching between phone calls, listening, learning. A spider in a web of information.

Silvia Loca comes by, sits in my patio, asks for a Pepsi or a cookie or a pan dulce, and we talk. More precisely I ask how she is and she responds before I've finished, her words tumbling out in circuitous rambles and meanders. When she slows for a moment I repeat one of the many snatches I've caught but not understood—she speaks clearly enough—and she's off on another volley of barely connected images.

She never stays long, half an hour at most, time enough to finish her drink or sweet cake. Then she's away, social appointments to be met in proper form before siesta time. She drops by other households too, receiving more pan dulce, gabbling on in every direction. Over the months I've known her she's stayed thin as any chicken grubbing in the Michoácuaro soil. She visits me three or four times a week, and talks about what she knows best, the people of the town. Some of them, at least; because many snub Silvia.

One who hadn't, who'd actually befriended her in some curious way, was Sálome Rivera. Silvia would sit in Sálome's parlor and, according to Silvia's rambles, they'd talk, often the whole morning. Rubén corroborates those visits, had disapproved of them just as he now sees as inappropriate Silvia spending time in my courtyard with the outer doors closed. "It doesn't look right. Anyway, Jorge, how can you follow what she's saying?"

That was just it. More and more I realized that the tangents, circles and connections pouring out of Silvia were precisely what fascinated me.

The rambling girl and the voluptuous moneylender, a compelling image from the moment Silvia first mentioned Sálome: "Sálome the good señora with the big breasts like those Mama never had."

"Sálome? You mean the lady who used to loan money?"

"My friend was very poor and very sad and she bought me grand clothes, these I am wearing now." Silvia stood, spread wide her two full ancient cotton skirts and gave me a dry curtsy. "She was my sister."

"Did you know her long before she died?"

"She's not dead. I saved her. She's very beautiful. She lends me money to buy firewood and rich jewels and beans and pan dulce and milk like I drank many years ago."

"Oh. I must mean someone else."

"She holds me very tight and she sings to me when I'm sad."

"What does she sing?"

"Songs. Songs she knows. Only she knows the songs."

"What kind of songs?"

"Sweet. She makes tortillas filled with honey for me. She lives with the bees, she sings to them, they give her honey. She's the mama of the bees. She opens her hands and flowers grow and the bees come to her and she closes her hands slowly and squeezes and she spreads her arms for me to come and holds me to keep the bees away and she fills the tortillas with fried beans and chicken with a mole sauce from the peppers from the market. The bees are everywhere in the market. I don't like bees. They make me hurt. Where it's tender."

Because of this reference I didn't know what to ask. Silvia had gone mad nearly twenty years ago when she was gang-raped. I wasn't equipped to deal with stirred-up memories. "Would you like another Pepsi?"

She smiled shyly, shook her head and told me I should repair the roof above my bedroom before the rainy season started. This was six months off and there was nothing wrong with my roof. As far as I knew. She searched clumsily through her two straw bags, muttering, "I'll find it, it'll keep you safe, keep you safe, keep you safe—" almost a chant. Then with a quick "Hasta luego" she marched out the door, thick skirts swirling.

After that she mentioned Sálome only in passing. Until a particularly hot week. Silvia asked for a Pepsi.

"With ice?"

"No! NO!!" She cringed into the chair.

"Okay, without."

I went for the drink, wondering at her sudden terror. When I returned with a glass her fear seemed to have dissipated.

Silvia drank. "Gracias." After a moment she said, "Ice is a knife."

"Oh?"

"A machete. A sickle. No one knows. This is our secret. Do you like motorcycles? My friend Ali Cran has a motorcycle. He takes me everywhere on his motorcycle. We fly through the sky. Sometimes I can see everyone. When I'm alone. Can you see everyone?"

"No, I can't."

"Would you like to see everyone?"

I nodded.

"My sister wants to see everyone too. They don't like that. It's very good you want to see everyone. Some I don't want to see so I make them hide. Then the roses and the corn and cactuses are my friends. I cut them down. I say to them 'Adios,' and they go to God." She laughed then, a hysterical nip of laughter.

I asked her why that was so funny.

"God is funny. In heaven there are only roses and magueys and bottles of pulque. There is no room for people!" A sweep of laughter.

I grinned. "Then who'll drink the pulque?"

"Gringo!"

This was the funniest statement of the morning. I watched her double over, shrill laughter building its own momentum, and wished I could catch a glimpse of the landscape she found herself in.

She wiped her eyes with her fist. "Loco," she said as her laughs subsided. "Loco. Muy loco."

"Who?"

"You like pulque?"

"Very much." Sometimes there's nothing better than its soft thin fermentation—

"Me too." Suddenly the joy was gone from her voice and, refus-

80

ing to look at me, Silvia squeezed her eyelids hard, and again. "I like pulque very much." She sounded, somehow, brave.

I nodded, waiting.

"Sálome loves me, you know. A sister. She knows—everything. She gave me a dress. Her dress. She knows how much everyone—would like my dress. She said I could get married in her dress. She said she was very happy because she had a good husband. Once she had a good husband. But it wasn't her husband." In her throat a laugh turned into a sob. "She gave me a glass of pulque. It depends on who gives you the pulque!" Tears flowed down her face.

I found a paper tissue in my pocket and wondered if this referred to the dreadful incident when she lost her rationality. It's said she was drunk when the men ravaged her. I reached over with the tissue.

She waved me off, wiped her eyes with her outer skirt, rubbed her nose on her sleeve and sniffed hard. "She loved me more than Angelita."

"Than who?"

"Angelita. She loved me more. More than Isidoro—!" Here she exploded again into laughter, but it was short-lived. "Isidoro." She shook her head. "Soft and fat and little. Loved her, he said. Put his hands everywhere. Sticky. Sálome said, Stupid Man. She didn't go from him. Didn't run away!" She spoke softly. "Sálome said a woman cannot run. She could see everyone."

Pepe's picture of Sálome in skin-tight pants and four-inch heels flitted through my mind. Out of place. Silvia too? In my courtyard, sharing with me these intimate shreds of memory?

"Sálome told me. Last week. Each day a glass of pulque, you will see everyone. Two glasses, everyone will see you. They must see you. No. No! Nonono!" She stopped herself. A small smile came. "Do you ever hide, señor?"

"Sometimes. I think everyone does."

"No."

"No?"

She shook her head and stared me square in the right eye. Whether she meant it's impossible to hide or I was too foreign to understand, I don't know. She got up and left.

I don't speak easily with Arsenio. Few in town do. But Arsenio sought me out. He's a dour man, makes you think he's considering you for absolution when you ask to make a long-distance call, bringing you to a state of grace by allowing you to pay the exorbitant international rates. Not so at the little restaurant down by the plaza between the cathedral and the jail. Here, several times, Arsenio asked permission to sit at my table, then requested the privilege of speaking to me. I found his out-of-character humility baffling, even mysterious. Of course I always said yes. One afternoon he explained in elaborate detail the best times of day for making long-distance phone calls to assorted places. Specifically, to my destinations. He'd remembered the precise locations of the dozen-plus calls I'd made in the previous weeks.

I came to understand Arsenio as a small-town snob, too grand to pass the time of day with people who had no phone and so were forced to use public facilities, yet a man who liked to be seen talking to the gringo in town about subjects that could never be understood by a mere Michoácuaran. Not that we ever debated Mexico City politics, or books, or the debt crisis, or that he asked about my writing. Actually he was little more than a stymied purveyor of gossip: a wealth of ancient detail hidden deep in memory, scattered, preserved, needing to surface. And I was a willing ear.

About Sálome he was eloquent. "Vivacious! Gentle! And how she would laugh! Until she got her own phone she came to the Larga Distancia and excited the whole lineup. She brought a natural kindness out in people, you understand? When she arrived, everybody, the men, even their wives, would insist she make her call first. She knew everyone by name. A few of the men she knew even better, you know what I mean. I helped her get her own phone. Sadly it meant she came to the Larga Distancia much less. Because she was, you know, very busy. Her business. Her"—Arsenio laughed; a man of the world—"her friends."

"Who were her friends?" I asked lightly.

A barrier descended over Arsenio's eyes. It would not do to appear indiscrete, no matter how deeply, how pleasurably he might ensnare the gringo in his finely woven vignettes. Self-censorship each time we reached new regions.

But over the weeks the frontier of the unutterable retreated. Forbidden material in earlier discussions became the natural subjects of conversation. Isidoro Lopez and Umberto Ponce were confirmed as Sálome's close friends: the former of the flesh, of the money belt, a little of the heart; the latter of the heart, of memories of political camaraderie, and till Sálome's death also of the flesh.

Several times I'd tried to press Rubén about his great-uncle and Sálome, with little success. Then one Sunday, unannounced, he took me to visit. We drove up the side of the hill. "For three years the old clod's been confined to the house," Rubén said. "Rheumatic arthritis in the hips and knees and feet." We parked, stepped through an immense carriage door into an age-old courtyard: impatiens and copa de oro, jasmine, bougainvillaea rich to the eyes, birds, butterflies, a tiny fountain; a private Eden. Umberto Ponce himself, his maid Teresa following closely, met us at the doorway. He turned the rollers of his wheelchair with hefty thrusts.

Dry-faced, eyes a thin brown, ninety-five years old, a slowness of speech that would prove to belie his wit, he'd not lost the ways of hospitality. We stayed two hours, nearly finishing a litre of Fundador, acme of available brandies. Rubén, whose stomach is a cauldron, drank his with a beer chaser, I took mine in fresh-squeezed grapefruit juice, old Ponce sipped his straight. In half an hour he was talking about the old days. He'd been a minister under Cárdenas from 'thirty-four to 'forty and had participated in hacking some of the old hacienda holdings down into parcels of acreage for landless campesinos.

I glanced at Rubén. He was scowling.

In earlier times Umberto had fought in the Revolution under Zapata, even participating in the formulation of the Plan de Ayala which charged the then self-proclaimed president, Francisco Madero, with treason. Fascinating stuff and I could have listened the whole afternoon, except Rubén broke in: "Tell the gringo about Sálome."

Old Ponce studied his cane. I noted my boots needed polish. Rubén sipped his drink. I examined my glass. It was Rubén's place to say something, not mine. I raised my eyes and caught the old man watching me. He squinted. "From whom do you know about Sálome Rivera?"

I don't know what made me choose. "From Silvia Loca."

After a moment he glanced back to his cane. "They were friends."

I had to say something. "Sisters, thinks Silvia."

"Yes." He nodded half a dozen times. "Does Silvia still speak with Sálome?"

"So she says."

"She is lucky."

"You do not." I couldn't afford to make this a question.

Umberto smiled sadly. "I am not crazy."

"You knew her—well?"

"For many years, señor." His smile grew to a quiet laugh. "We met at a party at Chapultepec Castle. Many years ago." He turned his chair to face me. "I was, I think, almost sixty, she not twenty yet. I heard her, you understand, before I saw her." He sipped his brandy. "Alemán had been President for three years. That miserable man. He had changed the name of our party. It's true. The name was the Party of the Mexican Revolution. He made it the Institutional Revolutionary Party. Can you imagine? And Sálome? I heard her across the room, a strong laugh, like an axe. She was hidden from me by three young government employees, técnicos. She mocked the idea of an institutionalized revolution. She spoke sharply: The end of Mexico! This was, you realize, an earlier time. Women did not use loud voices then."

He described the scene with intense clarity, the old thin man in his rolling chair surrounded by a crowd of flowers. I listened, motionless:

She wore a short imported yellow dress. Her hair was black. That one whose skin was the darkest in the room should be ridiculing the government of the nation insulted the three técnicos profoundly. Even the man who brought her, a self-proclaimed liberal among conservatives—a criollo, yet despite his white skin deeply sensitive to the needs of the new Mexico—found her shocking. Then he was shouting at her: We are nearing the middle of the twentieth century! We need to bring Mexico to power in the world, we are industrializing, we must have stability! and so on.

She listened, did not drop her glance.

Umberto had approached the group, eyes only on Sálome; the others had disappeared. "Would you care to dance?"

Turning, she began, "I don't—" and, seeing him, "—yes, very much."

"You should have been in the Revolution with us," Umberto said as his fingers touched her waist.

"I am." She grinned at him from the right side of her mouth. She saw the battle in his eyes, knew she wanted him.

He nodded. "Welcome."

She went to his house. After five days he asked her to marry him.

"No."

"But why?"

At fifteen, during the birthday celebration of a cousin, her uncle had violated her. Two years later she married a widower aged thirty-one. A lucky thing, her mother said, spoiled goods never finds a husband. When he reached his climax, if he was not completely drunk, he cried out, Ai mamacita! She was no one's little mother. After twenty months of marriage, out of nowhere, her husband turned white, then green, and died. Heart, was the official verdict. In one so young? It happens, explained Sálome's friend the medical examiner. After, she lived with the examiner for ten months.

Then she met Umberto. They were together seven years. They fought for the railroad workers, the nurses, against the church. And tried, unsuccessfully, to have a child. A happy union. Except every three or four months she went away—for a week, ten days, two weeks.

"Where are you going?"

"To be by myself."

They fought. She still went.

At sixty-six Umberto asked her a last time. He must have someone, one person in the world, to be near as his own skin.

"Am I not?"

"And a dozen years from now?"

"As close as if we married."

"No."

They said terrible things. Without apology. Sálome left, or perhaps he threw her out, Umberto didn't remember.

Sixteen months after she disappeared he married. Nine years later Sálome wrote him. She had worked a long time, her responsibilities were at an end. Could she come to live in Michoácuaro?

"I found her a home, señor. Ten years had aged her. And me. We met often. I was not enough for her."

Umberto stopped speaking. His brown eyes had gone shiny, wet. We sat once more in silence. I looked to Rubén. He nodded, got up.

In the car Rubén said, "Filthy old man," and laughed, almost with affection.

Later that afternoon I walked to the house where Sálome had lived. Three feet of sidewalk to walls painted red up to waist level, whitewashed above. Bigger, though, than the others. The windows were shuttered, the famous side door locked tight. Her roof, easily thirty-five meters across, gave a sense of inner immensity.

On the way home I met Arsenio, his wife Elena, their three little girls. His wife carried the little one, the two elder hung on his hands. He shook them free and grasped my arm, drawing me ahead. He told me in a pleased whisper, "Elena is pregnant!"

I congratulated him, laughing. "Have you made a son this time, or another daughter?"

His response was somber. "A son, God willing."

Dangerous ground, I suddenly realized. "Of course."

He nodded. "A man should not be alone in his old age."

I could barely keep from shaking my head in dismay.

He took me to the café and sent his wife and daughters home. I told him I had just met Umberto.

"Yes, Umberto." Some Umberto gossip followed, then led naturally to Sálome gossip. "She too had a daughter, you know."

"Who? Sálome?"

"Yes. Sálome the moneylender."

"Really! From which husband?"

He shook his head. "Nobody knows about this daughter, my friend. Only you. And me." He laughed.

Pregnancy must have put him in a sharing mood. Or he too had been nipping Sunday brandy. "Was the girl ever here? In Michoácuaro?"

"No."

"You're sure?"

He gave me a most superior smile.

I shrugged. Inside I felt disgust.

"Was Sálome always the painted woman in skin-tight pants?" I sipped tea. Pepe had come by with a washer for my slightly leaking faucet. I told him this was Rubén's job, Rubén was my landlord. Pepe said if he could help why shouldn't he. He'd taken to dropping by more and more regularly.

"I think—I believe I do remember this—in the last years she was more, you understand, made-up."

"She was losing her . . . ,"—I searched— ". . . charms?"

"She was growing older, Jorge. Like all of us."

"But in the beginning, when she first arrived in Michoácuaro, do you remember her?"

"I think—you know I was then a teenager, and I remember she was always a woman who wished to be seen as different, as—how should I say—as perfect."

I shook my head.

"Perfect." He thought a moment. "You understand macho, no?"

"I think so."

"The man who by one way of thinking is the perfect man. In Mexico we have no real word for a woman who is in this way perfect." He laughed. "No complimentary word."

Well, neither does English. For the male we even need to borrow macho.

"You know, Jorge, I have not thought about this before. But I believe Sálome made herself into the extreme version of how she thought a man wants a woman to be."

Long after Pepe left I pondered that. The swirls and tangents of the mind: Sálome so tightly embraces the need for love she takes to its extreme the logic of bodily allures and turns herself into a clown. Sálome's heart is not noble, it would have lost its kindness early. Sálome, born in 1930, a daughter of the post-revolution. New possibilities for Mexicans. But Mexicans are men.

A knock at my door. I was deep in writing. I cursed and put on my morning face.

Silvia. A huge smile, a fistful of hand-picked flowers.

I invited her in, went through the cookie ritual. She jabbered about gliding through the fields north of town. She had to follow a butterfly. She bit into her cookie. The monarchs were back for their winter hibernation. The world was very big, the air was sweet, cocoa was best for breakfast—

If she could bounce about, so could I. "Silvia, did you know Sálome's daughter?"

The smile slid away, the hand dropped to her lap, her eyes stared out beyond me.

"Silvia—?"

Her throat made a grinding noise, *hhrrrrrrrn hrnng hhhrrrrn*— Four or five times. Like a small motor trying to start. Or keep itself from speeding off.

I got up cautiously and knelt beside her chair. The sounds were dying out. "Are you okay?"

She whispered. "Her room is big. Curtains. Corners. She's hiding. She sang her songs. She is close. But I am closer than—than anyone. She is—far away. From Sálome." She shivered. "Where? Not here. *I* was there, señor. *I*. I was!"

"Yes, I understand, really, you were very close to Sálome, you—?"

"Sálome showed me her knife. Not again. She gave it to me. No more. She put it in my bag, this bag. You will never let them. Never never—" She stopped, looked down at her hands. Her fingers, blanched, sanded with cookie crumbs, two angular fists: waiting . . .

"It's all right. You're safe."

Her words popped. "The knife. Ali Cran. He took it away. Blood— pours. Freezes. Sálome is . . . cold." Silvia's breath came in gulps.

"Silvia. Ali Cran? Did he—hurt Sálome?"

Silvia looked down at me, startled. Her head quivered, tiny shakes, and she smiled gently. Serene.

SEVEN

Inside Mexico City

I KNOW THREE Mexico Cities, none of them well. Each intrigues me, each chills me.

When I go into the capital, more rarely than I want because its fabled smog enshrouds the city Monday to Saturday, I spend most of my time in a couple of the old cosmopolitan districts, areas built on top of the dried-out lake bed. The Paseo de la Reforma, of a grace equal to the elegance of any boulevard in the world, passes through the Bosque de Chapultepec, provides a glimpse of the Museum of Anthropology which houses the remains of civilizations alien and magic to my norteamericano (that is, European) trained eyes, and climbs into the Chapultepec Hills past proud mansions, some the homes of the once or the newly rich, some transformed into embassies, restaurants, expensive shops.

A dinner party in one of these grand houses comes to mind. Jaime León, a journalist/photographer/broadcaster friend—I'd stayed in his home for three sultry hazy days—brought me. His wife Luisa had been down with la gripa for nearly a week, sipping juices and broths. He hoped she'd be better right up to the day of the party but by early afternoon her aches and chills remained sufficiently in evidence for him to call his host, Gerardo Maldonaldo, who, singularly disturbed, noted that without Luisa they would be thirteen at table. Jaime described my work and suggested I come along. Maldonaldo invited me with pleasure.

A series of new paintings by our host, an artist of significant repute, had recently gone on exhibit. I'd coincidentally read a warm review of the show soon after my arrival at Jaime's and recalled words like cabalistic, glistening, atavistic. All at the same time? Clearly, despite the heat, I had a duty—at least some curiosity—to stop at the exhibit before dinner and take a look. I asked Jaime if he'd seen the show and thought I detected a sense of discomfort, a hesitation, as he said, "No, no I haven't." Though when he added, "I hear it's controversial, that's normal for Gerardo's work," all ambiguity disappeared.

The gallery was located in a section of town I didn't know, Coyoacán. A smart suburb, in the forties and fifties Coyoacán had been home to the stormy relationship—marriage, divorce, remarriage, immense love, many battles—between Frida Kahlo and Diego Rivera. I went by taxi to avoid a trip through unfamiliar districts without a competent navigator; deciphering a map while driving, a less than wise strategy at home, here becomes, like drinking unboiled water, a precarious act.

The taxi took me through the second Mexico City—old working-class barrios built up in the first two-thirds of this century, neighborhoods so self-sufficient they could have been independent little pueblos had the cost of living space not climbed in the last fifty years to an impossible premium, forcing the countryside between towns to fill in with homes and shops. Some of these areas, now designated as colonias, had in fact started life this way, complete with village church and ghostly graveyard. Overcrowded today and possessing few internal resources, they have received minimal assistance from the government in the way of health services, purified water, sanitation, garbage removal, and even less since the earthquake which overwhelmed an already debt-ridden economy.

The taxi stopped, the driver turned. The street he should take was blocked for repairs. He could double back but this would be a mile out of our way. He pointed to a building five blocks down, indicating, it seemed, our destination. I paid, got out, walked. Not a soul to be seen, and my goal, here in a section of Coyoacán strikingly similar to the poor barrios we'd just driven through, proved to be not at the assumed corner but eight streets further along. I was dripping with sweat by the time I reached the gallery. A small placard beside the door noted the building had been constructed in 1768, once housed the Sisters of the Sacred Heart, was nationalized by the constitution of 1917, and would be closed until 4:30. Perfectly normal for a Saturday afternoon, but living in a provincial town had made me forget such civilized matters. Obviously every sane art dealer, after a large midday meal, now lay sequestered in his natural state, motionless beneath a ceiling fan, waiting for the heat to lift before reemerging, encased in his white-shirt tight-collar dark-suit shell. I looked about for a café or restaurant, a bar, anywhere cool. Nothing. Hardly a tourist area I'd brought myself to. And more than an hour to go. How did a gallery in such a district survive? I could leave, of course—

Along the cross-street, a small rise. To the left and over, perhaps a hundred yards, stood some high trees, a couple of skirt palms, possibly a park. A bit of shade, I thought, perhaps a hint of a breeze. I made my way up the incline as I might have flailed through a steam-bath and drew parallel with the patch of green, only to discover I couldn't reach it—no street or alleyway, no access, only houses.

I found a not too dirty wall on the shady side to lean against. Earlier inhabitants of this upper area seemed to have been better off than the ones along the main street: large dark old houses here with high protective walls. Behind heavy gates I caught glimpses of several once attractive gardens. Beyond lay my little copse of trees, so almost in reach, and the green of it beckoned: I could have sworn I saw a rustling in their topmost branches, I felt it suddenly as a siren call, indisputable, clear. Between the park and myself there lay not more than two of these large houses. I could perhaps cross in silence through their back gardens as their owners slept the heat away, and thereby gain the trees.

I pushed open a gate. Inside, parking space just wide enough for an immense battered Cadillac from the fifties complete with tail fins and once-chromed twin exhausts; stacks upon stacks of excellent old orange clay roofing tiles, now very hard to get; two ancient refrigerators which even in their rusted state suggested coolness within; a gas stove against the side wall. Decades of debris. Silently I wound my way behind the house, in the lowering sun a spooky dim angular affair. No one. In back lay the remains of a once elegant garden. Paths from its four corners, edged in porous volcanic rock, converged at a marble fountain where three half-sized dolphins, tails curving outward, supported at their center a cracked empty marble bowl. On the far side, a three-foot-high tumbledown shrine half enclosed a statue of the Virgin. Weeds and brambles everywhere—except for a small area to the left of the shrine, a corn patch, the dry stalks bleached yellow. Behind the dead corn a segment of wall had tumbled away; my crossing point, made to order. Sweating gracelessly, I clambered over. On the other side, behind more thicket and bushes, the ground sloped gently down. This garden had been recently manicured, ten or twelve red oleanders trimmed with a caring hand, the copa de oro and tulipan blossoms swept away; someone had climbed the two fine skirt palms to cut the excess; old rose hips had been snipped from three dozen bushes. At the foot of the slope, in front of the whitewashed walls of a building, blue twinkled and I thought I saw movement. I worked my way forward, hoisted one leg, then the other, onto a low notch in one of the oleanders, and stared. Below on all sides rows of alcatraz lilies, dwarf bougainvillaeas, red and white and pink rosebushes, impatiens. More: between me and the house itself, embedded in a segment of flattened slope, lay an ancient swimming pool, kidney-shaped, filled with water, glistening in the hazy sun. Like the old white-walled red-tiled house beyond, the pool seemed a refugee from Dashiell Hammett's Hollywood, its side studded with ceramic octopi and mermaids, the surrounding mosaic patterns alive and cool. I was tempted to rush down, tear off my clothes, jump in; except—

In this blue artificial pool, a school of fish.

One of my great pleasures in life is fishing. I've fished salt and fresh water over more than forty years, and caught many of the species going. I can watch fish swim, leap, hover, for hours. But I'd never before seen fish in a swimming pool, hundreds of fish, churning the water. From my perch in the oleander I couldn't tell what kind. I'd have guessed mackerel or baby kingfish from the sharp white flash of their bellies, but how could anyone bring salt water up to this pool— Trout possibly, or a tropical species I didn't know. They were feeding, as on mayflies or some larva, rising to a hatch, whipping about. Hundreds of fish. A repeating blaze of silver against azure as their feed rose to or hit the surface.

But the fish were only half of it. There in their midst, oblivious to the frothing excitement, a rubber cap covering her hair, a woman slowly backstroked along. Hidden by the foliage, not daring to move, I watched. She crawled the length of the pool, turned, breaststroked back, then climbed out, pulled off the bathing cap, took a towel, dried herself. All perfectly normal. She wore an old-fashioned one-piece swimsuit. She looked perhaps fifty, maybe more. Dark hair, graying; on the fleshy side— Then, curiously, she kneeled by the pool edge, leaned over, spread her hands, touched the surface of the water and in a gentle version of her breaststroke made as if to spread the water apart. She did this perhaps a dozen times.

Finally she stood up, climbed some broken stone steps to the house and disappeared.

On the right the garden ended at a high uninterrupted wall. To the left, beyond more rows of flowers, the trees I'd taken to be a small park now stood within reach. But I no longer had a sense of high airy woods or trees with slender trunks. Instead the whole area looked closed in, dark, even foreboding. Tropical growth choked off all access. I checked my watch: five minutes past the gallery's opening time. I gave the pool a final glance. All lay calm, peaceful, the fish gliding silently below the surface.

I retraced my steps. At the gallery Maldonaldo's paintings hung in the ex-convent's onetime cells, rooms of various sizes off a flower-spattered inner courtyard. Each painting seemed like a pungent nut inside a dried-out shell. I had little time for a long critical look, arriving on time at the painter's home taking precedence over examining his work, so I quickly called a taxi and headed back to Jaime's for a cool shower and a tall drink.

"Gerardo Maldonaldo collects odd types," Jaime explained as we wound our way down paved-over barancas, through a maze of well-lit but signless streets, past expensively landscaped neocolonial houses. "The idea of me bringing a norteamericano professor disguised as a novelist pleases him greatly."

I shuddered at this notion of odd types. First of all, I was still only in the first stages of my novel. More uncomfortable, Maldonaldo's paintings, those in the group I'd just seen, bordering on the morbid, took as subject matter a relatively familiar figure, each in his or her "working" environment—a legless man with closed eyes begging in an urban street, an undertaker holding a large hammer nailing closed a coffin, a woman bank teller whose face exuded enmity or rancor kneeling in front of a kind of safe, a gardener tearing large white lilies out of the ground, these I remember best. Maldonaldo had rendered his subjects and their settings with utter realism. Two exceptions: On each figure an item of clothing had been meticulously cut away, a sleeve here, a piece of shirt there, to reveal skin describable only as bloated, blistered, ready to burst, the skin holding back immense tension or disease. Then, in one corner of each painting Maldonaldo had etched, as with a sharpened pencil or a palette knife, a line drawing of an object totally

93

out of place; at least on first viewing. A headless turtle for the bank teller. For the gardener a corset with stays. For the undertaker a stylized dangling penis. And a squid for the beggar.

"No, no," Maldonaldo told me as we sipped a frothy concoction of banana, mango and tangerine juice whose soft scent concealed a heavy dose of rum and tequila. "Don't worry, señor. Since completing that series in the winter I no longer use human models. Landscapes only. Just nature's grandeur now. Human beings are limited. As individuals we can never embody the best in the world." He laughed. "At least not us modern Mexicans. And if I may be so permitted, you pragmatic North Americans are no better. You have been destroyed by the limited precision of your language, we by the blurred contradictions in ours. Tell me, do you lay aside your analytical mind, señor, when you write your fiction?"

I doubted Maldonaldo cared to hear my full response, anyway I'd have much preferred for him to elaborate on the destruction of our—what? minds? souls? by the languages we speak, but before either of us could go on, the senior maid appeared at his side to whisper the readiness of the meal. He took me by the arm and escorted me, with a word to the other guests, into the dining room, murmuring all the while how pleased he was that I could join the evening's company, everyone else he had known for years, how stimulating to dine with a new guest. His white hair and light-grey suit complemented the table, dressed in crystal and silver; it sparkled below a chandelier with—I counted—twenty-eight candles. He placed me beside a woman I had been introduced to when we arrived, Liliana Trasmanale; it'd been difficult taking my eyes off her since. Her stunning three-quarter-sleeved black lacework dress seemed continuous with her crown of cascading raven hair. She seemed to be in her mid-forties.

"You must call me Liliana," she said immediately. Her English, impeccable, became our language of conversation. Perhaps in embarrassment at my halting Spanish, everyone at the table spoke considerable English, several as well some German which I admitted to knowing.

Liliana asked where I lived.

Boston and Montreal, I told her.

"Ah, Montreal. Beautiful city."

"You know it?"

"I did. Twenty years ago. Longer."

"What brought you there?"

"Oh, you see, my children. They went every year to the mountains north of Montreal. The Laurentians, if I remember their name? To summer camp."

Amazing. "And you came north with them?"

"And brought them back. We—my husband and I, he died some years ago—we would always spend a few days in Montreal. And Quebec City. Once we stayed in Boston, often New York."

"And why did you choose to send your children to Quebec, señora?"

"Ah, it's so clean, and the horseback riding, the water sports. Of course for their English as well."

"But why not somewhere closer? In the U.S.?"

She looked at me with black eyes and a tiny smile. I'd obviously gaffed. "But señor, all Mexicans send their children to camp in Canada."

Not a comeback available. I thought of saying as snidely as possible, Do they really? but was saved by a timely diversion, the entry of two maids, steaming tamales wrapped in corn husks, and wine; any incredulous or impolite response went unstated. The maids unwound the tamales and served each of us two; we were to add the mole sauce ourselves.

Señora Trasmanale had begun chatting with Maldonaldo to her left. I found myself intrigued by the conversation across the table, a stoop-backed man with a strange name, Cayetano, and a young woman I remembered as Cristina, the wife of an investment broker, Sergio; they were holding forth on the importance of María Sabina, onetime high priestess of the hallucinogenic mushroom cult in the hills around Oaxaca who had died some days earlier.

"It was very destructive for all Mexico, that she should have shown that reporter such things!" Cristina shook her head angrily.

I wondered if all cosmopolitan Mexicans consistently generalized about Mexico—and was drawn into the conversation. "You mean that article in *Life* magazine, many years ago?" I had a vague memory of it.

"In July of 1957, señor. It is very famous here." Cayetano leaned toward me slightly, his head low between his shoulders as if purposely exaggerating his stoop. "She revealed to strangers, a New

York banker and a French anthropologist, the secrets of the mushroom cult, perhaps you recall. For many centuries it had remained the secret of the Mazateca shamans."

"Yes, and as a result people from everywhere invaded every part of Mexico to search for mushrooms. We looked like fools." Cristina sounded both personally offended—some gringos had come digging in her rose-bed—and as if she were quoting a reputable source. I'd have guessed her to be born about the year the article appeared. "Thank god Sabina took her secrets to the grave," she added.

Many Mazatecas, I learned later from Jaime, practice the mushroom cult for curative reasons and "to purify the soul." But María Sabina was, as much as is known, one of the few to use its power for teleportive, "transmigrative" purposes. Her sessions were called voyages—"to the marvelous world of magic, light and the infinite," as Mexico's important daily, *Excelsior,* phrased it.

Cayetano glanced sharply at Cristina, but turned to me when he spoke. "Sabina, it seems, revealed her methods to no one, not even her daughters. But she did produce in the two foreigners the effects of transmigration. And for this one act she grieved, yes, and atoned, the rest of her life."

"I hope she suffered," Cristina murmured.

Cayetano ignored the young woman. "She taught us all. The Church as well"—he nodded to me, his eyebrows raised—"which as you know desperately needs to learn from the world. Did you realize, my friend, that in María Sabina's poblado, Huautla de Jimenez, even the village priest said a novena when she died. The Church embraced Sabina. And the cult."

"I hope they destroy each other," Cristina muttered; and, as if by invoking privileged authority she would guarantee annihilation, added, "So does Sergio."

"My dear Cristina, you must learn to temper your modernity." Again Cayetano turned to me. "Have you been in Mexico long, señor?"

"Since the evening before the earthquake. I awoke the following morning, walked into the courtyard, and the house swayed before my eyes. I assumed it was a special salute to my arrival."

The group at our end of the table laughed.

"Then you will already have seen we are a nation of many parts," said Cayetano. "Disparate parts. We have witches, computers, the Church—every kind of natural disaster. This is a source of pride.

Only, for us to remain a unified nation, we must blend all our catastrophes. Computers must be married to mushrooms and economists shall have to lie down with priests. Or else we're doomed."

I felt a stirring to my left, Liliana Trasmanale's side. But Maldonaldo stepped in. "We're doomed in any case, Cayetano. No one understands anyone but themselves, priests and computer experts no exception. We Mexicans in our ignorance"—he smiled directly at me—"are perfect members of the North American community."

Cayetano would have none of this. He leaned toward Maldonaldo, shoulders forward, head indrawn, a toad winding up to hobble. "Gerardo, it is clear an artist like yourself must always remain tied to his minutiae. So I understand why you cannot see—"

"Cayetano, are you calling me a realist?"

Accidental compliment or resounding insult? I couldn't tell.

"—how it is you cannot see that in the world of man, and"—to Cristina, who wouldn't look at him—"of women too, there exist patterns that can be gauged, modified, even, my friend, understood. The María Sabinas of this land represent only a small segment of a larger—"

"No!" The eruption came from my left. Liliana, her hair glistening ebony in the candlelight, reached out, pulled her wineglass toward her as if for a shield or to keep her attack from knocking it over. "In Mexico, yes, we live by the edge of a technological civilization. But our life is *precisely* here at that edge, as it must be—we are not of that other civilization. And on this side of that edge lie worlds no one understands. All about us. Inside us. Natural worlds. Human worlds. Buried, forgotten, lost. While we borrow from our neighbors across the edge the rational veil of their sophistication, we pull it over our eyes so we can see neither inward nor out."

I stared at her, incredulous. This, from an upper-class Mexican who sent her children to camp in Canada? I glanced at the others. Everyone at the table, even if silent, had joined this conversation.

She went on: "Oh, Cayetano, I grieve for us when even you speak such rubbish."

Maldonaldo leaned toward her then, his chin on his fists. "But Liliana, what of your Dior gowns?"

"You're a fool, Gerardo. We have to live in as many worlds as time and income allow. We cannot close our eyes to our own vast possibilities just because we're lucky to lead comfortable lives."

"With witches and ambassadors, architects and sorcerers?"

"Gerardo, you're truly an idiot sometimes. Jorge"—she turned to me; no mockery now; something more like sorrow—"please forgive your host his dimmed brain. He used to be a brilliant man. Before success taught him to traffic in evasions. And Gerardo"—her dark skin, I think, reddened, as she turned to Maldonaldo—"please forgive my tongue which loses its restraint when you speak of things you know nothing about. And I hope your guests will excuse me too." She pushed her chair backward, stood, stepped away from the table, turned, swept from the room.

Silence. Then Maldonaldo with a small sad smile turned to me: "I trust we do not bore you, Jorge. Doña Liliana and I have shared this conversation for many decades. Ah, I see we have something to eat at last."

Eyes turned toward the kitchen door.

The timing, perfect. Maldonaldo must have pressed a buzzer with his toe. A maid appeared, pushing in a sideboard on wheels: an immense baked-clay platter, lyonnaise potatoes surrounding a huge dorado on a bed of cress and cilantro. I couldn't keep from saying, "What a magnificent fish! How much did it weigh?"

"I believe, eleven pounds?" he asked one of the maids, who nodded.

I'd never seen a dorado that large, and said so. The maids served and—to the relief of several other guests—the conversation turned to the eating and the catching of fish. The dorado had been baked to perfection and, as we ate, I told my story of the woman in the swimming pool and her aquatic pets. After a few "How extraordinary!"'s our discourse broke into smaller groups.

Only Cayetano still seemed interested. "Now tell me," he said as confidentially as possible, given the table and the murmur of half a dozen lateral voices, "this swimming pool, where precisely did you find it?"

I explained, and how I got there.

"And—did you see any statuary?"

I thought back, tried to recall the scene, apologized for being so taken by the central image—

"Perhaps a figure, smiling, seated or stretched out, it might be leaning backward, possibly a bowl held in its lap? Chac-mool, he's called."

"Oh, the water god? No, nothing like that."

"Then perhaps a figure etched on, for example, a wall, wearing a complicated headdress, possibly a shield, in one hand he'd have a bow dangling by its string, on his back perhaps a kind of circular quiver filled with arrows?"

He certainly knew what he was searching for. I had to shake my head.

"And the woman?"

I described her figure, hair and age as I recalled them.

"Nothing unusual?"

I didn't know how to explain the strange swimming motion. "My inadequacy as an observer shames me," I joked.

He remained serious, however. "Think back, Jorge! It can be very important."

But no amount of urging could retrieve a memory that didn't exist.

Liliana returned at this moment. "Important for Cayetano," she smiled. "Less so for the rest of us."

I had no chance to ask what she—what either of them—meant because at the far end of the table Cristina's husband Sergio, a tall man with thick black curly hair, stood to raise a wineglass to the superb dorado and the health of our host. Soon Cayetano was arguing again with Christina, and I heard Liliana praising Gerardo for an excellent review in a paper I didn't know, and I talked aimlessly with the woman to my right, whose name I've now forgotten.

With dessert, ice cream made from zapote, a creamy brown fruit hidden inside an ordinary green apple skin, we edged toward another eruption. Gerardo Maldonaldo spoke of the earthquake: "A moment of disgrace for Mexico, as few before. A government, unprepared to deal with the smallest crisis in Oaxaca or Chihuahua, faced with death and conflagration in the capital. A President of the Nation, so at a loss he hides, he does not face his people for forty hours—forty!—after the catastrophe. Shameful."

Cristina trod on dangerous ground. "But after the earthquake everything in the country changed forever. Sergio says—"

"No!" Gerardo's fist thundered down on the table. Like Señora Trasmanale I reached for my glass, now to calm the sloshing wine against a second onslaught. "All remained as it had been. But for the first time, all was visible! Buildings crashing down to reveal government in chaos. Our resources, inadequate in every area— emergency health care, sanitation, financial recovery. Wherever one looked, at last we could see. Years, decades of corruption! We were drained, unable to respond, crippled. And to our eternal shame, deep in the bowels of the National Police headquarters, prisoners! Prisoners held incommunicado. Men who had disappeared—gone north—as the police had long ago officially reported. Disappeared! As if Mexico were El Salvador! The earthquake brought it to the surface."

Cristina needed to insist: "No! The government acted quickly. The financial structure of the nation, underneath everything, remained sound. Sergio said if only the—"

"Cristina! Do you ever think a thought of your own? Do you ever look about you on your own? Can you exist on your own?"

She glared at him. Silenced at last.

I felt certain I'd seen that hatred on her face before; but couldn't recall where.

We got up to leave a little after this, Jaime begging forgiveness, he was concerned about his wife's flu. Gerardo Maldonaldo insisted I call him the moment I next arrived in the city. Cayetano asked me to his home the following afternoon for comida, which translates as lunch but as the largest meal of the day begins anywhere between two and four-thirty, a later hour increasing the refinement of the setting. I was told to come early, he would show me his fine collection of sacred statues as well as his less impressive but still worth seeing pre-Columbian pieces. When? About three-thirty.

In the car Jaime feared I'd been embarrassed by the assorted company. Ridiculous, I said. Totally fascinating. I asked about Liliana. "Her husband's dead?"

"Yes, Manuel Cortiga, an architect with a fine eye. He designed Cayetano's home, you'll see it. Manuel believed in traditional styles, but modernized to fit the needs of the person who would live in it. An interesting man."

"Like his widow."

"Yes, isn't she. Could you guess her eldest daughter has just celebrated her fortieth birthday?"

I shriveled a little.

Arriving back Jaime found Luisa asleep and comfortable, so poured us both large Fundadors.

I asked how it happened so many tonight spoke German.

"Well, for example, the man across from you—"

"Cayetano—?"

"Cayetano Dominguez Portillo, he studied philosophy at the University in Hamburg. The mother of the woman to my right emigrated from Germany for love. The broker Sergio spent three years with the trade mission in Bonn."

Such internationalism somehow didn't fit with the rest of the evening and its talk of the occult. I said so.

"Why not? For example, as we sit comfortably here in this living room our maid lives up on the fifth floor with the maids of others in this building. I know from our Mariquita, whom I trust completely in these things, three of those maids are practicing witches, whatever they might do down here below with our food and our children."

I shook my head slowly. In the first Mexico City. We drank another Fundador.

I slept badly and awoke with a headache. Jaime had left for work. Luisa felt much better and would see the doctor in the afternoon. Arching one eyebrow she told me Liliana Trasmanale had called, she would be joining me at Cayetano's for comida, since she lived close by she could give me a ride. Grinning at Luisa, I phoned back and accepted.

Coffee cleared my head but not enough to let me find an idea for an appropriate little present to bring Cayetano. I drove, knowing this way well, to the Museum of Anthropology, my tenth or eleventh visit, and in the Aztec room located an eighteen-inch figurine which looked like the deity Cayetano had described, complete with shield, quiver, arrows: Tezcatlipoca, god of sin, suffering and sorcerers. I stared for minutes, not knowing what to make of it. Blank-faced, carved white stone with one foot broken away, no written elucidation beyond the name. I walked and mulled, ill at ease. I supposed I ought to take a look as well at the fine Chacmool, prehistoric god of fertility and the rains, of life-bestowing water, a figure central to the Mayans as well as the Aztecs— Suddenly I had to be outside. In the large courtyard I sat by the pool and listened to the wind rustle the reeds. Near some lily pads a fat goldfish darted forward, flicked about and disappeared. I knew what to bring Cayetano.

I followed the route taken by the cab the day before, my great idea bracing my courage, and parked just above the main road, first turning around; I didn't want to leave the car directly in front of the scene of my trespass. The sun, before the lunch hour still as hot as ever, somehow felt less oppressive. I could see a few people: two young girls in pastel dresses with ribbons; an old granny in her black finery carrying a baby or at least a package wrapped in three crocheted blankets, light green, pink, white; a boy driving a goat up the hill. I walked to the gate with a show of normal calm, always the best disguise, and as if checking the number glanced about. Inside, on the old cement walkway to the steps, a boy of possibly six, also wearing his Sunday best, pushed a toy fire engine; I'd not realized till then what day it was, no wonder the air seemed cleaner. Great; should anyone ask I'd be the gringo going visiting, my adventuring cloaked in Sunday virtue. Ostentatiously I glanced at my watch, where could my friend be— The boy's fire engine rolled badly. Finally with a gleeful shout he kicked it around the far corner of the house and disappeared.

I looked about, opened the gate quietly, darted in, quickly past the tail fins and tiles, around the side, out to the jungle garden— and froze. To the right, fifty feet off, two women. Hanging up laundry. Chatting. Laughing. I stepped back, waited by a bush. They continued their languid pace as the sun pounded down with all the vehemence of Maldonaldo castigating Cristina. Again the sweat poured. My headache returned. Leave? I could hear the boy again—

The women finished, walked slowly to the little shrine, knelt before it, prayed. I cursed religion, here with private cause. Long minutes later the women took their baskets and meandered inside.

Okay. Over the wall. The pool lay still, the water flat, empty. I worked around to the left, along the bushes. The house stood glistening white, silent. I angled to the pool edge, unnerved; expecting what? To be shot with arrows from Tezcatlipoca's bow? Or a round from a plain old urban pistol. I looked into the water.

Eight octopi, four mermaids; all man-made. No live fish. Where were they? Netted, shipped to market?

I felt a strong stab of disappointment. So much for careful research and the would-be present to my afternoon's host. I'd have to buy a bottle of wine. Had it been cooler I would've looked about for traces of fish scales, anything— If I stayed I'd throw myself into the water fully dressed.

I crossed toward the nearest shade to get out of sight of the house. I was heading straight to the undergrowth I'd taken for a copse when I suddenly realized the row of flowers beside me hid a kind of rut, a small hollow.

Three feet deep, eighteen inches wide. White impatiens acted as a kid of cover, protecting the water from the worst of the sun. Tiled as well. A chute; precisely, a fish run! The fish must live in the tropical growth. Did they come out to the pool to be fed?

Stop trespassing, get back. Clean up for lunch.

I had a sudden glimpse of myself fifteen years from now not having explored farther.

I pushed through a near-impenetrable jungle of sticky creepers, elephant-eared underwood, webs of vine. My town loafers kicked against decaying things, giant tendrils grabbed my wrists, minimal sunshine flickered down. An impudent twig knocked my glasses off and my suddenly desensitized fingers took a minute of terrified groping to find them. A bog pulled my shoe off, my hand found it, yanked it away from an insistent sucking sound. A source of water lay nearby. Two, three, eight more steps. My shoes squished, my arms swept through lush soft leafery into jelly, some mucouslike pine sap. Suddenly I'd had enough, would with pleasure have swapped knowledge of the environs for civilization and a cold shower.

Not to be. Drier land. The price, brambles with half-inch spikes. Not merely no exit, my entry too had disappeared. Thrashing, stabbed, I'd now have traded my beloved word processor in Boston for even a dull machete. And, for an icy beer, thrown in the printer.

Enough. I stood in the middle of some bushes in Coyoacán. A few blocks away I could buy color postcards, deodorants, a god-damn café con leche!

Okay. But I couldn't see out. I turned slowly. The full three hundred sixty. Nothing. Tried again, glancing low. About halfway around, at the base of several trees, a broadening. I still did the full circle; no, no sliding glass door to the sidewalk. Hunched over, protecting my face and glasses, I shoved through. Twenty feet of whipping opposition; then I stood. The edge of a pathway—leading directly back to the swimming pool. From the other direction it beckoned gently. I set off.

Onward. I've followed enough trails around the shores of lakes to know this little path had been trod for many years. The beaten dirt widened suddenly onto a "natural" pond, in the heavy shade half as big as the swimming pool. The glade bled moss across boulders, swept willows onto banks, raised ferns to challenge palms. Rubber trees to overcrowd three living rooms, dwarf tulipans burned hard orange, bougainvillaea in four colors, all these found somber reflection in the soft black water. How deep it was I couldn't tell. And no visible fish.

Inches from the water a thick slab of granite, three feet high, twice as wide, stood embedded in the ground. The side facing me was blank, weathered, as was the near end. The top, however, looked newly cut, or at least bared recently. I came closer. Four holes, metal rods protruding. Had another piece stood there? I leaned around to see the pool side, something carved on the face. I pulled over farther—

One shoe slid out, I reached to grab the slab, missed, slipped in the wet dirt, fell backward. The black water took me in, a cold shock. I lunged for air, splashed to stay afloat, keep my head up, glasses on; and clenched my toes to save my shoes. I took a few seconds to tread water and stared at the facade. Definitely a lower half. Of—? I could make out a semicircular object, and perhaps the stone-feathered ends of arrows. Feet, definitely, to perhaps the waist. A bow? Hard to tell, especially from my angle. I paddled to the path and pulled myself out.

Tezcatlipoca? If so, with his top half recently removed. A heavy bit of work—

I took off my loafers and poured water out of each, turned to the pool, stooped, felt a shudder of fear but still reached my hands in, splashed the muddier stretches of my pants, stood— On an impulse I knelt again and, as if completing some rite in appreciation of, even homage to, the statue beside me, made with my hands that breaststroke gesture I'd seen from the woman the day before. Then I got to my feet and walked away.

And stopped. The splash of solid things. I turned. The pond, alive with fish. They rose, swirled— In the shade, no flash or blaze from their bellies, instead a dull glow, pewter. More beautiful yet, chilling, the dark mottle of their backs below the ebony surface, grey dappled dorsal fins fluttering, the swish of many tails. Their movement slower, the swirls more studied than in the azure pool.

I had a strong sense they were calling me back, and took a step closer. But their interest, if it may be said this way, lay elsewhere. They seemed to arc before the slab.

Enough. The path led to the sun, the swimming pool. I lunged across the grass, free. Both liberated and cut off.

*　　*　　*

Liliana arrived minutes after I'd stepped out of the shower and dressed. "Cayetano has tried to reach you every ten minutes for the last two hours."

"Yes, didn't the maid say, Luisa went to her doctor, I—"

She walked away, leading me to the car. Still elegant, less imposing in daylight, wearing a white Uruapan dress embroidered with tiny flowers of a dozen colors and a scarlet silk rebozo over her shoulders, she drove me the ten minutes to Cayetano's home in Polanco, a center of expensive boutiques and fine houses. At another time I'd have allowed my attractive chauffeur and the streets lined with flowering trees to cast their spell, but now I felt chilled and sad.

Cayetano's house was large and airy. And strangely cool, given the heat outside; and its collection of sacred church relics hardly appealed to my uneducated eye. In the hallway a dozen stone saints stared down, unconcerned with our negligible existence. The living room, the largest of Cayetano's galleries, merely set in relief its owner's frantic impatience. The reflective intense man I'd so recently had dinner with now bounced in such agitation it nearly straightened his hunch: "Jorge, we must go. We must make a purchase and leave before the sun disappears."

"Am I invited for comida or an Aztec rite?" I joked; but I'd been hoping for a tequila or a brandy, ammunition against my sudden uncertainty, and a chance to describe in leisure my adventures of an hour before.

"We will eat later, you will be gastronomically rewarded. But come now, quickly. I shall explain as we drive."

Liliana took my arm. "This too is my friend Cayetano." She shook her head wearily.

I saw his car, a large air-conditioned Mercedes, and explained my tiredness; could I please ride in back?

Liliana would guide. "Do you have a map?"

"We will find it. Have faith."

He drove north. It seemed that an artifact of particular interest, a primitive pietà from the last third of the eighteenth century, made of straw, baked clay, corn stalks and husks, had turned up in that part of the city and was for sale.

Cayetano's earlier agitation and now his driving made me deeply uncomfortable. I excused myself and lay down on the seat. For nearly an hour I dozed. Images of fish in dark pools and stern guardian idols flashed through my mind. A series of ridges, mounds and potholes woke me. The car stopped.

I sat up, looked out. The side of a tan, sun-smeared hill, soil baked yellow, the road ahead impossibly rutted. To the right a street not accessible without a high-axle truck. Dwellings, hardly houses—plywood discarded from building sites, old boards occasionally covered with tar paper, roofs of corrugated plastic or tin, cardboard to keep out swirling dust but no protection against rain, all more or less held together with nails, rope and wire. A few bushes and cacti, some bougainvillaea, lush red geranium bolls on short stems sitting in old paint cans. Car corpses. Children with glazed eyes, crossed eyes, swollen bellies, skinny bellies, shirts and pants and dresses hanging loose, barefoot or in torn sandals. They surrounded the Mercedes. The third Mexico City.

"Jorge, will you come with me?"

"Sure, of course." I pulled myself together.

"Leave your wallet with Liliana."

We got out.

The dirty heat caught me in the nose and throat and the children swarmed around us, hands everywhere, demanding money, reaching into our pockets. Cayetano spoke to them sharply and they fell back, a distant circle. I felt only anger from them, a dense fury ready to burst out through eyes or mouths or through a dirty wound. Cayetano turned and spoke loudly to Liliana through the glass of the car door: "The pistol is in the glove compartment."

We walked from the car. "I will need your help, Jorge." He called to one of the older boys, and the boy pointed up the road some hundred fifty, two hundred feet. "You can see now, Jorge, why I did not wish to come here after dark."

We reached a shack distinguished from the others by its facade, yellow aluminum siding, twelve-foot lengths, eight or ten strips worth. Cayetano called, "Chucho!" Nothing for twenty, thirty seconds. Sweat poured down my sides and my chill wouldn't go away. A woman no more than sixteen, seventeen, nursing a blanket-swaddled baby, stepped halfway through the open doorway and with her head motioned us in.

My discomfort had grown since leaving the car. Inside the shack, ten degrees hotter, so dark I could see nothing, I was hit by an unstomachable cornucopia of stench, foulness, rot. Honest claustrophobia took over. I flailed about, found an arm, grabbed. "Caye-tano—?"

"You will soon be used to it."

"I have to get out—"

"Wait for me by the door."

Outside I leaned against the wall, luckily the shady side of the house. Inside I heard two men arguing with Cayetano. Eventually he came out and spoke to me in German. I was to go down to the car, ask Liliana for a hundred twenty thousand pesos and return with it.

"And the pistol?"

He gave me a look at first startled, then for a moment pensive. "No. But she will give you also a box of garbage bags."

"You're okay?"

"I believe so."

I walked quickly down the hill. Some fifty feet to the right of the car a small girl held a pink plastic bucket to a faucet on a pipe sticking up from the ground and patiently waited while water dribbled out. The other children sat, still back from the car, staring dully at my progress.

Liliana took several bills from a thick envelope in the glove compartment. She gave me the money, the box, and a scowl of stark disapproval. I returned, though more slowly. A hundred twenty thousand pesos, about two hundred forty American dollars, more money than any of these children would ever see at one time.

It took another twenty minutes. The sun, happily, had dropped low. They came out, Cayetano first, expressionless, after him the two men, huaraches, jeans, open shirts, unshaven, both wearing sombreros, grinning. They carried an object about four feet long, wrapped in the big black plastic bags. It seemed heavy. Cayetano nodded, we descended. No one spoke. At the Mercedes Cayetano gestured to Liliana, who leaned over the driver's seat; instantly the trunk popped open. Sheets of foam rubber lined the bottom and sides. The two men set the package carefully in, Cayetano placed more foam on top and closed the trunk.

He motioned me to get in the back, spoke some unintelligible words to the men, climbed in himself, started the engine, and we were off. No one said a word till we reached a large new paved road. There he picked up speed and turned to me. "Wonderful, Jorge. You will see. Thank you."

"Look the way you are driving." These the only words spoken by Liliana the whole way back.

Cayetano and I carried the garbage-bag-draped object from his car to the house. It weighed as much as a large child. We placed it on a carpet in the living room. The stone saints were still unenthusiastic about our presence. Liliana, implacable as the relics, watched us. Cayetano spoke with a maid, she brought me a towel and a cold beer. We would have the unveiling after my shower, then at last our—by now surely ultraelegant—comida.

Hot water helped dampen my aches. After the shower I found, laid out, a pair of white pants, a dark striped shirt and sandals. My own clothes had disappeared. They would be given me on leaving, clean and ironed.

In the sala Cayetano too had washed, now wore comfortable slacks and a loose shirt. Liliana, unchanged, sipped a margarita.

Cayetano stood. "Ah, Jorge. What do you think?"

They'd not waited for me. Yes, definitely a pietà. Seated on a kind of stool, lightly leaning back. The artist might have seen at least a sketch of Michelangelo's early work, or of the Avignon pietà. Lost or destroyed somewhere over the last two hundred years, the Christ was absent from the Virgin's lap. Her legs, the skirt of her dress, her chest and arms, constructed of cornstalks wrapped with straw then cemented with orange clay, seemed oddly pliable, as if the joints would bend. Bare corncobs bonded with baked clay shaped her head. A few shreds of what might once have been corn silk adorned her head; the baldness masculinized her above the neck. Her nose and eyes were of clay, as was her slightly open mouth; its smile showed a few embedded corn-kernel teeth. Leaning backwards, without the Jesus figure to complete her, she seemed awkward, yet sweet in a silly sort of way. "Well, Cayetano, congratulations." I kept myself from adding: I suppose.

He nodded.

Liliana muttered, "Disgraceful."

"Not at all. And don't begin again, please, that it is a stolen artifact. She hasn't seen the inside of a church in decades."

"That's not what I mean." Liliana got up. "I'll be back." Dramatically she turned and left.

I wondered how deep their argument had gone.

"Liliana enjoys her exits, don't you think?"

We both smiled. The maid brought another beer. I drank, and felt almost ready to forgive Cayetano everything.

We talked some minutes about the pietà. I wondered how he knew its age.

He made a few learned remarks about the straw.

I expressed interest in the clay: how could it have been baked in an oven without burning the vegetable matter?

Five days in the sun.

Ah.

We remained, for some moments, silent. I think Cayetano sensed what was to come, he couldn't speak, and I suddenly felt from him a panic, a kind of thick fear, powerful enough to trouble even the last sleep of our missing Christ. Time to tell my trout-and-god-of-sorcerers story; I made my fall into the dark water and subsequent mud-encrusted departure as comic as possible.

Cayetano didn't laugh. I waited for his reaction. Silence. "What's the matter?"

"Nothing." He smiled sadly.

"You know who she is? The woman I saw swimming?"

"Yes."

"Well?"

He shook his head.

After all I'd done— No, he was right. I laughed. Lightly.

Liliana Trasmanale returned. In her hand, a hammer. Before I could stop her she smashed sidewards against the head of the pietà. Clay shattered, corn and straw stayed in place. Again she struck: the shoulders, the chest, the belly.

I unfroze, leapt up: "Liliana—! for God's sake!"

She swung again. A hip cracked.

Cayetano stood beside her, "I know, Liliana, I know, my dear," but made no move to stop her.

She swung again. The dress fell away. Again. A clay leg shattered. "Jorge—pull away the husks—please."

I looked at her, incredulous. At Cayetano. His head hunched deep between his shoulders. He nodded.

I reached out to the Virgin's neck, yanked at the clay, at matted husks. It stuck, wouldn't come away.

"The head. Start there. Peel it off."

Two centuries of clay, straw, decay, held tight. Then the face gave. A shoulder and half the chest came with it. Inside, now exposed, gleaming dull silver, black, deep green, seated like the Virgin, leaning back, grinning, Chac-mool the rain god.

I pulled off more stalks and clay. I looked to Cayetano—

He shook his head. "For centuries the indigenous people of Mexico have hidden their victimized gods inside the statues of saints and virgins."

I stood back. The Chac-mool smiled at me, aloof, lascivious. Balanced on his belly, a bowl. To catch water. Or to offer it?

Liliana stepped closer. She pulled some clay from the top of the head, ran her hand down one cheek, down the shoulder, the arm—

EIGHT

Blood Feud

& OFTEN SILVIA LOCA would meander about the plaza, alone, around and again around, chattering to herself. The kids giggled behind their hands and behind her back. When she came visiting she was always restrained and respectful despite the saggy blouse and loose torn skirts. She is in her mid or late thirties, her face and hair probably hadn't made contact with real soap for a long time, in fact I'd guess regular hygiene to have been far removed from what went on in her mind. But for all that, especially when she grinned, she wasn't unattractive—could have been nearly beautiful once. Unlike most rural Mexican women of this age she seemed, as far as I could tell anyway, to have kept something of a slender figure beneath the baggy clothing—most likely because she'd never borne even one child, let alone the more usual seven.

Since the words she spoke came out slowly and clearly, she was a help to me in my early weeks in Michoácuaro. I was able to decipher some of what she said and I like to imagine she could understand my pidgin Spanish a bit. I'd taught Constanza how to make, among other things, oatmeal cookies, and once I asked her to give Silvia a couple; this proved to be a taste phenomenon Silvia had never encountered before, was ecstatic about, and returned for. If there were no cookies she'd be happy with a bolillo, a white-bread roll she gnawed little bits off as she sat in the corner of the patio and watched me, talking away.

She was the first person I heard mention Ali Cran. A friend of hers, she said: un muy buen amigo. I'd been warned about the alacrán, best to avoid it, kill any I saw. So at the start she left me a bit unsettled, being if I could believe her the good friend of a scorpion.

After I'd been here a few weeks I learned she was indirectly responsible for the bosque verde—the little green wood northeast of town—for its coming into existence in the first place. Here two square kilometers of trees have had twenty years to grow tall and tangled, and the brush is impenetrable. Nisi Calderón, who's often gone right to the edge, says the undergrowth is so thick not even ground fires could clear it, so little air can penetrate. Compare this wood with most of Michoacán, destructively logged, and you note the anomaly here: a pretty patch of land, crowned with both deciduous and evergreen trees, to the eye a mystery; at the same time a pleasure because it's not part of any reforestation program so the trees don't grow in dreary regimented rows. Within this chaotic wilderness supposedly lives the largest concentration of birds to be found in the state. Rabbits can still be seen at its borders and, I was told, early one evening two years ago little Arturo Mendoza, passing near the edge because he was expected home and had to cut the corner, saw what must have been a fox creep maybe thirty feet out from the underbrush. Arturo had never seen a fox before and it terrified him.

Nobody goes into the wood, for two reasons. The lesser, which as anyone in Michoácuaro will explain is nonsense, says the bosque is haunted. People such as Pepe agree it's simple to see how these fears come about: no one's been in there for twenty years so it's become an unknown place. Therefore it could be the home of hechiceras and vampiros and naguales—witch doctors, vampires, half men–half beasts, all "known" here. They'd be undisturbed in the bosque; and anyway, how can one know they aren't there, nobody's gone to look for twenty years. Add to this stories of strange lights shining over the trees at night, reports of burros and sheep wandering nearby never to be seen again, memories of heaving and moaning and terrible laughter coming out and in daylight too— taken all together, says Pepe, true or not, they're believed, so you have real grounds for fear.

The second, the important reason for staying out of the wood, is that years ago this piece of land came to be disputed territory, the object of a killing feud between the Rojas and the Sanchez families. The feud is said to be a punishment inflicted on them by Ali Cran.

Before he died Moisés de Jesús told me he didn't believe a word of any of those haunted bosque stories. Or at least that was how he began. I explained I'd driven by, seen an unusually green place, turned off on a dirt road for a little exploring, got as close as the cart path would let me, left the car and walked toward the wood because it was so inviting. But a campesino, appearing out of no-where, had warned me away, saying the wood was haunted.

M. de J. made as to pull me out of sight of passersby because he was going to impart some grand secret. He sat me down on the doorstep just inside his entryway and with a derisory smile explained how only country people would believe a word of that nonsense. Ghosts? Ridiculous. He offered me some of his homemade pulque and for half an hour I listened, nursing a glass while he finished a quarter of the bottle. I heard several rambling anecdotes about the wood, each beginning with a denial of any unusual happening, each ending with the kind of twist that leaves some real doubt—if not about the tale, at least of its telling. Such as: "My cousin Aurelia's second son, Carlos, is married to Bárbara, whose father is Isidoro Lopez-Clemente, a man of great wisdom and a devout Catholic who gives every year one-ninth of the earnings from his cane fields to the shrine of María de León at Aguafría. Isidoro knows well that ghosts are the foolish inventions of simple peasants. His land is only half a kilometer from the wood, but not on the sides where the Rojas or the Sanchez families live. Near to where you walked, Don Jorge. Isidoro has passed that wood many times and has never seen or heard anything unusual. Only one time. One time, yes, there was a small, a—you could call it, yes, a little strange." He sipped his pulque.

"What happened?"

"Now I think Isidoro had too much mezcal a nephew from Oaxaca had brought him for a fiesta. So I do not believe very much of this is true." He sighed, drank down more pulque, poured another glass, topped off mine.

I imagined his wishing this too were mezcal instead of our much milder drink, and chortled. "Will you keep me in suspense forever about this drunken friend?"

He spoke with great solemnity. "Don Jorge, this is not to laugh over. It is a matter of great concern, when Isidoro Lopez tells of such things—"

I waited. The surface of his eyes glazed vacant for a moment, as if he looked far beyond me. To the wood, possibly. To his friend Isidoro.

"About ten years ago Isidoro lost a pig. It was staked but the rope had frayed and torn. The pig, a hairy brown animal—I had admired it often and looked forward to tasting the sweetness of its flesh at the fiesta—this pig had wandered away. Afterward Isidoro complained about this rope, a new rope, he'd bought it only a year before, in the spring, how could it have torn. The pig should have been the center of the fiesta, the birthday of a son and daughter, the boy Estaban nine years old, she ten, born on exactly the same day of the year. The fiesta went on anyway, a neighbor's pig had to be bought and slaughtered. It was a noisy happy afternoon and evening. For Isidoro the mezcal from Oaxaca helped him forget his additional expense. You see, Isidoro is generous to the Church but he is not very generous to his neighbors, so a lot of the mezcal went directly to his belly, only his, and to his brain, making him laugh much, and very hard. He danced with everyone and fell asleep before midnight. By one in the morning all the others had left. About three he woke up. In the air above his bed was a light. It was somehow, you see, floating. In the middle of the light was his pig. Nice and brown and hairy. Wrapped in a glow of pink light. You understand me? Isidoro says he watched, fascinated and terrified. Slowly the lighted pig floated to the window, it was open, the pig hovered there. Isidoro was sure it wanted him to follow. In Isidoro's brain the impossibility of a floating brown pig fought with a great fear—what was this all about? But he wanted his pig back. So his curiosity won. He left the bed. His knees were wobbly with the memory of mezcal. Lucky he'd never gotten undressed or he'd have left naked because the pig was already over the barnyard, two meters above the ground. Across the field the pig led the way. Toward the wood." Moisés de Jesús closed his eyes, perhaps picturing the pig.

I waited.

"The only light came from the stars. And the pig. Isidoro liked this very little. Less and less. But he followed. He hadn't gone to the edge of the wood for a long time. Not because of ghosts or demons, no. Because of the feud. He did not want to get shot. At the edge of the wooded land millions of vines, solid brush, impossible to enter. But the pig floated to a certain space. The space was open a little, between brambles and branches. A real path, Isidoro said. By this time he was horribly afraid. But he still followed. He's crazy sometimes, poor Isidoro. They went a short distance. They came to an opening, a place where no plants grew, he could look straight up to the sky. The ground was black, no grass, not even moss. The pig lowered itself. Slowly. Isidoro looked down. A thing

114

was down there, white and very ragged. The pig lowered itself into the white ragged shape. Isidoro recognized the white. A skeleton. A white pig skeleton. The glowing pig settled into it. Took it over. Became one with its own skeleton, you understand. The light on the pig dimmed. Isidoro stared. In a minute it was dark. Isidoro shook with fear. Had he seen the soul of his pig? Do pigs have souls? Why had he been lured here? He was terrified, blinded. He lunged this way and that, where was the path out—everything was dead black, no moon. He never located the path, he rushed into the brambles and vines and bushes, all catching him and tying him down till he'd become a skeleton too. Somehow he got out to the field. He has a good sense of direction, he ran like a crazy man to his house, but two hundred meters away he tripped and fell and knocked himself out. They found him in the morning."

"A mezcal dream?" I offered this, hinting sympathy.

"If you wish." But he spoke the words with a little sneer: the gringo didn't believe.

I had only wanted to agree with my raconteur's assessment of Isidoro's no-nonsense character at the beginning of the narrative. More fool I.

Like Isidoro, the major reason people won't enter the bosque verde is because of the feud. Which, as I mentioned, was Ali Cran's creation. How this had come about— If I stayed here for a decade I don't suppose I'd learn half of what I want to know.

"And don't even bother trying," Rubén told me as we stood in front of the police station. Rubén prides himself on knowing a great deal about how Michoácuaro works; everything, he's said to me more than once, but I'm dubious. Still, when I told him Silvia visits three or four times a week, he nodded. "And she stays fifteen, twenty minutes."

I should have guessed he'd know this.

"She's crazy."

"I kind of like her."

Rubén cocked his head and looked at me with a squint. I couldn't tell whether he found me naive, or meddling too much in Michoácuaro's private life, or if those gestures I can't fathom are as much a part of him as his uniform. Still, I was about to push on except a car skidded to a stop in front of us. An extremely excited man in his early twenties leaned out the window; from his steam-engine

Spanish I caught only a few hard words, body, machete, blood, but his terror was clear enough. Rubén calmed him, led him into the station, glanced at me with a scowl that seemed to say, Understand now?

El Pescador carried the story a few days later. A taxi driver, a certain Juan Rojas Rodriguez, had been murdered. He was found behind the wheel of his car. His throat had been slit so deeply the neck was nearly severed; when discovered, the head dangled to the right at an acute angle. "The attack," Rubén Reyes Ponce, jefe de policía, was quoted as saying, "came from behind, the passenger having first struck the driver, then cut his throat." Juan Rojas was thirty-seven, married, eight children. And the sixth member of his family to die violently; three brothers, a nephew and his father, Fernando Rojas Gómez, had also met their deaths by murder or suspected murder. The article ended with a homily about the dreadful amount of drinking in the countryside. Eliminate alcohol and reduce this terrible violence.

Silvia Loca came by the next morning. She had torn the article from the paper, now unfolded it and showed me. Though only a day old the newsprint was near illegible, as if she'd run her fingers down it many times, mouthing the words, showing it around. She read it aloud then—or rather recited it from memory, the lines were that badly smeared. A kind of glow surrounded her, a secret pleasure; the murder had given her immense satisfaction. When she finished she said, "Ali Cran. Ali Cran. Ali Cran." She smiled with such genuine affection, what might she have become—

Did she mean Ali Cran was somehow responsible?

"Ali Cran. Ali Cran."

"He's your friend, I know he helps you."

"Ali Cran."

I haven't found out how Silvia and Ali Cran became friends, particularly after she and Nabór stole his baseball cap decades ago. But that they've been close a long time is clear: Ali Cran began for her, eighteen years back, a process of revenge. This I learned partly from Pepe one day at the Telecable office, and partly from Rubén, who had investigated the case as it progressed—a dubious term here—over the past eleven years.

In the autumn of 1968 when the last of the rains had gone, there'd been a fiesta at the Rojas rancho. In those days the Rojas and Sanchez families were friends as well as neighbors; and two years before a Rojas girl had married a Sanchez cousin, they'd moved near to Uruapan. The Rojas and the Sanchez lands shared a boundary about halfway between the houses where a spring came out of the ground. One of the responsibilities of the several daughters from each house was to fetch water. Nobody found the task unpleasant, the spring was less than half a kilometer away, always a chance for a few minutes' gossip with whomever showed. The place was in a bit of a glade, cool under some high trees. You could soak your feet.

There is disagreement on the reason for the fiesta. The rainy season had ended, the rains had been heavy, good time for a celebration. People began gathering in midafternoon. By nine it was long dark, a lot of pulque and tequila had warmed people's affections and blood and brought dozens up to dance. Probably eighty people from the newly born to the venerable sat or danced, played, talked, drank, ate. There was a small moon.

By the corral four girls stood separate, giggling, guffawing. The particularly ribald laughter of one, María-Silvia Carranza, who for the first time in her life had drunk pulque publicly, caught the notice of a group of young men known around town as "The Eight," four Sanchez sons and four Rojas sons. All born within six years of each other, at that time they ranged from twenty-three down to seventeen. They'd grown up together, were inseparable in all the worst and for all the best—in eternally sworn loyalties, in jealousy over girls, in fighting, in total commitment to each other against the world.

Toro Sanchez, the dandy in the group, his silk shirt half unbuttoned, called to a girl named Arcángela to dance with him. As they stamped to the tierra caliente rhythm he asked what Silvia was finding so funny. Toro said Arcángela swore him to secrecy but before he could agree she blurted out Silvia had bragged that she, Silvia, was the most desirable woman in all Michoácuaro, she knew all of the famous Eight wanted her. Afterward, Arcángela denied having said anything like this to Toro, denied also Silvia said such a thing to her. And the other girls corroborated all the denials.

Toro told his seven friends and brothers Silvia had said she knew they wanted her.The eight exchanged reactions: "You mean she wants us." "By herself or with her friends?" "You want to find out?" Guillermo Rojas, the eldest by four months, well drunk already, said: "She wants me." Pedro Sanchez giggled and smoothed his mustache.

Among the girls Marta swore she heard Silvia say, "None of those guys is very much," and Arcángela say, "How do you know?" and Silvia say, "I know." But Arcángela would swear on her little sister's grave she had no part in a conversation like that.

In minutes The Eight were milling around Silvia and her friends. Somehow a decision was taken, get a couple of bottles of tequila, go for a picnic by the spring. Later each would swear this was all they decided, a picnic, a little tequila.

At the spring the music from the fiesta was dimly audible. Silvia danced, the center of attention of The Eight and of her girlfriends. The scene would have been set for a performance, participants and audience both present. Still stomping and swaying, Silvia grabbed one of the tequila bottles, drank at it a long time; everybody later agreed on that. Then she danced more wildly, she swayed and shook in the near dark, she half unbuttoned her blouse—to cool off, that was all—dancing on alone.

Even then it might have stayed okay except Guillermo took the bottle from Silvia, drank, passed it to his younger brother Juan, held Silvia to him and for half a minute they swayed together— Then he stepped back, reached to his belt, undid it, unzipped his fly, grabbed Silvia and shoved and pulled her to the ground and yanked up her skirt. It didn't look like Silvia was trying to push him away, if she had the others might have helped. Arcángela said it was more as if the event panicked her, like stage fright—the sex, holding the center of attention. Guillermo was so drunk he had difficulty with his act. He got furious and slapped Silvia six or eight times. Being hit may have sobered her a bit. Not enough. But slapping her did help Guillermo, so finally he was done. Instantly another, Pedro Sanchez, was on top of her, and very soon the next, Juan Rojas, had pulled his jeans down. The whole scene quickly turned to terror, the girls tried to run away but Guillermo grabbed Arcángela by the wrist and muttered tightly, Nobody leaves till it's over, any of the girls try they join Silvia. By the fifth, skinny Simon Sanchez, Silvia's desperate attempts to scream had been stopped by a bandanna in her mouth and somebody held her shoulders down. The seventh, Toro Sanchez, the dandy wearing his new purple silk shirt, explained afterward the whole thing was making him sick but he had to participate or the others would call him chicken-piss. Some said he only didn't want to dirty his shirt. With the eighth, young Ticho, drunker than he'd ever been or would be again, Silvia was out cold.

After, the boys drifted away. The girls tried to carry Silvia back. She came to consciousness, lashed out, kicked, squeaked, screamed at them, scratched, laughed hysterically. And ran away. Isidoro Lopez found her in the morning in his barn. He'd already heard about the event, a bit of it, and he chased Silvia off his land yelling, Filthy whore! and, Shit-filled sow! and, Stinking scum-pot!

Silvia now went completely silent, often stayed motionless for days. Except, rarely, she would wail for hours, with tears or without. People conceded she'd gone crazy from the rape. For which no one was prosecuted since it was "impossible to place the blame."

Somehow Silvia was capable of communicating with Ali Cran. He would visit her two or three times a week, and speak quietly to her.

Pepe thinks Ali Cran's ploy came into existence at that point, and reconstructs it this way:

For over a week after the rape neither the Sanchez nor the Rojas brothers left their ranchos. Ali Cran spoke with them in the fields they worked. Both families still used the spring, but the old easy gossip had frayed away.

To the Sanchez brothers Ali Cran said Silvia believed that they, the Sanchez four, had organized the rape. One night she would get out of bed and with the Rojas four would lie in wait for the Sanchez four. At the spring. She has forgiven the Rojas four, Ali Cran explained, because they, the Rojas four, each of them, have abased themselves before her, apologized completely, begged forgiveness. And they have promised to cut the eggs off the Sanchez brothers.

To the Rojas group Ali Cran told the same story, but the other way around: Silvia says the Sanchez four have apologized, and so on.

Pedro Sanchez, taking no chances with the future of his pleasure stones, went calling, ready with a profound apology: he would lie on the floor on his stomach, she could kick him, beat him, tear his hair and—

At her door her father stood with a sickle, swung it wildly, screamed hysterically, tearfully, "You have ruined my daughter, my beautiful daughter, she will talk to none of you, I will kill you all!"

Pedro cringed, the father leapt forward, Pedro backed, ran—

One hot afternoon, in town, Roberto Rojas met Teofilo Sanchez on a narrow strip of sidewalk. Neither would step onto the road for the other. So these two young men who had once sworn blood oaths of loyalty for all eternity suddenly faced each other, one holding a ten-inch pigsticker, the other swinging a machete. Before they could be pulled apart Roberto had lost his left hand and three of Teofilo's ribs lay exposed. Attempting to separate them, two bystanders were slashed.

Now the families avoided one another. Each made certain no one was at the spring before one of its members left the house. Neither sent a daughter to the spring alone. For several weeks everything remained heavily quiet. Then at the plaza Guillermo Rojas, drunk again, bragged to a large company about how he would meet any Sanchez at the spring, fight to the death, that would settle their argument forever. Someone suggested it was mainly Silvia and her family who had been hurt. Guillermo with his pointed boots kicked the man in the shins and punched him in the neck.

At three the next morning Guillermo dragged himself home. His skin where visible was smeared with blood. Each step hacked agony into his body. He whined, excruciating pain, he'd been attacked by a man and a nagual, the nagual half man–half coyote and with a great scorpion stinger; he fought back and they knocked him unconscious, stung him ten dozen times— Worst, aaiee! he was castrated! In his cramp-tight fist, a piece of purple silk shirt.

The owner of the shirt, Toro Sanchez, died on New Year's Eve at a fiesta in tierra caliente. He had slipped away to the fields with a girl from a neighboring ranch. Three people she couldn't later identify attacked them, one grabbed her, carried her to a cornfield, left her; she was so frightened, didn't know where she was, only got back by stumbling toward the light from the fire. The other two had killed and mutilated Toro. The three were never caught. All the Rojas boys had alibis.

Michoácuaro cried, Enough! The newspaper begged the injured parties to show Christian charity and forgiveness. The Bishop spoke to the two families, then to Silvia, her father and mother. What was done was done and over, nothing could change what happened, this was God's will, perhaps Silvia's soul was undefiled even if her

120

physical condition could not be reversed. Now the killing had to stop. Had to.

Silvia's father, a pious man, said perhaps the killing was God's will also. Silvia's mother wept. The Bishop demanded a meeting of the three families.

Into a conference room in the Bishop's large residence came Silvia and her parents, the four Rojas sons and their father, the three remaining Sanchez sons and their father. The Bishop, grave, spoke first: If Silvia forgave everyone, here, now, all before all others, then the meaningless bloodshed would end.

Silvia sat silent, smiling. She moved her glance across the face of each of the seven sons. No one would meet her eye. She smiled, similarly, longer, at Ernesto, the Sanchez father. He had to look away. The same smile for Fernando Rojas. He couldn't look toward her, he gazed sadly at his sons.

The Bishop thought, This might just work. "We must proceed by assuming we all share, before God, the responsibility for all the acts committed. For what has happened, let us each, now, forgive each other. Let us begin anew." He turned to Silvia.

On her face the smile was gone, replaced with an expression of such pure hate the Bishop thought he saw the very Lucifer, naked and afire, staring out from those eyes.

He would concede his tactic had been useless.

Nevertheless it did look, at first, to be working. For nearly a year nothing violent happened between the two families. Then one morning Guillermo Rojas, who now drove a taxi for a living— everyone agreed he wasn't good for much else but he was okay as a chauffeur, he could at least sit—was transporting Isidoro Lopez, who had broken his leg, to the Aguafría shrine. The sun would rise in a few minutes, the dirt road had many curves, their progress was slow. Suddenly they were ambushed, four shots. One bullet hit the shatterproof windshield. Old Isidoro's face oozed blood in a dozen places cut by shreds of glass. Guillermo whispered to Isidoro not to move. The windshield, mostly intact, white with cracks, gave them cover. From the brush two figures carefully approached the taxi, assessing the damage. Guillermo leaned out the window and shot them both. They fell. He accelerated hard and drove over one of them. He brought Isidoro to the shrine of María de León, both took confession, Guillermo helped serve the mass.

On the road one of the young men, Simon Sanchez, lay dead. His brother Pedro was said to have gone north, across the Rio Bravo with a coyote who cheated him, to find work in Oklahoma. He wasn't seen again till 1979, bringing back an American wife, three children and enough money to buy a small ranch. While inspecting some land at the edge of tierra caliente he was shot by a sniper and died four days later.

The intervening years had been complicated. Many children had been born to the wives of those who remained of the infamous Eight, and children of sisters as well. Extensions of the family still lived nearby. As for the parental ranchos, a growing stretch of wooded no-man's-land separated them. No one used the spring anymore, no one dared. Wells had to be dug. By the little spring, bushes and small trees increasingly took over, tacit acknowledgment of the need for a physical barrier. The children would still meet, necessarily, in neutral areas—the road to town, or at school. A road meeting meant a fight. The teachers agreed to keep after school on alternate weeks either the Rojas grandchildren and children of cousins, or the Sanchez ones.

Three years before the death of Pedro Sanchez, Roberto Rojas the one-handed brother went out for a much-needed pee behind the Luz Cantina. After half an hour he hadn't come back. Once the appropriate jokes had been laughed at, the others went out and found him dead. More than a hundred gashes in his body.

Two years ago, in the spring of 1984, just before the rains began, Guillermo's taxi went off a cliff. The engine exploded on impact. His brother Ticho was driving their father Ernesto to his sister's place in the hills. Guillermo hadn't been in the taxi. Rubén investigated and ended up announcing, as it said in the *Pescador* report, there had been nothing wrong with the car.

One boozy night Rubén asked me how much I knew about automobile steering columns, criminologists had to know everything about steering columns. His questions indicated doubts he wasn't able to legitimize. But I don't know the first thing about steering columns.

Guillermo, since the moment of his castration by the nagual with the huge stinger, avoided all places where scorpions might be found. Dry adobe, musty corners, dark rooms and warm patios had become anathema. I suspect if he could have moved to northern Ontario he might have lived a happier life. Instead he died two years ago when he crawled into his bed, drunk as usual, without looking between the sheets. He was bitten by four scorpions. Big fellows even for around here, the story goes. How they got into his bed is unknown. They didn't kill him, but seconds after leaping from the bed in total terror his heart stopped, he fell over and was gone. Unusual for one so young, people noted.

Then when Juan Rojas's neck was slashed in his taxi only Teofilo Sanchez remained of the original eight. Teofilo had moved to Morelia, become a secondary school teacher. Over the years he was spotted once in a while visiting his mother at the rancho. He never wandered into town. He hadn't been seen at all recently, certainly not in the past couple of years, the time during which the last three Rojas men had died. Pepe can't believe Teofilo wasn't responsible, though. Or somebody he hired.

"How about Silvia herself?"

"Impossible. She's crazy. Come on, you've seen her, you've talked to her—"

A couple of weeks ago Teofilo was reported missing. His wife explained he had not returned home after an evening meeting of parents and teachers. The police had theories ranging from his leaving Morelia with a lady friend (he was a known womanizer; but all his señoras were home with their husbands) to his having embezzled funds from the school (he was treasurer there; but no money was missing). In Morelia, no clues.

In Michoácuaro, when word of the disappearance arrived, everybody knew, which is to say everyone talked about it, Teofilo being the last living participant in the rape. Small towns have long memories, and Silvia herself could be seen wandering around the plaza day after day, year after year.

Everyone spent a lot of time knowing in general what had happened to Teofilo but no one had specific ideas. Except, as it turned out, Rubén. But he wouldn't bring himself to act on his notion. Not directly, anyway. Since the disappearance he'd had a busy few days— a couple of break-ins, a stolen pump, a knifing at one of the ranchos, a man slashing up his brother-in-law in an argument over who owned a specific seven square meters of land. And a husband and wife going at each other with kitchen knives. So when Rubén came by one late Saturday afternoon I offered him a chair, told him to put his feet up and poured him a martini.

"Such a degenerate gringo weakness. And I am addicted." He

took the glass, shaking his head in pleasure. "Ah Jorge, what will I do when you leave."

"Mix your own pinche martinis." I was learning the language. I grinned, though with a hint of sympathy.

"No, no, you have the touch . . ." He sipped.

I don't argue with a compliment. "Salud." We chatted here and there for half an hour. I poured him another. We seemed serene.

Then, slowly: "Jorge, you're a criminologist. Do you know, I have an idea about this Teofilo Sanchez disappearance."

I was flattered he'd talk to me about one of his cases. But I felt a bit uncomfortable.

Rubén spoke slowly, musing, feeling out his words: "Well, I don't know who's responsible, of course. But I believe I know where our friend Teofilo is . . ." He nodded to himself. "Want to guess?"

A bit like grade school. I joked, "Houston? San Diego?"

"No."

"Then?"

"At the spring. In the bosque verde."

It almost made sense. But— "I don't understand. How could he have—"

He looked at me, laughed through his nose, shook his head. "What, Jorge?"

"I mean, why would—" I stopped myself.

He laughed again. A great joke. Laughed harder, took a sip of his martini, nearly choked as the gin went the wrong way. Much laughing, waving off my help. Calm again, he announced: "You are so scientific, all you criminologists."

I felt, suddenly, nothing like a criminologist; a new kind of peace. Unnecessary to disagree here. I knew I was thinking for a moment like the someone who'd left Teofilo by the spring. I said casually, "You going to take a look?"

He shrugged. The necessary excuses: No way in. Who'd believe such an idea. What, chop a trail through? People are terrified of the place. The police don't have money for unsubstantiated guesses. And so on.

I said I'd back his notion.

He nodded, noncommittal.

Within a day his excitement had gotten the better of his budget. Also he asked for—and, rare occurrence, obtained—help from the Federal Police. They hacked their way in. I went along, volunteering my machete abilities; not of much value, I'd never used one, but I wanted to see. Well, at the spring, a pretty spot, there was Teofilo. Dead probably a week. No obvious way he could have found his way in. No apparent bruises or contusions. A heavy smell of decay. Fully dressed. As if he'd been dropped from the sky. Only, even after a week, his face, what was left of it, showed dread. True terror.

The autopsy found nothing. No basic cause. Of course his heart had stopped, the reason given for death. But no explanation why, not simple like Guillermo and his massive coronary. No poison, no wounds. No natural internal causes.

Rubén had warned the federales, young kids mostly, not to speak of what we might find. Of course one, in his late teens, had been so frightened by Teofilo's face he couldn't not babble about it. From then on everyone in Michoácuaro agreed, Teofilo had died of fear.

A few days later, passing through the plaza from the market, I saw a small crowd chattering excitedly. Ahead of them a slender woman of perhaps thirty-five. She wore a cotton dress, had short hair, and moved simply, lightly. With her a man of about the same age. I walked over. Silvia. Looking like a normal, attractive woman. Talking to the man beside her. The others couldn't stop themselves from staring, and following.

"I've just spoken with her." Pepe, appearing at my side. "She remembers very little about the last eighteen years."

"Amazing."

Pepe didn't answer.

"Who's the man with her?"

"Him? Ali Cran."

A usual-looking Michoácuaro man, middle-dark skin, slim, a mustache. A jacket, half unbuttoned shirt, jeans, pointed boots.

NINE

El Racimo

🪶 " 'PEPE!'

"I knew the voice and wanted no connection to Nabór, its owner. How often after all do I come to my father's house? And how little chance to speak again with my friends, many of them here together, people important to me, Jorge. I've known them all since childhood. Oh yes, they come up to town to the market, Frico, sometimes Faustino, but there on the road we were a group again, so many of us. The little farmhouse that was once a sugar mill right outside Ojo de Agua, less than thirty kilometers from Michoácuaro but really a century away, this is where I was born. Now we stood in front, talking without needing to be careful, and wind swirled in the dusty road. The words flew out from our memories, Jorge, the old feelings for each other clear in each phrase and smile or raised eyebrow. Of course if you didn't know us everything was hidden.

"It felt natural to recapture this so quickly again. Frico, my friend Federico, told me about the plans for the first communion of his second daughter, Martita with the crossed eyes, very sad, but in the country they don't think of it like that, as sad, it's all part of life in the usual way. You know, for me this is at the same time wonderful and terrible too. Because her eyes can be fixed—not here in Michoácuaro, but if the girl lived in town, or at least went to school here as I did, a doctor would tell Federico to take her to a specialist in Morelia for a small operation and the child would be perfectly normal. Except in the country she's normal anyway. Just like Octavia who was born with red hair though neither Frico nor Lupe have such hair or the grandparents either. But there's no question whose child she is, for Lupe only Frico is possible, everyone in the poblado knows this. Just as the whole village knows Frico's success is from his own work.

"We played together every day for ten years, Jorge. No, more. He

126

was closer than my brothers. Now he owns nearly three hectares, which is six times how much his father-in-law gave him when he married. All the land is full of trees and all the trees are full of avocados, fine avocados. But they sell now for so little, from Ojo it's impossible to control the market price—

"No, that's another story. Yes, Nabór. He called to me. I didn't want to talk to him. He's never been a friend, not even when we were children. He destroyed a bamboo flute my father made for me with the reed placed so when you blew in the sound piped out perfect. Only my father in the village could make a flute with the holes exact, each note. He knew how many months the bamboo had to grow, still wet enough to work at it but already drying so it didn't become brittle after it was cut. This flute, my first, was a very Mexican flute, made exactly like this, I've never seen them anywhere else. I learned from my father to play some wonderful melodies on it. Like 'La Muguete,' you know it, Jorge? it goes—

(he hummed an indecipherable little tune, ~~′/ ~~′/ ~~′/ ′ and repeated it)

"—no, no one knows it except me, I used to think my father invented it for me. The flute, Jorge, Nabór stole it when I left it with my schoolbooks one afternoon by the big pool in the stream that flows past the old mill, the irrigation water. We would splash in it after classes on hot days. Wonderful and refreshing, except you had to keep moving or the leeches would stick to your legs and other places and make you bleed. Well, Nabor saw the flute and ran away blowing into it and calling out to me, I can still remember his stupid voice, 'Pepe always takes his thing off when he swims, it's a very thin one, the girls don't like Pepe his thing is so skinny.' Then he was gone, disappeared through the dry corn before I could get my shoes and pants on. I knew where he was running to, his grandmother's adobe house, his secret hiding place where he figured no one would ever find him. He covered my flute with lard he stole from his grandmother's pot. He found their goat Alma, who was already old, more than twelve, and pushed the flute up Alma's vagina. And Alma was very unhappy bouncing around with a flute sticking out from her like a little flagpole. When my father and I got there we saw Nabór chasing after her, yelling, 'Make music! Make music!' My father caught him and took him by the hair and dragged him over to poor Alma who had stopped running around. She bleated a screech of desperation as she tried to sit on her rump and scratch out this horrible stick. My father held her tight against Nabór and pulled out the flute. I know Alma prayed for the salvation of my father's soul every night after that. Then he wiped the lard from the flute onto Nabór's face and hair. He pulled down Nabór's pants and wiped it on his buttocks and between his legs. Nabór screamed louder than Alma had because my father tortured him with wonderful threats, Nabór was terrified by where my father might put the flute for the next part of the punishment, then Nabór pissed on my father's hands and onto his pants, he was so— Look, Jorge, if you want me to tell you this story which is serious and will soon become terrifying, truly it will, then stop laughing. Listen, you can't possibly hear me if you're making so much noise! Anyway don't feed me all these martinis and you won't—"

Laughter was shaking me so hard my bladder nearly brought me to young Nabór's embarrassing state. Pepe is usually the most urbane of men, veneered with a suavity far from his Michoácuaran roots. I used to wonder what keeps him here. He would have been a middle-success professional in most cities of the first, second or third world—only middling because he would never kill himself in his work, too much else in life remains important. Yet success comes to him easily. He speaks French more than adequately and it would return to near native if he went back to a francophone country (three years in Strasbourg, business administration—also there, from his Munich girlfriend, reasonable German; and one year in Quebec City, international communications). His English comes originally from his mother, a gringa who arrived out here from Mexico City after marrying Pepe's father. In some ways she became more of a village person than her husband, Pepe says. He makes it a point of professional pride to deal with his Telecable colleagues in their language whenever he goes to the U.S. I can't really say how well he speaks English. He's decided my still dreadful Spanish won't improve unless I use it constantly, and he's correct. I assume his English is of the highest quality because when I search for a word in Spanish he gives me three or four English alternatives immediately, including the one I'm looking for and one that's more precise. Then he translates the right one into Spanish for me. I hate him sometimes. He's a gentle pedagogue and my vocabulary does grow, my grammar slowly improves. Occasionally my English vocabulary too.

And more. Pepe helped get me past some of the worst moments

here—the loneliness and guilt. Alaine spoke Spanish a little, school-taught but enough to make her want to visit Latin America. I had always turned toward Europe; next time we'd go to Peru and Argentina and Nicaragua, wherever. And now I'm the one who lives here, newly a friend to an urbane Mexican who has also looked to Europe, and I think he understands. He seems cloaked in urbanity and sophistication, yet when he's telling a story complete with a dozen names and places I'm never able to keep straight (it doesn't matter, finally, the important ones keep returning), he can lapse instantly back to his Michoacán rambles. Or, as he says, rise to his roots. So I'll give him his lead here, and his voice—at least the way my memory hears it just now—as it echoes through the courtyard of my eighteenth-century Spanish colonial house in Michoácuaro where my novel is slow in coming and if I get this down right I'll feel less like my time slipped away completely while drinking with the likes of Pepe on a normal workaday pull-up-the-typewriter-and-get-to-it early afternoon.

"On the old road in front of the house we were kicking small stones at each others' feet like we used to twenty-five years ago, standing around talking, the wind cutting hot sand against our feet, Tolomito and Frico, and Carmen who married Ciro who went north and keeps sending her dollars but it's clearly guilt money because he has a woman in Bakersfield, rich, he wants to marry her, a Chicana, her father owns a farmacía. Ciro's father Faustino, who stood with us, says his son is imprisoned by the farmacía, in Mexico if you kill a man you go to prison for a year, two, but in California if you marry the daughter of a farmacista you become nearly a gringo. Which is like being in prison for a lifetime.

"And Ciro's best friend from those days, Gustavo—he's the brother of Elena, who was once very beautiful and now is extremely fat but still not ugly, this happens to women in the villages, many of them—Gustavo joined us on the road also. He became a policeman, very serious about his job, his professional position as he calls it, he is a sergeant. He believes his place in Ojo de Agua is to help the poblado. Sometimes this becomes more possible, sometimes less. If I had stayed there, for example— In spite of everything that happened to Gustavo which I'll tell you about he still is a fine-looking man, his sister's features that he's kept. He has nine aunts and for each he's the favorite, which gives him strong allies, their husbands.

This is important because everyone knows he's never gotten along with his lieutenant Adolfo, Adolfo Pitol, who truly has a little-village brain and is responsible for civilian law for many hectares around. Really second-in-charge since we all live within the jurisdiction of our own jefe de policía, our friend Rubén Reyes, your landlord Rubén—

"Now where was I? Yes, Ciro's father Faustino there with us on the road. He speaks only softly these days, he's very sad about the boy, as he calls him, though Ciro is my age, two months' difference, Faustino had set his racimo of bananas down in the dust, it was heavy, twenty kilos anyway, and he told me Ciro—"

I shook my head—

"No? But really it weighs this much. Faustino and my father, who's now seventy-eight and still goes to the fields every day, they're close friends, have been for sixty years, Faustino has great strength, his arms—"

I explained I didn't understand racimo—

"Ah! A racimo, I think the English is 'raceme'— Jorge, must I educate you in your own language as well? The racimo is how bananas grow; you know, from a central axis, no branches but with the flowers and fruit coming out from the stem directly. Like a—I think you call it *lily of the valley*. Yes, so we talked and beside me was standing my brother Julito's sister-in-law Trini, who I'd been in love with for two years and I never spoke to her, not the whole time, not till I fell in love with—

"No, I'll tell you nothing of that, these martinis are almost the perfect truth potion. I've never except for my compadre and my own sister spoken to another person about Trini. You tell this to anyone in Michoácuaro I swear as much as I hate violent acts I can get very drunk and then I could shoot you even if it must be in the back while you sleep. But you know, they're not perfect, these martinis, because about some memories I still as you see can hold my tongue.

"Nabór. I've told you how we were, a group, we grew up together, these are people I can speak to about serious things. Like to you, Jorge, but of course this is different. For a few minutes we were in a wonderful place, people I hadn't seen together for many months, years even. And then I feel the hand on my shoulder and behind me a voice,

" 'Pepe!'

"Naturally I ignore it and immediately ask Faustino if Ciro still lives in Bakersfield, I've heard nothing since his last letter to Gustavo six months ago. I know everyone wants to hear how much Faustino will say in front of his daughter-in-law. I don't turn to welcome Nabór to the group. But I can smell the beer on his breath—Tecate, the macho pee-water he began to drink at eleven and since fifteen I don't think the stink has left him even for a day. But then I see how everyone has become uncomfortable. People are shuffling their feet and suddenly no one looks at anyone else. Finally Faustino speaks to all of us—even I think to Nabór behind me, but I didn't turn around—Faustino talks about his friend Pachuco who always has terrible luck, last month one of his four cows fell into the stream above the adobe and died and rotted and poisoned the water so two sons had to go to the hospital, and his wife lay sick for nine days. We were all nodding, Pachuco's luck was truly miserable. Someone asked about Pachuco's daughter, had she had the baby yet, her third, she's eighteen, when right at my ear—

" 'Pepe!!'

"It was impossible then to avoid him. " 'How are you, Nabór.'

" 'Pepe. Come. We'll have a beer together.'

"He wore an old corduroy sport jacket falling to halfway down his thighs and buttoned to the center of his chest, no shirt underneath, and jeans and worn huaraches. Except for a mustache so overgrown it covered both lips he looked about the same as when I'd seen him three or four years earlier.

" 'Borito'— I think now I shouldn't have used the diminutive, probably my voice sounded not like I was speaking to a person I cared for but to someone else's child who has just been naughty again— 'I'm spending a few minutes with friends. You've broken into the middle of this conversation. I haven't seen my good friends for a long time and I want to—'

" 'Gringo!'

" 'Me?'

" 'It is like I said. The gringo is too good to talk with his old friend Nabór, he comes here one day in the year and when his old friend Nabór talks to him he says, Adios, Borito; Chingada Borito. You gringo *Peeeeter—!*'

"The mistakes you make when you're young, Jorge. My mother would call me Peter when she felt very affectionate, or if I was sad. Never with someone else around of course. The name belonged to

131

her grandfather and she used it at good moments or to scare the monsters away. But when I was perhaps ten I told—actually told, can you imagine, Nabór always made life horrible for me so I must have been trying to rouse his jealousy, I had a kind of magic name and he could never get one—I bragged about my name to Nabór. He never used it till the afternoon on the road. But you have to understand, Jorge, I've lived here all my life. As long as Nabór. Except for the years I went abroad to study, and that miserable rooster had no right to call me a gringo, I belong as much to Ojo de Agua as he— I'm sorry, 'gringo' is a bad thing to call another person even if you are one. Unless you're a good friend. It's a complicated word. I won't apologize because it is so and right now I've drunk enough to say it: you, Jorge, are a gringo but you are not a gringo—you see the difference, no? So when I say to you 'gringo,' it's that I say you're my friend because I know in truth you're nearly a Mexican, a Mexican who didn't grow up here but a Mexican in the soul who was born in the wrong place. But when Nabór says 'gringo,' he doesn't mean gringo— He means, gringo! Which you must not call any Mexican.

"So Nabór and I stand there. The wind slices sand into our necks, between our toes, it isn't important. We walk around each other. We don't take our eyes from each other, if one even blinks too long the balance will disappear, the other will have the advantage. We talk in careful words that mean nothing and everything, words that aren't important but are very dangerous. He says bad things to me. I say to him worse things. His retorts are three times as bad. Finally no words are possible. I turn to my friends and— It's terrible. No one is there. They've disappeared! Into the trees. Into the stream. Into my father's house. Quién sabe? No one, Jorge. And so I turn back to Nabór and I say—no, probably I screamed—'You see what you've done. All of them, you've driven them away, you've—'

" 'Because of you they've gone, gringo. The gringo makes the campesino go away. We live here and are very happy by ourselves. Only when you come to see us, then you bring your gringo noises and smells and all my friends disappear. Drink with me, Pepe.'

"It was no longer a request. Even the jaunty threat from before had disappeared. Here was an order. I was very angry, I began to stamp around and I shouted at Nabór the only way a human being so sterile in the brain as Nabór could come into the world was his mother must have committed terrible acts with the family mule which was surely the most stupid mule in the world in positions so obscene— In the next instant my eyes were half a meter from Nabór's very old—but from that distance it didn't have to be very accurate—his Colt pistol. The round open muzzle. A big hole."

I recognize but often deny that Mexico is a dangerous place. Not so much the violent deaths, which my back-home profession calls to my attention. And no more perilous, probably, than many places at home. But there we do a good job of hiding the danger away. Some neighborhoods are "secure," people believe, and feel shock, outrage, even a kind of violation when the boundaries between safe and vulnerable are transgressed; and that some disease might enter there— The law explicitly condemns certain activities and if you want to avoid trouble you don't get involved in drug trafficking or prostitution, robbing or embezzling from banks. Of course it's easy enough to make a bad move or look as if you have, but if you live more or less safe and narrow day after day you can often avoid the breakdown of the Old Legitimate Principles. Especially if you're rich enough, in which case your margins can get a bit broader.

In Mexico on the other hand there's less distinction, especially in the smaller towns, between, say, where a wealthy man lives and where a poor man lives. An elegant house can be found in any part of town, adobes without electricity next to mansions. And danger, its skinny finger pointing now to life now to death, scratches lightly when you cross a street which is clearly one-way east-to-west, that's the way the arrow points, which is no guarantee a tequila-filled or more often fully sober ornery s.o.b. doing eighty west-to-east in some drag-race in his mind isn't going to obliterate you with his high-axled Cheyenne wagon. And who'll say he was wrong except for a few prissy-faced gringo lovers: Look, you insist on crossing the street in the middle of dangerous traffic and you think you're safe because some chingada arrow says traffic usually comes that way not this, well you're a fool and the only good fool is a dead one, so go the clichés but you don't hear the homily since they're washing the street down to thin away the blood because it brings flies.

Death is easier here.

"Jorge, I don't like guns. I've argued about this many times with your friend Rubén, the big-time landlord he's becoming, always the tough-guy jefe de policía. When we were fourteen one time he found his Great-uncle Umberto's rifle, you know Umberto fought with Zapata? Rubén found the rifle and insisted he must clean it because he wanted, do you know Sancho's wife? No you wouldn't, she was already twenty or twenty-one at the time and Rubén— No, sorry, that's a different story—

"Yes, a small glass— Gracias— Basta—!

"Ai, Nabór. The pistol. He pointed the big circle of the barrel twenty centimeters from my nose. I was truly terrified. But I've been afraid before. It's a good thing to know how to be afraid and I have no problem with fear. Or not till afterwards when I'm always ten times as frightened as in the moment. But this time I didn't know how completely terrified I would become. Because one thing no one had told me: since the last time I saw Nabór he had killed three men. Three that people in Ojo de Agua knew about.

"Even in my ignorance I saw the danger I was in. I made it very clear to Nabór that in the world outside Ojo de Agua he had no friend closer than myself. I spoke to everyone I knew of his loyalty and strength and generosity, to many fine people from Michoácuaro to Madrid. When they thought of all that was best about Mexico their minds would naturally form a picture of Nabór. He was right, we must have a beer together. He could tell me all the good and the sad things in his life since I had seen him last. And of course a gringo like me belonged in this place much less than a real Mexican.

"But now he didn't want to have a beer. Anyway, not with me. It made him angry, people telling him the way he thought was right. Because he knew he was right. He didn't need to hear this again. So he wasn't going to kill me. Not now. He would do it late one night when I thought I was safe in my father's house. If he didn't find me there he'd get on the bus and track me down to my home in Michoácuaro. He'd put a knife in my heart. If I tried to run he'd shoot me dead.

"He walked away. I stood completely still, not breathing. For ten minutes I would have said, But this isn't possible. Finally I walked I think very slowly, I have no memory of moving, to the room I used to share with my two brothers that we all left long ago. I fell on my bed till my heart slowed to normal, easily an hour. Do you know, I hated myself for complimenting Nabór, for saying the world saw him as the embodiment of Mexico. In the kitchen I found my father. He listened in silence as I spoke. Faustino arrived then for a glass of pulque and the two of them explained about Nabór's three victims. As they talked my heart crashed against my ribs.

"The first, Claudio Espinoso, his name people only learned after he was dead, he came from tierra caliente and they met in the little cantina where Nabór spent the afternoons from Monday to Saturday. On Sundays he went for the day to his grandmother's adobe to clean the place for her. She had bad arthritis and died of an infection last year at the end of October just before the Day of the Dead, so for twelve hours it became a joke in the village to say now they wouldn't have to make two trips to the cemetery. He swept out her old stable, home for her burro and a few chickens and sometimes a pig when she could afford one, he trimmed her banana trees and picked the fruit in season— Yes, Claudio Espinoso and Nabór, they became instant friends at the cantina, you know the one? halfway down to tierra caliente, with the yellow front. After the first litre of tequila they discovered they were compadres of the blood, closer than brothers, clearly a moment of great truth. They would have to drink a fine tequila to this revelation. Old Faustino explained to me carefully all that happened:

"Claudio Espinoso said, 'Now, hombre, I will buy this next bottle. We will celebrate.'

"Nabór said, 'No, the next bottle is for me to buy.'

" 'No, in tierra caliente the one from far away buys the bottle always. When a man gives his daughter to the son of his cousin from Santa María. When I sell a mule that will limp in three kilometers to a campesino who cannot tell the difference. When two who have not known each other swear they will be friends forever— Today I am from far away. I will buy the bottle.'

"During Claudio Espinoso's fine words strange cactus juice spirits must have crawled about in Nabór's heart. This was clear from the way he sat and how he moved his hands. Everyone in the cantina had turned to watch. Two or three who were more sober suddenly discovered they needed to go out for a pee. Claudio Espinoso had stopped speaking. The blood had drained from Nabór's face. He said, 'We are not in tierra caliente.'

"All who heard this agreed: Nabór was giving Claudio Espinoso a last chance. But the poor man, deaf and blind to everything about him, insisted to the end on proving his generosity. He actually called for Jaime Sola who owns the cantina to bring a new bottle. But

Jaime had found it necessary to smoke a cigarette on the front steps by the window. Claudio Espinoso's eyes searched everywhere for Jaime but he saw only silent stares on all the faces, men pushing back in their chairs. Faustino says Espinoso must have understood at last. His eyes filled with tequila and cigarette smoke. When he turned to Nabór water came down his face and he saw the big Colt pistol pointed directly at him. First at his neck, then at his stomach. At his neck again. Always very close.

"Nabór said, 'You have insulted the way we live in my poblado, señor,' and fired. The first bullet hit Claudio Espinoso in the shoulder because he spun about in his chair. The second hit him in the side, the third in the throat. By the time el jefe Rubén arrived Claudio Espinoso had bled to death.

"Do you realize, Jorge, within two hours everyone had heard the story of Claudio Espinoso. Half of Ojo didn't believe Nabór could do such a thing. The other half knew Claudio Espinoso was a dangerous criminal from tierra caliente and it was good Nabór had done this.

"The next victim was Manuel Ochoa Gómez. Seventeen years before he had married Ida. They made five children, all boys. So Nabór said he had to kill him because Manuel was impregnating the women in Ojo de Agua with only boys and this would make it impossible for life in the poblado to continue because there would be no women to make pregnant— I know, Jorge, it sounds stupid beyond anything you can believe, but Nabór had been drinking for three days and he would always make an idiot of himself when he was blind drunk. Ida was scared, too, because she had hit Nabór in the face with a whip handle eighteen years ago. This was the only way to make him stop courting her, then she married Manuel. So perhaps Nabór thought he had to kill Manuel because the moment of revenge had waited long enough. Quién sabe?

"Now Nabór swayed and stumbled through the poblado decapitating fence posts and little banana shoots with his machete, yelling 'Manuel! Manuel! You are destroying Ojo de Agua with your cock, you're pointing it in the wrong direction!' Faustino and Frico and two or three others tried to talk to him, his old friends too, and his compadre Luis. They calmed him a bit, he even agreed he would go to his grandmother's adobe if they brought him only a small bottle more of tequila. Everyone agreed one last tequila would definitely make Nabór sleep for two days and when he woke everything except his head would be well. So Luis found a bottle, poured most of it into a pot—which proved to be a large mistake—brought the bottle to Nabór, took him to his grandmother's little adobe and lay him down in the stable. Nabór drank the tequila in three large swallows, grinned at Luis and passed out.

"The following day Ida's oldest boy, Sergio, found Manuel in the cornfield below their little house stabbed many times but with Manuel's own machete. When they found Nabór he was fast asleep in his grandmother's stable. He has of course never said he killed Manuel. The poblado grew increasingly worried about young Sergio. He slept all the time with his father's machete.

"The next was Agnostio, Nabór's brother-in-law and neighbor who married Severa eight years ago. She could not have children so he would beat her all the time when he drank. Like on the day he was sharing a bottle of mescal with Nabór in the kitchen. They had a small argument about who owned the ziranda tree between their properties, one of the oldest trees in Ojo de Agua, a small ziranda but big enough. You cannot tell easily where the roots stretch from. The wood is hard and valuable. Nabór wanted to cut the tree down. Agnostio said the tree would not be cut no matter who it belonged to. Nabór took the pistol I now know the barrel of very well, he put his finger on the trigger and brought the gun very close to Agnostio's heart, squeezed and blew Agnostio's brains out through the top of his head.

"My father said to me about this, 'Now I know why you felt so frightened about the barrel of his pistol so close to your eyes. He might have shot your eggs off, then what kind of a man would you be!' He and Faustino laughed till they cried. Then we all drank a glass of pulque, became very serious, spoke of ways to protect me from Nabór, but came to no conclusions.

"There is a question I didn't need to ask because I know the answer very well but which perhaps you're thinking: Why didn't the police come to arrest Nabór? Were there no witnesses? Of course. The first time, as you know, many. The last time, Severa was washing potatoes three meters away. With Manuel we all knew Nabór had killed him whether he could remember or not. Well? You must understand, Jorge, the popular sport in Mexico, in Michoácuaro in little ways, in the government and the civil service much more, I will not begin to suggest the extent, is La Mordida, La-Morrr-di-i-i-i-da! *the bite, the bribe, the payoff*. We all have it, except here in

Mexico it is visible everywhere, a great institution, very shameful to us, Jorge. But I remember it well from living in France, too, and in Canada. It didn't have a beautiful name there but it worked the same way, big and small. In Canada especially it was not polite to speak of it. And when I visited in New York a friend from Naples who I'd met in Strasbourg, he took me to a baseball game, the Mets against St. Louis. You could find no tickets in the world for three days before but somehow he got hold of two directly beside first base. I asked him how he'd managed them. He looked at me for a moment like I was four years old, then he said, 'Pepe, where do you live?'

"I waited only for the sun to go behind the sugar barn and went to bed. Jorge, if there are two thousand four hundred eighty-three sounds between when the sun disappears and when the light comes again, I heard them all. I was certain not every one but surely three in ten were the sounds of Nabór deciding the moment to shoot me had arrived. Of course I'm not paranoid, I knew very well if he truly wanted to kill me he would have done so on the road, Nabór isn't capable first of thinking about shooting and second doing it. For him that's one step too many. Realizing this I came close to sleep at last a few hours before the sun rose. Except a rooster that couldn't have known which side of the chicken to put his prong in began to crow and my mind wouldn't relax. All the time new sounds squeaked about in the grass outside my screen, the wind like drunken breathing or the rattle of a man who has been stabbed. Worst, the memory of the second murder shot through my heart: Manuel who Ida married instead of Nabór, and he'd waited sixteen years to avenge being jilted! In the morning I cut short my visit, in Michoácuaro at least I could lock my front door. Whatever good it would do.

"I can tell you I slept badly for many nights, Jorge. If only I knew why, exactly, Nabór wanted to kill me— I was even afraid he would invade my dreams as well as my imagination. But this he didn't do. Except for one time. Along the road in front of my father's house. I walked there, shirtless. The wind stabbed sand into my chest and my face. Then it wasn't sand, it was a sharp stick, bamboo, Nabór hacking at me with pointed bamboo. He slashed through the skin, many times from all directions as I walked. There was blood, yes, and very great pain, at the same time a strange satisfaction too— Until I woke up.

"Usually I would lie silent. Sometimes I could feel my brain caught between two or possibly three places. The bed first, safest there I thought, but I drifted, back to the road by my father's house and in front of my eyes was the hole in the barrel of the Colt. And from the road, back along the years I have known Nabór: maybe I would find some moment, some incident, use it to deflect him, or show him how little I mattered to him. Sometimes I was certain by now he had forgotten. Me alone in my bed, what could he want with me? He had more important things to do than killing me— For example, to find the money for La Mordida, a hard señora with ongoing demands, not large ones but appearing every month like cramps. Because, Faustino had told me, his grandmother always paid out for him. When she died she left Nabór the money to cover his debt. But every day, even Sunday now, he went to the cantina, he had drunk up his capital till nothing was left. I used to imagine the picture, Nabór stealing from beggars or robbing tiendas for a few pesos. I found from this a bit of relief till I thought: What if he decides that I, to stay alive, have to pay his debt? So my mind ran away, returning to the old days in Ojo de Agua, the friends in common, I would find some go-between perhaps—? But only Carmelita came to my mind, also Elena the sister of Gustavo— I remembered: I had taken them both from Nabór!

"And why did I not go immediately to Rubén Reyes Ponce our mutual friend, in his grand powers of jefe de policía for all Michoácuaro. He could certainly find a way to eliminate this threat of Nabór. But what should I say, how do I describe a threat made in the middle of a sandy road, a drunken fool who says, One day soon I will kill you. One must know such a pig from many years ago, one must know him as the scum who sticks a flute up a goat's cunt. If I told Rubén such a story, he would laugh and put his heavy arm on my shoulder and say anyway he had no control over what happened down in Ojo de Agua, I should speak to Lieutenant Adolfo Pitol. Then our Rubén would pour me a tequilita.

"So what could I do? I went to work always looking a little behind me, at night I lay silently awake. Do you know, for probably ten or twelve weeks the only withdrawal from my fear was the radio, a long evening of music—almost never the television. Music made me think of other times, fiestas, certain days in France, a fine meal, a beautiful woman. It is of course dangerous to live with one part of the mind only, to search for only one kind of escape, to allow only a single pleasure to touch your senses. Yet I did this.

Till one night, as I listened to the radio convinced Nabór had de-
parted finally from my life, there came into my shoulders, which
understood a second or two before my brain, a few strange cold
twitches against the sheets. I felt chilled far far beyond the end of
my toes. Then at last my ears heard the music on the radio, a flute.
The campesino melody my father had played for me, that he taught
me:

~~'/ ~~'/ ~~'/ ' // ~~'/ ~~'/ ~~'/ '

I leapt from the bed screaming and swept the radio to the floor. It
shattered and the sound disappeared.

"Jorge, it was terrifying to discover, to realize in this way why
Nabór wanted to kill me. I hadn't seen my father since the time
Faustino told me about Nabór, nearly three months. Ojo de Agua
is so close, but still— I could not think of what else to do, I couldn't
escape, I had to face the danger. Before light, shaking, I drove to
the poblado.

"My father was not surprised to see me. His first words were, 'If
you want breakfast see if the hens have given us eggs.' He handed
me a basket. They had, and I made an omelet for him and me. We
sat silent. We never talk at breakfast. His coffee is very good. Finally he said, 'If you've come to kill Nabór you can't, he's in jail.'

"An immense shiver shot up my back and along my arms and
out my fingers.

"My father told me this: Nabór had not paid his mordida for four
months. His friends with the policía understood his income had
disappeared and chose Gustavo to speak with Nabór. Gustavo could
make a stone understand its place. So Gustavo explained yet again
how his superiors of course knew these deaths had been accidental
but it's always difficult to forget to conduct an investigation, surely
Nabór could find enough— Nabór it is said then felt a terrible fear.
Instead of lying, yes, soon he would pay, then going out and bor-
rowing or stealing a few thousand pesos, he screamed at Gustavo,
and beating at his head with a chair he shoved Gustavo out the
door. The sergeant, a reasonable man, turned, tried to come back
in. Nabór shot at him with the Colt. But since Gustavo stood six or
eight meters away Nabór had no chance to hit him. Gustavo retreated. In three hours they all came back in the police car, a pickup,
Gustavo driving, Adolfo Pitol the lieutenant next to him, three deputies crouching on the bed. But Nabór's shack stood empty. Severa

next door said he had come with his pistol and taken a bottle of tequila from her cupboard. She knew where he had gone. They drove along the burro track to his grandmother's adobe and surrounded it. Pitol ordered Gustavo to call out.

" 'Nabór!'

"No answer.

"More softly Gustavo called, 'Nabór, amigo, come out, we're on all sides.'

"From inside, a garbled shout, Nabór already deep drunk: 'I'm on all sides too!'

"Pitol looked at Gustavo. They both nodded.

"They approached the front door and stood to the side. Not that they feared Nabór's Colt, but still— Gustavo pushed at the door with his foot. It opened two inches, three. Inside a rope kept it from moving further. Gustavo explained the rope was looped around a nail in the door frame. Pitol gestured: reach in, undo it. Gustavo curved his hand around the frame, found the nail—

"A noise like a shaft of wind slicing through cracks in adobe. On Gustavo's face, great surprise. Then his mouth and eyes open wide. His arm comes back. His hand is gone. Blood pumps to the ground. He screams—

"Adolfo Pitol shouts. The others come running. One with a sickle pushes at the door. The holding rope is gone. He kicks the door open.

"Nabór sits in the chair, his face a total grin. His right hand grasps the machete, blood along his arm. In his left the Colt, hanging, too heavy to fire. Between his legs an empty bottle. They shoot Nabór, hit him five times."

Pepe shivered from telling me this. I poured him a full martini. He didn't object. A truth potion; but more. I poured myself some too, and stared at him: My friend Pepe. My informant about Michoácuaro, Pepe. My narrator. Pepe who brings me into his life and makes me feel again, some laughter and some fear of dying. Pepe who left Michoácuaro behind but returned— Why? Because of his father, old friends, roots? Pepe who has found himself a female friend every year or two of his adult life but has not married. Pepe who runs the Telecable which brings for good and dreadful the outside world to little Michoácuaro. Pepe who feels for his poblado Ojo de Agua not quite shame and not quite guilt, no longer need, yet hardly freedom; love probably, and fear. Pepe surviving the on-slaught of a murderer, a kid he grew up with— The many unstable connections of his life.

"Jorge, Nabór didn't die. He was given five years and three months in jail. One for Gustavo's hand. Nothing for Claudio Espinoso, that was self-defense. The judge decided the argument with Agnostio by ruling that the ziranda tree did belong to Nabór, so three months for disturbing the peace of Severa's household. And four years for the death of Manuel. It could not be proven that Nabór had killed him, but the judge argued he had planned it and as a result had removed the head of a household from his proper place in the poblado.

"You'll understand I felt a great relief. Again I could be with this friend, another one. I could walk anywhere in safety.

"And then last week here in the plaza I met Frico with little Martitá, they had taken the bus in for the market. I spoke to him about the girl's crossed eyes, a simple operation. Frico said he'd think about it. While I was convincing him Rubén joined us and asked me when I could have my workers bring the Telecable up to his hacienda in the country, he's restoring it. 'The cost will be high,' I told him.

"Do you know, Jorge, at this exact moment I felt a hand on my shoulder and a jaunty voice laughed and said 'Pepe! Let's have a beer!' "

TEN

Scape

A PALL HUNG over the town as I walked to the post office. For fifteen hours the day before the fires had burned out of control. Now they threatened to flare up again. Only the morning's lack of wind held the flames in check.

Over a period of three weeks in tierra caliente, the campesinos had been burning off the cane. Our usually clear air hung bleary with smoke. The burning process, a necessary prelude to harvest, irritates those of us with other concerns.

Sugar cane grows as a solid fibrous stalk, around here one to two inches in diameter and twice as high as a man's raised arm; the tiny serrated blade of its brilliant green leaves can slice like paper into flesh. For the crop to approach profitability, seedlings are planted less than a foot apart; sometimes campesinos weave a maze of narrow trails through the brake for access and passage. From my rooftop patio, the acres of cane far below look rich and soft. But when Ali Cran's dog Furtivo chased a rabbit into a cane field he never came out. Not even the buzzards could reach him. The campesinos found a dog's skeleton during the harvest, flesh gone to the worms. "They had a delicacy of Tivo," said Pepe; every day he finds more to laugh at in the world. "Dog meat trimmed thin as stroganoff."

To harvest cane, first burning off these razorlike leaves is essential. The lowest stay sharp and go dry, the little upper shoots retain their sap; the fires burn slowly, eating away the razor edges below, leaving the sticky cane stalks accessible. The smoldering leaves produce my particular oppressor of the last weeks, thick debris-laden smoke. A fieldhand will allow the fire to do its work while he scythes down burnt-off cane half a mile away, or takes a nap. The flames, unregulated, creep away. Then along comes a pernicious breeze—

Constanza had asked her son to stop by and say she'd be a few

143

minutes late this morning. I waited a couple of hours. When she still hadn't come I headed down to the plaza with some letters to mail. I felt no concern, though tardiness wasn't usual for her.

On the face of everyone along the street, an indrawn pall and sense of weariness.

The post office, part of a warren of interconnected services, shares walls with the cathedral on the right, municipal offices to the left, and the social security clinic behind. The maze continues—police station and jailhouse right of the cathedral, the church-run school behind it, all sharing walls. Of the public buildings only the bank across the street stands separate.

My needs this morning could luckily be met without bureaucratic or social involvement. In fact I'd kept myself apart for nearly ten days now, my novel at last taking off. I wanted beyond all else to avoid time-consuming conversation, often wonderful stuff and rich with local lore, but not desired now. I waited in line. The tone of the postal clerk, ranging from dreary to morose, in keeping at that moment with the bare floorboards barely hiding the dank earth beneath, kept me from exchanging more than a "Buenos días." I dropped my letters in the mail slot, thereby reestablishing contact with the world beyond Michoácuaro, and left.

Walking up the hill I saw Constanza ahead of me, her shoulders low, her step dragging. I called to her, she turned and waited. When I looked at her face, puffy, eyes swollen, I again cursed the fires; but suddenly felt something worse might have happened.

She wouldn't speak—couldn't, I think, for fear of a new storm of tears—till we closed the door from the street and stood in my courtyard. She opened her mouth, said, "Señor—my niece—my niece Chabela—" She pushed the heels of her palms over her mouth, covered her face with her hands, tears poured out, a panted wail, another, another.

"Constanza—! Constanza . . ." I reached out to her and she slumped against my chest, heaving terribly, gasping for breath. I held her, making soothing noises with hushes and in English, my limited Spanish not having had to sound these essential sympathies till now. At last the gale of tears abated. I led her to the kitchen, sat her down and poured a shot of brandy. She took it, raised it, the tears welled. She sipped, very slowly. "Now. Tell me."

Constanza looked at her glass, beyond— Slowly she gave words to the grim story. Isabel, called Chabela, lived about fifteen kilo-

144

meters from Michoácuaro in a poblado near the area where one of the fires had gone out of control. Every weekday she went to town on the bus that stopped at the dirt road coming from her home a mile's walk away; she attended the church school. Often on the way back she would stop at the home of a friend, the house no more than a couple of hundred meters off her road, they'd study or more likely play together. She always returned home before dark. Yesterday she hadn't come back. Her father, her uncles, then the entire poblado had searched all night long, badly hampered by still burning ground fires. They finally found her body around eight in the morning at the edge of a smoldering cane field, badly bruised, her clothes charred, her hair— Constanza could not go on.

Had the girl fallen, been knocked unconscious, burned?

Constanza shook her head slowly, spoke to the floor. "Señor— They say—stabbed—and strangled—"

A chill swept me.

Constanza whispered, "And—they think—violated."

In the afternoon I heard a fuller and, in its implications, more frightening version of the events from Rubén. He sprawled out in a chair on my patio and said he'd come by to avoid furious Michoácuarans who had assaulted his office all day yelling for him to find the murderer, and instantly. "It is unbelievable. Here. How could anyone do this to a child here."

"Here?"

He looked at me with the impatience of one who has explained a thing a hundred times. "You've been here how long, Jorge? Seven months? Eight? Do such things happen in Michoácuaro? In Monterrey, in Mexico City, there you'll find men who murder children. But here?"

Rubén had recently returned from Cuernavaca where he took a seminar in sources of criminal behavior. Over the last weeks he'd grumbled about the uselessness in a small town like Michoácuaro of the analyses he'd listened to.

I spoke casually. "Perhaps even here—"

"No, no, here a man kills another man in a cantina, it happens all the time, or his wife when he hits her too hard. Or she'll stab him twenty or thirty times and he'll bleed to death. But a little girl—aiee!"

Little girls in this part of the world grow up quickly. At twelve or thirteen they bloom with great beauty, by eighteen they've had two children of their own and begin to wither. Rubén knows this far better than I. Still, he was disturbed. A hard-edged man, control comes easily to him.

"That a man from here could kill a child, and now a second, in my—"

"What! Another one? After Isabel?"

He shook his head and in irritation shoved air toward me with his palms, warding off such questions as if my denseness might be catching. "Before. Last week. Ten days ago."

"Right here?" No one had mentioned anything—

"Not here in town, no, no. Down in tierra caliente. The other side of Ojo de Agua, thirty, forty kilometers from here. But it's my jurisdiction." He slumped down in his chair, shaking his head. "Give me a beer, will you?"

"Sure but—what happened?"

"The same thing. A child—twelve, I think—she'd been to see her grandparents, on the return along the small stream is a path, there he caught her. She dropped a bag of two mangos so Adolfo Pitol who is in charge for Ojo knew where to look, the man dragged her into some bushes and raped her and killed her or the other way around. And to make sure she was dead he held her face under the water and left her in the stream. But she didn't drown, she had already died of asphyxiation."

One story more terrible than the last.

But Rubén was wrong. As he must have learned in his seminar, this sort of thing can happen anywhere. I gave him a bottle of beer. "I've heard absolutely nothing."

"Pah! You must be the only one. There's not even a telephone in the poblado where she was killed and the news reached my office before I got back. Get on the street sometimes, Jorge. Learn about this town. Go into the fields."

"And your investigation—?"

"It advances."

I took a beer too, opening the bottle slowly, concentrating as I poured to keep the head from spilling over. "Maybe this second death will provide new evidence."

"Yes, yes, perhaps . . ." He suddenly slammed his beer bottle on the table. "That chingada Basta Hernandez!"

The Rubén Reyes Ponce I know is clever, rarely lets you sense his feelings, has been known to twist the law to suit himself and squeeze his enemies. Now here he sat, anger undermining his control as easily as in any man. I spoke quietly: "What's Basta's complaint?"

"That girl, the first one, Amanda, her mama is Basta's cousin. He says the woman is nearly out of her mind with misery." His tone softened; he shrugged. "It's true. I've tried to speak with her twice, three times. She doesn't answer."

"It must be terrible." I waited. "What did Basta say?"

Rubén slapped the edge of the table with the flat of his hand. "Can you believe he screamed at me—screamed! and in my office— that if I didn't catch the murderer of Amanda then Ali Cran would find him."

I'd met Basta, a pleasant enough young man who, when his father died a couple of years ago, inherited considerable wealth in farmland and other assets; still, in town he held no power to speak of. But he and Ali Cran were compadres and that kind of special friendship means a great deal, especially, I imagined, to someone like Ali Cran. When Furtivo lost his way in the cane, people say Ali Cran located the dog as if by magic, but too late, he couldn't reach him even by the maze of pathways, so he sat at the edge of the field making growls and whines—gentle, soothing sounds, say the campesinos who heard. He stayed by the field until he knew the dog had truly died.

But Rubén's anger— When they were younger Ali Cran and Rubén had been close and I wasn't aware they'd become antagonists. So what was the problem? I asked him.

Again that look of despondence and a weary shake of the head for an ignorant gringo. "Jorge—I don't need another Sálome case on my hands." Rubén has never found her murderer.

"If Ali Cran is really all that clever why don't you ask him for his help?" The moment I spoke I heard my mistake; a favor from Ali Cran would be instant town-wide news and involve great loss of face. And worse: I think Rubén suspects Ali Cran himself of Sálome's death.

"No, Alicito would only confuse the case." Cool Rubén again. "And in the process, the murderer could elude us. With Ali Cran there are always complications."

Three days later, no progress.

I'd met Isabel, a pretty, dark-skinned child of probably twelve with black hair, parted in the middle and bangs in front, so rich and thick I was sure it would glow in the dark. Chabela had accompanied Constanza a few times to help with some of the larger cleaning jobs. From the door to my study she'd watch while I wrote and, when I noticed her, dart me a cheeky grin, then flick shyly away. The news of her death, though I barely knew her, had hit me hard. Till a few days ago the girl, both the girls, had played and complained and been just like everybody else. The deaths, Isabel's particularly, haunted me—all the more sharply, I think, because I wasn't personally involved.

I had yearned for this kind of distance, an ideal from my back-home perspective: the perfect novel-producing environment. So I arrived here, optimistic. The novel—ironic it should be about victims—had bogged down again, all my ends gone loose.

Early in the evening I walked down to the plaza to buy a copy of *El Pescador*. I stared at the Spanish words, their meanings bleeding into each other. On the way back I stopped at Pepe's. He lives a few houses from me in a magnificent home. In the center of Michoácuaro the houses, eighteenth-century Spanish colonial, usually abut directly onto the sidewalk. One enters such a house through a walkway to an internal courtyard. Pepe's is fronted by a high cement wall topped with embedded broken glass. A double metal gate, the only entryway, opens onto a drive through a small wonderland of lush trimmed grass, tall palms and flaming orange tulipans. Crimson, purple and white bougainvillaea spread along the lateral walls, in the shade double and triple impatiens soothe the eye. The house itself is low-slung, glass-walled in back overlooking a patio with a pool carved out of the granite. Inside are half a dozen large rooms each commanding a view of the garden or of a sweep of valley to the hillsides beyond. Flaco, Pepe's blind gardener, brought me unerringly around back.

I had interrupted a meeting, or at least a drink. On the patio sat Dr. Felicio Ortíz whom I'd met, Pepe, and a man I recognized as Alejandro Cruz Ocampo, known as Ali Cran. I apologized and said I could come back. Pepe wouldn't hear of it. Rubí, Pepe's maid, Constanza's daughter, appeared with two glasses. Felicio poured me a tumblerful of tequila and another of spicy red sangrita chaser. It had become impolite to leave without drinking.

I stayed late. Ali Cran and Felicio threw themselves into vying with each other for our laughter. Pepe, who restrained his own narrating inclinations, swore all the stories were true. One raconteur could barely hold still while the other finished, so eager was he to tell a better tale. It proved a hilarious gold mine of an evening.

Along the way I learned Felicio Ortíz had retired twice, once when he'd retired and again—his great joke—last year when he'd retired. The first time, at sixty; he left behind the lucrative surgical practice he divided between Mexico City and Houston; he was rich enough, he told me, and his American investments would keep him that way. Fortunately he came to Michoácuaro where people needed a doctor and in the next twenty-four years learned from curanderas and brujas—good and bad witches—and his patients as much as he had from medical school and thirty-five years of life in operating theaters.

I also discovered the mysterious Ali Cran had a normal daily life. He owned two small ranches and raised milk cattle, goats and chickens. Using dyes he produced from plants, ore, insects and seashells, he often spent long hours in his weaving workshop where he combed wool and spun cloth according to methods evolved locally hundreds of years ago.

I had a glimpse, too, of what I'd interrupted. They'd been talking about the two rape-murders, and what could be done. I had apparently arrived just as they'd conceded their frustration.

The doctor, short, spry, in a light shirt, white pants and military boots, sat forward, alert and prepared for anything. The fabled Ali Cran, about thirty-five, wearing faded loose jeans and a light-blue ribbed shirt, struck me as strangely unimposing as he slouched, drink in hand, listening. But when he grinned at me I was swept by a sense of easy generosity—whatever he needed I knew I would get him. I wondered if the others had grown immune to him by now.

Such was the competition between these two that when they reached what became the evening's ultimate tale, they argued for ten minutes over who should tell it, without revealing a single clue as to its subject matter. Pepe determined they would share in the telling. With some grumbling and another drink, they agreed. And who would begin?

"By virtue of superior wealth, whiter hair and less time left on this earth for telling his truths and lies"—Pepe pointed—"Dr. Felicio Ortíz."

Felicio nudged Ali Cran sharply. "If this one keeps on playing his jokes and his travesties, which many people do not find humorous, I would not wager on his life expectancy. No, I shall begin because it is my story."

"You'd never have had a story if I hadn't—"

Pepe raised his glass for silence.

Felicio turned to me. "I did not arrive in Michoácuaro to practice medicine, Jorge, no, I came to write my memoirs. But to be a doctor once, you can never not be a doctor. If people come for your help— Understand me, I am not a particularly generous man and—"

"On that we agree." Ali Cran folded his arms and sat back.

"—yet, if a person is ill or hurt, one must respond, no? I am a man of medicine, I'm good at this profession, as even our shameless young friend here will admit."

Ali Cran nodded lightly.

"Increasingly people came asking for help. I did what I could. A great deal more than the quacks in this town with licenses to cut up flesh and prescribe poison for people and cows alike. When I think—"

"Not everyone, Lici, is as perfect as—"

"The story!" Pepe held up his hand. "Or lose your time."

"The problem for me in those days, Jorge— I had retired. From work, but not from my calling. Still, if I charged these people, these campesinos, I lived among them in those days— My house, do you know it?"

I shook my head.

"Over there on the side of the hill, you can see it in the daylight, do you know when I built it I—"

"Alicito! Take over. And stay with the story."

"But Pepe, now comes the important part—"

Pepe stood firm.

Ali Cran nodded in Felicio's direction. "He didn't want to earn money. He's rich— He could play doctor without charging. But if he did not charge, the campesinos would think he was a terrible doctor, his work was not worth charging for. And if someone was to think el doctorcito was not perfect, aiee! So he charged, you understand, but very little. In those days, twenty centavos. Last year, fifty pesos. It was all the same, each in their time bought a loaf of bread. Yes, he took their money, and so began dreams of being rich a second time—"

"Not true. Pepe—"

"Alicito, don't ruin the story for Jorge."

I threw up my hands in mock despair. The whole evening was thoroughly captivating—

No, they made it clear, I too had to play by the rules: a perfect audience must demand a perfect presentation.

I realized then the evening's stories were not only for my benefit.

"He placed all this money in a jar. The jar he set on a shelf. Every day Lici looked at the jar, and the jar looked at Lici. Every day the jar said, And what will you buy with your earnings, señor?"

"Don't dramatize."

"What? Such rebuke from you, doctorcito?"

"Onward, Alejandro."

"Very well. El doctorcito Felicio is a man of conscience, a humanitarian, a philanthropist. The end of the year has come. This money must go to some noble cause. But Doctor Felicio lacks not merely the imagination, also the capacity for intrigue. Time to call in an expert."

"Yes! Time! Felicio, your turn."

"Pepe! He can't possibly describe my idea with the subtlety and cleverness it takes to—"

"A very simple idea, Jorge. Ali Cran suggested I give the money to the prisoners in our incomparable jail, that delightful institution which I am certain you've seen—?"

"Oh yes." Two days after arriving. I'd been to the municipal office to photocopy my tourist card, went around the corner to the police station to leave a message for Rubén about a leaky faucet, and there it was: guarded by two grizzled toothless gunmen in straw sombreros bearing antediluvian rifles, an open doorway to an unlit space. At the back of this, steel bars from floor to ceiling, behind them a single cell: dirty whitewashed rear and side walls, a high window, wooden floor, toilet in the corner, tiny sink and faucet. And ten or a dozen men. Vicious criminals every one, Rubén had said, incarcerated for everything from burro theft to unarmed bank robbery, can you imagine? When they get out they're good for nothing except shipment over to Uruapan to become guards at the maximum-security prison there. He had laughed uproariously at his joke, hilarious to him since the two men at the door with the nineteenth-century breechloaders were themselves ex-prisoners from the penitentiary in Uruapan. I nodded to Felicio. "A pretty place, our jail."

The doctor agreed. "These men in the cell would receive, with the money I'd collected, the chance for a great fiesta during the Christmas season. A small idea, elegant only in its simplicity. And so I spoke with Rubén, who thought the idea—I did not tell him who gave it to me—he thought it was not so good, because it had never been done before. I will say nothing, Jorge, against your landlord, but he is not a man of imagination. Therefore, he could think of no reason to refuse me, and families always bring food to prisoners so my contribution meant he would have to give nothing, no matter how little, from his treasury. And we went ahead. At this time there were fourteen prisoners in the cell, some awaiting trial, some already serving sentences of up to five and a half years. One of them, the head of the Prisoners' Association, as they called it, his name was Ricardo—"

"Roberto."

"This Ricardo even sent me a note, I still have it, a kind of receipt, everything bought with the money, chickens and chilis and tomatoes and onions for stew, a sopa of rice, the beans and vegetables, even the spoons and forks and napkins with red poinsettias printed on them—of course no knives, which is why it had to be a stew. And ten bottles of tequila and twenty of Coca-Cola to drink it with. And six new tapes of music. The fiesta began in the middle of the afternoon of Christmas Eve day. Now this Ricardo, it turned out, was—"

"Time! Alicito."

Ali Cran nodded and prepared himself by grinning at Felicio, who shook his head at Pepe's unfairness. I saw the end of the story lay near, that each had wanted the pleasure of relating the best part. Because after the end—

"Our prisoners are generous men, Jorge. They have very little. But they will divide it among all who are hungry or thirsty. So fourteen prisoners and four guards shared a grand meal and drank

152

very much. And as Felicio was about to tell us, Roberto is no fool. He—"

"Ricardo."

"Roberto. I know his sister. Roberto Lagarto."

"Ricardo. I treated his father for pneumonia."

"This Señor Presidente of the Prisoners' Association, he had a great plan. By eleven-thirty that night any person who passed by as I did on the way to midnight mass could see most of the prisoners leaning against the bars and all of the guards sitting right inside the doorway cradling their rifles, everyone fast asleep. If you had gone by at twelve-fifteen and looked carefully, which of course no one did because at that moment all the people of Michoácuaro were on their knees in the cathedral, you would have seen four sleeping guards and three drunken prisoners who Roberto Lagarto had not persuaded to postpone their indulgence. And if you had been at the mass and if you paid close attention to others in the huge crowd as you walked out after celebrating once again the birth of the Baby Jesus and thereby felt cleansed in the heart and spirit—"

"Get to the point, Alicito."

"—you would have noticed eleven men not wearing their best holiday clothes. Five of them carrying bottles of tequila. Walking with you through the cathedral doors, out to the plaza, into the night."

Pepe, who knew the story well, was chortling as much as I.

Telling tales helped them, Pepe and Ali Cran and Dr. Ortíz, flee momentarily from the earlier anger, the sadness, the mute frustration—this the first intention of their evening.

Felicio, still irritated, smiled despite himself. "With forks and spoons, Jorge, they had lifted floorboards and dug through the dirt. They reached the schoolyard by eleven but found the gates locked, they had no way to climb over the walls and the broken glass. So they waited. And while the Bishop's choir sang its litanies they broke into the cathedral through the door the schoolchildren use. Rubén was furious. Later he caught two of them. The others vanished."

Rubén came by the next afternoon, a little smile curling under his mustache. He looked pleased, at the same time antsy, and thanked me for my advice of a few days earlier. I reminded him he'd done all the talking. He shrugged this away, paced about and told me there'd been a break in the case, they'd soon have the man, another girl had been raped—

"Oh no!"

"All is well, she's alive. Only she won't tell me who did it. Her mother is saying it didn't happen at all. That chingada señora would rather let the man escape than admit her daughter has been damaged."

"How'd you find out?"

"The girl, Guadalupe, she got away from the man, she told a couple of friends and one of them told her mother who came to me. A few people have sense."

And are terrified for their own daughters, I thought. "You've talked to Guadalupe?"

"First with her mother there, and she said right to my face the story from her friend is untrue. But when I spoke to the girl alone she wouldn't deny it, only she said nothing at all. She burst into tears and kept her lips tight shut." He shook his head. "She's older than the first two. Thirteen or fourteen."

"You explained how important for others, her friends—"

"Of course, of course. And I could have made her talk to me. But there are easier ways." Again the smile. "The Bishop is speaking to her at this moment."

The Bishop, as it turned out, got nowhere with Guadalupe.

Ali Cran's idea was for Doctor Felicio Ortíz to talk to her. He had brought Guadalupe into the world.

The next morning, early, alone, the doctor drove to the girl's home, a three-room adobe about twenty minutes from town; the mother was now keeping her daughter out of school. He knocked on the closed door. It opened, the father appeared.

"Señor, I would like to speak with Guadalupe."

The father immediately called the mother, a broad dour woman from whom Felicio Ortíz had pulled six children, five of them living. The mother stood in the doorway, her arms folded. "Can I help you, doctorcito?"

"You know why I have come, señora. It is important that I see Guadalupe."

"She is not ill, doctorcito."

"I am certain of it, señora. But she may be pregnant." Felicio gambled on the immensity of his bluff; only the smallest chance

154

she was and even if so he'd have no way yet to tell. "I must examine her immediately."

The woman glanced at her husband, he looked very sad and old and shook his head, helpless. She, her eyes suddenly filled with tears, already weakened by the earlier procession to her home of the jefe de policía and the obispo himself, succumbed to this final assault.

Felicio examined Guadalupe. Apart from the rupture of her hymen she seemed physically all right, even self-possessed. "Tell me what happened."

The girl, Felicio told Pepe afterwards, was eager to explain. Literally overnight she'd become the center of everyone's attention and concern, she hadn't been allowed to talk about any of what happened, now everything poured out, fear, pain, pride in escaping.

The man had been standing on the path at the edge of the cane only three hundred meters from her house. He wouldn't let her by. When she backed away he jumped after her, grabbed her, she started to scream but he shoved a rag in her mouth. Then he knocked her to the ground and yanked her dress up and her underpants down and pulled his pants half off and lay on top of her, he stank of tequila. She knew exactly what was happening, if her friend the doctorcito would promise not to tell her mother she would reveal to him she had done it already with a boy she liked very much— she and Colocho, which of course wasn't his real name, they'd done many things together. But the man hurt her a lot and she'd heard about the two girls who were killed so she knew when he finished she had to get away instantly. She was scared but she had a plan and it would work if she was quick enough, because she knew from what happened with her friend Colocho the man would be weakest right after. So when he rolled off she jumped up and he tried to catch her but he tripped on his pants and she ran into the cane where she knew the trails. He tried to follow but got lost, once got very close, he wanted to cut across from one trail to another but was caught by the leaves. She described the man to Dr. Ortíz, tall, skinny, maybe as old as her papa, dirty brown pants and a dark shirt with short sleeves, hair getting thin on top, and he squinted. "You'll recognize him with no difficulty, I think. He'll have many scratches on his hands and face. And if he didn't get his pants pulled up properly—" Amazingly, she giggled.

Who should tell Rubén? The jefe wouldn't allow the doctor into the jail, Ali Cran couldn't be trusted, Pepe simply refused. They came to me. Rubén had no reason to doubt his tenant.

Rubén's dark face went darker. "You have no business in this affair!" and "Felicio Ortíz has no right to examine witnesses!" and "Ali Cran is right at the edge of being arrested as an accomplice!" Then, armed with this information, Rubén placed two deputies at the door to the bank and strode in. He spoke to the manager in his private office. The manager asked his secretary to call the senior clerk, Benedeto Pérez, to leave his deposit window for a moment and report to the manager's office. Perez, however, had just stepped out, an important errand to the municipal building. One of the deputies, Manolo, had followed the tall man to his car, where the deputy jefe explained to Pérez he had been parking illegally, he needed to show his registration papers—

Pérez insisted he had left the car in this place every day for the last three years, from the moment he had begun work here—

The deputy examined the driver's license with great care, asked Perez if he always wore glasses when he drove, perused the registration papers—

Rubén arrived. "The scratches on your hands, Señor Perez, where did these come from?"

"My—my cat. My cat likes to fight with me."

"And those on your neck?"

"Rubén, in the name of God, what is this?"

"Jefe, señor. Jefe. These scratches . . ." With his fingernail he scraped at the powder covering a thin line of clotted blood below Pérez's ear.

"Jefe, I shave with a razor, please—"

"Señor Pérez, please take off your jacket."

Pérez, sweating now, asked why.

"It is a formality. Take off your jacket."

"No. No I won't."

So, as dozens of men from the plaza approached cautiously for a better view, Manolo grabbed Perez by the arms and twisted them behind his back, Eliseo the other deputy pulled the jacket off, Ruben undid the buttons on his sleeves. On Pérez's forearms, dozens of long thin paper-cut slashes.

"And these, señor? Do you shave your arms? And perhaps your legs as well? You are under arrest, señor."

156

"For what?"

"You will be charged in my office."

"Rubén, I have my rights—"

"Señor, you have been enjoying too much norteamericano television."

They took him away.

All was not over, however. Rubén had charged the bank clerk and locked him in the cell on the evidence, highly circumstantial as he well knew, of some scratches together with the brown workpants and a dark short-sleeved shirt from the trunk of Pérez's car. He needed Guadalupe's identification but for her sake would not bring the girl there till it was dark.

Minutes after Pérez joined them, the prisoners had learned from the guards the charges against this man. At first Rubén heard only taunts, the liquid Michoacán accents strong, phrases as if curling upward at their end; all seemed okay. But then a scuffle, then a high-pitched scream. By the time his deputies reached the cell, Pérez lay under a pile of pummeling bodies, seven of the nine prisoners revenging two dead girls whose parents some of them knew. The bank clerk's right shoulder was dislocated and he bled in slow throbs where his earlobe had been bitten off.

Rubén removed Pérez from the cell and handcuffed him hand and foot to the cot where the guards slept, against their strenuous objection. By now word had spread throughout Michoácuaro: Our jefe de policía has caught the rapist! Within half an hour a large crowd gathered at the jail door. Many angry cries, some straightforward calls for instant hanging.

Constanza reported to me they had caught Chabela's murderer, he was in the cárcel. "You must go and see."

"Why? What should I do there?"

She didn't understand my questions. "Come!"

I'd never before seen a mob build from anger to raged frustration to near hysteria. Hatred grew as I stood watching from the steps of the bank. Ugly clichés took on a dreadful immediacy:

Two eight-year-old boys beating each other, heads, shoulders, against the sidewalk; then jumping up and in unison shouting "Kill him! Kill the rapist!" half a dozen times till one slugged the other and they bashed themselves back to their private battle.

A woman at the edge of the crowd, barely twenty, her belly swelling, lips pulled back, teeth clenched, held a tiny child in one hand and cradled a baby in her rebozo; such virulence on her face . . .

An old man with one leg leaning against the wall beat his crutch tip against the sidewalk, a festive tattoo in rhythm with the crowd's taunts.

But: a boy and girl close by, unaware of me, each maybe fifteen, drawn back from the crowd, holding each other tight, powerless, horrified.

Someone threw a rock. Another. A rusted wrench hit the door, bounced back. Three women brought forward the mother of Amanda, the first of the murdered girls; a community-sponsored taxi from Ojo do Agua had driven her here minutes before; her agonized weeping fired the crowd yet further. Chabela's parents arrived, her father tried to talk to the crowd, convince them to go away, force the man into the shame of a trial. But the crowd had heard the prisoner was not even in the cell, he lay only meters away, somehow he would elude them! The presidente municipal tried to argue with them but he could find no leader, no spokesman; the mob was becoming its own brute thing.

Inside, Rubén the hero felt torn: accept his civic responsibility for guarding the prisoner? or save his neighbors the trouble and cost of a trial. The crowd wanted this pig: why not let them have him? But no, Rubén Reyes Ponce was too much a professional, anyway the girl Guadalupe still had not identified Pérez. Could he face his fellow police chiefs as the man who gave his prisoner to a mob? Yet many among his colleagues, in this situation—

Which did not change his practical problem: a cellful of prisoners ready to tear Pérez apart, the man himself easily accessible if the mob broke the door in.

He made his decision. "Eliseo, bring the truck to the back. Chico, get me every set of handcuffs in this place. Manolo, stay with the guards, no one enters."

Rubén told the inmates they were going for a ride. The Prisoners' Association head made an official complaint: they weren't supposed to be moved without court approval. While Chico covered the group with his automatic pistol, Manolo placed a heavy bag on the front seat of the waiting pickup. Eliseo escorted the prisoners one by one to the bed of the pickup and handcuffed them by the right wrist to the guardrails. Then deputies and prisoners together drove quietly out of town. And Rubén made a phone call.

From in front I saw nothing of this departure. I did, however, watch the television crew, Pepe's people, arrive, set up—

In San Sebastián, forty-five kilometers from Michoácuaro, the jail was already overcrowded, as Rubén had suspected. So on the alternative orders from their jefe the deputies drove forty more kilometers north, another half dozen kilometers off the highway, stopped the truck in the middle of a field and, while Chico again held the group covered, Eliseo opened the bag and handed around three of the four bottles of tequila. In this way, one raised hand attached to the guardrail, growing ever drunker, the prisoners would spend the night. In the cab the deputies opened their own bottle.

Rubén unlocked the weapons case, checked his arsenal's only submachine gun, an Uzi; yes, properly loaded. He waited, paced, listened to the mob. When his deputies had been gone half an hour he grabbed a chair, unlocked the jail's front door, set the chair down, stood on it.

The crowd quieted, though individual voices still yelled they wanted Pérez. Rubén shouted for silence but wasn't loud enough. Finally he raised the Uzi and fired half a dozen rounds in the air. He got their attention.

Rubén Reyes Ponce addressed the mob in an accent so thick I understood almost nothing. Pure Michoacán, said Pepe, suddenly next to me; indeed all Rubén's sentences ended with their curlicues intact. But the sense came through sharp: he would kill anyone who tried to take his prisoner from him. When he finished he fired two shots straight up, a pair of staccato exclamation marks. He stepped down from the chair, shoved it inside, locked the door.

Nothing less than a scene from the Old West. Plus a TV crew.

By evening few people remained. An armored van arrived from Uruapan and took Pérez away.

He remained there, awaiting trial. A few weeks ago he and two other prisoners climbed over the penitentiary wall and ran off into the night. Within hours they'd been recaptured. But in the truck bringing them back Pérez, attempting to overpower a guard, was killed.

Dr. Felicio said to me, "It was very easy, no? for the three to escape from such a secure place as Uruapan. Perhaps someone gave them a ladder to climb the wall." He laughed.

Yesterday I read in El Pescador that the sentence of one of Pérez's co-escapees has been reduced. The other will be paroled next month.

ELEVEN

The Underside of Stones

🐾 OFTEN WE MAKE discoveries without realizing what has happened. Something new, something never before seen or said, flashes clearly in the mind. We think, Sure—! or, Of course, that's right. But, beyond affirmation, we usually find no phrase to capture our new understanding. So we let the moment pass. It fades. We forget.

Once in a while, though, remembering and recording become the highest priority. Sometimes stories are born this way.

A couple of weeks after I'd arrived in Michoácuaro, Moisés de Jesús introduced me to Pepe's gardener, Flaco. Flaco is blind but, people seem to agree, knows his job better than anyone else in town. I needed advice about which flowers and leafy plants would grow best in my elegant but then still-bare courtyard; Flaco made several excellent suggestions. Since that time he greets me as I pass, "Buenos tardes, Señor Jorge," often before I've noticed him weeding in Pepe's impatiens beds or among the oleanders.

I asked him once, "How do you know it's me?"

He laughed. "From your walk."

"My walk?"

"Yes, señor." A pause. "Yes."

In the silence—his discomfort, my amazement—I felt him withdraw, as if he'd said too much. "What do you mean?"

For a moment, nothing. Then: "The walk, señor. That's all."

"Is my walk so different from your walk, or your brother's?" His brother Salvador, a burly jolly man, works in construction.

Flaco laughed hard. "It is very different, señor. Salvador and I, we walk the same."

I sat on the grass beside him. Though I'd never compared the solid stride of Salvador to the toe-probing shuffle of Flaco, anyone could tell they were different. I said this to him.

He thought for a few moments, then nodded. "You are right,

señor. In your way. Salvador and me, we walk differently." He wrinkled his brow. "But we walk alike also." He hacked at some obstreperous crabgrass with his scythe. Then he laughed, happy with himself. "Your walk is only different."

I wondered what passing image of clumsiness had slid through his mind, that he should find my walk so humorous. "Different how, Flaco? Tell me. I'm fascinated."

He shook his head. "I don't have a word for it, señor."

"Well, describe it then, how you hear it, how you can tell."

His hands worked now, keeping as busy as possible. I had made him uncomfortable. He could find no way out except by telling me to mind my own business. He nodded to himself, still working on his weeding and, I supposed, on his notion of walking. "It is only, I know your kind of walk, señor."

"And what kind is it?"

He turned to me and his unseeing eyes—if I can put it so incorrectly—looked directly at mine. Into, even behind, mine.

I felt naked. I adjusted my glasses; a stupid gesture.

Flaco's face seemed caught at a place between anger and unhappiness. "It is a—gringo walk, señor."

Now the laughter came from me. "What's a *gringo* walk?"

"Your walk, señor." He nodded to himself, smiling.

"Where do you know a gringo walk from?" As far as I was aware, no other gringos lived in town.

Again the weighty hesitation.

Surely he knew I'd not taken offense, that I found his notion merely strange.

This time he didn't face me, he scraped at the soil with his fingers. When at last he spoke it was with the voice of a child admitting he had spied on the grownups. "From Don Pepe."

"But Don Pepe isn't a gringo, he's as Mexican as—as you are." Technically correct, I realized, but more than likely untrue as far as Flaco was concerned. Though Pepe had lived in Mexico all his life, his mother was born in Chicago.

"Yes, señor, most of the time, yes, you are right. But—"

"Yes?"

"It is also, Don Pepe does not walk the same way always. Sometimes he walks . . ."— Flaco searched for the right word—" . . . different."

"How—different?" I was totally intrigued.

161

Flaco looked more relaxed. Interested also. He knew all this but, I wondered, had he ever thought it through? "Mostly, yes, he walks like most of us in Michoácuaro. Like Salvador, like—me." He grinned suddenly, as if he'd scored a difficult point. "But sometimes when Don Pepe wears his suit I can smell the suit but I don't have to, I know he's wearing it because I can hear his walk. It's the walk for the suit." He stopped, thought— "No, this time it isn't the gringo walk, I have no word for this walk. It is his serious walk, nothing more. Nothing like the gringo walk. The gringo walk comes only when he is alone, when he's tranquil, when he believes no one sees him." Flaco laughed lightly; as he spoke I sensed a strange pride. "But I hear his footsteps. I—" He stopped. Had he suddenly realized how much he'd given away about his employer? Turning to me, his face again fearful, his mouth opening— He fought the words back, as if he had no right to speak them.

I put my hand on his shoulder. "Don't worry. I won't tell him anything you said."

He looked over to me, almost shyly. "Gracias, señor."

But his distinctions intrigue me.

Recently Pepe showed me a new book, just out, poems by a Michoácuaro writer, Rafael Mirate Dominguez. "You've heard of him, Jorge?"

"Oh yes." His records are played often at private gatherings around town, as well as in the plaza. And I remember Rubén mentioning him when he told me about Ali Cran and Serafina. "I even recognize his voice."

"Remarkable, no?" A kind of sadness, a nostalgia, had come into Pepe's words. He held the book lightly, looking at its brown mottled cover with unembarrassed affection, and nodded half a dozen times. "Such a pity, a shame."

"His death, you mean?" From what I understood, this would have been about four years ago.

"Yes. Ai, Jorge— An incredible loss."

"I understand the funeral was huge." Rubén had said people came from all over Mexico. The Governor of Michoacán gave the eulogy. Traffic in town was chaos.

Pepe laughed grimly. "Rafael would have hated it. Lucky for him he couldn't be there."

For some Rafael was not only there, it's assumed he led the singing at some of the spontaneous wakes. Nisi Calderón from across the street told me he heard Rafael's voice the day after the funeral. A record of it, I was sure he meant. No, no, when he heard the singing he was at a rancho in tierra caliente, they have no electricity there. Surely a tape running on a battery? Nisi Calderón shook his head wearily and looked away. End of conversation. I'm certain I reconfirmed for him the blind deafness of the entire gringo race.

"I'll lend it to you." Pepe handed me the book, a paperback with thick cardboard covers and printed on fine vellum.

Rafael Mirate's book of poems was handsome. If the level of his writing reached the quality of its binding, some serious reading pleasure awaited me. I turned a page, noted the dedication: For Ali Cran, brother and scoundrel. I laughed; in one bawdy, affectionate phrase he had addressed the largest part of Ali Cran's reputation. "I look forward to reading it."

"The poems are sometimes complex."

I reread the dedication. "He died about four years ago?"

Pepe nodded.

"And the book's just been published?"

"This month."

"The poems were collected before his death?"

"I don't know. I don't think so."

"Curious dedication. Direct to Ali Cran."

Pepe shrugged. "It's what he'd have wanted, I suppose."

"Hmmmm." Probably true—

"Shall I put one of his records on?"

"Please." I watched Pepe walk away as I'd done often since my conversation with Flaco. I couldn't see anything Mexican or gringo in his movements.

Rafael Mirate's voice filled the room. I do enjoy his songs but developing a taste for his crackly timbre has taken a while. The sound gives me the sense of a mirror, its surface scratched as if rubbed with coarse sandpaper: look into it, the image is a blur; you feel what you're looking for is somewhere on the other side of the glass. Too, it made me think of the range of audible sound, for example what dogs can hear but we can't, at least not consciously. As if he sometimes sang beyond the edge of our hearing.

Mirate sings about life in tierra caliente, the daily existence of campesinos there, about early love and its pain, about too many children and not enough water, about changes in nature and changes people make, about magic creatures, spooks, witches. "Unseen Love," a typical example, the first cut on Pepe's recording, tells of a young man who dreams about the woman he will one day wed, a fine lady with hair so black as to be invisible. Since in the dream he sees himself marrying in a great cathedral, he goes to The City to look for her. He returns once a year to tierra caliente, admitting his love still eludes him. We hear the song from his point of view, then in alternate verses from that of the girlfriend he leaves behind; she loves him desperately and will marry no one, she'll grow old with only her passion as company. One moonlit evening after he's returned for the sixth time, as they walk through the countryside and he laments his inability to find his dream-woman, he sees the stars and moon reflecting off her black hair. He cannot see the hair itself but lights are shining there and he knows he has found his prophesied love.

Pepe returned with a couple more beers. "I think that is a very strange song. Once on television, a science program, I saw an animated young man, he photographed what he called the aura around leaves and moss, and the heads of animals, people too. He'd invented some filters for this. He showed the pictures. You could see a bit of light, yes. But he talked about colors and intensity. I couldn't see any of this on my television." He smiled. Pepe is the first to criticize the quality of the service he provides; but he only passes on what he receives.

"You think Rafael is singing about that here?"

Pepe shrugged, poured the beer. We listened on in silence. The next cut was a ballad, simple, funny, about a campesino who sells a donkey, but the animal won't stay sold, she keeps returning to the previous owner.

I drank. "Did you know him well?"

"Well? Not really. When we were young he was older. Then I left, and later he rarely came into town. He stayed down in his rancho most of the time making his instruments and composing new songs, always new ones." Pepe stared out, eyes unfocused, looking in. "And his poetry. When Rafael wrote, in the words he saw no difference between poems and songs. You see, for him a poem changed into a song when the poem found its music. So none of his songs are in the book here, you understand. With Rafael, once a poem had its music it was no longer a poem, it had become a song and its music must never be taken away, this would be a mutilation." Pepe nodded to himself, in approval—as if enjoying his explanation. "A shame. Some of his best poems he made into songs. But he never recorded them so they aren't in the book."

"He must've become famous when he was young."

"In other parts of Mexico, you mean? But he was known here before then as a poet, even while he went to the university. He studied architecture. Interesting, no? Left after two years and came back here. Know what he did to earn his living then? He ran the cinema house. He was the projectionist, sold tickets, decided which films to show. So he had most of the day to write his poetry. He loved watching films, they gave him the world. But he didn't want to leave, he wanted to be here and at the same time to see the world." Pepe laughed. " 'More,' I remember him saying, 'I want to see more and more of these.' He brought in some wonderful films, Jorge, from Japan and Sweden and India and Italy. But no one came to see them, just me and some friends. He was nearly fired many times for his choices. So he brought in terrible films too, *The Ten Commandments* every six months at least, with Charlton Heston, can you imagine, and many films with Jeff Chandler, with Lana Turner, Bible films, the Fathers liked these. And gangster movies and westerns."

"Did he enjoy those?"

"Everything. He hated only being told there was something he could not do or not say. Or sing." Pepe laughed. "Yes, yes. I remember." What, he didn't say. "After his songs started to sell he bought the ranch in tierra caliente and he lived there. He didn't leave, except to record new songs. Once in Mexico City they convinced him he should stay, live there. Because his audiences wanted to see him, watch him perform. But he lasted only three months, he had to come back. Really he never went away. Till he died."

"He got lost in tierra caliente, somewhere out there, is that what happened?"

Pepe stared at the floor. "So sad." He shook his head. "And unnecessary. A rattlesnake, you know that too? He understood snakes. It shouldn't have happened."

We listened to the lyrics, now lush and melancholy, about two women, deep friends, each with more than ten children. One dies, the other mourns. Then a strange song about a bruja, a witch, who sees her village grow diseased, she tries to cure her neighbors but they resist her, she comes to understand she has to take into herself all the poisons from their bodies but knows it won't help and she can no longer live among them. Then a strong macho song about the importance of never backing off from another man's challenge. Finally a haunted melody about a young fellow who goes north to earn a lot of money as dowry for his sister but the coyote who should guide him across the Rio Bravo to Texas says the water is too high, too turbulent, takes his last few pesos and leaves him on the Mexican side; when he tries to swim over he drowns and his ghost returns to tell the mother now the sister must marry poor. That kind of music.

I left, infected by a sweet sadness. Pepe had said I should talk to Rubén or Ali Cran about Rafael, they knew him far better.

Rubén, I suspected, had no interest in telling me much about Rafael. He seemed removed from just about everything these days except the hacienda he was rebuilding—still was buying land up bit by bit, by hook as well as, I sensed, by crook. After the one time he'd talked about Rafael, Rubén I think felt he'd given away too much of himself, of his private self. Better not to mention Rafael to him.

Though we'd met that evening at Pepe's, Ali Cran remained a stranger. I forgot about Rafael for a while.

One afternoon, taking a break from work, I found Moisés de Jesús sitting in the courtyard among my geraniums, roses, impatiens. No knock on the door, of course. He's like that.

Don't leave yet, he said. No Buenos tardes, or Qué tal? or even a glance in my direction.

I'm not going anywhere.

You will.

You mean when my year is over?

Nine months. Ten. Not enough time.

I agree.

No no, you are thinking about your novel.

And you—?

About how little you know.

Moisés de Jesús, my self-proclaimed tutor. I waited.

Don Jorge. You are still very stupid.

I suspect a number of people in town think the same; M. de J. is the only one dares say so. Yet only he pays me the respect of placing "Don" before my name. I continue to get a dash of perverse pleasure from this. I shook my head wearily. And what have I done now?

You still believe stupidity is an action.

I let that ride. I can't help feeling you have a cure for me, amigo.

No. You have a cure for you. But you are too blind to see it.

Blind, stupid—next you'll be telling me I'm loco too.

It wouldn't hurt you. Something to work against the venom you are filled with.

He has pronounced virtually every person in Michoácuaro stupid beyond endurance. Only I, gringo or not, and one or two others, we have the potential of being rescued. And such rescue has been for M. de J. the sole purpose of his presence on the face of the earth. This afternoon, however, he was getting to me. I looked at him sternly. You must have a very low opinion of your prospects if you won't find anyone better to talk to than an ignorant gringo.

Stop looking for compliments, Don Jorge.

Then stop insulting me. If you've got something to tell me, say it.

He sat for a while in silence. I'd have guessed him to be planning his next move if I didn't know he usually arrived with a scenario ready in mind. Still, he was clever at acting out his moments of spontaneity. He turned to me, scowled, nodded. Get your car.

I drove, he guided. The afternoon glowed, warm and green. We left the highway by a reasonable dirt road which turned into a sequence of small rills, rounded smooth and deep by uncounted seasons of rain, sun, wind. I stopped the car and told him this was it, whatever we were looking for, now we go on foot.

He grunted.

We got out, he pointed, we walked. I didn't ask, Where to; his answer assuredly would've been, If you had any intelligence you'd know.

He led the way, half a dozen paces in front, along a gradual but steady slope through high bushes and low trees. I watched his gait: light, almost hovering above the ground; was this Mexican too? I had the feeling he could will himself from one place to another, this walking merely a concession to my company. I followed, breath coming easily despite the climb, careful where I stepped on the gullied dirt. Ten minutes and we reached the crest. I recognized the place from the stories: the rim of the old volcano.

The crater, perhaps a hundred yards across where we stood, had over the millennia filled with water. Now, below us some twenty-five or thirty feet, the lake lay black and flat. At the edge the darkness faded first to a silvery aquamarine, then inches from the edge to sky blue, and finally to light brown where it met the sandstone. High above, two zopilotes, lazy old vultures, floated in light circles. I shivered a bit—from the sense of the water's unmeasured depth, from memories of anecdotes that held it in awe. Here on certain windless sunny days the water turns to a whirlpool, sucking swimmers into its vortex; here when all good Michoácuarans honor their deceased at the cemetery on the Day of the Dead, water monsters cavort in obscene rituals; here Ali Cran's supposed tail is regularly trimmed.

Moisés de Jesús stooped and suddenly sat, feet dangling off the edge. He pointed to the space beside him. Sit down.

Heights frighten me. I squatted, then lowered myself onto my legs flat on solid ground. He'd left a silence heavy with the implication that it should be filled by me. So I said, A beautiful place.

He didn't move.

Second-guessing M. de J. is a worthless exercise. Right then I didn't care. I let him know this: Also terrifying.

What do you see?

I played his game, talked about the lake as it appeared to me, the bank opposite higher than on our side, the flat blue sky, the birds, the stories from the lake's crater—

He interrupted me. Forget other people's lies. Look up. What's there?

Well, sun. And the sky, birds . . .

What else?

What do you mean?

You talk only about objects, background. Are you truly blind? Or do you mock me, Don Jorge?

What else? Maybe I'm seeing what you want, but—

Everything in the space before you.

The—buzzards?

The air!

His blast hit me hard. I was glad to be sitting on solid ground. Oh. Yes. The air. Even though I couldn't exactly *see* it—

What do you think keeps the zopilotes up there? Are they hanging by threads the gods pull at? Air! Right before your eyes. He calmed himself. You do see it. No?

I'd never thought about seeing air. Feeling it, warm and caressing as here or blasting at me in an icy wind back home, yes; hearing it whine through crevices and forests, yes; and smelling it full of clover or jasmine, or cigarette smoke or sewer gas, yes also. But he was right: without smell or feel or sound, real air currents up there held those birds afloat. Could he truly see them? I stared. A huge space between me and the blue background of sky. I willed myself to see air. I failed. I said, Okay, I can certainly *sense* the air.

As if acknowledging some as-yet-to-be-enacted scenario or, for all I knew, watching his perverse plots floating in air currents totally invisible to my eyes, he nodded. All right, Jorge.

I felt like I'd passed some sort of test.

He got up. Come.

We walked a short way down the slope back into the bushes, then took a trail to the right, following the crater's rim but below it. We reached a clear area six or eight yards long and possibly half as wide, and he stopped.

Look up.

The sky, a blue hole between treetops, hovered clear of sun. I felt dizzy and hoped he wasn't going to ask me what I saw. Nothing. Blue.

In six hours the moon will be at the center of that space. Tonight is the full moon. Why do you think dogs yowl at the full moon?

I stared at him. I don't know. What kind of question—?

Because the moon is speaking to them, telling them they are dogs, they live as slaves to others, to you and me, Don Jorge, they have lost their freedom. The dogs are angry at being told the truth. Yet they do nothing but complain. Yowl. And we, hearing their pain, suffer also.

I grinned. And how do you know this?

I know. He turned, walked on.

I followed. No argument possible. The path descended slightly. Ahead, M. de J. had stopped beside the bank of a small stream flowing from a crevice in the volcano rim.

He stared at me. His eyes seemed troubled, the certainty that had produced his earlier anger gone. He nodded to himself and sat on a small boulder at the stream's edge. It is a strange world, your rich Norteamerica.

I agreed with him on that, certainly; so nodded.

You see only outlines. You see no substance.

How do you mean?

Outlines are exact. They fit against each other precisely. Like your tools, and your machines.

Well— I thought about Japanese accuracy and German engineering—and suddenly realized he would include Germany and Japan in what he meant by Norteamerica.

Each detail, exactly correct. When I was a stevedore in Veracruz, I loaded your machines, I admired them. And your weapons, your guns.

I remembered he'd worked the docks for twenty years. And that three times he'd been pistol champion in a series of all-Mexico competitions.

You have made a great deal of money from your perfect machines, your sciences.

I started a joking answer about how I'd not seen a penny of that cash—

He cut me short: Don Jorge, I understand your illness. He'd become the specialist, giving his diagnosis; wise, absolute. You suffer the disease of precision.

I'd always taken precision as a fine thing, essential to my work. Why such deprecation here?

You aren't blind. Yes, I was wrong to say you are blind. It is only, you see very little. Only what you have learned to see. I have thought this, that there is hope for you. I was right. Come here.

Suddenly I felt uncomfortable. I'd always been pleased when I could be precise. Now such precision mattered much less. Suddenly?

Don Jorge. Over here.

Refusing would have been obvious cowardice. I walked to where he sat. Something was going wrong.

He stood up, his face now less than a foot from mine. He raised his hands and suddenly his fingers pressed against my temples just as on the day we'd met: pressure, but not squeezing. His eyes, a washy blue surrounded by blood-free white, stared into my right eye for what felt like a minute but couldn't have been more than seconds; then to my left eye for as long. Or longer.

I didn't dare blink. Blinking could signal concession. My eyeballs burned, went grainy, shot with fine streaks of blurring liquid like onion juice. Finally a tiny blink pulled at my lids. I had no way to stop it. I felt myself shiver, my knees and ankles went weak. I squeezed my eyes shut. And quickly opened them again.

He relaxed his grip, and his stare. It is as I thought. He nodded. Now, Don Jorge. This stone I was sitting on, here. Look at it.

I felt myself caught between anger and absurdity. He was browbeating me. I'd let myself be intimidated. I wanted to tell him to go to hell; but for what, asking me to look at a stone? I dared to say, Why?

He spoke gently now. You will understand. Look. The stone. What do you see?

An ordinary stone, greyish-brown, possibly as big as a baseball, longer than wide, some old moss green-blue on the right side. I said all this.

Yes. Now. Tell me. What is underneath the stone?

That question somehow broke open for me the whole of his scenario, his entire weird volcano-rim entertainment. How the hell should I know? And why should I care? What did you bring me up here for anyway—?

He watched me, silent.

I couldn't take my eyes away.

He spoke me a list: an earthworm nine centimeters long, three wiggling grubs, roots in the pattern of a white cobweb.

I shook my head. Come on, this is too much. A worm. Thanks a lot. I let out a breath of anger, tried to disguise it as a laugh.

Still he stared. At last he let his eyes drop. You are lost. Truly. He walked past me, back the way we'd come.

I didn't turn. I felt a fury climb my spine into my brain, all the more irrational because I didn't know why. An overwhelming desire cursed through me—to scream at the air currents invisible in the sky, to damn them into submission. It took me minutes to pull myself together. I walked toward the car.

Twenty-five feet— I had to go back.

The stone sat a few inches from the stream. I checked its edges. Solid in the ground. It hadn't been moved for a long time; years, anyway. I tried to lift it. Impossible. A lever. I broke a small stiff branch from a tree, worked the tapered torn-off end into the damp soil at the base of the stone, pried, lifted. Three attempts and I had the stone loose. I reached down, pulled it toward me, it came away.

In its cavern, the patterns of white roots. Protected in their web, four grubs and a worm.

I stared. No idea how long. I slid the stone more or less back into its groove.

I ran down to the car. Moisés de Jesús was nowhere in sight. I called. No answer. I searched along every path I could find. I must have called fifty times. No one.

I waited. Then gave up and drove back. Very slowly.

The battle with Moisés de Jesús, if that's what it was, had bothered me in ways I couldn't explain. But I did feel as if my plans—to get away from deadening sorrow back home, to actually concentrate on nothing but writing—had been upset; certainly for the time being. Worse, I could feel an irritation, subversive in a small way, tiny but potentially dreadful, asking—what?

Since I couldn't persuade my own muse to sit by me I borrowed another, and worked my way slowly through Rafael Mirate's poems. His language seemed simple in vocabulary and in construction. Still, I felt the sense slide away as I read. I knew the songs were poems set to melody; I understood the songs, I thought, but these . . . Possibly Mirate's voice itself provided the necessary insight, pointed the way into the meaning of the verse; possibly he'd never found melodies for the more opaque poems, those collected in the book. At any rate, reading his verses had become a frustrating task.

The next day, when I still couldn't write, I decided to throw myself seriously into the Mirate phenomenon; a project. I would buy tapes of his songs, listen at length, see if they could provide greater insight into the poems. One music shop in town, not a thing by Mirate, all sold out, go to Morelia. At first I felt frustrated, irritated. Then the thought of an hour's drive, getting out of here a while, talking English with Mark—I hadn't seen him since Dolores's funeral—all this would do me good. I called him, we agreed on a long lunch, and I felt better.

I sat behind the wheel, the engine warming. On the seat beside me, a list of tapes recommended by Pepe, some film for development, my glasses for driving. The police pickup stopped in front of me. Jefe Rubén got out, came alongside, bent to the open window, grinned. "How are you, Jorge."

Today I didn't feel like talking to Rubén. "Pretty well. You?"

"Leaving town, Jorge?"

"Just going over to Morelia. Buying some tapes. Your old friend

Rafael Mirate." The words out, once more I wished I'd kept my mouth shut.

Rubén scowled. "No, no friend of mine. I knew him. But he got too big for his pants. Too smart."

"His music's pretty good."

"Some like it, yes."

"Well I'm off, then." I released the brake. "Adios."

He backed away from the car, I slid into gear. The temperature gauge still hadn't come off cold and I hoped the engine wouldn't stall out. I pulled away slowly, waved without looking back, waited till I'd gotten around the corner before putting my glasses on.

The drive, through tall pine forests, proved as always beautiful, and today quieting. Because the itch at the back of my mind had spread, broadened. Why wasn't I able to write? I don't like having my intentions undermined.

In Morelia I quickly found a half dozen tapes I wanted, dropped off the film, called Mark, and he suggested we eat a lunch of white-fish aboard a motor launch while touring Lake Pátzcuaro. A bit of a drive, but—

We boarded the launch about one. There was an anguished half hour while we talked about Dolores, they'd been so happy— Now tequila soothed the pain a little and we passed on to happier topics, even laughing—perhaps too heartily—a number of times. The fish were delicious, the rhythm of the launch easy, the sun glowing; only a couple of rough-and-tumble ten-year-olds, carousing with-out regard to boozy adults, brought some momentary ire into the afternoon. Mark and I got into a pleasant argument with two people at the next table about the whitefish. He insisted Lake Pátzcuaro was fished out, the little sprats now had to be imported from other parts of Mexico. The others claimed no, that very morning they'd seen fishermen come in with a catch.

And as if to prove their argument, the water to our right sud-denly shimmered in activity—a school of fish, possible cousins to the ones we had eaten, fluttered about less than an inch below the surface. We all stood, leaned over the rail to see more clearly: whitefish, or merely perch? The ten-year-olds had to see too, push-ing through. One of them grabbed up to the rail for support just as I bent down to tell him to take it easy. The side of my face met

173

his hand, his fingers slid under my glasses and yanked them away. They flipped high in the air. I lunged as they arced down, I nearly fell overboard. Mark caught me, the glasses hit water and sank as if sucked into the depths.

I came close to throwing the kid after my glasses. His parents apologized profusely, of course they'd pay to replace the glasses, terrible embarrassment. Would that I'd been able to find the proper verb tenses! I'd have liked to wax dramatic, past-conditionally and future-subjunctively, about what to do with their infuriating kid— But I couldn't, so didn't.

A great irritation; in truth, hardly a disaster. We returned to Morelia immediately, went to an oculist, new glasses would be ready in five days, and Mark took it on himself to drive me and my car back to Michoácuaro. He returned by bus.

My reading glasses enabled me to work, but without distance glasses I felt at a loss. The sharp outlines and confines of the world were gone. I couldn't make out details more than a couple of yards away. Yes, approaching blindness. M. de J.'s ironies bit hard.

Shopping in the market I tripped over a curb twice, stepped into a hole between paving stones and twisted my ankle. Shapes I once took for granted melted into each other, determinacies mellowed.

I listened to the tapes. With my eyes closed. I began to get a feeling for Mirate's universe. I read the poetry again; its cosmology took on some shape.

Far from any science or whatever his preparation for university, the poetry seemed based in a belief that nature is a home to spirits, of which there are four kinds: those found in air, on land, in water, and under the ground—harking back more to the Greeks than to a pre-Columbian world. By spirits he means real forces in the world which, though they are not yet understood, can be readily experienced by commonplace people like you and me, brother and sister, hermano, hermana, so goes the refrain of one poem called, appropriately, "Spirits." In fact those real forces, those spirits, have already been experienced by you and me, hermano, hermana. Often. By earth he means every reality on the surfaces of our lives. Water means any place where things change—a notion which made me grimace as I thought of Lake Pátzcuaro. Underground for him is where spirits give structure to nature and human life—and he sees no difference between the two. About air he seems least clear; here one may find the link between this planet and the rest of the uni-

174

verse, as well as the space where earth, water and underground meet.

Pepe came by. We drank a tequila. I presented him with my observations.

He seemed intrigued; yes, in terms of Rafael's songs it did make sense to him. "He understood much, our Rafael." Pepe's tone had suddenly taken on a note of respect, even wonder.

"He certainly created his own universal systems," I allowed.

For a moment Pepe seemed elsewhere. Then he looked at me, and nodded. "Do you ever think, Jorge, it's possible to understand too much?"

My reaction, stifled, was to laugh out loud. But Pepe's voice somehow cautioned against this. I shrugged. "Never really thought about it." True enough; knowing as much as possible has always been one of my unexamined priorities. "Have you?"

Pepe nodded. "Yes."

"And?"

"I don't know."

We talked on for a while, he finished his tequila, I offered another, he refused and took his leave. I sat down with the novel. Once more, nothing. Worse than nothing: reading what I'd already written depressed me.

I spent some more time on Mirate's specifically Mexican Spanish and its layers of reference, concluding only what I already knew, that Mirate is a poet and singer of a romantic pantheistic sort. Or to put it another way: I distracted myself, at moments even enjoyably, till my new glasses were ready.

Three days after the launch incident, at last back into writing— a few small changes in my text and attitude had improved the manuscript greatly—I heard a knock. Irritated at the interruption, I went to the door. Ali Cran. "Please. Come in."

He stepped into the courtyard, glanced about at the flowers and plants, nodded in what seemed like approval: "You've done a good job." Later I learned Flaco had told him how I'd asked for advice.

"Thanks." Why was he here? "I've enjoyed the work."

Ali Cran explained he'd known the house before I moved in. Then he fell silent.

"Can I offer you a beer? Coffee?" No doubt sooner or later he'd get around to the reason for his visit.

He accepted a beer. And sat.

I went for a couple of bottles. I'd been looking forward for some time to talking with him but had never extended an invitation. I felt intimidated. Not of Ali Cran himself, it had been easy enough that time with him at Pepe's. Rather the stories surrounding him gnawed at me.

He wished me health and drank down half the bottle. Then he sat and looked at me, in silence. Not an unfriendly stare; as near as I could make out. A little smile crossed the bottom of his face. His eyes, though, seemed uncertain. I wondered for a few moments if he himself knew why he'd come by. The silence went on. Should I start talking? Or sit here like him, stare out over the courtyard, feel the warm shady air on my arms, enjoy the beer? As host I felt impelled to speak, carry the weight of this nonconversation. "Some bread and cheese?"

His head shook slowly but his eyes didn't leave me. "You are interested in Rafael Mirate?"

"Yes. I've been reading his poems, I saw they're dedicated—"

"Would you like to see where he died?"

"Yes. And—where he lived."

Ali Cran nodded. He lowered his glance to the beer bottle, lifted it, drained it. He rose from the chair with a liquid spring. "Come on."

We walked through the courtyard and out the door as if I'd been waiting to go all week. And perhaps I had.

His old Jeep stood in front. We drove toward tierra caliente. The roar of his engine made conversation difficult. At one point I shouted, "Are we going far?"

"No!" he yelled back.

Another time I asked how he knew of my interest in Rafael Mirate.

"Pepe!"

Not the best circumstances for chatting.

We roared through Ojo de Agua, on to a dirt road I didn't know, fair condition, no problem for Ali Cran's Jeep. After half an hour a smaller road, little more than a double track, bouncing, wheels whirring as they caught traction. At the bed of a dry wash he stopped. We got out. Silence.

"We'll continue on foot." He led the way. Ali Cran's walk, a kind of self-assured striding, proclaimed ease of mind and control of place. I wondered if this too was a Mexican way of walking.

We marched without speaking ten minutes or so through rocky terrain, wet season grazing land at best, hard to believe anything might ever shoot up green here. Gullies cutting through stone, tufts of ancient bushes dwarfed in self-protection against bare sky and sun, occasional cacti. With a lot of water, sugar cane country possibly; now, close to desert. A light dry wind hinted at endless erosion. Between Ali Cran and myself, a different wordlessness from that in the truck: here a sense of the unimportance of speech.

He led the way toward what looked like a depression. I saw it ahead, deep, full of stones. Some twenty feet away he stopped. I came alongside. He pointed, whispered, "Watch. Those rocks."

I stared, saw only three huge boulders, they seemed flat on top. But without my damn glasses I couldn't make out any detail.

"We'll approach slowly."

We walked side by side now.

"Look! There—" A hoarse whisper.

At first I could make out nothing; then I saw movement, though in a blur; a sense of slithering, some sparkle against the sunlight, and in the breeze a sound like TOKK-TOKK-TOK-Tok-Tok-tok-tok-tk-tk-tk-t-k. The snakes, I think there were two, on the middle rock, winding themselves down out of our view; to their mind, a safer place.

"Here." Ali Cran waved his hand across the hollow. "He died here."

We walked closer. Below the three flat boulders, many smaller rocks and some few bleached branches swept down by the rains, now wedged in.

"I found him leaning against that rock."

"How— That is, why here?"

He shrugged. "Is it such an unpleasant place to die?"

"I only meant, how did you find him?"

"The zopilotes."

"Then had they already—"

"No. I was looking for him. He wouldn't have been dead very long."

I stared. Not an unpleasant place . . . I suddenly had a sense about this hollow, that it held secrets other than Rafael Mirate's. The edges of the boulders shimmered, though not with serpentine movement. Something else. I stared, but couldn't see clearly. In the broken branches, shapes as of misformed animals, the arms of a

177

man or woman, a double-size skull, beneath all this a scurry of movement which I sensed was a squirrel; here? I cursed my sight, my lack of glasses—

From the corner of my eye, motion. When I turned, nothing: empty air I would have said but for the memory of M. de J. Yet I'd have sworn I saw, well, an image, perhaps a person. But no, impossible; the sun, a bit of swirling sand.

Ali Cran had been watching me, again the smile as in the courtyard, still with the uncertain eyes. I caught his glance, nodded, smiled back, looked away. Said nothing, I wasn't the guide here. The downstream rim of the hollow beckoned to me. I walked to the edge. Below, where the rent in the earth narrowed, another glimmer, a flash, slithering. The place was a rattlesnake pit— "Did he fall in, somehow?"

Ali Cran stood behind me. "He would come here often. One of two or three places like this. He knew the snakes. His voice charmed them. He sang to them."

"He—sang?"

"All his songs. First to the snakes. His friends." Ali Cran's smile now took on a hard tinge. "No. He didn't fall."

"Then—?"

He shook his head.

My eyes swept down across the dry range, over to the little hills. North of us I could see green, the edge of irrigated land. Down below, after the next rise, or the one after that, there'd be water again, and more cane. Here, dryness, desolation. The snakes and Rafael—what?

I heard Ali Cran say, "Jorge?" and turned.

"Yes?"

He had his arms folded across his chest. No more uncertainty in his eyes. "Jorge, what are you doing here? Really?"

Here? Alone above a hollow filled with snakes? With this strange legend of a man standing beside me? Despite the sun, the dry wind, I shivered. Yes, how had I let myself get here? I tried for a joke. "Is that an existential question?"

Cold. "In Michoácuaro. Now."

"Well, you see, I'm writing a novel—" But he knew that.

"The truth, Jorge. Here. You can write a novel anywhere."

Fair enough. But why was I in this conversation right now? "I don't really have a better . . ."

Suddenly he stood very close to me. No closer than Mexicans often stand when in conversation with friends. But now his body, five inches from mine, became one clear limit; the other, perhaps a foot away, the hollow below. "What do you write about in your novel? Us?"

His question drew out my only answer: "Yes." Until I spoke the word, I hadn't understood. I heard the echo in my memory and felt suddenly excited. And immediately afraid.

He nodded but didn't move. "And you came here—?"

I have no idea, now, while writing this, if I believed he might push me into the hollow. Yet the moment had to it such a life-and-death quality his words drew from me an answer I probably couldn't have uttered under another circumstance: "I think I'm—I'm trying to see myself more clearly. Myself as I—was—from up north. Me and—other victims. Of—"

"Why?"

"To know better what I'm—what I'm doing now—when I'm with the world—around me."

He thought a moment, stepped back, turned away.

I felt calm, even clean. With my sleeve I wiped the sweat from my face; strange not to remove my glasses first— During that evening at Pepe's Ali Cran had begun one of his stories by saying, "Nothing in life changes by itself. We make things happen."

I said to him now, "You promised also to show me where Rafael Mirate lived."

He nodded. Slowly, in answer, he swept his arm across the landscape, pausing for a moment at the hollow, committing finally the full circle.

I stared to the horizon. "Here?"

He gave a barely perceptible nod.

"But I thought—" Then I saw. And panicked. At the periphery of my vision, he was about to sit. On a medium-size rock with a kind of crack running down it. I leapt toward him— "Don't!" I grabbed his arm, pulled him away. "There's a scorpion in that crack!"

He turned calmly, looked down. In the shade of the crack, true enough, a healthy large fellow, possibly two and a half inches long pincers to stinger. He hovered there, stared at us, as we at him. I have no idea how I knew he was there.

Ali Cran reached his hand toward the monster. I started to say No! but held back. He shaded the boulder with his body, scratched at one side of the crack. Slowly the scorpion crawled out. Ali Cran lay his hand flat on the stone's surface. Tentatively, but directly, the scorpion meandered toward it. With one pincer, then the other, it touched the skin of his finger. Then it pulled itself up, head and pincers, legs, long arced tail, into the palm of his hand. And sat there. He shaded his palm with the other hand and came toward me. I fought my impulse to back away. Keeping the animal out of direct sunlight, he showed me; as he might show off his girlfriend, or a new baby. "We are brothers."

Nodding in rapt appreciation, believing all legends, readying myself to jump if that would do any good— I wondered if scorpions can leap, like tarantulas.

He returned the animal to its rock and said we had to go back.

Driving, we spoke no more about Rafael. Or the scorpion. Ali Cran hummed Rafael's song about the young man who sees his betrothed in a dream.

I watched the passing countryside. Its muted outlines seemed larger, more open.

He dropped me at my door. I thanked him.

"Sometimes," he said, "it is necessary to know what you are seeing," and drove away.

Where to find Moisés de Jesús? I looked for him in the market, around the plaza, even at his family's plot in the cemetery. Nothing. I got up at five in the morning to catch him sweeping. My sidewalk already shone clean and wet in the streetlight. The next morning, an hour earlier, he'd come and gone. I went to Morelia on the bus, picked up my glasses. Precision of line and shape returned. Moisés de Jesús was nowhere.

I returned to the volcano's rim, to the place where we'd sat. I stared out over the water. As flat and black as the previous week. I took my glasses off, put them in my pocket. So they wouldn't fall into the lake, I told myself. I sat, bravely, at the edge, my feet hanging over.

He found me.

I could feel him behind me, didn't turn around, waited.

Well?

Well what?

What are you doing here?

For a moment I felt like giggling. Looking.

180

All right. He sat beside me, a small grin on his face.

We both stared at the water. It felt thick, like a blanket. I thought I heard it hum. I said, You see under stones?

He was silent. Then: By looking.

I looked out. At?

Pause. The light. And: The smell. Pause. The sounds.

We remained silent, watching the water. The sun slowly dropped behind the far high rim. I said finally, I've been listening to some songs. Rafael Mirate.

He lived with the snakes.

Yes. I saw them. They killed him.

No.

I waited. He didn't go on. They didn't bite him, poison him?

Yes. But they didn't kill him. He killed himself.

Why?

He stopped singing to them. He gave himself to them.

During the next days I felt a well-being about all that was happening. Less the stranger. As if I'd finally seen the person I'd brought with me to Michoácuaro, seen myself changing and approved of the changes.

One afternoon, a week or so later, I headed down to Pepe's place, light of step, light of heart. Flaco, trimming grass around the orange tulipan, turned to me, waved. "Buenos tardes, Señor Jorge."

TWELVE

A Wall

WRITHING THROBBING ANTS, three or four thick in some places, prickled the wall black. Carpenter-ant size, half an inch long. Glossy specks of jet. Bunches of them, as if gathered in glades or clearings, and at left-center a solid mass. Ten, fifteen thousand? More.

When I looked closer, some weren't black. In the morning air, its weary sunlight dense with the approaching rainy season, other ants shone a deep maroon luster as if their bodies, burnished, sported uniforms, or armor.

This was war. Ants, clutched in lethal embraces, annihilating their opponents, battled to the death on the vertical plane before me. Entwined limbs searched out weakness, and silenced life. In the clusters deadly skirmishes raged, fragments of the larger slaughter.

The wall, a Mexican wall, was made of adobe, covered in cement, patched in plaster, whitewashed, scab-red the first three feet up from the sidewalk. It stood ten feet high, twelve or fourteen wide. Here and there the surface had fallen away.

Years ago I saw a theatrical adaptation of *War and Peace*. Raked at such a slant the actors nearly slid into the orchestra, the stage had been transformed into the Battle of Borodino. Recorded cannons roared, hundreds of foot-high tin soldiers served as inert props, and we the audience were entertained by a panoply of strategy and maneuver. Now, on this wall, the sharpest possible rake, a silent carnage. Along its base amid plastic candy wrappers and tangerine peels lay the bodies, several hundred, thousands. At two points, foot-wide piles half a dozen corpses thick. Here, there, ants dropped to the ground. Some, stunned, wriggling, in seconds pulled themselves to their feet and again were climbing the wall.

I singled out a tiny conflict spearheaded by one smart red fellow, marching through as if on his own schedule. At the margins of battle he found an isolated enemy, weak and struggling. He struck, and his adversary fell to the ground. Three times he did this. No sense of the larger battle, no effect on it.

Neither side as far as I could see had gained control; the massacre rolled on, seemingly by mutual consent. What lay at issue here, what vendetta, what territory? Where had they come from? Why this wall as battlefield? I could see no reinforcements arriving from any quarter. Would it go on till one side had decimated the other? Countless ant-world structures here, murderously at work, invisible to me. Only the event itself, this Armageddon, and its troops oblivious to the human onlooker. Just as well. Had they noted me, turned, decided I was the enemy— Twice I've been bitten by these ants. The venom stings for days.

Noting my irrelevance here and the analogies elsewhere, I left the ants to their massacre and climbed the hill. I'd been on a mission of minor assistance and was now late in returning. But in Michoácuaro time is measured by need and daylight rather than in minutes. So my concern for Nisi Calderón, who was perhaps dying, made me move along at last just as earlier it had allowed me to stay and stare at the ants. Nisi, if truly departing this world, would take leave at his chosen time; it mattered little whether I arrived with the promised groceries at 10:45 or 11:15.

Neither Nisi nor his wife Marita are friends, just neighbors to wave to—she far warmer than he, Nisi usually on his doorstep or dawdling by the curb, watching, investigating. They live across the street from me and a few entryways up, their door like most along here usually open. I can see him hovering, checking out the few visible details of my life. And some say of Nisi he has second sight, an ability to foretell the future. Or parts of it; his prediction as to when the sewer repair on the street would be completed proved three weeks short.

The time of his demise, however, he knew precisely: the afternoon following the night when his dog Palo would die. Palo, seven or eight, looked healthy if mangy, no visible worry about his passing. But Nisi Calderón saw both their ends looming and had taken to his deathbed over a week ago. He looked a lot worse than Palo.

I'd not seen Nisi, with some relief, for a while. This morning on my way for tortillas I called "Buenos días!" to Marita in the usual neighborly way, and the whole story spilled out. She sounded somewhere between fury—she had to serve Nisi in bed, feed him, take out his bedpan—and panic, deeply concerned, unsure how much to worry; she even asked me if his complaints were justified. The doctor had come, found nothing, but when her poor husband tried to stand up his legs collapsed under him.

I arrived with the groceries. The door stood open. I called. No answer. I went inside, set the bag down on the dirty kitchen table, looked around. They had three rooms, each off a narrow entryway open to the sky; plants in pots lined the space, pleasant enough, but since it ran north/south they had less than an hour of sunshine a day. I called again. Still nothing.

Then a throaty response from the second room. He lay in a double bed, one of two, the other perfectly made up, unused; probably left over from years back when the last of their children left home. A greying sheet covered him to the neck. His face a scraggly paled brown, a tequila nose, eyes drained chestnut set against blooded whites, a disarray of thin hair, the white of his stubble. The tangle of features, turned in my direction, gave the barest sign of notice, less of welcome.

I nodded his way. "Buenos días, señor. How are you?"

He closed both eyes.

"I brought some groceries. Is the señora here?"

He spoke slowly, from the bottom of his throat. "I am dying."

"No no—"

"But until I die, I am immortal."

"You're a philosopher, señor."

"Knowing when you will die, you can do anything."

I wondered how long, lying there, he'd been mulling over his fated semipermanence. His face gave little away. I asked, "And what, señor, are you doing?"

"Waiting."

My cue to leave. "May you wait in health and peace, señor." I smiled and raised my arm in a parting gesture. "Adios."

Since meeting Nisi I've marveled at the name chosen by his parents for this man, shriveled here to a ferret: Nisi, short for Dionisio, god of frenzy, wine and eternal saturnalia. Now, walking from his bedroom, I thought instead of his Aztec ancestors and their version of immortality: the privileged candidate, favored by the priests and therefore we presume by the gods, selected for the sacrifice of his living heart one year hence, would pass the seasons in glory and indulgence, preamble to supposed paradise and eternity.

I stepped onto the sidewalk and nearly collided with Marita. She, blinded by tears, heard my voice and burst into a gale of sobbing. I took her wrinkled elbow and led her to the kitchen, explaining I'd spoken with her husband and he seemed in fair health.

But Nisi was not the reason for her anguish. She had just met Rubén Reyes Ponce, her landlord also. He had demanded she and Nisi move out, and immediately.

Surely a misunderstanding, I suggested.

No, no misunderstanding. He had not raised their rent for years, though the law gave him this right. Out of his great generosity— ha! wept Marita—he had not taken, and now would never ask them, for the hundreds of thousands of pesos due. But their new rent was to be nine times as high. And the first installment must be paid in three days! Rubén had shown Marita columns of figures which proved him correct by statute; yes, the new rent was demanded by municipal law. She couldn't read but Rubén understood these things, surely he must be right.

Why was he doing this?

In the next half hour I heard fragments of sentences, piles of words, wailed repetitions. It seemed there'd been no problem till Rubén heard Nisi was dying. Rubén then began by raising the rent, and along the way refused to let Nisi die in his house: Nisi's ghost would haunt the place forever.

Ridiculous, I told Marita. Rubén, a rational man, didn't believe in ghosts, in haunted houses. (I had to keep the irony out of my voice, explaining this.) He goes to police seminars to improve his grasp on the science of criminology, he has invested a part of his municipal budget in modern crime-fighting equipment—

Every calming phrase from me brought Marita closer to hysteria. Only by promising to speak with Rubén myself could I quiet her.

The incident disturbed me disproportionately to Marita's problem. Though a friend, Rubén has grown distant lately; others tell me he's been abrasive to them also. I had no fear he'd raise my rent, he was already gouging me, not a huge amount in North American terms but here a small fortune, probably fifty times as much as Marita paid. I wasn't complaining and wouldn't; but still—

I'd once asked Rubén how many houses he owned. We'd been drinking beer in the courtyard.

He considered my question. "Eight." He took a sip of beer, and added, "Or ten."

About the rent raise Rubén would be technically correct, he knew all the ins and outs and round-abouts. Inflation in the last ten years has been horrific; in 1976 the peso was 12.5 to the U.S. dollar, in 1982 it leapt from 26 to 135, in the eight months I've been in Mexico it's climbed from 350 pesos to nearly 500. And Mexican products standing on a Mexican shelf untouched by international fingers, gasoline drawn by Mexican oilmen from Mexican wells, the rent of homes in Michoácuaro, all have jumped in price at more or less the same rate. Of course the minimum wage hasn't kept up. How my neighbors on fixed salaries and pensions continue to lead normal lives I don't understand. So yes, Rubén would know dead-on by how much he could raise the rent. But to fear someone dying in his house, that sounded perverse. Luckily it wasn't my mess. I'd ask a few questions, but becoming involved would be a mistake.

The last month hadn't been easy on Rubén. He'd just completed his investigation of the Sanchez-Rojas feud, and it had drained him. Then two kids found the body of a young woman twelve miles north of town, her head shaved, fingertips burned off with acid. An outsider, so her case has gone to the Policía Federal; still, Rubén gets raspy when his turf is used as a dumping ground for nonresident corpses. A lover's quarrel or a drug ring death, he says. Worse, last week a Michoácuaro elementary school teacher and member of the Civic Council, Angel Dario, was found murdered. According to Constanza, who is the town's best gossip, Dario turns out to have been more than a teacher and municipal advisor. In addition to Leticia Gómez, a large woman still in her childbearing years and mother of his seven children, Dario's cronies knew him to have another wife in Morelia, he'd had two children with her; and in Ojo de Agua he'd kept up relations with a sexy ex-student who'd recently married but remained Dario's demanding lady-friend. Under normal circumstances the incident would have been treated in the usual way, Constanza explained—a crime of passion, the guilty party charged, then released to the custody of a brother or compadre.

Two complications. Dario had been bribing someone to protect him. No one knew or would say who. Since La Mordida, the "bite," in this instance hadn't had its effect, the one who'd messed up would be called on to pay a hefty penalty. Second and more unpleasant, Dario's Michoácuaro wife Leticia, a formidable woman in both opinion and size, was screaming for revenge. It seems Dario was found naked, tied spread-eagle around a tree, his testicles cut off and shoved down his throat. No arrests had been made, and trouble brewed.

So Rubén had problems. I'd promised Marita to speak with him but didn't say when. I tried to work, stared at my typewriter, but unfinished thoughts crowded me, jostling my concentration. Not Rubén but— The ants. Down the hill, around the corner. The wall. Unscarred by battle. Nothing of the fabulous war from an hour before. Bare faded whitewash made a lie of my memory. Borodino, Flanders, Gettysburg; my wall. Returned to wind and sun.

Except, on the ground, corpses. Fewer than before, and these being borne off, red by red, black by black. I trailed two black stalwarts carrying away a comrade; twenty minutes and fifty feet later they still had reached no nest. I gave up. Now at the base of the wall nothing but fruit peelings and candy wrappers. A clean battle, this. No one paid mordida here.

A curious thing, La Mordida. It's faced me only once since I arrived, following sharp upon a moment of terror in a glorieta, as traffic circles are called. They are true glory-holes, Rubén points out: enter innocent, get good and roundly screwed. Cars come from five or eleven directions, no one and everyone has right of way. The idea is to get round to the other side hitting nothing as you spurt and brake along. But if somebody bashes you and you're still alive and can prove he hit you first, you own him for life. So I waited till I saw an opening, accelerated and was in. But I'd arrived without tactics. Cars roared at me from the next entry, sliding in front, delivering up their bodies for insurance, one 1957 Plymouth after another. Naturally I made the worst possible move, I stopped. Screaming of brakes, screeching of horns, curses all but drowned out by roiling engines, in front of me an obscene line of cars flashing by in multiple couplings so tight they made group sex seem prosaic— I sat terrified, and grinning—a hole in the traffic, some neophyte satyr missing his cue! A shot of adrenaline cut with gasoline and I was out the other side.

Safe. I breathed again.

More fool I. Two hundred feet of relief, then behind me a siren and flashers. For a moment I thought I'd be presented with the Successful Tourist Driver of the Year Award: I was prepared to accept it in full humility, knowing others had given their lives competing.

187

Wrong. Two cops. Out of the car, señor. License. Registration. One, beefy, in his early twenties, a heavy automatic hanging from the right hip and a handsome billy club from the left, worried me. The other, however, was my man: late twenties, pressed uniform, clean-shaven cheeks and a nice smile—truly an asset to his squad. I could see he cared about my predicament. He explained half a dozen times—I nodding, speaking even less Spanish than usual, playing dumb tourist—it was illegal to stop in the middle of a glorieta. Yes I understand now, I told him, garbling in my brokenest Spanish, Sorry, won't happen again. But Mexico's clean-cut entry to the twenty-first century found my apology completely inadequate, kept making we-must-keep-your-license noises, kept indicating a ride to the municipal courthouse was definitely next.

Under such circumstances the application of two thousand pesos on these wounded conventions serves as pretty good salve—or so I'd been told. Trouble was, I couldn't believe this straight-looking cop would take a bribe. I knew for certain I'd make the situation worse by offering. So I held off until he, holding my license and registration, turned back to the squad car. I called to him then— desperation hand in hand with daring—how much would my fine turn out to be. He came back, grinned and explained this would be the judge's responsibility. I wondered, I wasn't familiar with the customs of his country, did he think it possible, could I give him the money for the fine, to pass on to the judge. His grin matured into a gentle smile such as would make any mother melt and he told me, since I did not know the traffic laws, he would plead my case with the judge. I found a two-thousand-peso note, handed it to him, was this too much? Oh, on the contrary, just right. And I was gone, having bribed a cop with five dollars.

I don't like getting involved in squabbles so why I'd allowed Marita to drag me in I can't say. Perhaps because a couple of months ago I'd been angry with Rubén. He had indirectly caused great anguish to Pepe by not curbing his veteran lieutenant, Adolfo Pitol. Pitol could have undercut the situation between Nabór and Pepe but, because he was taking mordida, only complicated it.

The police station, stuck between the municipal offices and the jail, is usually a sleepy place, one or another deputy with feet on his desk, an ancient rifle across his lap, reading a lusty comic book, and maybe a couple of hangers-on drinking coffee. Today the place stood empty, silent, except for two prisoners in back and Rubén on the phone, an open file in front of him, smoking nervously, nodding, listening; no interjections. Unusual. I caught his eye for a moment, otherwise he ignored me. He put down the phone, saying only, "Okay."

"I can come back."

"No. Stay. Coffee?"

"Thanks, no—"

He shrugged. "And your novel? Is it boring you, that you come to see me?"

He was no more belligerent than usual so I started in about the Calderón rent, none of my business, but—

"Yes, you understand well, Jorge. It is none of your business."

"Still, they're poor people. Now of all times when Nisi Calderón is dying—"

"Precisely! I've no need of a higher rent! I want the man out of my house." He paused. "It's simple."

"You want to move a dying man—?"

Rubén scowled, rubbed his hand across his forehead. "That woman leaks words."

"And tears of desperation."

"No. I want him away. He's bad luck, he's a witch."

"Surely you don't believe in that—"

"It's not what I believe. Don't be so stupid. Who will rent the house after a witch has died there?"

"But if you—"

"Jorge, go away. I have many problems today. You are a nuisance."

I got up, a little off balance. Usually Rubén waters down his sense of my norteamericano naiveté with a joke or comradely grin; today, nothing. As I left he only nodded, not even looking up from his file.

I've come to feel comfortable here, a minor adjunct to the landscape yet not wholly out of place. I live my own way, at ease, my earlier life discarded. When I need contact with the outside world a few people, no matter how busy, have given me warm welcome. Rubén was—has been—one of them.

Pepe is another. He'd been away nearly a week, Telecable business in Houston, and was due back this evening. I worked late, decided

I should wait till morning to drop over, he'd be tired. Anyway, I could see lightning over tierra caliente; the rains might start at any moment. Automatically I prepared for bed and, equally thoughtless, walked out my door and through the thickening air down to Pepe's house, listening to thunder growling in the distance. The road, thin yellow in the dim midnight street lamp, was deserted except for an attractive threesome coming up the hill, a man in his thirties, his pretty young wife, between them a small girl in a party dress holding onto both parents. They walked by, I returned their nodded buenos noches with mine, and as they passed I noted the steel glint of a long-barreled pistol strapped to his belt. Daily life in Michoácuaro.

With Pepe's gate still open and lights beaming from the kitchen I decided a visit was permissible, so let myself in. I found him cursing out his maid Rubí, Constanza's daughter. Unusual; he's the mildest of men. I thought about sneaking out but he saw me.

"Buenos noches, Pepe. Welcome home."

He glowered; only a moment, but long enough for me to wonder if all my ties here had been cut. Then he smiled and dismissed Rubí in a kinder voice. "Jorge. Come, sit. What can I give you to drink? Make it strong, I need to complain."

Complaints about someone else's world I can handle. I took a large tequila. "What's going on?"

He slumped in his chair. "I'll tell you." His head shook. "This country, ai— This country is going to hell. Mexico— You see, Jorge, once we were a noble land. Now—" He shook his head. "We are destroying ourselves."

I sipped my tequila.

"On the bus back from Mexico City this evening—I didn't take the car, I don't like to leave it at the airport—it was dark half an hour, no more, a first-class bus, Jorge, crossing the mountains to Toluca. We were robbed."

"What? Somebody stopped the bus?"

"They'd all bought tickets. Just after the pass one of them forced the driver to pull to the side. A small track, he knew exactly where. Then four more stood up, they had guns and they worked in teams of two, the fifth stayed with the driver. They took watches, money, everything, engagement rings. No, no wedding rings, these they left. They were polite, I must say that. They said please when they pulled my watch from my wrist. No panic, except one woman, she was crying, moaning."

"But—no one was hurt?"

"No. They took the keys from the driver when they left. They told him where he could find them, on a stump two hundred meters away. He must wait for half an hour, if he didn't someone would shoot him." He snorted a laugh. "But do you know, before they ran into the forest, they gave us each a thousand pesos? So we could get home from where the bus would leave us."

I shook my head, bemused.

"In Toluca we had to speak to the police. Very unpleasant. I told them three hundred American dollars was taken from me. They said I lied."

"Bastards."

Pepe shrugged. "Three hundred pesos, three hundred dollars, what does it matter. I won't see it again."

"A lot of money."

"A lot, yes." He mused for a few seconds. "I wonder, will they truly buy food with it."

"Why do you say that?"

"One of them said he was sorry but his children had to eat."

I laughed at this, a cliché of motivation justifying crime. Then I wondered, maybe the robber had studied sociology—

Pepe shrugged. "Yes, it sounds funny here with a glass of tequila. But I assure you, Jorge—"

"No, don't misunderstand, just one of my old categories, coming back—"

He went on, his tone divided; and the tequila wound him down. His words, his inflections, gave me less a sense of anger, more a tired sadness.

To change the subject I told him about the ants.

He had no explanation. "Sometimes they swarm."

When I left I felt better. The lightning, still flat and distant, hadn't stopped, nor was it closer. I slept heavily and awoke groggy but by early afternoon had found my way back to work. Then Rubén came by, much as he used to, plopped himself into a chair in the courtyard and asked for a beer. I wanted to work but this proffered renewal of friendship felt important.

Still, I would not be the first to mention yesterday. "How long do you figure till the first rains?"

191

"Soon. Very soon." The small talk meandered along till he said, "Jorge, I was not in a good mood when you came in."

I shrugged. "No problem."

"This woman they killed, it's a difficult thing . . ."

"They?"

He shook his head, stared at the beer bottle. "I cannot speak of it. The investigation is going on. There are federales everywhere."

"Least you have help."

"I don't want them here! They put their feet, their noses, in everyone's business. This is a small town, Jorge. People hate them, the pinche federales with their uniforms and automatic rifles—"

I nodded. "I understand."

"It's marijuana, of course. The girl was a messenger. They think she tried to go into business for herself."

"They know who she is?"

He shook his head.

No real interest in the girl. Rubén the jefe de policía, letting me see through him; a window without glass, as they say here. Rubén had come by for more personal reasons. Transparent, but calculated. Be careful, I reminded myself. "Another beer?"

He waved a refusal, stopped, nodded. "Yes, damn it, a beer. Gracias."

I served us each a cold bottle. We tried to drink the muggy air away; failed. Still, it tasted good. I let the silence prod him.

"Jorge, you're an intellectual man. Let me pose you a question. A theoretical question, you understand."

"Sure." I nodded with careful nonintellectual ease.

"Let us suppose you, you who're beginning to understand Mexico a tiny bit, let's imagine you are one of my deputies. He's been given some information. Important information in, we can say, a murder. Of— A young man. A young man of respectable family. This information, you are the only one to have it, you and the person who gave it to you. You aren't acquainted with the—that person, you're not sure how much to trust him. Now, you know the reputation of our Policía Federal. They're good at their job. Many are very good. Some are good, some less good, some not completely honest—you understand, not to be trusted. Information sometimes finds its way not to the investigators but to those investigated. Of course I'm not telling you anything new."

I gave a noncommittal nod.

He nodded back: two gentlemen of the world in abstract agreement. "Now my question is this: How, by passing on such important information, do you know where the dangers lie? For you?"

"It's a hard question." He wasn't looking for my answer.

"Very hard. From the first, even now as jefe, I've always done what was necessary." He shook his head. "You agree, no? the problem is very complicated. I have to think about such things. It helps me to deal with my young deputies."

I nodded solemnly, wondering what he'd found out. His newest deputy was three years younger than Rubén. "I suppose one of your deputies, if he had a piece of information, he'd have to be certain he could trust you, too."

Rubén burst into a laugh, a roar, a relief. He shook his head. "You are truly funny, Jorge. Very clever."

I accepted the compliment with grace and wondered at what sensitive point I'd touched him. "Anytime." We chatted on, friends again. Except for two or three private references punctuated by his chortles he didn't return to his theoretical problem. I decided to test our new amiability: "You know, you'd really be doing an old lady a lot of good if you let Marita stay in her house."

Had at that moment the thunderstorms over tierra caliente compressed themselves into a black mass at the center of my courtyard the atmosphere couldn't have been denser. "Jorge! Stop! The man has to go, there is nothing else!"

"Okay—okay sorry—"

"I told you—he's a witch, he's enchanted! He'll contaminate any house he lives in, he'll bedevil every house I own! Including this one, this lovely courtyard, do you want it filled every night with demons? I will not have a witch die in my house!"

"Look, Rubén—"

"What is this? Has he demonized you already?" Rubén jumped to his feet. "I thought you were too clever for this, Jorge. That man and his wife, they're conspiring against me, they've trapped you too somehow— Well, they won't get away with it, if they don't pay their rent in two days they are out! Out! Be careful, Jorge, if they've bedeviled you you'll have to leave too! They're dangerous—" He set the beer bottle down hard, turned on his heel, strode away.

I shouted, "Rubén, don't be ridiculous—"

He slammed the door and was gone.

I felt shaken by Rubén. Still, this deep-set fear of supernatural forces intrigued me; the earlier business of no one renting his houses because they, not he, would be afraid of spirits, was a great subterfuge.

The next day I pounded on the Calderón door till my knuckles ached. No response. I realized then I'd never seen it locked. I tried banging with a rock. Still nothing. Finally I called, announcing my name.

Immediately, behind the door: "Are you alone?"

"Yes." Had she been there all the time, terrified?

It opened an inch, two. "He sent a man."

"The jefe?"

She nodded, drew me inside, locked up again. "I am—frightened."

"How is your husband?"

She led me to the bedroom. Nisi looked as if he hadn't moved since my last visit. I greeted him quietly. He pulled the sheet tighter around his chest. "Nisi, Marita, I've spoken to the jefe. It's useless. I'm very sorry."

Marita began to sob, quietly. She wiped her nose with her apron. I thought, if Rubén could see them, right now, he'd know even his tiniest paranoias were unjustified.

Nisi Calderón made a sound then, "Blrr, buhlrrr—"

Marita sat beside him and with the sheet wiped his brow, her skinny fingers swollen at the joints.

He pushed her hand away, drew himself up higher on the pillow. He coughed. "Rubén Reyes—will die before—I do."

More morbid clairvoyance. I smiled. "You will live a long time still, señor."

She looked up. I caught her eyes. I think she believed me. I'm sure she wanted to, despite the bedpans, despite their years of arguments. "Señor, Nisi said this, about the jefe's death, also to the man sent by the jefe. The man will tell the jefe. The jefe will be even more angry." Tears flowed again.

"No no, I'm sure not—"

She led me to the door. I wished them good health and good luck. She nodded, cast her eyes down. "Go with God, señor, just as the jefe walks with the devil."

*   *   *

After eight months and hundreds of hours of talk, probably twice as many bottles of beer and a great deal of tequila, I know very little about Rubén Reyes Ponce. His paradoxes intrigue me: a belief in the techniques of his profession set against an apparent terror of witchcraft; machismo covering uncertainty, and the reverse; his need always to be in control, yet from outside his world I could see, feel, the threads, rewoven daily, every minute, which he uses to hold himself tightly in place. At a happier less sober moment I may ask Rubén to explain more of his life. A number of times in the past he's begun to open up—his respect for me as "intellectual," which allows him too to participate in abstractions, lets him talk in such terms.

About three months ago in one of our conversations, Rubén told me a tale of himself as a young man, literally teetering at the rim of the extinct volcano. The place had terrified him. Here, he told me, he had met fear and fought it. He had walked the rim on the inside bank.

I asked if every Michoácuaro boy, to prove himself a man, underwent this test.

No. Rubén at fourteen had to prove he could commit an act no one else had attempted.

I wondered about that path already there.

This had given him the idea. The tiny path, one shoe wide, petered out after a few meters. For a far greater length shoes hindered progress, only rough edges in the rock kept him from falling in. The far side, the high steep wall, was the worst: fifteen meters below the rim, seventy or eighty above the waterline, there the only toeholds he could find. Finally he'd defeated it. No one had seen him. He told his friends. Some believed, others didn't. No matter; Rubén knew.

Pepe once warned me, Never accuse a Mexican of not being macho. Either he will kill you, which will be terrible for him. Or he will break into tears, which will be worse for both of you.

Some months after I first met Rubén he took me to a quiet place in the rolling country north of town, an unusual curved plain between two hills. The soil after four hundred years of cultivation was

195

still so rich it could produce three crops a year. Springs appeared from unknown depths. At the center of this little stretch stood a circle of trees, possibly forty feet in diameter, their trunks not six inches apart, their branches completely intertwined. Here Rubén had courted his first wife.

I looked between two trees and marveled: a space completely enclosed, a natural shelter if one could get inside. What strange forces would have caused the trees to grow this way? Over my time here I'd heard any number of tales of magic, strange healing rites, enchanted creatures causing great evil or unhoped-for good. In proper fashion I'd listened politely; when asked if I believed the tales, I explained they fascinated me, I would like to hear more, but till I'd seen some of this magic myself— Now as I stared at the trees a sense of awe swept over me: an enchanted circle? I asked Rubén.

He laughed. Silly gringo, he said, and in the best of humor slapped me on the back. A stockade! A stockade for storing grain, to keep the animals out! Branches had been cut, turned into fenceposts, stick a piece of wood into this soil it's so rich anything will grow. Branches, Jorge, now they've become trees, my uncle Umberto built this enclosure thirty years ago! He chuckled all the way back to town.

A couple of days earlier I'd bought a newspaper at the plaza. From the perspective of Michoácuaro, weighty international matters retain their importance for a long time; last week's strife in the Middle East, unread, remains fresh today. I'm still saving papers from a month back. Now one item caught my attention and I wished I'd read it earlier. In the state of Veracruz, about sixty-five miles from the port in rough jungle-covered hills above the coastal swamps, seventeen federales on a drug bust had been ambushed, shot to death with automatic rifles. Shells from a bazooka had been found at the massacre site. Marijuana smugglers were suspected. How could the criminals have known of the raid, critics demanded. Federal and local police stood united in an ongoing investigation.

Rubén's theoretical problem—

So I gave him the many benefits of doubt, all doubt, here in his country, and drafted a few words of apology; for "minding his business." I invited him to lunch the next day at Las Rosas, a restaurant on the road above town. Constanza dropped the note at his office on her way to the market. And returned with his acceptance.

Our entire meal, until the violence, was first-rate. We drank a well-rested tequila, Rubén not squeamish in his intake at my expense. He would not let me repeat, in his presence, my apology—admitting most emphatically that he too had been at fault. He knew my concern for Nisi and Marita, and while he couldn't agree, we must never let such differences stand between us. He sounded sincere, I took him at his word. I'd done my best for them in the face of Rubén's recalcitrance. We agreed to disagree. Now filled with good will, he laughingly told me about Nisi Calderón's prediction, that Nisi would outlive him. We stared out through the large open windows at Michoácuaro below us, tierra caliente beyond. In the distance huge black clouds flickered with electricity, threatening magnificently. Yes, we lived in a beautiful land. Rubén's Tampiqueña steak, delicate and tangy, and my guajolote con mole more than satisfied our appetites, and a thick dark beer washed beef and turkey down well. We rocked lightly on the backs of our chairs, at peace with each other and the world. A light flan, accompanied by a Fundador, then a second, a third, brought us we agreed to a point as close to true friendship as we from such different worlds could ever hope to achieve.

Beyond Rubén I sensed the woman, red dress, advancing; in her hand a very large pistol. I felt her eyes too, black and raging with hate, unimpeded anger throbbing its way toward Rubén, isolating him. Only knowing, somehow, that I was invisible to her—plus, I suppose, the afternoon's alcohol—gave me the chance to move. "Look out!" I leapt up, shoved Rubén hard at the shoulder, he turned, saw. His chair balancing on one leg slid from under him as she fired. I heard the blast, closed my eyes and rushed her, slammed into her as hard as I could. I think the backfire of the pistol wheeled her, knocked her backwards onto another table. Perhaps my shove felled her faster.

In the evening I visited Rubén in Michoácuaro's little hospital. The bullet hadn't lodged in his body but passed laterally through three ribs, they were broken and in danger of infection. "Not from the bullet," Ruben snorted as I walked into the room, "but from this filthy place." He was sure he'd be out the next day.

Watching him in bed, bandaged and hurting, I talked, waited a few minutes, then decided and took the plunge: "Well, Nisi Calderón's prediction was wrong, you see. So he can't be a witch."

Rubén squinted at me. "What do you mean?"

"You're still alive, aren't you?"

"So is he."

We agreed to retain our truce.

Pepe came to see me that evening. "The whole town is talking about you."

"I hope the outraged widow doesn't revenge herself on me next."

"No, I hear she's grateful. She says now that killing Rubén would never have brought back her pig of a husband—the tree was his cross. I'm quoting, you understand." Pepe grinned. "But others in town wouldn't have minded if she'd—"

I shook my head. "Has Rubén really been taking mordida?"

"From Angel Dario? They were close friends, Jorge. No, Dario gave Rubén information. About properties he could buy cheap and which tax land was available around his hacienda."

I still didn't understand. "But Rubén did agree to protect Dario? How?"

Pepe shrugged. "His position. His office. If anyone gives Angel Dario a hard time, the man will answer to the jefe de policía Rubén Reyes Ponce. That kind of braggadocio." Pepe shook his head. "No, in this instance, not mordida. Not directly."

"In this instance, Pepe?"

"Rubén has never taken mordida, Jorge. You understand?"

Again I listened for a condemning edge to Pepe's voice, again only sadness reached me.

He spoke softly. "Perhaps his lieutenants, one or another in the outlying districts, Ojo de Agua, Santa María—"

"And from them—"

He shook his head.

Next afternoon Constanza came by to tell me, she realized I'd be concerned. Nisi Calderón was dead. Everyone knew it would happen, his children had come to his bedside this morning, he died with their hands in his, they watched him pass into his last sleep and they held Marita as she also watched. Because the dog Palo, the night before, had lain down at his master's bedside, whimpered twice, and stopped breathing.

Rubén allowed Marita to stay on in the house. At the old rent. He knew no one else would live there. Let the widow deal with the ghost.

I went back to the wall where the ants had battled. I don't know—
in tribute, perhaps, to Nisi Calderón. Without that errand for Marita I'd never have seen them. The wall stood bare. As I looked at it,
searching for traces of what I'd witnessed, a few large drops of rain
spattered the dust. Pathos aside, it felt right.

THIRTEEN

Edge of the Mind

TWICE I'VE VISITED Ali Cran on his land. After our last encounter I'd hoped for an invitation but had no reason to expect it. So when he said come to lunch I felt flattered.

The first time, about three weeks ago, he picked me up in his high-axle Jeep. Most afternoons now the clouds break open between three and four, but I figured we'd be comfortably seated well before then, overlooking a no doubt magnificent view, awaiting our comida. Ali Cran would most probably hold forth with tales of clever pranks and strange events while I, listening in fascination and testing my reactions, silently sipped my tequila. The projected picture pleased me.

Our destination, his rancho Dos Arroyos about thirty miles from town, lay well into tierra caliente. For the first three-quarters of the way, on tarmac, the tire tread whined, the chassis squeaked, groaned, crunched, and talk proved near-impossible. We turned onto the dirt road at a shack restaurant that featured tamales and pozole, heavy on the corn and chicken, hot every day, but was closed till the world dried out again, more or less mid-September. Rainy season, begun about ten days earlier, had already turned miles of road, powdered clay hard packed for eight months, into long strips of mud-porridge. Now in first gear Ali Cran worked at twisting the tires from rocky outcrop to draining water. Most of the time they dug through crusted soup in search of gravel, underground boulders, a solid shelf. The Jeep ground forward mainly, sometimes sideways.

"Not so bad today! Last week it—"

I lost the rest to grinding tires and cringed at the thought of the return drive in the dark.

The sun had been up over six hours, cracking the chocolate mud. Dry warmth sucked breathing holes out of the three or four inches of dark cream below the baked surface. The air, after two sultry months waiting for rain, glanced lightly off my skin. At least in the shade. Clean, so clear you think a new dimension has just caught the corner of your eye, the light enchants, magnifies. At one-thirty in the afternoon, a sharp blue sky. By four all would be gray on black, jags of lightning, a leaden deluge; for an hour, possibly more. Then with luck the already low sun would reappear as the clouds receded, heading for wherever they live when not pouring rain on us, and angled light would smear their black bottoms gold, crimson, purple—a magic denouement before the first stars.

Thoughts, mind-pictures as we bounced along; perhaps overwrought, but I'm grasping for images to remember with since I head home in a week, and my nostalgia at leaving is settling in.

The first twenty miles had taken less than half an hour, for the final ten we'd need more than fifty minutes. The Jeep swerved and slid; twice I felt us go out of control. But I held tight and tried to think other thoughts. About, for example, the invitation. Despite Ali Cran's renown, his friends and associates, those he trusted, were few. Would I have to pass some kind of muster this afternoon? And the obligation: I didn't realize the trip would take so long, and double for Ali Cran.

Two or three hundred feet to our left, at the crest of a ridge to the north, a lone figure, hatless and unmoving, watched the road, the Jeep. He was far away yet I had a sense of something familiar about him, possibly his stance— No possibility to speculate because now, ahead, lay a high triangle of land: Ali Cran's rancho, a broad wedge above two streams; hence the name Dos Arroyos. "They meet about a kilometer below," he shouted. "Most of the year this one's a dry bed, the other trickles."

We crossed a bridge, twelve swaying planks. Beneath us the "dry" stream thundered over boulders and through erosions, thousands of muddied gallons making way for the afternoon's inevitable storm. A winding uphill track brought us to the far side of the house. We got out, greeted by swirls of wind and two large barking dogs, dark grey with black swatches, so similar in appearance I asked about their breed.

Ali Cran laughed. "A pure mountain mix."

I didn't find it so funny as, with lips drawn back, they nipped at my legs. Just a joke between friends? I batted them away. One leapt for my hand and missed by a snarl.

Now Ali Cran was making throat sounds, long-short-long, three times, and they backed off, rebuked but in no apparent disgrace.

Impressive. "You really do speak to them."

"They're good watchdogs. When strangers come, especially those with a different smell—"

I chortled. "You mean they don't like extraños."

He gave a kind of one-hand shrug, an avowal thrown away.

The elegant veranda, hooded to eight feet out and running the length of the house-front, impressed me. I said so.

"Yes. It keeps off all but the rain that blows sideways." He waved over to a young woman waiting there and we walked toward her. She wore a black skirt richly embroidered around the hem with threads of half a dozen colors—work of the Indians around Uruapan, I guessed—and a white blouse that shone of acrylic. From her shoulders fell a handsome white and black rebozo; against the wind? "My wife."

Glancing somewhere between us she raised her eyebrows, then turned my way. "I'm called Gitana."

Of me Ali Cran said, "The norteamericano writer you saw on television."

Gitana smiled then, first at her husband in—what, some kind of surprise, or appreciation? but hadn't she expected me? Then to me, open, easy: "Good. The rain is coming. Welcome to Dos Arroyos."

Good? because we'd arrived before the storm? I felt my sense of cohesion, of continuity, erode a little.

The veranda faced south, down across the valley. I let my stare sweep from the west, the clouds still distant but rolling our way, to a low point between two hills: a semicircle of horizon.

"These days"—Gitana pointed to the notch—"the sun returns just there."

We stood in the large front room, Gitana and I. She offered a cold beer, "To wash the mud from your throat," and left. Ali Cran had disappeared. Curious: I had no memory of leaving the veranda. Three fat chairs here, comfortable-looking, and woven wool carpets; and two large doors, one open, leading out the back to a garden.

The room's striking feature was a display of masks covering two walls. Easily a hundred, some the kind used in Christmas posadas, Mary and Joseph, devils, the good and wrongful townspeople, a large mask of the evil Malo. Others too, less representational, men

202

with animal features, pig snouts, flopping donkey ears, and primitively wrought faces painted green, purple, sky blue, yellow snakes for cheekbones, black-lizard eyebrows, and animal grotesques, a rabbit with fangs and snails as eyes, a more or less human face with leaves for skin. Chilling, hung high so my glance turned up, a double mask, two chubby pink faces, jolly ladies attached by the temple and cheek sharing at the center a single ear. Dolores—Dolly and Loris—smiled before me again . . .

Ice touched the skin of my forearm. I jumped, pulled away—Gitana, with the beer. "You were up there, no? On the wall." She laughed lightly, handed me a mug, dark and cold, and raised hers. "Salud." Ali Cran appeared with his own and drank from the bottle.

They led me beyond the doors to the back. The house, relatively new—that is, not another reconstructed pre-revolutionary hacienda—had been built piecemeal over the years, one room, another added, one more as needed, till for shape and protection Ali Cran had connected the units to create a square, open at the center. On three sides a portico, a fourth to be constructed; this year, they said. The internal space had been first a storage area, then an enclosed court. Now, Gitana's contribution, it was a courtyard garden of vegetables and herbs, red, white, yellow flowers to soothe the eye, and medicinal plants.

"Ah. You're a curandera, then?"

She smiled easily yet somehow downward, as one might to an inquisitive but slow child. "Here it's important to know such things." She showed me onions, carrots, three kinds of peppers, cilantro, tiny zucchini, potatoes—"This is our life." And thyme, and in each corner a bush of rosemary six feet tall and as big around; the garlic patch, anise, epazote (known to us by the ugly name "wormseed"), four fine nopalito cactus, turmeric, chamomile, sage. She pointed, stroked a leaf and held blossoms my way for admiration, described her garden with the kind of detail that said it was in its many parts home to her senses—

Suddenly against the darkening sky, still blue overhead but with the sun increasingly threatened by black, she seemed exquisite. Minutes before, an attractive woman to be sure; now in the altered light, a rhinestone comb pulling coal-shiny hair back from her forehead and temples, black eyes glistening silver and amber, cheeks smiling though her mouth sat straight, slender neck, wrists—I was dazzled, held for a moment—

203

They showed me the rest: Three simple bedrooms off the central court. The kitchen with large cooking surfaces and a round table to seat ten. Ali Cran's weaving workshop where he combed wool from his own sheep. Two large storage areas, one for maize and the grinding mill, the other filled with drying coffee, crates of beans, along one wall half a dozen racimos of bananas. A pharmacopoeia, leaves, flowers, roots, brown-grey dry things, whether animal or vegetable I couldn't tell though I recognized the bottles they were stored in, Nescafé and mayonnaise jars, clear gin bottles and maroon reclosable Christmas beer bottles.

Along the way Gitana remained a powerful distraction; though no fault of hers she made it impossible to concentrate on Ali Cran's explanations. The first time a woman's presence had taken me over in a very long time. The wife of my host. A dangerous attraction, and I tried to veer away. Clouds covered the sun as she led us to the far portico. Only then did I begin to wonder about my fascination. Because her bare feet were large, her waist no longer slim, in fact her body seemed to have little of the softness and warmth I'd somehow attributed to her. Why then my intrigue with a few outer details? But she had only to look me in the face when I'd been silent a couple of minutes, ask if I hadn't understood her Spanish, and again I was entranced. I now think it wasn't so much sexual as hypnotic—no removal of consciousness, rather its opposite. I don't mean her words, these slipped by as she described the medicinal value of that plant or the dropping market price of avocados. No. I mean the candor in her voice. When I asked a question, What happens in this room, Why do you dry coffee beans on the ground, she cut to the heart of my mundane inquiry, as if she had understood it, and me, completely.

At the same time I felt ridiculous, listening in silence, holding my beer mug with two hands, all but gaping.

Ali Cran walked with us. He spoke less now. A smile, I think bemused, came and went across his face. He asked, as the rain prepared to swamp us, "Would you like to see the animals?"

I looked uncomfortably at the sky. "Do we have time?"

He glanced up also, as if till now he hadn't noticed. "Fifteen minutes, I think."

A sudden spear of lightning, followed in too short a time by its thunder, left me dubious. Well, this was his show. We passed through a rear exit in the wall opposite the living room.

Straight ahead the cow sheds, a large pasture beyond. To the right up the hill, and downwind from the house, the pigs. "One sow is very pregnant." Gitana spoke and Ali Cran nodded.

On the left in the distance a small herd of sheep, twenty-five or thirty. Further on, around and above the cattle, an avocado orchard, heavy green trees black in the light. "Come." A blast of wind caught us sideways as they led me toward the cattle. He pointed "For milk."

In the sheds two boys, one adolescent, the other nearing twenty, looked up suddenly; distracted from what? Our excursion took on speed, stopping a moment as Ali Cran touched his hand, several times his temple, to the forehead or ear of each cow. Eighteen of them.

"What are you doing?"

"I suppose you would call it—listening."

We moved with new purpose through the stalls. He gave orders to the boys. Otherwise he said little, the tour now for his needs, checking the animals. To calm them, I decided, before the rains hit.

He looked at the hanging sky and nodded. I finished the last of my beer, he grabbed my arm in one hand, Gitana's with the other, and we ran hard to the rear of the house. As we entered the inner courtyard large raindrops shattered. From under the portico we watched the heavens release a massive waterfall. Beyond, the far side of the court all but disappeared.

We made it to the kitchen only a bit splashed. I met María— "Cook and teacher, Jorge." María dropped her head a moment, smiled lightly and returned to the sink. I asked for the bathroom. "To get rid of more mud." Gitana pointed and I made my way.

Washing, I discovered company—an orange-yellow cat with a round face who rubbed against my ankles, sudden compensation for the earlier threats from her cousin dogs. I bent down to stroke the animal, her appreciation showing all along her back as she purred and stared me calmly in the eye. Thunder slammed the house and she drew away, still watching me, opening her mouth just short of a yawn, closing it again, repeating the movement, all the time meowless, as if wanting other sounds. I gave her a last head-scratch, then one on the belly, and myself a final look in the mirror: the reflection, darker now, had traveled a ways in the last months, my wan and sallow face gone at last.

Would I learn the reason for the afternoon's invitation? And what of Ali Cran, his larger-than-life status, here a respectable hardworking small rancher? Did his fame with animals amount to commanding dogs with a throaty rumble, and "listening" to cows? I enjoyed him well enough and his wife enchanted me. The kitchen smelled wonderful. It drew me back to the others.

We sat not at the central table but around a little one in the corner beside a stove fired with wood; curiously satisfying now, May in Mexico, as rain returned the world to flood. Ali Cran poured a golden liquid from a bottle with no label, the four of us toasted and I drank tequila smoother than my imagination will recall, I'm sure, next month, thousands of miles to the north.

Gitana asked about my life before coming to Mexico. I became absorbed in speaking with someone who sincerely cared. I believe she understood, in its own terms, the complexity of a life of university bureaucracies and action committees, of my increasing remove from the scientism of criminology, and I told her such insight impressed me—Michoácuaro seemed so distant and foreign.

"Why? We are both norteamericanos, no?"

"Of course. But—"

She shook her head and asked me about my life in town.

Had I known her better I might've argued. Instead I went where she led. "I don't want to leave. But in a few weeks, I must. Back to my old haunts."

Her response came sharply, instantaneous: "Cleaner." She stared toward the living room, the masks. She nodded. "Emptier. Fuller."

My insides, augured. I wanted to hear more, Gitana's version of me, a long and intimate talk with her. But María brought the meal over and served. Her dark face, flat nose and black eyes hinted at a smile. Rubén's story of Ali Cran and Serafina suddenly hovered. María sat with us, we ate; talk turned, justly, to the food. In the center of the table, two hot sauces, green tomato, avocado; keeping warm in a padded cozy, huge tortillas. We each had a large bowl filled with thick shiny brownish liquid, small pieces of light-colored meat, and tiny squash, calabacitas, lightly cooked.

"And what's the stock?"

"Lamb. Do you like it?" Gitana's voice, soft, sounded concerned.

The stew tasted delicious. Some of the pieces of meat were smooth and creamy, others lightly chewy with a lingering breath of sage. I gave it pure praise. "What part?"

"The stomach lining and the pancreas."

I love sweetbreads, have eaten haggis, and this was yet more delicate. If some kind of food test loomed, the hors d'oeuvres were delicious. "Interesting combination. And a fine peppery broth."

"Good for settling the moods. No, María?"

María's smile deepened. She nodded, said nothing.

"Which moods?"

"The harsh ones. The excited ones."

"That your attack dogs bring on?" I couldn't stop the tease but wished I had.

"You knew. They like to eat gringos."

I looked for the undercutting grin. Nothing. Ali Cran's attention belonged to a delicious bit of tripe.

Gitana broke the silence: "I think they would also bite a Chinese man."

Ali Cran looked at her in surprise. Now he smiled. "Of course they would." He swept his arm around her and kissed her cheek. Another private smile touched María's face.

The table's mood lost its edge. The cat appeared, meowed once, leapt onto my lap. I stroked it, a reactive gesture, and the animal lay quiet.

I reached for another tortilla. Out of the corner of my eye I caught Ali Cran and Gitana exchanging a glance. Suddenly I felt so far outside, so separate from these people— I plunged back in; a shallow dive. "Yes, your cows. What did they tell you this afternoon?"

"That with the rains the grass has at last begun to grow. That today it will rain a long time. That you don't eat their meat."

A small chill hit me. True enough, I'd given up on beef. Was he— "How did they know?"

María got up, took the serving bowl, left us.

Ali Cran grinned. "They smelled you."

And passed on to him what they'd learned? Somehow he had heard, perhaps from Rubén, I'd stopped eating beef. Or it was a lucky guess. "Then they have very discerning noses?"

"Much more intelligent than they seem. Especially milk cattle. Their life is carefree. And here, they eat well."

"Why especially milk cattle?"

Ali Cran leaned back, reached in a pocket for a cigarette pack. "Do you really want to know?"

Gitana stood, began to clear. A spell broke.

I hesitated, a bit of politeness while she took my bowl. I let the talk about how I smelled from the perspective of cows pull my mind far away, to safer ground. In fact, openly asked, I realized I did want to know. "Yes. Please."

He lit a cigarette, drew on it. "Cows, bulls, they aren't stupid. Beef cattle know their fate. They eat well but no one asks anything of them. They're suspicious. But they learn nothing from the other cattle. None, you see, have made a return trip from the abattoir. But when their parents and their cousins disappear, when knives slice into throats, they feel it also. Because of this—" He saw my scowl, stopped.

I was fascinated, though unwilling to admit it— "Feel? How can they possibly?"

"Ah." One syllable, heavy in disappointment. His eyes connected with mine, right to left and back again, shifting but holding. "You doubt this."

I couldn't pull away. Far stronger than fear, a sense of potential discovery made me go on: "No. Not doubt. Just—how can it be?"

He nodded, sucking in both lips. "Birds migrate. Ducks, geese, these you know. Swallows, orioles, gulls, many species. And not far from here, in the east of Michoacán, eight or nine hundred trees, four acres on the top of a mountain, this is the winter home of the monarch butterfly."

I'd seen them. Thousands, probably millions of monarchs.

"Every year they return. Not the same butterflies but the next generations. From New Jersey and Minnesota and Oregon. Five, six thousand kilometers. How do they get back? Did their parents whisper the secret? Or draw a map?"

Migration has been studied, more will be learned. I'd seen them en route too, swarms of butterflies, golden brown clouds of monarchs. I'd heard them: the buzzing of ten thousand wings, a sound like no other in the world. But not now the issue. "And with cattle—?"

"They can feel death. Even hundreds of kilometers away. They know their time will come. Not the dairy cows, they've learned such death happens, every day, but not to them. To beef cattle, yes. They turn into tense nervous beasts. Their muscle, their meat, has filled with malign fluids, dangerous to them and when eaten to the human body also. Here at Dos Arroyos we eat only goat and sheep. And chicken. Stupid animals, they run in the fields all day with no tension in their bodies. This is good for us."

"And your cows, they've—talked to you about this? The fear?"

His eyes seemed to intensify their gaze. "In their way."

I saw no chance to argue except outside his terms of reference—become rational, pragmatic. Except right now I didn't want to. "I see."

"Do you?" He looked away, releasing me.

So I could say: "In truth, Ali Cran— No."

He laughed lightly. "Come. To the other room."

Gitana, clearing, helping María, smiled, warming me. "I will join you soon."

We got up. Rain still barraged the house. In the living room fireplace, flames ate away at long logs, cheering the space yet transforming it into a stage as for small conspiracies. The light flickered on the cheeks and noses of the masks, darkening hollows and eyeholes. A hundred new faces; I felt hemmed in, under alien observation. We sat again, Ali Cran poured a sweet anís—after the meal a settling drink, he claimed—and for minutes we stared into the fire. I could wait.

He startled me. "Jorge. I never saw your television interview. You said a person was inside the statue, yes?"

"That's right." I could explain this now as an absurd alternative, as trying to be witty. And in my then terrible Spanish. "A bit of a joke."

He leaned forward, the grappling look again, and he had me. "But Jorge. Did you see a man in the statue? Truthfully."

His stare left no room for banter. "Yes."

He sat back, his face directed to the ceiling. In the firelight I could see him look far beyond the roof.

I watched dancing flames transform wood into heat, felt dozens of faces behind me scowl, grin.

"Jorge"—the voice much further off than the next chair—"how did you know?"

What to do, explain I'd been chatting over the months with a dead man? Moisés de Jesús hadn't said not to. Yet to reveal all that now to Ali Cran— In the months since the interview I'd assumed, hoped, people's curiosity would die away. On the other hand I wanted to go on exploring the Ali Cran myth, and the murderous statue seemed part of this world.

At last, for M. de J.'s sake I told myself, I explained my discovery. The incredible details rang of normalcy, now much as when they occurred. Speaking, I wondered where that person had gone, the norteamericano criminologist who came to Michoácuaro ten months ago. And where this one would go—

Ali Cran listened silently and gazed into the distance. He turned suddenly. "The man in the statue. I've seen him, them, too."

"Yes—" I had wondered.

"Strange he'd reveal himself— And that you, from your world, were able to see him."

I laughed. "Nobody else jogs around the plaza at four in the morning."

"They kill, you know, when they're seen. Or try to. There have been many men in the statue. Twenty-five or thirty that I've noted. Mostly at night. Twice, during fiestas, in the middle of the afternoon. He's very thirsty, that one. I've thought, it must be a requirement for those who are allowed into the statue, the ability to drink deeply."

The conversation veered to other subjects. Two more glasses of anís. The cat came in, rubbed against me. And the rain stopped. A sudden clear evening, a fine low sun. I made departure noises. Ali Cran explained that Antonio, one of his helpers who had a girlfriend in town, would drive me back.

He went off. I looked in the kitchen for Gitana, found neither her nor María, returned to the living room, examined the masks. The cat meowed. I picked her up, stroked her under the chin.

Again she darted her head back, explored me with a long look, again moved her jaws in that beyond-yawn gesture, open, closed, again, again. "Well, what is it, what d'you want to tell me. Yes?" I felt Ali Cran behind me and turned. "She's very friendly."

"She likes you."

"What's her name?"

"Gitana."

I laughed. Nervously. I set the cat down.

"The Jeep is ready. Antonio's a good driver. He knows the road well."

We went outside. Stars already claimed the darker sky. I stepped into the Jeep.

Ali Cran held the door. "Gitana apologizes, she says adiós. She and María, they're involved with the pigs. A birth."

I asked him to give her my thanks. To María too.

* * *

The second invitation, a couple of weeks later, arrived in an envelope, delivered by Antonio: Would I come again tomorrow, for comida; and plan to stay overnight so we could spend the evening talking. And if I didn't mind, could I drive to the restaurant by the turnoff, there'd be a protected place to leave my car. I scribbled a note of acceptance and gave it to Antonio.

Since that day at the rancho, Ali Cran and Gitana—the two Gitanas!—had scrambled through my mind. Moisés de Jesús too. I'd tried to find M. de J. at the usual spots; I visited his grave at dusk, twice, in the hope he'd put in an appearance; unlikely, it was one of his least favorite places. Still, I felt the subject wasn't yet—ha!—dead. In a pleasantly subverted frame of mind—try to watch cows after hearing Ali Cran's discourse on bovine intelligence—I tossed a toothbrush, pajamas, a sweater into a plastic bag and headed for the restaurant. Ali Cran and his Jeep arrived minutes later, with Antonio. We parked my car a kilometer away by the adobe of a cousin of Ali Cran's and drove off across the mud. Talking again proved difficult. I stared over the greening countryside. No clouds yet.

Deep ruts in the road, a washout, all maneuvered deftly. I looked forward to the long evening, to the tequila, to Ali Cran's stories, even to his masks. Would Gitana, the human one, spend more time with us? A mile or so from Dos Arroyos we stopped near a grove of trees. Ali Cran jumped out, signaled me to follow with my bag. Antonio drove away. What was this? I recalled the dry wash at Rafael's place of death, Ali Cran inches from me. In the grove, tethered, saddled, two horses, one small, brown, silent, the other larger, black and sleek—the famous Apostata?—watched as we approached. Ali Cran petted and spoke soothing words to them both. Yes, well, one does speak to horses.

He turned to me. "Do you ride?"

I nodded. Once, fifteen years ago. A handsome brute that handled me gently; the first half hour. Now I patted this new monster, Sancho, on the cheek. He seemed docile enough. "Nice, but why didn't we take the Jeep?"

"We're going to the other rancho. Lomas Secas."

I remembered: two ranches. "Is it far?"

"An hour perhaps."

I looked at the sky. Still no clouds. But they come quickly— I stuck a foot in the stirrup and hauled myself aloft on the first try.

But I'd set my plastic bag down so started to dismount. Ali Cran bent from the saddle, scooped it up, and we were off.

Five or so miles between hills and around cane. Then the cane gave way to brown earth, plowed fields, seedling corn. Just a single crop a year here. And when the rain went, eight months of lizards, snakes, hawks, buzzards and parched ground. Now little movement, no sound except the horses' hooves. Never-plowed land, bleached despite the weeks of rain, was followed by new green, and knobs of red and yellow flowers, tiny bursts unidentifiable at my height. Miles of flat prairie and loose shale. My tailbone began to feel the distance as Sancho loped along. The stirrups twisted my feet inward, I could already feel it in the knees. Tomorrow—

Then, through a narrow barranca showing signs of recent flooding, a small valley lay below us: an oasis. Three distinct greens, and at the far edge a flash of blue. Ali Cran pointed, explaining as if I'd asked, "Bananas. The lighter side is cane."

In front of the ranch house, a long, low affair also with a veranda along its facade, was lawn. Here? As we rode, abreast for the first time, he talked: he'd won the rancho long ago in a poker game; good riddance, its previous owner said. For two years he hadn't gone to look at his winnings—he knew the region, arid, deadly. Then his friend Rafael asked to see the place and they'd ridden out together. The decayed building gave a home to bats, rats, lizards; the corral fences had long since rotted; and once-plowed fields, the nubbly prairie, lay barren. There was supposed to be a spring. They found it where a few birds gathered by some meager brush. Rafael had studied the hills protecting the valley from the north and west, and said, "Bananas." Ali Cran observed the land for a year, then another, and agreed. Around the spring, a well when properly cared for, he built a retaining wall, found he'd have water for six or seven months, till December, early January. He planted corn, had one good crop the first year, with irrigation ditches got two in the second. He reconstructed the house. The retaining pond was too small for the rains so he built a reservoir, it took three years. By April the level went low, but for the last five years it had held carp, which flourished. And the banana trees—after eleven years, more than eight acres.

We stopped at a small corral at the near end of the ranch house. I climbed down, noted the first clouds above the western hills, and stretched. Easiest horse ride of my life. A dog rushed to greet us, black, bouncing; followed by a woman, past forty, still handsome, her long hair drawn back in braids wound into each other. She took the horses' reins, tied them to a rail. The dog licked Ali Cran's hands and left me alone. A preliminary rumble of thunder. Ali Cran said, "This is Beneficia, my wife. My friend Jorge."

A talking cow I'd have been near ready for. A second wife caught me up.

Beneficia shook my hand hard, said, "Mucho gusto," led us indoors. One long room divided by a huge fireplace, its pipe chimney passing through the ceiling, big windows making it lighter than the usual adobe. To the right the kitchen and an eating table, on the left a comfortable sitting space, good chairs, a central table, gas lamps.

"How did you bring all this out?"

He looked at me, the naive child, as Gitana had: why does one ask such a thing? "Mules, donkeys—"

I chose tequila over beer, Ali Cran filled my tumbler and we drank. This, the white stuff, harsh and clear, befitted the land.

Beyond the sitting area, two bedrooms. Beneficia showed me to mine. A door on the far side led out, the privy stood beyond.

It seemed fairly obvious: Beneficia was the true or perhaps ex-wife, Gitana the mistress or second wife. I would ask Pepe when I got back to town.

Taking my glass I stepped outside. The tequila had burned silver on the way down. I took another swallow. The liquid went smoother now, the hour on horseback must've left my throat raw. Or my esophagus had lost its sensitivity. Always a danger, that.

Beyond the privy, a field. There, watching the house, a woman, no hat, unmoving. I knew I'd seen her before, her stance, the skin of her face lighter than most campesinos' yet she was dressed in a dark Indian skirt. I sensed I didn't want to have anything to do with her—somehow I didn't feel ready. I shut the door, unpacked a clean shirt, my toothbrush, my notebook—

No. Privies should be tested in daylight. I stepped out. The woman was gone. A clear path over, cacti and burrs hacked away for several feet on either side. Two one-seaters, each as clean as desert and oasis allow. I started back—

Movement around the side. I have no memory, no sense of what kept me from looking straight over, fear of rattlesnakes, hovering strangers, I don't know. Yet by the corner of the wooden wall I

213

made out, from the edge of my eye, orange. An animal or—I stood, waited. The movement continued. A face? I felt it imperative not to turn, not yet. The motion itself, the rising and falling of a person, a dog, sleeping. No, a cat. Yes— Same orange-yellow of the round-faced cat, Gitana, at the other rancho? Close, anyway. A cat. Still I didn't turn. Because I could see, peripherally, over the cat face, a mask. Or was the cat face itself a mask? Probably a projection. When one isn't seeing—

Had I made out a yawning movement, just where the jaws would be? At the time I didn't think I imagined the voice. Obviously I must have, talking cats aren't part of my menagerie. Listen, it said. Carefully. To them.

It spoke in English.

I recall nodding. If I couldn't look, did I dare talk? Was I out of my skull? I didn't need this. Still I didn't turn—

The jaws, or the mask, or my overstrained mind's eye, said: Remember, your sweeper.

Well, if I could chatter with a man I knew I'd buried, why not to a live cat? Ali Cran supposedly had such conversations every day. I'd seen two, after all—a growl for dogs, a head-cuddle for cows. What had gone on with those cows anyway? No question I was losing my mind, M. de J. was a dead man, but this cat— Departure from rural very foreign Michoácuaro, two weeks off, would come none too soon.

I needed to get hold of myself, locate that rationality which all my life had let me look at things directly and know what was there. Surely this moment had a perfect explanation outlined in solid black with two exclamation marks slashing down.

I didn't turn my head.

It said, Later, more, again?

With a question mark at the end was how I heard it: a voice so intimate it could ask me about me.

The orange-yellow mask face softened like a light bulb set on a dimmer switch. For the first time, I panicked: would it vanish altogether? Yet I hadn't wanted it to begin with— I turned.

A cat. Only. Stretching lazily in the sun. Paying me no attention. Not yawning.

I walked over, knelt down. Close enough to Gitana to be her twin—which she or he probably was, Ali Cran could have divided a litter. I stroked the beast. It squeezed its eyes shut in, I assumed, pleasure. "A curious one, aren't you." Me speaking. No answer from the cat.

Whatever had happened was gone. One feline, one human. The latter sane. More or less.

I went back in. We ate. I learned about the economics of dry-country farming. Bananas paid for the upkeep of Lomas Secas but the cost of the reservoir hadn't yet been repaid. Sugar cane grew well but wouldn't bring in its costs without government subsidy; should this be taken away the fields would go to corn or more bananas. Beneficia lived here all the time, silence and the absence of others satisfied her. Once a week, with Ali Cran or alone, she went to the city—meaning Michoácuaro, larger places angered her. She'd lived six months in Mexico City and found no pleasure there. Morelia gave her little more.

Still no rain. The clouds, a distant bluster, now approached on a slant. Gusts of wind slapped past the open door. Ali Cran took advantage of the late-arriving rain to inspect the dam; Beneficia had mentioned a small leak.

I started to help clear. No, I had to sit, I could talk to her from the table; or not, as it pleased me. Possibly she preferred silence? No, she liked to talk, yes, loved it—as long as I promised not to stay a week. She laughed.

I had prepared myself, before arriving, for Gitana again. Instead I told Beneficia about my writing, my pleasure at living in this part of Mexico.

She nodded. Comfortable wordlessness set in. I went to the window, looked toward the banana grove. The sky, still half blue, gave off cold light. The air was warm.

From the sink she asked, "Have you seen Dos Arroyos?"

"Yes," I answered nonchalantly, "very impressive."

"A fine courtyard, no?"

"Yes."

"Did you like Gitana?"

"Of course."

"She knows herbs, and plants. Not many of the younger ones do. Soon we will not understand our own land."

Silence again, less easy. "Did you teach her?"

She laughed. "Gitana teaches me."

"You see her then?"

"Of course. She's Alicito's wife also. We're good friends."

215

Nothing more natural—

"It would be impossible to live with Alicito all the time. He has much energy. He does many things."

"Yes, to have built up this rancho—"

"Extraordinary, no? But living with him only, no one else? Impossible. You understand, Señor Jorge, he sleeps sometimes four, sometimes two hours a night. And he's not satisfied, not him, with only five senses, he has to have twice as many. He gives one no rest."

"I'm sorry, I didn't understand. It must be my Spanish. Twice as many senses?"

She exploded into laughter, stopped herself. "Then it's my Spanish too. Yes, perhaps in English he would only have five. Or two." This sent her into further laughing pleasure. She wiped her eyes with her apron.

I laughed too, but only at her good humor. "That means—ten? Ten senses?"

She nodded.

"May I ask, what are these?"

"The first five you know, yes? And the others, we all have them, he says, only we've forgotten. Retaining. Tracing. Uhm, patterning. And—and—oh, thrusting."

Which made no immediate, if I can say it, sense. Running them through my mind— "And the fifth?"

She repeated them, remembering— "Oh, and predicting."

Great. A fortune-teller. "And what's tracing and patterning? Or thrusting?"

"Thrusting. He does it often. To make you feel a certain way. He can look at you and how he looks—you'll feel comfortable, or you want to leave, or you can even feel love. Did you for example like Gitana?"

I hesitated. "She impressed me. Very much."

"You see? And patterning, that's—"

"Wait, wait! If he's thrusting, it's not like something coming to him—like, well, sounds do."

"Ask him that. He says he thrusts what he wants for the person to feel, and it comes back to him. Like reaching over to touch a tree. I don't understand. But he does it, I see it all the time. Often it irritates me. Not just me, Gitana also. We get angry at him. So it's not us, our imagination, it's Alicito doing it."

"What happens? When it's irritating?"

"We leave for a while."

"Where?"

"Oh, we visit our other husbands."

Of course. And they take their orange cats with them too. "And patterning?"

"He can see, but not with his eyes. He can see the patterns in people around him. How their lives work, how they're shaped."

"Oh." What else to say? "And tracing?"

"That one I like. I use that too, a bit. He taught me how. He can see the disappeared things that have happened, in a room, the traces of what went on, he can see them and describe them. If there was anger, he can see it, or— You understand? I'm not saying it well, I don't have the words."

"You mean, when he comes in he'll know what we were doing? Talking about?"

"Yes. Yes exactly."

"Then, should you be telling me this? Here?"

"But he wants me to."

"He does?"

"Or else I wouldn't."

And then I simply couldn't formulate another question. Which seemed fine with Beneficia. Ten senses. I felt emptied.

Soon—three, ten minutes, half an hour?—I heard rain hit against the roof tiles. Ali Cran arrived, and a moment later the deluge. As if, I thought, by design. He made no mention of the room's previous conversation.

Beneficia, inside, sewed by a gas light. We sat on the veranda, Ali Cran and I, tequila in hand, watching the rain. White tequila, a common bottle, a hefty kick. Same mighty rain. I felt him waiting for me. "Beneficia told me about your extra senses."

"Ah."

"Intriguing."

"But they're not mine, Jorge. I live with them, yes. Everyone has them."

I waited.

"Half are barely used."

"But you use yours."

"Many did, once. We've forgotten."

"We?"

217

"Even my grandfather. Not so long ago. Without such senses he wouldn't have survived." He was silent a while. "We too, sometimes. As babies, yes, before our senses are used consciously. But each of us, we unconsciously use them. A little bit." He laughed lightly. "We know things without understanding why, feel things we cannot see, remember things we never knew. You know this, Jorge."

"What's retaining?"

"Ah. It is, how to say this— It's how your body remembers."

"I don't understand." I felt myself more and more part of some mystical Sophoclean dialogue, youth to the master—

"You had a wife, Jorge."

"Yes."

"No children."

"No."

"Did you love your wife?"

In the rain I saw Alaine, the tubes to her arms—and before, pale—and before, her hand reaching for mine— I closed my eyes. "Yes."

"And—you still feel this love?"

I did, then. A fine distant whisper of love. Alive, but— Weak. I nodded, twice.

"You came here alone. To write your novel."

I said nothing.

"And you love your writing."

"Very much."

"This writing, it is like your whore, who you love?" He laughed, rough.

Somewhere that irritated me sharply. "If you've got two wives, can't I have a mistress?"

"Of course, and may you love her too." He got up then, stood between me and the rain. "Jorge, what sense do you use when you love?"

"Well—all of them. I mean the five we normally—"

"And that thing you feel there" (he gestured chest high) "and there" (poking me in the stomach) "and there" (flicking his finger at my crotch, just missing), "what do you call that feeling?"

"A . . . sensation—"

"Jorge. Which of your five?"

"I'm—not sure."

"Very well. Now. How did you know what I was talking about, when I spoke of this feeling, this love you felt for your wife?"

"Well— Memory."

"Where? There?" He tapped me on the head.

I had to think. To refeel. And figure out what—

"Not there, no. This—memory, which is not from the intellect, this is retaining." He sat down. No sound but the rain, suddenly loud. I heard him say, "With it you can remember why you are alive, and human, it's a part of how you're free. Or it can control you."

In my mind connections flashed, Alaine, her fingers, thin and dry— I tried to hold on, the hand moved away; faded . . .

He refilled our glasses. We sipped tequila in silence. The rain stopped. In minutes the clouds blew away. The stars were immense. Without speaking he got up and walked around the side of the house. Silence.

For a long time I stared out across the lawn, northward to the dry hills. Nothing came clear. With and without glasses. I went to my room, sleep or dreaming might help. I lay down fully dressed. Immediately I knew sleep wasn't there. I wondered where Ali Cran had gone, to what project or pleasure. Ali Cran, as if he were two people—two ranches, two wives. Even two cats. If children, then scattered across the countryside.

Outside, steadily, the world grew lighter. I stood up. The moon, near full, cast long hard-edged shadows toward the west. I would walk for a while.

Along a small path, slanting down. By the side of the banana grove. The reservoir, its dam. The moon from the water doubled the light. I sat by the edge. No movement, no sound, except mine. I stared at the water and felt a calm sense of waiting.

For how long I don't know. I realized the landscape had changed, beyond the house, by the horizon, movement . . . Against the dry hills, the woman with no hat. Too far away to discern details but I knew this person. No, no fear. Here at this time of night? Now she stood still. I shrugged her away, actually moving my shoulders. Although she had as much right in this place as I.

Seconds later I glanced up again. Much closer. Moonlight glinted off the pale skin. A man's. He didn't move. The same face. Still no hat. A white formal shirt. Indian trousers, black. Where had he come from, so quickly?

He approached. Not walking, simply moving. He stood beside me. I recognized him then, as I see, every day, my face and body in the mirror. But his cheeks, his brow, were whiter, softer. We walked toward each other, some slow kind of ceremony. We stopped, reached over. Then, I can say it only this way, where our forearms touched, he stepped into me: if such a thing is possible, we blended. I felt no shock. No doubts or questions.

Nor do I remember how I got back to my room. Only, in the banana grove, the fronds were like masks, laughing.

Salida

🔆 THE TREES ACROSS the valley, soft green heads on the side of the hill: I think they spoke to me this morning.

I'm leaving tomorrow. In one sense it'll be an easy departure: pack the car—typewriter, boxes of books, clothes—and go. I bought little, a couple of good kitchen knives, flowering shrubs, pots to put them in. Big handsome pots, space for roots to spread. Now the plants are given away—to Pepe, always room for more there, my three hibiscus and the tulipan; the azaleas to Constanza, who is ruthless about pruning and uprooting; a rose, gold flecked with crimson, saved for Silvia if she chances by; my white double impatiens for Rubén's wife. None for Moisés de Jesús, he'd probably dump them on his grave.

So I go. Simple. Except for the people—

And now the trees. From my rooftop patio I sat watching the sun rise, saw light paint the colors sharp. The air softened. Below, bushes glistened where drops of rain lay caught. I took my shirt off and my glasses, closed my eyes, let the sun warm me to the marrow.

Pieces of the year. In mind-pictures and memories. As fragments in my files, neatly typed. I saw clearly what I'd felt for months— essential to write down these stories while still living here. Over the last days my sense of Michoácuaro's shape and cohesion has already begun to drain away, travel plans and upcoming domestic bureaucracies drilling holes in my senses. By the time I'm three thousand miles distant— The year, moments scattered, my fear of losing many of the pieces: The visiting dragonfly. The sign at the station, Do Not Put Toilet Paper In The Toilet Bowl. And on the first-class bus to Mexico, Keep This Bus Clean Throw Garbage Out The Window. In my courtyard, the day the thyme was eaten, by whom or what I never learned. The old woman in the field under a ziranda tree, on her back on a brown blanket covered to the armpits with a baby

221

blue sheet, arms folded across her chest, stone-motionless as I drove by; should I have stopped?

I heard the trees. Not words, more a sonority of movement. Wind blowing through leaves but at the same time more, very little wind comes to the valley so early. I opened my eyes, reached for my glasses. Stopped. Waited, and listened. A sway of sound, too easy to call it moaning, though this as well, yet nothing we'd call pain. Sense came with the listening, words but not in a language I spoke, or knew. Except, sitting still on the patio, I did understand. That these were words, I mean—not their intention. No, despite the lessons of Gitana, Ali Cran, Moisés de Jesús, I still can't think of trees with intention, or will.

I have spent hours in the last nights awake and listening. In daylight, staring at shapes, what makes them, how they change. Loosening up on my will to rationalism, allowing it to stretch, holding to it more lightly. And where should such a practice stop? I mean in the sense of knowing what, these days, we can afford to lose. What does the mind forge for us, and what, forged, dare we undo? And where do we step into madness, or the religions?

Are you thinking, Trees might talk . . . ?

Leaving gives measure to time: another year over, a few physical beginnings, some defined ends. Yes, the bursitis is gone, vanished. The novel, back in March I admitted it to myself, has become these pages, these chapters. And Pepe, Rubén, Ali Cran, Felicio, Silvia, Constanza, Moisés de Jesús: people, lives, discovered. A large new part of me. I've gotten much more than I gave.

If I stayed another year— I've thought of it. M. de J. has visited three times this week, it's his single theme: Don Jorge, you can't leave yet.

Amigo, I've got responsibilities, my money's all but gone—

What do you need money for?

For one thing, to pay for your sweeping.

I'll do it for free.

Now you tell me.

Stay, Don Jorge.

I shook my head. From him would be the strangest parting. If I wanted to I could explain away, with careful if sometimes strained reason, nearly everything else over the last ten months. Including a chant from trees. But M. de J. showed me an alien path. Its branches lead to terrain previously unknown in my experience, a different yet surely human landscape. The past year, often strange but its moments in fine proportion, now seems an exotic kind of racimo in time, growing away behind me. I stepped across the old boundaries when I admitted to his post-interment presence. But what else to do?

His hoarse voice echoes, stay. And what? Learn better Spanish, necessarily. Rethink, or rather think, the next ten, twenty years of life—if worldlier affairs, toxins and bombs, don't take that time away. Meet more people here. Buy a house? Social relations. A telephone—but how to avoid the interminable hassle of inscribing myself, waiting, petitioning petty bureaucrats, probable mordida— And if successful, duplicate my life at home?

A piece of it.

But I'm not ready to stay.

Leaving people means, most important, cutting oneself away from their lives, their affection. It also means leaving their stories. The narratives you've read, they aren't over.

About four months ago, late morning, I sat at my desk. A large dragonfly buzzed into the room, jagged back and forth, couldn't find the door out, sped to the window and daylight, bounced off the screening. Brick-brown, double wings flicking sunlight, stunned, it quivered on the sill. I watched. Shaking off the crash, it began to crawl—along the sill and, as a breeze swept through the window, up along the screen; exploring. I came close. Halfway along its torso, little red spots a quarter inch in diameter, one on each side. A foot up the screening it pushed off, past my face, airborne again. The jags, the swoop to the window, again the crash. It fell to the ground. A few seconds to sort itself out. Another flight. Smash.

Time for me to intervene. I found a clear plastic bag. The dragonfly began its climb along the screen. I enveloped it and its environs with the mouth of the bag and it crawled inside. Out in the sun I let it work its way up the plastic; it found a ledge, warmed itself. Two minutes and it flew—a slanted path, a jag down, back higher up. It hovered, zoomed, disappeared over the wall.

The next day, about the same time, a hum in the room: hovering, inches from my ear, yank away bat it off could be a wasp a flying roach— The dragonfly, returned. Or a different one. He stayed in place for possibly fifteen seconds, that long, then swung round in front of me, high and fast—this time finding the door immediately. I ran out as he shot up, higher, over the roof and out of sight. A curious coincidence. I forgot about him. Four days later he was back. At the same time. He turned his side to me and I saw the two spots, sharp. A marking of this particular subspecies? He hovered above my page as if to learn the secrets here. Then swish, and gone.

I went off to Mexico City. After a week I came back, but the dragonfly didn't.

All year the world of our newspapers has gone on without me. As it does normally for most people here, Rubén much of the time, Constanza, Ali Cran; Pepe brings some of the world in and distributes it about town, he attends faraway conferences, but where is his interest in the larger world, except as it affects Michoacán, the debt and so the inflation—

A harsh pairing, I making stories for export about daily life while the economy of the nation decomposes about me. Avocados: I watch them grow plump, dark, heavy on the branches, as world markets fall. Cane: brilliant green, lush, unsellable for the price of growing it; subsidized, which means larger cane yield which increases the surplus which drives down the price. With tortillas and frijoles the basic diet here, hundreds of tons of beans and corn are imported annually from the U.S. Tomorrow if I can stop jotting these notes I begin my return to the land of supermarkets instead of markets, washer-dryers instead of washing, money instead of time. And Ali Cran's many senses, will they stay here?

I wonder if I understand projecting. The morning I left Lomas Secas, Ali Cran and I walked through his banana grove, all masks and mirrors far away. One bunch of fruit, thick, green and heavy, the knob at the racimo's end a shiny purple-black, caught my eye. He left me for a few minutes. I stared at the bananas, something about them— Stopped looking, tried to sense the whole of the orchard, my bananas extended— In this way I sensed the bunch grow larger, lighter green, leave the tree, pass through a space. I thought of Isidoro's pig except my bananas didn't float, more as if they'd found a comfortable place. Then the racimo lies in a market, Michoácuaro perhaps, yellowing, separating, the bunches fade to a kind of greyness my eyes can't penetrate . . . a bunch, however, taken by . . .

Rubén's wife Bárbara and these too disappear . . . except one held by a child, overdressed, Bárbara's daughter Mercedes? too much banana, she chokes, is rushed away— The image darkens over.

Warn Rubén? Rubén, I had a vision of your daughter choking on a banana when Ali Cran brings his crop to market. I could hear him laugh, clap me on the back, thank me with an exaggerated sincerity, take me by the arm, sit me down and pour us each a large tequilita. "Jorge, seen any more snipers in the statue?" We'd both drink to that.

An incident I'd not like to see happen, I told Ali Cran. "Why not take that racimo somewhere other than Michoácuaro?"

Ali Cran shrugged. "You're being paranoid."

"Probably."

"If it's not my banana, it'll be another. The child has been taught greed. Or maybe not a banana, it could be a piece of steak."

Today I said goodbye to Rubén. He arrived with a bottle of tequila, the grand old brown nectar. "Take it home, Jorge. Drink it and remember us."

I offered him a glass right then. He looked tempted, but caught himself and declined. I didn't mention the bananas. We drank beer. He asked me to send him a postcard sometime.

Yesterday I threw out hundreds of pages of false starts. More pieces of a year.

Ali Cran arrived to say hasta luego. Suddenly we fell deep into an argument. I'd simply said, "Alicito I don't have the words to express how I feel, just—"

"So? We have far more feelings than there are words for."

Not even the chance to offer him a beer. From out of nowhere he lectured me, huge charges: I allowed the tyranny of language to control me, I cowered under it. I'd accepted as natural the hubris of words, had made it mine, was at the edge of believing that the words of my language, of the Spanish I wanted, that these are capable of describing a day, or the worth of a human being. "People live in the space between words, hombre."

A new Ali Cran, not the man who labeled his senses. Or another part of him? I told him I'd worry about his hubris and tyranny. While driving north.

"Jorge, write your stories. Don't leave behind the largest part of what you know." An abrazo, a grin, and he left.

In that instant I think I understood. A story can never be an end in itself. But there is no way to reach beyond a story without telling it.

Constanza's way of talking about her family, friends, life, her way a few minutes ago of saying goodbye: I'm suddenly thinking of her speech patterns as an attempt to get beyond, or through, words. She repeats what seems to be the same thought or idea over and over again, but each time from a minimally shifted perspective, someone else's possibly, or her own but recalled from earlier moments, then all the thinking collected as she speaks, not collated but heaped, talked around and around but, because the time of talking is now, never back to the earlier sense. Till all the space between the words is filled in, or seems to be. Today she cried, great rolling tears, she too asked me to send a postcard, and laughed through memories which became part of the repetition, till she'd built it up again, for us in the courtyard, her remembered moments, her sense of the months she's known me, not as I recalled them but equally as true.

In the beginning I had great difficulty listening to her. My tendency was to abstract, find the core, move on. I tried to take a phrase, a couple, get back to the known pattern the words were a symptom of; at first I misunderstood her regularly. But listening to the repetitions, hearing the structure as itself a language— I have just realized, sometimes Rubén too speaks this way, and Pepe. When they don't shift to my speech patterns, which they have been taught, and have mastered, Pepe to near perfect.

In the courtyard ten days ago, taking a break, a peaceful afternoon, I tended my geraniums and roses, nostalgia for flowers also a part of departure. Though well into the rainy season, certain plants need more careful watering than a regular afternoon deluge; I held my pruning knife at the ready for any wayward stem.

A thunk and loud clatter on the courtyard stones. I spun about. A rock, round, about an inch in diameter, came rolling to a halt. Thrown over the roof and into the courtyard—good aim, too, it had missed the roof tiles entirely, and me, from the chip it made in landing, by only four or five feet. I picked it up, uncertain— Rushed to the door, out— No one. I pretended to close the door, come back in. I waited. Some schoolkid hidden in a doorway, scooting away when he thought himself safe? But nothing moved on the street. I felt a moment of sharp loss for Nisi Calderón's weary figure, if he'd still been guarding his stoop— But Nisi, no Moisés de Jesús, as far as I know has stayed in the ground. Back to my plants.

The next afternoon, about the same time, again a rock. Less rounded this time, about the same heft. I was passing through the courtyard, heard the impact, it bounced rather than rolled. To the door, open— Three schoolgirls walking up the hill, too far away; coming down, an old lady with a tortilla basket.

My neighbors one or two doors up the hill? I'd never said more than a buenos días to them. Get involved now, a week and a half to go, in a wrangle? I asked Pepe.

"If you can ignore it—"

Midafternoons I stayed out of the courtyard. Angry, a bit nervous. Why should they? And how could they see me? I had explored, couldn't figure where a catapult might be placed. Even with mirrors . . .

Then today, clattering across the roof as in frustration, an hour ago a small stone, no bigger than a pebble.

This evening, bags and boxes packed, I'm unable to escape the need to record. I have a sense of rural Mexico, that here is a country outside time; I mean as measured by clocks and weeks. Technology brought in by our norteamericano time, yes, it's here. Pepe's omnipresent TV, all the machines electricity runs, stake trucks for hauling, these create their own schedules. But ten kilometers away daylight and darkness is the dominant cycle. Sunrise means work. Eat the big meal at two, it takes till then to market and cook, much later means cleaning up after sunset. Human activity, near-medieval, is collective: family in all its directions, church, the government-run social hall. Where I'm heading tomorrow, we're all supposedly free individuals—work, money, respect; for oneself. True, we are responsible for our children too, till adolescence ends. But then they're on their own.

The world up north, hi-tech, hi-civ, hi-soph, is wondrous for the ultraprivate life: when we are formed by the desire, when the desire is formed into us, for personal satisfactions and fulfillments, yes, we have much. This same world, seen from down here, has two faces. For those who must stay, who see its self-chosen TV images, it dazzles; its ravages are rarely grasped. But returning, after living in Michoácuaro, to the home of the images—words fail. I see myself stare at, see clearly, with which senses I don't know, all that hi-everything: wealth, decadence, death.

If I'm visible I'm still here, even to the rock-thrower. When they no longer see me—

Not that "I" am necessary to their lives. But they've become important to me. And I am beginning to understand one role I might have played for them. Because usually they have nobody from outside their daily activity against whom to test their—again I can't make the words fit—what? their place in history? their existence? to test just *that*. Explore, examine. Which they cannot do with neighbors, family, those like themselves. So they can't place their identity, its uniqueness.

A postcard is a reminder: he would have laughed that way—; in his funny Spanish said this—; we must remember to tell him . . .

Pepe has a better view of the sunset than I. I walked down, well aware I'd not be doing this again for a long while. I met Flaco, he wished me the best possible trip, we shook hands and he embraced me gently.

Pepe and I talked carefully, weighed down by the lack of time for new stories. When he came north, of course he'd visit—depending on who paid for his trip, how flexible he'd be. Since my arrival the peso has dropped from 320 to the dollar to nearly 600. Assuredly one day he would come to see me, quién sabe— "And when will you be back, Jorge?"

Also the problem of money, and the time to get away— "But sooner than later, yes, I promise." We drank two beers, watched the sun drop, disappear. The sky still shone. Tomorrow's sunset, for me, will be multiple miles to the north.

Of course I'll come back. But returning will be the way one visits the lives of distant friends. The trust grown from this accidental admission, that glass of tequila, a shared story—all was being uprooted at the very moment we stared over to the hills. I walked home, sensing the cement and gravel under my feet go loose. I sat on my patio, stared at the stars, listened again for the trees. But they seem to be silent tonight.

*   *   *

A postscript.

I left this morning, a late start, merely loading and driving away not possible. Pepe came by, Constanza made us coffee. I dragged boxes to the car. Silvia appeared, I gave her the rose, she asked for a cookie as well. Señora Calderón brought me a quarter of a cake— very good to eat while driving. Basta, Ali Cran's compadre whom I barely knew, shook my hand. As did Eliseo—I'd no more than nodded to him since my night at Rubén's casita; now for a moment I wondered if the jefe had sent him.

At 11:15 to half a dozen waves I drove from the curb, up the hill and out of town. I stopped at a turnout, looked down at Michoácuaro. The statue on the square, tiny. The clay tiled roofs, the valley road to tierra caliente. The hills beyond. Slowly I drove away.

Beside the car, keeping pace, a dragonfly. Brown. I wiped my nose, speeded up. At the curve Michoácuaro disappeared. The dragonfly shot ahead, swerved and zoomed down to the valley, its wings vibrating life.

ABOUT THE AUTHOR

George Szanto was born in Northern Ireland, and has lived in England, the United States, France, Germany, Canada, and Mexico. Presently he divides his life and writing time between Michoacan, Mexico, and Montreal, Quebec. Mr. Szanto writes stories, novels, plays, and criticism, all of which explore irregular ways of looking at the world. His novel *Not Working* was named one of the five best first novels of Canada in 1983.